SIREN SONG

At Diego's touch, the wall gave way, and a soft, eerie light from within sent a shaft to meet them. He pressed forward into the room, where flame-colored liquid bubbled up in a central pool and the walls glowed with phosphorescence. Roots and rock formations twined and curled into strange designs in the rough shapes of animals and men. And there was a humming was so loud, so perfect, so beautiful that after a while Diego thought he must be hearing the voices of the angels he had once read about—and they were telling him things. He listened so closely he could not hear his father screaming.

By Anne McCaffrey and Elizabeth Ann Scarborough
Published by Ballantine Books:

POWERS THAT BE

Other Titles by Anne McCaffrey
Published by Ballantine Books:

DECISION AT DOONA
DINOSAUR PLANET
DINOSAUR PLANET SURVIVORS
GET OFF THE UNICORN
THE LADY
PEGASUS IN FLIGHT
RESTOREE
THE SHIP WHO SANG
TO RIDE PEGASUS

THE CRYSTAL SINGER BOOKS
CRYSTAL SINGER
KILLASHANDRA
CRYSTAL LINE

THE DRAGONRIDERS OF PERN® BOOKS
DRAGONFLIGHT
DRAGONQUEST
THE WHITE DRAGON
MORETA: DRAGONLADY OF PERN
NERILKA'S STORY
DRAGONSDAWN
THE RENEGADES OF PERN
ALL THE WEYRS OF PERN

With Jody-Lynn Nye:
THE DRAGONLOVER'S GUIDE TO PERN

Edited by Anne McCaffrey:
ALCHEMY AND ACADEME

POWERS
THAT BE

ANNE McCAFFREY

ELIZABETH ANN SCARBOROUGH

A Del Rey® Book
BALLANTINE BOOKS • NEW YORK

A Del Rey® Book
Published by Ballantine Books
Copyright © 1993 by Anne McCaffrey and Elizabeth Ann Scarborough

All rights reserved under International and Pan-American Copyright Conventions. Published in the United States of America by Ballantine Books, a division of Random House, Inc., New York, and simultaneously in Canada by Random House of Canada Limited, Toronto.

Library of Congress Catalog Card Number: 92-54992

ISBN 0-345-38779-1

Manufactured in the United States of America

First Hardcover Edition: July 1993
First Mass Market Edition: June 1994

10 9 8 7

We dedicate this book to Neva Reece
for holding down the Scarborough fort
(and supplying the cats with TLC) while
we wrote at McCaffrey's house in Ireland.
Thanks from us both, Neva.

1

Stifling in the crowded processing center of Petaybee's spaceport, Yanaba Maddock eyed the side door as a drowner would eye a drifting spar. Unobtrusively making her way to it, she hoped it wasn't locked. It was, but the lock was not proof against the skills she had acquired in her years as a company soldier, investigator, explorer, training officer, and, most recently, long-term resident of a medical facility. Automatically checking to see if her activity was being noticed, Yana slid the door open just wide enough to accommodate her thin body. She paused to pull on her gloves: she had been warned in the briefing—and she always took briefings seriously—of the danger of bare skin sticking to frozen surfaces.

For a moment she leaned back against the slide panel, to secure it in case she had been observed. Then the cold air hit her.

She knew from previous cold-weather training not to inhale the freezing blast that whipped around the corner of the building and slammed into her face.

"The temp-er-actch-chur of Planet, Terraformation B, commonly called Petaybee, at certain locations during certain points in time during the winter can range as

1

low as minus two hundred degrees fare-in-height," the computer aboard the shuttle from ship to port had cautioned. "That's cold, troops. Do not touch metal objects with your unprotected epy-dur-mus. Do not run, or the air will freeze into small icicles in your lungs and lacerate them. Wear or carry your winter gear with you at all times. Do not count on a nice warm vehicle for warmth. For one thing, there is a shortage of nice warm vehicles on Petaybee, because machinery that doesn't freeze and crack in the extreme cold is expensive. For another thing, even the expensive equipment breaks down, and you may find yourself stranded. The temper-atch-chur at Kilcoole SpaceBase today is minus fifty degrees fare-in-height. Some of the locals have been known to regard this as relatively tropical by comparison with what they consider *real* winter. Bear in mind that summer to these same individuals consists of two months of fairly constant daylight as warm as fifty-five to sixty degrees above zero, still twelve to seventeen degrees colder than regulation shipboard settings of seventy-two degrees. So button up your outer gear, 'cause the wind blows free, and take good care of yourselves, remembering at all times that your ass belongs to the company. That is all."

Yana had smiled to hear the computer briefing given in the gruff voice and speech patterns of a senior NCO, but she was no more inclined to ignore the warning than she would have been had it been issued by a flesh-and-blood top sergeant. Minus two hundred, huh? Good thing she'd gotten here during a "heat wave." Icicles lacerating her already trashed lungs would do nothing for her convalescence.

Fumbling with outerwear that had been broiling her

in the facility, she pulled her scarf across her mouth, flipped the hood to her head, pulled it down over her forehead, which was fast becoming wooden with cold, and tucked the scarf securely up to her eyes before she tied the hood under her chin.

Cold though the air was, and despite a taint of over-heated oil and space fuel from the snow-rimmed plascrete landing pad, the freshness of it—warmed by her breath as she inhaled through the muffling fabric—was clean! One of the small joys of her life were those first moments of breathing fresh, unadulterated, unrecycled *air*: the real stuff.

She inhaled through her mask, tentatively at first, because her lungs were still not working as well as they should—one of the reasons she was the perfect candidate for Petaybee in the eyes of her employers. Gradually she began to take deeper breaths; she wanted to flush the dead air of a spaceship out of her poor abused lungs. They would have even more of a chance to heal here in Petaybee's unpolluted atmosphere than in the rarefied aisles of that medical complex back on Andromeda Station.

She took in one deep breath too many and started to cough, gasp, and choke until her eyes teared with the spasms. Panting with short chest inhalations, she managed to get control again. The tears froze on her cheeks and she brushed them away. Grimly she thought that you could have too much of a good thing—even air. And she had better get back inside: for all she was wearing garb appropriate to the new climate, she could feel her fingers and toes numbing. She spared one look at the horizon, the great bowl of a blue sky without so much as a defense shield over the spaceport, and the ice-covered land and wondered if she really had made the right decision.

Slipping back inside, she pushed the hood off, pulled down the scarf, and scanned her nearest neighbors. Only one of them seemed to notice that she had left and come back. He blinked and frowned before turning his attention to the screen at the far end of the long hall where the names of those to be processed were blinking. Y. MADDOCK was one of them.

She moved forward, squeezing past people until she came to the more eager layers of folk, packed tightly as they waited for release.

"Maddock, Y," she said to the official, offering her plastics.

"ID," he said without looking up from his terminal.

She extended her left wrist, and with rough fingers, he turned it so he could see it, bending her hand painfully.

"You're cold!" He looked up now, seeing her as a person, not a number.

She shrugged. "Leaning against that door."

"Humpf. Didn't you attend the briefing?" He frowned. "Don't touch metal . . ."

"Even inside?" she asked with the innocent inquiring look she had used to flummox brighter men than this one.

He frowned, and then the terminal required his attention, her plastic having jumped out of the processing slot. It skidded halfway across the worktop before he caught it. Yana kept her face straight: he looked the sort not likely to appreciate chasing anything, much less plastic.

A slip of film extruded from the slot by her hand.

"That has your work number, which you will memorize, work assignment, living quarters, ration status, travel and clothing allowance, and the name of your official guide as well as his office hours. Your travel pack has already been delivered to your quarters." Then he paused and startled her by smiling. "You can take one of the waiting vehicles outside the terminal, Major Maddock. Welcome to Petaybee."

Amazed by both the courtesy and the unexpected smile, Yana thanked him and moved smartly out of the way to make room for the next person in line.

A translucent roof shield protected the area outside the passenger terminal. It was filled with the sounds of confusion and impatience as the processed arrivees, most of them lugging their precious 23.5 kilo personal-allowance sacks, searched for each other or for transportation.

"Yellow slip, huh?" someone said in her ear, pulling her hand down to peer at it.

The someone was a young girl, so bundled in furs that only her face was visible, and that slightly obscured by long wisps of fur and, possibly, her own hair. She appeared to be in her early to mid-teens; her keen gray eyes were alive with intelligence and interest.

"I'm cleared for yellow, too," the girl added, and her mittened hand shoved a plastic square under Yana's eyes. The woman grabbed her hand for a longer look at the official-looking plastic. The girl didn't resist, though her eyes widened slightly at the strength of Yana's grasp.

The plastic-covered printed documentation licensed Buneka Rourke to convey passengers in an authorized snocle within the environs of the port but no farther.

There was a large A in the right-hand corner and a renewal date sometime later on in Petaybee's year.

"How much?"

Buneka Rourke blinked and then grinned companionably. "From here to your place, it's on the PTBs."

"The PTBs?" Yana wasn't sure she had heard correctly.

Buneka's grin broadened, and her eyes twinkled with mischief. "Sure, PTB—the powers that be. Petaybee," she added. "You didn't know that's where this planet got its name?"

"The briefing said it was Planet, Terraformation B," Yana said.

The girl waved her mitten dismissively. "They would manage to make it sound dull. But it's really named after them—the Powers That Be that move us from A to B or Z or wherever they gotta plug holes or clean up disasters or fight wars. C'mon. Let me get you out of this mess and give you a proper welcome to Petaybee." The girl tugged at Yana's sleeve, pointing to a battered-looking but clean orange/yellow snocle with fluorescent numerals, MTS-80-84, that matched those Yana had seen on the plastic ID. But as Yana stepped off the curb, a big figure intervened.

"Yellow ticket? I take yellow tickets." The man glared menacingly at the girl. "You doan wanna ride with this flitter-face. She turn you over into snow drift. No one find you. Yellow ticket deserves big, warm snocle." He gestured toward a large, sleek affair.

"I've already—" she began.

"Terce, she's legally mine."

"You ain't cleared for yellows," the man said, hunch-ing belligerently over the girl. He was a tall enough man, but the furs made him even more bulky.

"Am, too." She waved her ID at him; snarling, he batted at her hand, dismissing her qualification. "I got a passenger all legal, Terce," she went on. "You weren't even here."

Yana deftly inserted herself between them and made eye contact with the intruder. "I've already accepted Rourke's assistance, but I thank you for your willingness to transport me."

"I gotta, dama . . ."

At first Yana thought he was swearing at her and then realized that he was bowing with great subservience. There was an edge of anxiety in his voice and manner.

"You're safer with *me*," the girl said, glaring such a challenge first at Yana and then at Terce that Yana sensed that more was at stake than just a fare.

"Look, girl, another yellow ticket." Terce gestured toward a man whose yellow ticket was plainly visible in his hand, "you take 'im." Then he took a firm hold on Yana's upper arm and began to swing her toward his vehicle.

Deftly, almost automatically, Yana disengaged her arm and then strode across to the battered little MTS-registered snocle.

"Dama, dama," Terce cried, real concern in his voice.

Yana ignored him, lengthening her stride when she heard the triumphant exclamation from Buneka, followed by the sound of boots slithering across the snowmush behind her. Yana hit the door release on the passenger's side, then paused a moment to catch her breath before she slung her sacks onto the rear storage shelf. Still chuckling over her success, the girl slid into the driver's seat.

"You'd better button up. This thing takes longer to warm up than Terce's fancy sleigh."

"And I'm safer with you?" Yana asked at her driest, as she rearranged her hood and scarf and belted into the seat before slipping her hands back into the fur mittens.

The girl's eyes crinkled. "Well, Terce is known to do 'errands' for folk. My hunch is he was there on purpose to collect you. If you'd wanted to go with him, you could have, of course, but you didn't. So you didn't know he was there to meet you. So ... you're safer with me—especially the way he was acting. He's not very bright." Her remark was couched in a kindly tone but held a hint of caution nonetheless. She glanced over at Yana, her eyes bright, alert.

Well, Yana mused. An hour on the planet and intrigue starts already. Never a dull moment, no matter what the spaceflot about Petaybee was. PTB! Powers that be. She chuckled at the thought but let that also be an answer for her driver.

The chuckle turned into one of her coughing fits, and between spasms she fumbled in her sack for her bottle of syrup. She was suddenly weak with the effort it took to draw enough breath between explosions that threatened to blow her ribs apart. The fur mittens made her hands clumsy, and she almost dropped the bottle before she could peel a mitten from her shaking hand and get the plastic cap off. As soon as the syrup began to coat her pharynx, the spasm eased. She cradled the bottle in her hands, against her chest. The preparation had a lot of alcohol in it, but she still wouldn't risk it freezing.

The girl slowed the vehicle and looked back at her

with wide eyes. Poor kid looked as if she were wishing that she had let Terce take her fare.

"Are you—all right, Major?"

Yana gulped another swallow of the syrup, this time feeling the warmth spreading into the poisoned cavities of her damaged lungs. Every time she coughed, the images flashed through her brain of the graphic films the doctors had shown her when they had explained why she was no longer fit for active duty. As if the fact that she couldn't laugh or hoist a duffel bag without a paroxysm of coughing wasn't evidence enough of her disability. Still, she was alive, which was more than the others were. She recapped the bottle, tucked it into her parka pocket, and pulled the mitten back over her hand. It was already going numb with cold. She noted with satisfaction, however, that there was no blood on either mitten.

Catching the girl's anxious look, she said, "Don't worry, Rourke, it's not contagious. Took a little gas at Bremport Station was all."

"From the sound of that cough, you must have had a nasty time of it," the girl remarked, speeding up slightly again but proceeding more cautiously than before, as if afraid the jarring would set her passenger off again.

"You might say that," Yana said, thinking of the others. The hell of it was, she had been through a lot worse in her younger days and had come through without a scratch. Bremport was supposed to have been a routine training mission—new recruits, a couple of them from Petaybee, she remembered. She remembered just about everything from that mission, over and over again.

Using the technique she had learned a long time before from one of her old sergeants, she switched her focus, letting her eyes rest on the panorama of blue and white nothingness, the featureless landscape soothing her, helping her blank her mind, the cold in the air matching the cold inside her.

Ground-hugging vegetation pierced lumps of snow with frozen spines. Then she noticed that the snocle track was on ground slightly lower than the rest of the terrain.

"You guys dig a new road here, huh?" she asked her driver.

Rourke snorted. "Not a bit of it. Do you think they'd be spendin' money on improvements for the likes of us? This—is the river!"

"No kidding?" Yana looked out and down. Where the snow had blown away in one patch, she saw the translucence of powder blue ice. "Anybody ever fall through the ice?"

"Not lately. Even this late in the winter it's still between minus seventy-five and minus thirty most of the time."

"If everything is frozen, what do you do about drinking water?" Company leaders automatically considered such details.

"Oh, that. I'll show you." The girl grinned and continued on.

After a few moments the ground had more rise and fall to it. Beside it, stunted trees, rooted and branched in billows of snow, began appearing closer and closer together until they formed a sparse forest on either side of the snocle. The girl veered the machine over toward the trees, and around the next bend, Yana saw a little pavilion set up on the ice, smoke rising from a hole in the top. Rourke had been decreasing the speed of her snocle and now drifted to a gentle stop.

The tent shook slightly from within and what looked at first like a bear emerged.

"Sláinte, Bunny!" the bear said with a wave, dispelling the illusion. The fur-clad man lumbered forward, lifting his great fur boots high above the snow. His face bristled with icicles from the ruff around his mouth and nose, which was only lightly frosted, to his beard, eyebrows, and mustache, which were thickly encrusted with ice.

"Sláinte, Uncle Seamus!" The girl waved back and cut the motor. The man's eyes flicked up through his personal icicles to glance at Yana, a searching look for all its brevity. "This is Major Maddock, Uncle. She's going to be staying at Kilcoole."

"Is she now?" He included Yana in his wave, and she nodded at him.

"Do you have some thermos or two for me to take to Auntie, since I'm passing her way?" Bunny asked.

"Now, that would be very good of you, Bunny. I've two now, and I'll have more later when Charlie and the dogs come along. This dama doesn't mind stopping on her way, does she?"

"Nah! She won't mind. Will you, Major? You wanted to see how we got water. Come look in the shed."

Moving a little more slowly than she would have liked, Yana climbed from the snocle. Out here, on the river, the cold immediately clenched its fist around her face and thighs, the only parts of her that weren't encased in synfur. She hoisted the muffler around her nose, but the sweet smell of woodsmoke still came through. She wondered if it would set her coughing again. But there was Bunny, encouragingly holding up the flap of the tent and pointing to the fire burning in a circle around the rim of a long black hole in the ice. An insulated container on a length of line stood beside the hole, along with two other containers, which Seamus now gave Bunny.

Yana took a couple of steps toward the tent before the smoke from the fires wafted toward her. She felt her throat seizing up and stepped back, silently cursing her weakness. How the frag was she going to survive on a cold planet if she couldn't breathe in the presence of fire?

Bunny, her shoulders bowed as she hauled one of the thermoses with both hands so that the container bumped against her shins, nodded to Yana to return to the snocle. Yana was relieved not to put her lungs through any further ordeal. She turned with more enthusiasm than was prudent and her feet promptly slid on the ice underlying the thin covering of drifted snow. She placed her feet more cautiously then, and managed to make it back to the snocle without falling.

Seamus set the other water thermos in beside her and ran a mitten across his face, an accustomed gesture that dislodged some of his facial icicles. "Welcome to Petaybee, such as it is, Major. You need something, you just ask Bunny here."

Yana nodded. "Thanks." It was just possible that, if her official guide turned out to be anywhere near as inept as she herself was in this environment, she would find Bunny's unofficial assistance more useful.

They arrived at Yana's new quarters long after darkness had fallen, though by Yana's calculation it was no more than late afternoon. She looked at the small single house standing alone on pilings beside others of similar construction. It had one window and one door that she could see in the gloom, and the window was small. Whatever. It was bound to be roomier than some of the berths she'd had, and compared to her place on the ward at the space-station hospital, it looked palatial, as well as incredibly private.

Bunny hefted her duffel out of the snocle for her and pushed open the door. The interior was spare, white as the outdoors, and contained a cot, a small table on which rested her survival pack, a chair, and a stove for heating and cooking.

"It's too late for you to inprocess today. Sorry it took so long," Bunny said. "Look, wait here and I'll get some blankets. You'd better take this water, too. No one's given you your ration." She nodded toward the thermos on a shelf beyond the stove.

"That's for your auntie, isn't it?" Yana asked. "And I can scarcely take your blankets, too."

Bunny shook her head. "They won't care about the water, and I can spare the blanket. You'll be issued your own tomorrow."

She drove away in the snocle and, in a short time, returned on foot, carrying a bundle of puffy cloth and a packet. "Smoked salmon strips," she said, indicating the packet.

"What?"

"Fish. It's good," Bunny said patiently. "You'll like it."

Yana's day had started back at the station hospital nearly thirty hours earlier, and she couldn't face anything more taxing than rolling up in blankets and going to sleep as fast as possible. "Thanks," she said.

"Okay, then. Shall I pick you up in the morning to meet your guide? I could get the blanket then, too."

Aha, Yana thought, a little blackmail here to ensure the continuing custom. Very enterprising. "That'll be fine," she said with a weary lift of her eyes that would have to pass for a smile. Bunny showed her how to light the stove before she left and promised to help her organize more fuel the next day.

Without waiting for the room to warm up enough for her to remove her outerwear, Yana arranged the chair at the head of the cot, sat down, and stretched her legs out on the bed. She had chewed only a couple of bites of the oddly spiced salmon strip before she fell asleep, as she had for the last few weeks, sitting up.

Bunny Rourke returned to her aunt's house after delivering the blankets to her client and returning the snocle to its special shed.

"I'll need to check it out again in the morning," she'd told Adak O'Connor, the dispatcher and guard.

"No shuttles due from SpaceBase for another week," Adak said, removing his headphones and turning away from the radio that connected him to SpaceBase and the few other places on Petaybee that had such advanced equipment. He scowled at his record book, which contained the schedules for the port and kept track of the whereabouts of the vehicles—both of them. Bunny was licensed to drive one, Terce the other: they were the only authorized drivers to and from Kilcoole. The shuttles belonged to InterGalactic Enterprises, known as Intergal, the omnipresent if not omnipotent corporation responsible for the existence of Petaybee, and the boss of all Bunny's people. Bunny had qualified for her license only because one of her uncles was an important man and owned his own snocle as *well* as dogs. When Bunny's parents had disappeared, Uncle had taught her to drive the snocle to help her make her own way in the village so she wouldn't be a burden. She was Uncle's driver on the rare occasions when he preferred the snocle to his team. She also made the trip out to his place to keep the machine running for him and repair it when it broke down—usually from neglect. Her uncle was a brilliant man but not mechanically inclined. Bunny took after her Yupik granddad: she could fix anything. And six months ago, on her fourteenth birthday, she had obtained her license to ferry passengers from SpaceBase to Kilcoole and back.

"I know there's no shuttles," she told Adak, "but my fare has to inprocess in the morning."

"Can't she walk or go by sled?"

"Nah. She's an important dama. An officer. But she's puny. Said something about being at Bremport."

"The massacre where the Shanachie's boy was killed? Ah, the poor dama. And how is she puny?"

"She coughs. Bad. But she seems nice. Anyway, the snocle is authorized for official functions, so I want to take her round to the outpost as quick as possible so she can settle in, like."

"Good child. You've taken to this dama, have you?"

"She's sleepin' this night under the quilt Auntie Moira made me."

"Then by all means take the snocle in the morning, but mind you, no sight-seein'."

"Thanks, Adak," she said. "I'll bring you one of

Auntie Moira's cakes in the morning when I come, shall I?"

"That would be very welcome, Bunny. Good night now."

"Good night," she said, and headed back to the shed behind her aunt's house.

Ever since her older male cousins had turned a little too inquisitive about her development, Bunny had preferred to sleep out here, in back of the kennel where Charlie kept his team of noisy and protective dogs, who warned her of anyone approaching. She wasn't really scared, though. Most of the people who came to see her brought her things—fish or moose chops, zucchini or tomatoes in the summer—though some came just to visit. She was personally related to a large percentage of the village, and she knew who would help her and who to avoid. There were a few people she didn't want coming to her place—Terce, for one, but he was scared of Charlie's dogs. Mostly, everyone looked out for her. That would have made her feel like a child except that she looked out for them, too. That was how it was in Kilcoole. She was actually very adult for someone her age, trusted with the responsibility of living on her own and holding down her own job.

Approaching her house, she was greeted by the hounds, who set up a good welcoming howl as she walked quickly through them, unclipping the lines from Pearse and the lead dog, Maud.

She was pleasantly surprised to see smoke rolling up from her chimney to the sky. As she followed its path she saw the lights were on display tonight: a simple pale green band whipping across the black sky, dancing and twisting and sequined with stars. The smoke from the chimney smelled grand—nutty and warm. Maud whined and stuck her long muzzle in Bunny's pocket. The dogs were more used to Bunny, who had time for them and who usually fed and exercised them, than they were to Charlie, who was their owner. Bunny petted Maud absently. Even with her stove getting a head start on the chill, without her quilt she would need the dogs for warmth tonight. She would let them in to get toasty by the fire while she ate her supper.

The big red dogs with their thick soft coats took up most of the floor space in the little shed. It contained her berth, a scrounged unit cut out of one of the dead ships at SpaceBase, a shaky tabletop pegged into the wall and placed so she could sit on her berth to eat, plus the stove and the shelves she had built from old storage crates to hold her few belongings. She had the three books left her by her parents, a set of tools—a gift from her uncle upon obtaining her license—and a selection of shells, rocks, and mushroom-shaped tree tumors, as well as hand-me-downs from the cousins and what little gear she had. On the table was a mare's-butter candle; it gave a fairly bright light, though it didn't smell very good. Her shed was built of stone, of which Petaybee had plenty. She had caulked it with mud two breakups earlier and reinforced it with some plasti her Cousin Simon had scrounged for her at the SpaceBase when he first joined the corps, before he shipped out. The plasti had originally been used to repair the bubble around the SpaceBase garden, and it did well in the cold, never cracking or contracting.

Something plopped down beside her onto the table and mewed up at her. She reached down to stroke the rust-and-cream stripes of one of Aunt Clodagh's cats, though which she couldn't say since so many of the Kilcoole felines were orange-marmalades. The cat pawed the door, and Bunny smiled and followed, chattering to the cat.

"So Clodagh already knows about my passenger, does she, and left you here to tell me to report? Glad to, cat, as long as there's a bite in it for me."

The dogs in the shed had ignored the cat; the ones in the yard did not bark as it led her through the kennels. No one's dogs ever barked at Clodagh's cats. They went where they pleased and knew where everything was and what everyone was doing—as did Clodagh.

2

The official guide—only a second lieutenant, Yana noted—stood up when she entered the room.

"Major Maddock," he said, saluting and flashing her quite an energetic smile. "Lieutenant Charles Demintieff, first Petaybee military liaison officer, at your service, dama."

"Relax, Lieutenant," she said. "I'm reporting to you, not the other way round."

"Yes'm. It's just that I've read your file, and we don't get many heroes back here."

"Most heroes don't make it back anywhere," she said.

He laughed as if she had said something extremely witty. "Then we're luckier still to have you, Major. Colonel Giancarlo from SpaceBase snocled in this morning to welcome you personally. When you've had your chat with him, we'll go over the routine stuff."

Walking into the adjoining room, Yana felt as wary as if she were entering the bridge of an enemy-held ship. If the SpaceBase brass wanted to talk to her, why hadn't he done it at Inprocessing and saved himself a long, cold ride?

The colonel, in contrast to the lieutenant, did not look

happy to see her. His insignia was one she had seen only occasionally: Psychological Operations, a euphemism for the Intelligence branch. She reported, and he waved her into a chair while he continued typing something into a terminal.

"Well, Major," he said after she had been sitting there long enough to become impatient and uncomfortable in her heavy gear. "What do you think of Petaybee so far?"

"Seems friendly," she said cautiously. He was testing her somehow, but she wasn't sure for what. "The air is clean, pretty cold. Fairly primitive technologically. New recruits from here need extensive training in the simplest equipment, and it's pretty obvious why, from what I've seen of my quarters and the village. Am I missing something?"

"If you are, you're not alone," he said, his eyes shifting from the terminal to hers and boring into them. "There shouldn't be anything here that we didn't put here. This planet was nothing but rock and ice when Intergal claimed it. The company terraformed it, upgrading it from frozen uninhabitable rock to a merely arctic climate. For the last two hundred years, it's been useful as a replacement depot for troops, a relocation center for the peoples who were being displaced by our other operations. Because the climate is rough on machinery, only SpaceBase contains much in the way of modern comforts. The transportation needs of the inhabitants are mostly supplied by experimental animals bred for the purpose."

"Experimental?" Yana asked. "Like lab animals?" She had been born on Earth but had spent her childhood being shunted with her parents from one duty station to the next. Lab rats and monkeys were somewhat familiar to her, along with a number of different alien species, but she was unfamiliar—except from pictures—with the beasts she had seen on her way here today.

"Not exactly, although I suppose their ancestors did some time in a lab—originally. The company hired Dr. Sean Shongili to alter certain existing species to adapt to this climate. That's how the resident equines, felines, and canines, and many of the aquatic mammals, come to be here."

"I see," she said, but she didn't. The dogs obviously worked as sled animals, the cats to keep down rodents. But she couldn't understand why Petaybee supported equines, too. Horses, from what little she knew of them, seemed rather inappropriate for such a climate. And considering the need for hacking and burning holes in ice to secure water, wasting such effort on domestic pets seemed totally unproductive.

"Well, Intergal doesn't, entirely," the colonel said, as if he had read her thoughts. "The animals we commissioned are here, but there have been sightings of other types that indicate perhaps Dr. Shongili and his assistants were a trifle more creative than was covered by their authorization. The current Dr. Shongili, also Sean, is certainly an odd bird, not what you'd call a team player. We've monitored his records, however, and can't find any evidence that he's been exceeding his instructions. We could, of course, move him, but this is not a research area favored by many in our employ, and the Shongilis have done so well at producing viable species for arctic conditions that we're reluctant to remove the current Shongili without more concrete evidence. Trouble is, unauthorized species are not the only anomaly. Something else is going on here—our satellite monitors have detected deposits of important minerals on this planet. When we dispatch teams, they either can't find the location of the deposits, or else they simply don't return."

"That's why psyops is interested?" she asked, relaxing a little.

"You got it." Suddenly he grinned at her, an expression that did not make him any more attractive. "That's where we can help each other, Major."

"Sir?"

"You're here this morning technically to be demobilized. You're a medical retiree due to spend the rest of your days on this iceberg, which is unfortunate for you. However, your experience as an intercommand investigator, and your earlier work with preliminary datagathering landing teams, is of some interest to us, despite your disability, as is your record of combat experience. You don't realize it yet, of course, but being a combat veteran carries considerable cachet in this place where most families have at least one, and usually several, relatives in the corps. Furthermore your genetic stock is similar to these people's." He eyed her, and Yanaba knew he was assessing the sprinkle of white in the black hair that Bry used to claim had an auburn cast under bright light, the high cheekbones, the rather bleached-out olive complexion, and the slightly tilted green-gold eyes. Her body had once been lean and athletic, but weeks of illness had reduced her to brittle gauntness at a weight she might have enjoyed had her strength not deserted her along with the extra kilos.

"How's that?" she asked, mystified.

"The people on this continent are a mixture of Irish and Eskimo—we've resettled cold-weather natives all over the planet to assist the others in assimilation. In this area it's Eskimo: in other settlements, ethnic Scandinavians and Indo-Asians."

"I don't exactly fit then," she said, smiling as tolerantly as possible.

"Well, of course, you were practically born into the company, but your father was Irish and your first name, *Yan*aba—"

"*Yan*aba," she corrected. "That's Navajo—my mother's people. It's a war name, like a lot of traditional Navajo names. Means 'she meets the enemy.' The Navajo, by the way, were desert dwellers, not snow people."

"Close enough," he said. "Desert can get damned cold midwinter." He dismissed her objection with a wave.

That told her she had made a tactical error by showing up his ignorance before she heard what he wanted. But she had a fierce loyalty to her family. All she had of them now was the history recorded in the computers for her by her parents before their deaths. It was about all she had had in her life that hadn't been Intergal-issued.

"We think you can fit, Maddock," he told her. "And we want you to do just that, because we need to know what's going on. We want you to get to know the people, find out what or who exactly is responsible for these problems: if Shongili is concealing experiments in producing new life-forms on this planet, we need to know about it. If the geologic survey teams are being deliberately ambushed and eliminated, we want to know that, and we want to know whom we have to deal with. You don't have enough technical knowledge to locate the deposits yourself, but we want you to find out who's preventing our teams from locating them. If there's some kind of sabotage or incipient insurrection brewing, help us put a stop to it."

"Wouldn't it have been more effective to recruit a local informant?" she asked.

Giancarlo snorted. "There's something screwy about all of them. They all stick together all the time, and every time I've had one of them in my office for any length of time, they start sweating and turn red. Why would that happen if they're not scared, hiding something? Even Demintieff sweats like crazy every time he comes in while I'm here. This office is always freezing when I arrive, and even while I'm here, he keeps that outer office way too cold. These people also have gatherings that nobody from SpaceBase is invited to, and if you ask one of the new recruits from here about it, they just shrug."

"You haven't actively interrogated anyone yet, then?"

"No real excuse so far. What would I ask? Why do you people sweat so damned much, and how come I don't get invited to your parties?"

Yana nodded.

He leaned forward and stabbed at the desk with his finger, as if the gesture would somehow make his words plainer. "We need someone loyal to the company to gain their confidence, find out what's going on."

"What if they just sweat because they're used to the cold, and they have orgies or something at their parties and don't want to mingle with outsiders out of embarrassment?"

"Major, perhaps I didn't make myself clear. You were injured at Bremport; you saw what happened there. I shouldn't have to tell *you* what swamps of insurgency these colonial planets can be. Unauthorized life-forms *have* been spotted on this planet. Research-and-development teams *have* disappeared into nowhere. You can't tell me these circumstances aren't related. What you have to tell me instead is how they *are* connected with each other. Do you read me?"

She nodded, cautiously, and evidently mistaking her caution for hesitation he pressed on.

"You said something about your quarters. They're pretty standard for down here, but we certainly have the wherewithal to make them more comfortable. Also, you're not full retirement age yet, nor eligible for full pension."

"I have a medical discharge, sir."

"Not exactly. Not yet. Actually your disability status as of now is"— He tapped a key. —"only twenty-five percent. That won't generate much of a pension. If you were on covert active duty, however, you could do a lot better. We could even throw in hazardous-duty pay."

"Sir, with all due respect, while I wouldn't sniff at the money, the doctors back at the hospital . . ."

"You can't contact them from here, Maddock. And in the event you need further, fairly expensive care, the transport from here back to there would be beyond your means, unless, of course, Intergal foots the bill. I'll expect progress reports via Deminticff on a weekly basis unless, of course, something comes up that I should know about instanter. Demintieff will take you around, introduce you to people . . ."

Whatever this guy's specialty was, Yana reflected, it wasn't the gentle art of psychological persuasion. He was about as subtle as a photon torpedo. But she owed Intergal her life and had spent her life in its service. She wasn't going to turn them down just because this hammerhead thought he was blackmailing her. Besides, she *could* use the pay.

"With respect, sir, I think maybe Demintieff should do the bare minimum of guiding me around. Seems to me I'd be better off on my own. I'd be less suspect to any possible terrorists within the area if an indigenous civilian helped me acclimate rather than a uniformed professional."

"Good thinking, Maddock. This conversation never happened, of course." He dug a sheaf of old-fashioned hard copy from a case at his feet. "However, this contains a full briefing on what we know and suspect thus far. Familiarize yourself with it and burn it."

"Yes, sir."

"Enjoy your retirement, Maddock."

Bunny Rourke was sitting on the edge of Lieutenant Demintieff's desk when Yana and Colonel Giancarlo emerged. Neither Bunny nor Demintieff was perspiring unduly as far as Yana could see, although at the sight of the colonel, Bunny fled through the doorway with barely a nod to Yana.

"Demintieff!" the colonel snapped.

"Sir!"

"You're to report to SpaceBase. Congratulations, son, you've been chosen for duty shipside."

"But, sir . . ." The lieutenant, formerly so cheerfully obsequious, looked as stunned as if the colonel had suddenly kicked him in the balls. He evidently did not feel that congratulations were in order.

"Grab your gear on the double and you can ride back with me, soldier."

"Permission to say good-bye to my family, sir," Demintieff said with some difficulty.

"Permission granted as long as you can do it within the next forty-five minutes. Duty calls, son."

"Yes, sir."

"Maddock, in view of this man's reassignment, you are authorized to requisition civilian assistance during your civilian orientation process or until the position can be reassigned."

"Yes, sir. May I suggest my driver, Miss Rourke, sir?"

"Sure, Colonel, Bunny will look after the major," Demintieff put in, rather gallantly, Yana thought, in view of his own evident distress. "She's my own sister's cousin-by-marriage and a very good girl."

Seeing this side of Demintieff, and realizing how well-connected he was locally, Yana cursed herself for making suggestions before she got the lay of the land. He would have done as well as Bunny from the standpoint of gaining the trust of the villagers, but now he was being sent away from home, an assignment he obviously did not relish, to provide a reason for the change in routine. Damn fool shouldn't have enlisted if he didn't want to serve shipside, she thought fiercely, but she had trouble meeting his eye. Giancarlo returned to the inner room, and Demintieff's eyes were brimming shamelessly as he turned toward her.

"Dama, would you and Bunny mind very much givin' me a lift up to Clodagh's? My gear's there, and Clodagh'll see to it that my family in Tanana Bay get notified."

Yana could only duck her head as the lieutenant

scooped up a tightly wrapped bundle from his desk, started to hand it to her, then carried it out to the snocle.

Bunny was starting the engine when Yana and Demintieff emerged from the building. She started to say something when Demintieff climbed in beside her, leaving Yana the back section, but Demintieff cut her off with "Take me to Clodagh's quick, Bunny. They're shipping me into space." In his distress, his voice had thickened into the same oddly precise brogue coloring of Bunny's and her Uncle Seamus's speech.

Brilliant start, Major Maddock, Yana told herself. Everybody on this damned planet seemed to be related to everybody else.

"Okay, Charlie, but I'll have to drop you and Yana off and take the snocle back. I'm only checked out for another fifteen minutes. I'll hitch up the dogs to take Yana home and bring you back over here."

"If there's time. Giancarlo may requisition your snocle to take us back to SpaceBase, though Terce brought him out. You'll look after my dogs, won't you, Bunny? They already think you belong to them, and I want them to be well cared for; they've been with me since they were pups." He dug through layers of fur and found a wallet, then handed her a wad of bills. "Here's to help you with their food."

She released one hand from the wheel and accepted the money, stuffing it in her parka. "No problem, Charlie. I'll keep on looking after them. You didn't know about this reassignment?"

"No idea. He decided just like that."

Yana found herself leaning forward, wheezing into Demintieff's ear: "You'll be going to Andromeda Station to inprocess and for assignment. When you get there, unless he's gone now, the master sergeant in charge of deployment is Ahmed Threadgill. Tell him Yana Maddock sends her love and reminds him of the time she alerted him to the Ship Police raid. He'll know what I mean." Ahmed would know she was calling in the favor and that he was to look after her friend. It wasn't much, considering the way she had caused however so inadvertently the situation, but it could keep his hide intact.

"Yes, Major Maddock. Thank you, dama."

She clapped him on the shoulder, a little feebly, and sat back until Bunny skidded to a halt outside a house a little larger than Yana's own quarters. The morning's exertions had left her panting and trembling with fatigue, but she still took note of this house. The snow in front of it was full of huge, strangely shaped lumps, and the crusted snow all around them was lightly dotted with what looked like some kind of shit, which vaguely shocked ship-bred Yana. Stiff oval nets with points at each end hung over the door, three pairs of what were unmistakably skis leaned against the side of the house, and from the back of the house issued a high-pitched keening, like a woman screaming.

"I'll take you back in a minute, Major, if that's okay," Bunny called back as Yana climbed out of the vehicle. "Besides, you'll want to meet Clodagh. She was asking after you last night at supper."

Charlie Demintieff grabbed the bundle of cloth from the snocle, and Bunny drove away.

The screams erupted again and Yana hung back, tensed, listening. Charlie, who had already taken a step toward the house, turned ponderously in his furs, saw her staring, and touched the elbow of her coat with his mitten.

"That's just the dogs," he said, his mouth spilling clouds of condensation into the air, as if his words were freezing there. "When our dogs were first made, our grandfathers called them banshee-dogs because of that sound, but they're just saying hello."

Yana nodded, hearing her own breath rasping in her ears above the screams of the dogs, and willed herself to relax and follow Charlie to the house. A feline with rust-and-cream markings stood on the roof above the doorway and looked down at them as if considering a pounce. On another corner of the house sat the cat's twin, resembling pictures Yana had seen of the gargoyles decorating ancient Terran architecture. Another of the creatures sat in each of the windows flanking the door.

Just as Charlie reached the door, it opened before him and was filled by the largest woman Yana had ever seen. Of course, people on shipboard were required to keep their body weight to a certain level, a requirement necessitated by the narrow passages, small hatches, and the close confinement of the rooms. Also, anyone in space had to be able to fit into the suits and, should it become necessary, the cold-sleep shells. The rigors of shipboard life plus the uninspiring quality of the nutritious but mostly tasteless rations guaranteed that regulations were easily met by all personnel.

But this woman! She was like a planet herself, or at least an ovoid meteorite, a large round entity unto herself—imposing, to say the least.

"Charlie," the huge woman said as she opened the door. "I hear you're leaving us." She threw a hard look over his shoulder to Yana, as if divining her role in the matter.

The woman fell back, and Charlie Demintieff stepped into the house, holding aside the standard-issue gray military blanket that covered the inside of the door so that Yana could enter.

Demintieff stripped off his hat, muffler, and gloves and loosened the front of his coat; Yana followed suit. The house was small and close, but not as warm as Yana would have expected. Nevertheless, as Giancarlo had indicated, the woman's upper lip and brow were dewed with perspiration. Yana wasn't sure, however, if the moisture on Demintieff's face was sweat, tears, or melting ice from his hair and eyelashes.

The woman embraced Demintieff, her caress oddly delicate and tender for such a massive being. Demintieff returned her embrace with every evidence of affection.

"Don't worry, Charlie," the woman said. "Natark is hitching his team now. He should be in Tanana Bay by tonight."

Demintieff showed no surprise that the woman had anticipated his news, but simply said, "Thanks, Clodagh. I just wanted to say good-bye. Bunny's taking my dogs."

"Good. Good. Bunny treats them well," Clodagh said, making no further attempt to comfort him but seeming to share his sadness. She offered neither a look nor a word of false encouragement that he was likely to return: they all knew he probably wouldn't.

"This is Major Maddock, Clodagh."

"Ah, the dying woman," Clodagh said. It should have sounded tactless except that her tone was vaguely ironic, indicating that she was only referring to Yana's

own opinion of herself, as if they had already had a
long discussion about it. A soft smile and the penetrating gaze of Clodagh's tilted blue eyes also showed that
she meant no offense but simply cut straight to the
heart of Yana's concerns as she had to Demintieff's.

"Come, sit, have tea. Charlie's sister and the rest of
the family are on their way. Bunka will bring you to
supper tonight, if you'll come, but right now we have to
talk about Charlie."

Even as she spoke people began arriving, until the
room was crowded with bodies that smelled of wet fur,
smoke, and wet dog. Clodagh's house boasted a big table with four chairs set close to the stove. Yana, still in
her parka, was soon stifling from the heat of the stove,
but as the room filled up, she had no elbow room to remove her coat. One of the cats jumped up on the table
and began sniffing her coat and her face. She let her
hand drop to its marbled fur and it purred and took her
gesture as an invitation to settle onto her thighs.

Meanwhile, furs and scarves and quilted fabric
brushed by her and she wondered that people didn't
singe themselves on the hot stove as they wished Charlie Demintieff farewell. Yana's debilitated lungs labored
harder as the room filled, the lack of oxygen smothering
her. She began deliberately taking deep breaths as first
one and then another of Charlie's friends and distant re-
lations stepped up to crowd around him near the stove,
envelop him in a furry hug, and step back away to make
room for the next person. Yana couldn't imagine having
so much family.

Clodagh stood among them, not as tall as some of the
men but distinguishing herself by the space around her.
Her hair, Yana noticed, was quite beautiful, cloaking her

shoulders in shining black waves, the black of a hue that somehow was not too harsh with the woman's fair skin. Her cheeks were pink with the heat now and she was perspiring freely, glowing like some benevolent sun. She didn't appear to be as old as Yana, and yet she effortlessly carried an air of the kind of authority generally conferred only by well-seasoned maturity.

Just as Yana thought she was going to have to fight her way through the crowd for air or black out, people began filing back out the door with last good-byes for Charlie, and suddenly it was the four of them again, Clodagh, Charlie, Bunny, and Yana.

"We have to hurry," Bunny told the dejected-looking young officer. "I need to drop the major and get you back."

"Okay," he said.

Clodagh put something in his hand with a soft pat before he pulled on his mittens. As they were leaving she said, "Major Maddock, will you come to supper tonight with Bunka?"

Yana nodded and waved, and turned back toward the path between the houses to face four excitedly yapping dogs strapped to a low sled.

"Climb in, Major," Bunny said.

"You're kidding. There's not room for all of us."

"You ride, and Charlie can drive. I'll run along beside," Bunny said, "just as far as your place."

Yana looked at the low, insubstantial-looking sled and the four wriggling, whimpering dogs, who were having their pointed red ears and muzzles scratched by a kneeling, sad-faced Charlie Demintieff. Their faces looked more like those of foxes or cats than those of the dogs Yana had seen pictured. Their coats were very thick and their legs fairly long and muscular, but their paws were covered in little booties. Every time one of them could get close enough to lick at Demintieff, it did.

"How far *is* my place, anyway?" Yana asked. She had not formed an impression of any vast distances within this town; on the contrary, the snocle rides had been brief.

"Just down the road," Bunny said, gesturing. "But you're not used to the cold and . . ."

"And I'm an invalid?" Yana asked, hitching her muffler up higher on her nose. "The dying woman, eh? Not dead yet, Rourke. Not by a long shot. You take Charlie back—and Charlie?"

"Dama?"

"Don't forget to look up Master Sergeant Threadgill and tell him what I told you."

Charlie nodded once, briefly, his chin set. Bunny tumbled into the sled and settled herself for transport while Charlie, one last time, whistled to his dogs, who obediently trotted off toward the company station.

Yana sighed, sending a plume of her breath up against the crisp blue sky, and began trudging in her heavy gear in the direction of her new quarters. Damn Giancarlo anyway. If he wanted her to spy for him, did he have to start off by doing something that, if the truth were known, would alienate the whole village from her? Of course, there was always the possibility that he, like Yana, had had no idea that Demintieff was *one* local boy who happened to be stationed close to home because he wished to be. But Giancarlo should have known before he went off half-cocked. If this assignment had any significance at all, he definitely should have had Demintieff checked before he decided to replace him. That kind of rashness could blow this mission.

Mission? This was supposed to be her new life! Not that it looked as if it was apt to amount to much. She ought to thank Giancarlo for giving her something to occupy her mind, to keep from going nuts here on this ice ball.

Feathers of smoke curled up from the houses; if there were any shops or supply stores, they were indistinguishable from the dwellings as far as she could see. Each step in her bulky primitive clothing was like walking in heavy gravity. She couldn't bend her head easily to see the path before her, or her muffler would fall down and her hood ride back on her head. But by turning her head slightly, she saw that many of the houses contained kennels full of dogs and had mysterious-looking lumps out front just like the ones she had seen in Clodagh's yard. Two of the larger places had not only houses but outbuildings, and in one of the yards two horses were zigzagging back and forth in the snow. Yana thought there was something strange about the horses, but she couldn't quite decide what. Never mind. She'd return to her quarters and read the briefing. She needed to find out what was regular about this place before she could determine what was *ir*regular.

She made it to her door with only one slight mishap, when she slipped once more on the ice and had to recover from a coughing fit before rising. She hadn't hurt herself seriously otherwise. How could she, with so many layers of clothing? A passerby—impossible to tell if it was a man or a woman in those wrappings, but the person was short—stopped and waited for her coughing fit to abate, then gave her a hand up. She felt like a bloody baby, and wanted to slap the person's hand away, but as soon as she was on her feet the person said in a muffled voice, "You got to walk a little duckfooted when it's slick like this."

She watched the person waddle away; then, feeling sillier than ever, she fell into a waddling gait until she reached her own door, the last one on the row.

Something bright flashed ahead of her as she opened the door, and she stiffened, until she heard a thud from the direction of the table and beheld one of the orange cats sitting upon it, nonchalantly cleaning the snow from furry paw pads.

To her relief, the log she had left burning in the stove earlier that morning was glowing coals. She wasn't sure how long such primitive material was supposed to last, but she had the impression it needed refurbishing frequently. She stripped off coat, gloves, muffler, and coverall and sat down on the chair in her uniform. She had best strip off the insignia. She sighed. That would be admitting to her present status. Whatever. She wondered what she would do for clothing here when her uniforms wore out. She had no other kind of clothing, having been shipside most of her life. Considering the assorted outerwear she had seen in Clodagh's, perhaps the locals had indigenous sources and supplies. She would have to ask Bunny where she got her furs. Meanwhile . . .

She spread the brief on the table, while the cat looked on inquisitively. The report contained a short history of Petaybee and its settlements, as well as maps showing the resource sites and the spots where the missing survey teams had last been seen.

Petaybee: third world from star XR798 in the Valdez system. The original evaluation team found no life-forms, sentient or otherwise, on the planet: the rocky surface was largely frozen during most of the solar year. The Whittaker Effect was suggested as the best terraforming package for the planet and was inaugurated. Colonization was feasible, and procedures were initiated as the planet warmed. The only land-masses available were in the polar regions, where the climate was subarctic, with a long extremely cold winter, temperatures frequently as low as or lower than -100 degrees F, summers barely two Terran months. Daylight is intense and almost constant during the summer, but dwindles rapidly into total darkness for most of the winter. Suitable colonists were chosen from ethnic groups accustomed to such conditions.

Knowing Intergal's ways, Yana doubted the "ethnic groups" had been asked their choice in the matter. She kept reading.

. . . following initial seeding, adjustments were made on-site by company staff members among the colonists. The team determined that although the planet could support life of a primitive sort, most low-level machinery and electronics would not withstand the cold. Therefore, biological alternatives were developed. Company botanists perfected food and fodder crops, and other domesticated plant life specially designed for the Petaybean growing season. Summer thawing of rivers and shorelines is facilitated by the planet's network of subterranean hot springs, which

to some extent warm the surface water, which becomes warmer as it deepens, preventing all but the shallower streams from freezing to their total depth. This deep water, along with hot springs occurring on the planet's surface and open year-round, and small quantities of melted snow, provide hydration for plants, humans, and animals.

Company geneticists also altered existing animal species to conform to the requirements of the Petaybean climate. The following species were developed under company auspices: Petaybee curly horses, for nonsnow and heavy-duty transport; fox-hounds, intelligent hybrid dogs for pulling sleds; domestic felines, originally for fur-bearing purposes but later to control the vermin, the development of which was not authorized. Additionally, fur-bearing species able to sustain themselves in the wild were introduced and specially adapted for the climate—wolverines, wolves, bears, lynx, as well as caribou, reindeer, wild sheep, and moose.

Sounded right to Yana. Just about what one would expect a fully stocked subarctic Earth clone to have. She had done the Service and London interactive holos as a kid. The only thing missing so far was the malamutes, as in Malamute Saloon, and the fox-hounds seemed to be standing in for them. Too bad there wasn't a continental mass along the equator that would be more temperate. But even with long-term terraforming, one couldn't always choose appropriate sites for continental masses, though she didn't know the geology involved in supporting Gaias.

She skimmed past the description of ocean and river

dwellers, noting that some long-extinct species on Earth had been revived for this planet, making the terraforming valuable for that purpose if no other, in her estimation. Five kinds of whales populated the ocean: orcas, humpbacks, grays, rights, and the small so-called pilot whales, as well as dolphins, otters, seals, walruses, and all of the fish and plant life necessary to support them. The only odd thing about Petaybee was that the oceans were still many times warmer deep down than they were upon the icy surface, since considerable geothermal activity was still taking place following the terraforming. This same activity accounted for volcanos, hot springs, earthquakes, and the odd domes the Irish-Yupik-descended colonists of this continent called "fairy hills," the report noted.

Yana flipped forward. Nothing irregular here yet that she had to memorize and eat. Nothing she shouldn't know—or be able to ask about, for that matter. If it was here and it was authorized to be here, it was no doubt a matter of public record.

The next aberration she found was a notation that it had been unnecessary to develop a methane-based energy system when, by the time enough colonists had settled the planet to make such considerations a priority, it was discovered that the smallish alder trees transplanted to this planet had somehow mutated far beyond the alterations of the company botanists, into a completely new hardwood that made unusually long-burning and hot fuel. That explained why her homefires were still burning, anyway.

But in the last part of the report, she began to wonder if the computer's word processor hadn't gotten scrambled with some kid's IAH game. One of the expeditionary team members, prior to her complete disappearance, had reported via land-to-ship voice transmitter that she had seen what appeared to be a unicorn. Unicorns were definitely not among the authorized species for this planet, or any other. The official theory, the report went on to say, was that the woman had suffered from snow blindness or hallucinations induced by hypothermia. This climate was hostile to those not bred to adapt to it, the report rationalized. One team member who did return from that expedition appeared to have aged at least a decade and had patently gone insane, babbling about hearing voices from the soil and tree roots, though the reports he gave of crystal caverns led the authorities to hope that there was some thread of reality in his ramblings.

The locals, both company employees and dependents, denied knowledge of crystal caverns or any of the other anomalies but did admit that sometimes they too suffered from cold-induced hallucinations, particularly when out on the trail with their teams.

Yana rubbed her fists through her hair and put the report in the stove. Like a lot of company paperwork, it didn't actually say much that couldn't have been conveyed in a short verbal briefing. Disgusted, she watched the papers burn, the cat poking its nose around her arm to see into the stove as well.

"I'm going to have to take you back to Clodagh's tonight, kittycat," she told it. It blinked golden eyes at her. "At least with so many like you stalking about, she's unlikely to have missed you."

Just then there was a thump at her door, and she called out to whoever it was to come in. By the time she realized no one was coming and had closed the stove door to investigate, the area in front of the house was as empty as it had ever been—but a bundle of wood sat beside the stoop.

Yana pulled it inside, although it could as easily have remained out in the dry, freezing air. She wanted whoever had brought it to know she had found it and planned to use it, since so far she wasn't sure how she was supposed to acquire provisions and today, at least, she didn't have enough energy left to investigate. She had given the bed quilt back to Bunny, thinking she would get a new one today. Belatedly she realized that the bundle Charlie Demintieff had been carrying might have contained her thermal blanket and other authorized survival gear. In the confusion, it had been left at Clodagh's.

The cat looked up at her expectantly, and she sat back down at the table, wishing she had a console to work on. Nothing to read, write, work at, or interact with unless she wanted to put all those clothes back on and tramp about in the cold. The cat looked up at her and mewed.

"Just as well we're taking you home tonight, beast," she told it, giving it a stroke. "Otherwise I'd go buggy, landed with so much solitude all of a sudden."

As if it understood her, the cat chirruped and hopped down from the table, where it began chasing the toggle string of her parka with every evidence of great concentration and ferocity. It leapt high with front paws spread and twisted in midair to land squarely upon the coat's drawstring. Then the cat sat down, gave its paws a lick, and looked up at her expectantly. Other than the coat's drawstring, there wasn't a single thing to dangle or roll in the cabin.

Finally Yana took off her webbed uniform belt and dragged the buckle on the floor for the animal to hunt, while it did its best to entertain her. After a while, they both fell asleep by the stove, Yana with her head on the table, the cat curled by her elbow, while the winter-muffled village of Kilcoole remained unnervingly free of clanging, computer beeps, and the hivelike activity of spacers.

Yana's sleep was light and her dreams fragmented with scenes of a surgeon using a horn growing from his head as a scalpel, twenty young troopers convulsing while clawing at a hatch as poison gas slithered into a hold that looked something like a crystal cave, and a tiny man she knew was Charlie Demintieff being pounced at by an orange cat.

Diego Metaxos hadn't been all that thrilled about being dragged down to Petaybee to watch his old man in action as a geological surveyor. In all of his sixteen years, he had never been planetside, and he expected life on Petaybee to be as dreary and routine as life on board ship. But when he saw the place, he was glad he had come, and when he met the dogs, he was even gladder. By the time the lady let him drive her dog team, he had been convinced that this trip was the most brilliant thing that had ever happened to him.

At first he had been freaked out by the whole idea of the expedition, and with good reason. Even the shrink on his dad's ship had told him that he had had a lot to be freaked out about recently. First of all, his mom had fallen for a company exec who liked Mom fine but didn't want any other attachments. Mom, a senior astrophysicist, had never exactly been the warm type, and

Diego had spent most of his life moving with her from ship to ship, or watching her come and go from various assignments while he sat in front of a teaching computer. Lots of the places Mom was assigned, there had been no one his own age, and very seldom did he find an adult who wanted to be bothered with someone else's kid. At the last couple of stations, he had begun to pal around with a few of the younger corps troops, listening to their casual conversation and admiring the hard-core way they handled themselves, but he was always conscious that he wasn't really one of them, and in case he forgot it, his mother made no bones about her displeasure in his choice of company. Then, too, about the time he started to gain a little acceptance and make one or two friends, they moved to a new station. He then had to fall back on the resources he had developed since he was a little kid, a good imagination and a quick brain. He didn't really need any friends. Both his mom and his dad were brilliant, self-sufficient people, and he was, too. All he had ever needed was computer access, and he could entertain as well as educate himself. He was good at languages, having started out speaking both Spanish and English from when he was a little kid, and he enjoyed reading actual old hard-copy stories in both languages when there was nobody he wanted to hang around with, so he got by.

He had gone to visit his dad and Steve about once every calendar year, and that was okay. He really loved his dad, even though he was a little on the perfectionistic and ultraserious side, except with Steve. Steve got him to knock it off, to relax and laugh a little. Steve was always finding neat things to share with them. He had given Diego his first hard-copy book—a Spanish-language text of *Don Quixote*—for Diego's ninth birthday.

"Pay close attention to Sancho Panza and Dulcinea," he had kidded Diego. "I'm a little of both." He struck a flamenco pose.

No wonder Dad and Mom hadn't gotten along. Even if Dad hadn't discovered he was gay, he and Mom were too much alike, both studious and serious and very literal-minded. So Diego didn't mind Dad and Steve's arrangement all that much; it just had never occurred to him that he might end up living with them.

He had just begun to get used to *that*—and he had even come to find out that Dad had wanted him all along but had been second best when it came to custody because in the eyes of company management theirs was a less-preferred sexual orientation to Mom's. Diego didn't see what difference that made. Nobody tried to tell *him* which way to swing, even if he had been ready to do any swinging of any kind. So far, he hadn't met anyone who instilled in him a desire to implement the procedures his manuals and texts described.

So he had just been getting used to his new situation and settling in when Steve had come down with some kind of virus just before Dad was due to take off for this mission to investigate something or other on Petaybee. *That* was when Dad had gotten the bright idea that Diego should come along, too, as his assistant instead of Steve, and "broaden his horizons."

In fact, he hadn't actually seen a horizon before, since he was *in* it, by dirtside reckoning. Pointing this out had caused Steve to rasp at him not to be a smartass and to give new experiences a chance. So he had come along, and to his surprise, the landscape of Petaybee looked more open and spacious than, well, than space.

But where space was black, Petaybee was blue and white, even when it turned dark, as it quickly did on their way from SpaceBase to the dinky little town where their guides met them. The sky was sort of dark ivory, and he could still see Petaybee's sun, like a small snowball hanging in the sky, as well as its two moons, one organic and one company-manufactured, in the sky.

Being here was sort of like being *inside* the moon, all pale and shining. SpaceBase was a hole and the town was ugly, but the countryside was really pretty fascinating, and the snocle ride into Kilcoole seemed all too short. The place was so much like something from his books, and yet so different that he knew he would never forget it even if he didn't decide, as his father obviously hoped, that he would become a great geologist like his old man.

Then, when they started unloading the equipment from the snocle, and a whole fleet of dogs, about fourteen to a sled, pulled up in front of the station, he started getting hooked.

The dogs were the most beautiful creatures he had ever seen. They were red as a Mars moonscape but delicately featured with foxy, intelligent faces. At first their barking scared him a little bit, but then the lady—when she spoke he could tell she was a lady—driving his sled said they were friendly and he could pet them if he liked. They were soft! The tops of their coats were a little icy, but when he took his mitten off and dug into their fur with his hand, it was as soft as anything he had ever felt, and warm enough to keep his hand from freezing before he stuck it back into the glove. As he was bending over to pull the mitten back on, the dog licked his face. "Hey, boy!" Diego said, and hugged him.

"Girl," Lavelle, the driver, said. "That's Dinah, my leader. She likes you, and she's a good judge of character."

"Leader?"

"The dog I talk to, and the one who tells me and the other dogs what's going on up ahead, what to do. As you can see from this arrangement, mostly all the other dogs see is the rear end of the dog in front of them." The dogs wagged their curled feathery tails and grinned as if that was a great joke they all shared.

He rode with Lavelle while his dad rode in the sled in front of them. The other members of the expedition, two women, one a seismographer and one a mining engineer, and the man his dad said was a soil mechanics specialist, all of them Doctor Somebody-or-other, rode in the other sleds.

It was a great ride, bundled along with the supplies into the furs on the sled, bumping and whisking over snow and ice while the dogs ran ahead, tails bouncing. But the best part was when, once they were well out of town with nothing much in the way, Lavelle let him drive.

"When you want them to go, yell to Dinah, 'Hike!' and 'Gee!' if you want them to go right, 'Haw!' to the left, 'Whoa!' when you want them to stop. Dinah will do it and see that the others do it. She's a smart pup. You stand here." She showed him the rough hair-hide strips along the runners where he could put his feet without slipping. "The brake is here. Step on it if you want to stop, but you won't stop very quick on ice."

The other sleds all passed them, but Lavelle didn't care. As soon as he had his hands on the handlebars and his feet on the treads and Lavelle had strapped on the nets made of wood and babiche—rawhide strips—he shouted "Hike!" to Dinah and off she went, the others pulling with her, whining a little at the sound of a new voice.

Dinah was, as Lavelle said, a smart dog. She wasn't about to let the other sleds stay ahead of them and passed them easily, falling in behind the first sled, the one his father was riding in.

The run to catch up was the best part, with the wind biting into his face and blowing his breath back, the whole white-and-blue world framed in the icicles clinging to his lashes and the ruff of his hood. As soon as they slowed down to fall in behind the other sled, he got cold, then bored at having to stay so far behind. Lavelle, loping beside him with a funny knee-high gait to let each cumbersome snowshoe clear the snow before she set it down again, began telling him about the great races her grandfather had told her about, the ones they used to have in the old days in Alaska, which was part of a country back on Earth.

"One of the biggest races they had back in those days developed from a dogsled relay that took emergency serum from a big city to a little town called Nome far away," she told him. "People admired the stamina and skill it took to do it, and so they made a race out of it. Whole towns sponsored dogs and their drivers, and people all over the world knew about it. Another race they had ran along the route the mail sled used to take. It spanned two countries, and drivers from all over brought their teams to compete. In both races, they still took a little mail with them to deliver at the end."

"Why did they need to send the mail by dogsled?" Diego asked. "That's silly when they could use computers."

"Some places they didn't have computers, sometimes," she shouted back. "And sometimes folks just liked to prove they could do things in the old ways and still survive like their ancestors did. They were learning to be tough like them, you know?" She grinned, a very white grin in her sun-darkened face. "Tough like us."

He grinned back, but he thought privately it was a little backward to do things the hard way instead of learning new skills. But then, he was now doing things the old hard way and *he* was learning new skills.

They camped that night and he listened to his father talking about rocks and stuff for a while, over rations that were much the same as what he ate on the ship. Then Lavelle slipped him a stick that smelled strong, but very spicy and interesting.

"Eat it," she said. "It's good. Smoked salmon. I caught it and smoked it myself."

He nibbled on it and she sang him a peculiar song about catching that particular fish. She said the song was her own song, though the tune was to an old Irish song her Grandmother O'Toole had taught her, "The Star of the County Down."

The chorus went:

> *"From SpaceBase down to Kilcoole town*
> *On out to Tanana Bay*
> *The wild fish swims but I caught him*
> *And he's our food today."*

He fell asleep quickly in the heated shelter. The next morning when he woke up, looking forward to maybe driving the dogs again, soft powdery snow was sifting down from the sky. He knew, scientifically, that the snow was part of this world's ecosystem, but at the same time it seemed strange that he had spent so much time above this planet and had never been on it before. His father explained that snow was white rather than clear because it was a dense accumulation of light-reflecting frozen water crystals, but Lavelle showed him that each flake was a different, beautifully ornate design. He had to ride in the sled because Lavelle said they were nearing rougher country, and she had to be vigilant for the place the expedition was seeking. She promised to let him drive again on the way back.

He spent a lot of time lying in the sled, catching flakes on his mitten and trying to memorize the shapes before they melted.

"Maybe tonight at camp I'll make you some snow ice cream," Lavelle said, bending over him so that her breath blew icily into his face. "I've got some seal oil and dried berries with me, and a little sugar."

"*Seal* oil?" he asked.

"Yeah. Gives you instant energy on the trail. Don't knock it till you've tried it."

He pulled a face, and she pushed his ruff down over his eyes.

But the storm picked up as they moved, and twice the Petaybean guy, who seemed to be Lavelle's husband, asked Diego's father and the other men if they wanted to camp, but they said to keep on, that their instruments were showing them the way. The snow no longer fell in single, beautiful flakes but in clumpy sheets, so hard that it was all Diego could do to see the tails of the dogs in front of him, never mind the other sleds. All around him the world was white, and the sled moved more and more slowly, while Siggy, as Lavelle called the Petaybean guy, tried to break trail, keep track of the sleds, and persuade everyone to stop.

The ride had become much rougher, and although he couldn't see anything, Diego knew they had left the plains, because the dogs were tugging the sleds up and down little hills and, finally, up a long, long pull.

He heard Siggy yell something, and then he heard Dad cry out and the woman in front, Brit, whistle and call "Whoa, you mutts! Whoa! Oh, shit!" and multiple sounds of slipping, cracking, and sliding, but by that time the dogs had reached the summit and were plummeting down, too.

A man screamed, and several heavy things rolled and tumbled just as the sled was suddenly airborne, and Diego felt himself flying more surely than he had ever flown in the spacecraft he had lived in since he was a baby.

Lavelle called, "Whoa, Dinah! Back girl!" and Diego felt her hand pull on his ruff. For a moment she had him; then the sled jarred again and she fell, and his hood was free, and he was falling from the sled, rolling, tumbling, into the snow, over and over, until his feet struck something soft at the same time his head struck something hard, and there was darkness.

3

Yana tried to take the cat back to Clodagh's that evening when Bunny picked her up, but the cat refused to cooperate. When she tried to pick it up to carry it outdoors to Bunny's waiting sled, the cat escaped, firing a warning volley across her knuckles with its claws, and hid.

Yana explained this to Clodagh while the big woman finished stirring the contents of a pot on the stove. Delicious smells came from the pot and from the oven.

"Keep him," Clodagh advised her. Looking around the room at the four identical felines lounging on various furnishings, she added with a slight smile, "I have extras. Besides, they go where they wish and do as they choose. You seem to have been chosen."

"Yes, but what am I supposed to *do* with it?" Yana asked.

"Feed it," Bunny answered. "That's the important thing. And let it in and out as it likes, unless you want to keep an indoor tray for it."

"They do all right outdoors for prolonged periods," Clodagh said. "They've been crossbred for that, so they don't lose their tails and ears to frostbite the way their ancestors did. But they usually prefer a fire and a lap most of the time. They're good company."

"Mm," Yana said noncommittally. "I need to find out where to get things: food, clothing, wood. Someone brought a load and left it beside my door. Do you know who it was so I can thank them?"

Clodagh shrugged. "Could have been anyone. One of Bunka's relatives, maybe. Someone who knows you need more than the PTBs provided for you. Speaking of that, don't forget your pack tonight. Not that that flimsy blanket will do you a lot of good. You'll need a proper one."

"Where can I buy one of those?" Yana asked.

"Not at the company store, that's for sure!" Bunka said. "They don't have anything there but obsolete spacer stuff." She crossed to Clodagh's bed and pulled aside the standard-issue blanket to reveal another—full of lovely soft yellows, blues, and pinks—underneath. "Here, feel."

Yana leaned over and felt. The blanket was thickly woven or knitted—she had no idea which—of some heavy, long-haired material. It would be wonderfully warm.

"It's beautiful," she said.

"Speaking of that, here comes Sinead and my sister Aisling now," Clodagh said. "Sinead gathers the hair for spinning from the horses and dogs and sometimes the wild sheep she hunts and Aisling spins, dyes, and weaves the hair into the blankets. Perhaps they'll make a trade."

Another woman entered the room. She was almost as round as Clodagh; her face and hair bore a resemblance to Clodagh's, as well, but the newcomer had a much dreamier look about her. She was followed closely by a small, wiry woman who helped her off with her wraps.

"Welcome, sister, Sinead," Clodagh said, smiling at the two women. "We were just talking about you. Have you eaten?"

"Nah," said the shorter and slighter-built of the two women, shucking her outer garments off with great dispatch. "We heard you were entertaining tonight and came to gawk." She stuck out a hand to Yana. "Sinead Shongili here. Nice to meet you. Did you make it home okay without falling again?"

"You were the person who showed me how to waddle!" Yana exclaimed.

"None other. And this lovely lady is Aisling Senungatuk," Sinead said, fussing a bit over Aisling, who was settling her ample form into a rocking chair Clodagh had pulled from a corner of the room. Aisling smiled warmly up at her partner and indicated that she was comfortable.

"Yana was just admiring the blanket you women made for me, sister," Clodagh told Aisling.

"I'll put you on my list, Yana," Aisling promised in one of the loveliest voices Yana had ever heard.

"Yeah, the blankets they send you from the company are all crap," Sinead said. "I need to gather some more material for weaving, but my Aisling can make you the most gorgeous damn blanket you've ever seen, can't you, love?"

Aisling nodded, her eyes dancing when she looked at her partner. "You bet."

"I'm afraid I haven't got much to trade you for it," Yana told them, "apart from some obsolete insignia. Had to give away any souvenirs, and bring only what I couldn't do without. Baggage allowance didn't give me any latitude there. You don't know where I can get a small computer, do you?"

Sinead gave a merry laugh. "You've got to be joking."

Clodagh said, more gently, "Oh, no, dear, that's not for the likes of us, goodness me no. Nobody here in Kilcoole has such a thing. We're just poor ignorant ips you know, and the PTBs like it that way."

"Ips?"

"The inconvenient people," Aisling elaborated. "That's who they got to colonize this place. They wanted our land on Earth, you see, and promised us a new place in exchange. Frankly, we had nothing to say about it. Evicted, we were. No one could afford to own land anymore. So we came here, as they intended." Her eyes dropped as she finished the statement; then she turned an apologetic look to Clodagh. "Sorry. It doesn't do to get me started. And we should be going now. We didn't really mean to interrupt supper. We just came to see if there was anything we could do to help." She nodded in Yana's direction.

"Thanks," Yana said, and Clodagh showed them to the door, Sinead darting three steps forward and two back for each measure of her partner's statelier progress.

When they left, Clodagh pulled a bottle and some cups from the shelf over the cloth-draped cabinets along one wall and asked, "Will you be havin' a drop with your supper, dear?"

"Pardon?"

"Clodagh's home brew," Bunny said. "It's good. Gives you good dreams."

"I don't know. With all the medicine I've had lately . . ."

"It'll do you good," Clodagh said. "Has medicinal properties. You can't get sick drunk on the stuff—just a little pleasantly blurred. You look as though you need blurring, my dear."

"Clodagh's the local healer, so you can trust her on that score," Bunny told Yana.

"Just a little then," Yana agreed. The spicy smells from the stove were making her long to put something in her mouth. If not food, then drink was not a bad alternative.

But with the drink came a heaping bowl of some sort of noodles and a red meat sauce, accompanied by hot, crusty bread. She burned her lip on the first mouthful, something she had never done with prefab ship food.

"This is delicious," she said when she had had a few cooler bites. "What is it?"

"Moose spaghetti," Clodagh told her.

There was another knock at the door. Bunny hopped up, slurping in a strand of spaghetti, and opened it. A rush of cold air and a parka-clad figure entered the room at the same time.

The person, a woman, pointedly did not look at Yana as she unbuttoned her coat.

"Sedna, how's it going?" Clodagh asked her.

"Oh, fine. Just wondered if you had some mare's butter I could have. We're about out."

"No problem. Say, Sedna, have you met Major Maddock yet?" Clodagh asked.

Sedna shook her blond curls and then allowed herself to look squarely at Yana, a look which told Yana that meeting her was more the point of the visit than the mare's milk. She thought she vaguely recognized the woman from Charlie Demintieff's send-off earlier that morning.

"Major Maddock," Clodagh began.

"Yanaba, please, Clodagh, or just Yana," she said.

"Yana, this is Sedna Quinn. How's your boy's earache, Sedna?"

"Better, Clodagh, since you made up that poultice."

"You got time to eat?"

"Nah, I got to get back and help Im scrape that moose hide. I'll bring you some—"

"Well, say, if you're that busy, why don't you take some of this moose spaghetti home for supper? That way you won't have to fuss."

So Sedna sat at the edge of her chair with her coat half-buttoned while Clodagh dished up a containerful of the pasta.

"So, Bunny, pretty sad about Charlie, huh?" Sedna asked.

"Yeah, too bad. I hope he's gonna be all right. It'll be lonesome up there, I bet. I wish they'd given us time to send him off good, make a song for him. He'll miss the breakup latchkay and everything."

"I'll make a song for him, even if he won't hear it," Clodagh said.

"Maybe you could record it or write it down and Bunny could take it in when she's back at SpaceBase," Yana suggested.

Sedna straightened her back, gave Yana a pitying look, and said primly, "A song has to be sung from one person to the other to be any good."

"I'm sorry," Yana said. "I don't know your customs yet. It's just that I could see how much you all liked Lieutenant Demintieff and I know how important it is to

a soldier to hear from friends, whether they're dirtside
or on some other facility."

"It's okay, Yana," Clodagh said. "Sedna, Yana's going to be staying with us here so she'll find out soon
enough. The fact is, Yana, nobody here knows how to
record much less write."

Yana sputtered with surprise. "They don't? You
don't? But how the hell can that be? The Petaybean recruits I've met all know how; Bunny surely must know
how to have passed her snocle test."

Bunny shook her head. "That's all done on comm
link—verbal and visual cues. And of course the company teaches the soldiers to read, at least enough to get
by in the corps, in basic training and at the officers
academy down at Chugiak-Fergus, but other than
that . . ." She shrugged.

"Surely the colonists who first came here . . ." Yana
insisted.

Clodagh shook her head. "Only those who were high
officers in the company already. Oh, sure and some of
our great-grandparents maybe knew a little bit at one
time—maybe as much as the company teaches soldiers
now—but back then, so the songs tell us, everybody
had fancy machines to talk to them and show them pictures of what needed to be done. The company apparently didn't think we needed the machines as bad as we
needed other stuff when they sent us here, and such
things were far too dear for the likes of us to import
once we were here. So there's just a few of those machines on the planet, the ones the company needs to
keep here for their own business. As for your *written*
books, well, I don't suppose anybody had a clue where
to find many of *them* anymore, except for the special

ones the scientists had. So we sort of fell back into just talking and singing and telling about what happened, like people did way back a long time ago."

"We do okay without that stuff," Bunny said, with a defensive edge to her voice that was immediately tempered by wistfulness. "Except, sometimes, like now, but still there are *some* people who can . . ." She turned to Clodagh.

"Including, if I'm not mistaken, your own Uncle Sean, Bunka," Sedna said. "Is that so, Clodagh?"

"Of course. He's a Shongili." To Yana, Clodagh explained, "The Shongilis were originally of Inuit stock but already had careers as valued Intergal scientists when Petaybee was founded. Sean's and Sinead's grandda was the most respected man in our hemisphere until his death." With what seemed undue pride she nodded emphatically. "Shongilis definitely can read— books and books if they want to. Even Sinead can— Aisling's seen her do it, but said Sinead told her mostly she'd rather read animal tracks instead and rely on her own sharp ears and long memory for stories and songs like everybody else."

Bunny bounced up and exclaimed, "I forgot! That's right! Uncle Sean can not only write, but he has stuff to write with *and* a recorder. He could do it!"

"Your uncle is an important man, a busy man, Bunny," Sedna said, horrified. "He's got problems to solve for the whole planet. We can't go bothering him with every little thing."

"Charlie being shipped out isn't really a little thing, though, is it, Sedna?" Clodagh asked. "No, I think that's a good idea. If Yana knows how to read and make recordings, too, and if you'd help us do it, Yana, we wouldn't need to bother him very much. He could just loan her the machine. You think he'd do that, Bunny?"

"He will if I ask him and tell him it's your idea," Bunny said. "I'll go up to his place in a couple of days, next time I don't have any fares to and from Space-Base."

"Maybe Yana'd like to go with you. I bet Sean would like to meet somebody else who knows writing."

"How about it, Yana? You're not scared of the dogs, are you?"

Yana shook her head, grinning. "No, I'd like to ride in that contraption." As advertised, the home brew was starting to blur her.

Sedna, a container of moose spaghetti in hand, said good-bye; she crossed at the doorway with yet more drop-in guests, one of whom Yana had already met. Bunny's Uncle Seamus was less encrusted with snow and ice this time and was accompanied by a tiny woman with short, wavy silver hair.

"Sláinte, Clodagh! Bunny said you were having the major over for dinner and Moira and me wanted to bring her some fish. Here you go, Major," Seamus said, and handed her a string of stiff frozen fish as if he were handing her a promotion to executive vice-president of Intergal.

"Thanks, uh . . . Seamus," she said, pretending to admire them. She didn't have any idea what to do with them, so she hung the string over the back of the chair, where it was instantly the object of much interest from the cats.

"Get away, you lot," Clodagh said, wading through orange fur to rescue the fish. The cats stood on their hind feet and batted at the string as she held it aloft.

"Better hang them outside until she's ready to go, Seamus."

"Right," Seamus said, casting an odd sidelong glance at Yana. She waved and said thanks again, and planned to ask Bunny later about the etiquette involving gifts of fish.

They stayed a short while longer, and while they were there two more people came by, a rakish-looking girl introduced as Arnie O'Malley and her little boy, Finnbar, who chased the cats. Finally, all of the extraneous guests left, the girl calling, "Wait'll you see my new latchkay dress, Clodagh! The lads will be making songs about me for years to come."

"That Arnie, always showing off," Bunny said disgustedly.

"What are these songs everybody talks about?" Yana asked. She was full of food and on her third glass of home brew and was feeling pleasantly relaxed and even a bit sleepy. "Are there a lot of musicians in this town?"

"Nah, only old man Ungar and his bunch," Bunny said. "But everybody makes up songs."

"Everybody?" Yana had never personally known *any*body who wrote songs, or admitted to the practice.

"Yes," Clodagh said. "We make songs about everything, even one about the reason we make songs, but that particular song belongs to Mick Oomilialik. Maybe he'll sing it for you at the latchkay."

"What's that?"

"Oh, it's a big feast and sing where we get together to talk things over. My Inuit ancestors called such a thing a potlatch and my Irish ancestors called it a ceili, so one of the first batch here combined it into latchkay. Anyway, everybody makes songs to sing then about what's happened during the last season. Sometimes villages get together and share food and news."

"So you only have them once a season?"

"Except for weddings, funerals, and other special events, yes."

"Well, what might you write a song *about*, for instance?"

"Charlie having to leave is one kind of thing. I might write a song pretending I was Charlie."

"And you can make up music and everything?"

"Oh, no, not usually. Mostly we use the old tunes. And there's drumming, too," Bunny said. From Clodagh's wall she pulled down a circular drum, holding it in one hand and using the other to extract a stick from the back of the drum.

"Our drums can be used like Inuit drums and beaten with a wand in strict time," Clodagh explained, "or if you want to use it like an Irish bodhran, you beat it with that little stick. Or your fingers, if you're real clever. When a song is first presented, we use only the drums so everybody can hear the words. Later on, if the song's owner permits it, others sing along and other instruments join in."

"I can sing her one of mine," Bunny said.

Clodagh looked mildly surprised. "Okay. I'll drum. Which one?"

"About getting my snocle license. Irish Washerwoman."

"What?" Yana asked.

"Oh, 'Irish Washerwoman' is the tune," Clodagh told her. "Our ancestors liked each other well enough but it was easier for the Inuits to adapt to the Irish music than it was for the Irish to adapt to the Inuit. Of course, some of us don't have the voice for Irish melodies, so then we sing in the Inuit way."

"It's more like chanting," Bunny said. "So our singing is like us—all mixed-up. Anyway, here's my song:

"Oh, I'm getting my license to snocle today
From the big shots although I'm a Petaybee maid
You'll forgive me if I'm very vocal, hooray!
But I'm getting my license to snocle today.

"That's all there is," Bunny finished. "But I sure was happy about it, even if it's just a short little song. I didn't want to brag too much."

Clodagh said, "Here, I'll sing you a song in the other style.

"Before it awakened the world was alive.
It brooded in a shell of ice and stone.
Alone, thinking of its own mysteries,
Deep dreaming.
Jajai-ija."

Clodagh was chanting slowly and deliberately, and the effect was that of an eerie tune, similar to some styles Yana had heard on shipboard holos and in company pubs throughout the galaxy. The last note of the verse was very low, almost guttural.

"Then came the men with their ships, their fire
Awakening the fire within the world
Sundering rock, cutting river channels,
Great holes were gouged for ocean beds.
Jajai-ija.

*"Painful was the awakening, the beginning
As only beginnings can be painful
But the pain roused the world from dreaming
Melted its blanket and dribbled water in
The mind of the world
Jajai-ija!*

*"Awake, the world grew leaves
Awake, the world grew roots
Awake, the world grew mosses and lichens
Awake, the world knew wind.
Jajai-ija!*

*"Then came more men and the world grew wings
The world grew feet and hands.
The world grew paws and claws.
The world grew feathers and fur.
Jajai-ija!*

*"Noses smelled the new world and mouths tasted it
Fangs tore it and fins and scales swam through
The new waters. And the tails of the world
Wagged, happy that it had been given a voice.
Happy that it woke up.
Jajai-ja-jija!"*

Yana nodded appreciatively, while pictures of ice caves and snow plains and various disjointed animals somehow connected to the planet's surface kaleidoscoped in front of her eyes. The blur had become audible as well as visual. When Clodagh was done, Yana smiled and thanked her for the song and the meal and refrained from saying that the Corps of Engineers terraforming department might well wish to adopt that song as their anthem if they ever heard it. Clodagh began clearing the table, and Bunny pulled on her parka.

Although Bunny was willing to drive her home, she let Bunny take her dogs straight back to their kennels and walked back. Blurred and blithe, she carried her pack and her string of fish, enjoying the snapping freshness of the air, thinking that maybe the world in Clodagh's song had lungs, too—healthy ones.

She hung the fish outside the door, as they had hung at Clodagh's, up high, the effort costing her another coughing fit that doubled her over in the snow until she was afraid she would freeze to death. She crawled inside and started to spread the blanket on her bed, then saw by the moon's light through the windows that there was already a soft brown fur spread over it, the cat peacefully curled on top of it. Yana gratefully joined the little animal, glad of its steady, contented breathing and its warmth.

Warmth. Diego shuddered to life, staring out through eyelashes frozen together, feeling himself dragged. He rolled over. He hurt bad. His dad had him under the arms and was tugging him, sliding him, inch by inch, over the springy, snow-covered surface.

"I'm okay, Dad. I can do it," he said, and rolled over, away from his father. Dad looked as if he needed Diego to pull him in turn. His lips were cracked and bloodless, but there was a great deal of blood elsewhere, frozen on his face and parka ruff from a cut on his forehead.

"Cave," Dad said, shouting against the wind. "Under—the ledge. Limestone—"

"Tell me when we get in there," Diego yelled back.

Somewhere very far away dogs howled, and he thought maybe he heard voices, too, but they didn't sound close. That Dinah was something, though. Maybe Lavelle would let her loose, so she could come and find them.

"We'll be okay, Dad," he said, as much to reassure himself as his father, but even to his own ears his voice sounded no louder than a whisper compared to the wind.

They crawled toward the piece of shadow looming under the side of the hill amid all the white. Snow drifted and blew in front of it.

His father took a laser pistol from his pocket. "Wild . . . animals," he said, and they crawled into the opening.

They huddled inside, listening to the wind howl outside. Diego's dad looked bad to him; he seemed to have doubled his age in just a few minutes. His black hair was iced over, and the thick black eyebrows that normally made his dark eyes seem so penetrating were dead white with encrusted snow and ice. His expression was not so much scared as dazed, and the blood from the cut was running again, pretty freely. Diego's own face was wet, too, as was the ruff on his parka. Then he realized that was because it was warmer here in the mouth of the cave.

"Dad, let's go on back in. It's warm in here.

Come on, let's keep out of the cold till the storm's over."

He felt more like his father's father than his son then, and that was as scary as being stuck out in the blizzard. But Dad nodded a little stiffly and followed him.

The passage sloped sharply downward for a time, and it was very narrow. Dad had to squeeze sideways and kneel to get through one part, but it had grown so warm that Diego took off his hat, mittens, and muffler and stuffed them in his pocket and unfastened his parka. About this time he began to hear the humming from inside the cave, as if it housed some huge machine. For all he knew, maybe it did. The company had made this planet, hadn't they? At least that's what they claimed, though Diego privately thought it was pretty weird to create such a physically inhospitable place.

The path bent sharply to the right, then to the left, and seemed to stop. Diego groped toward the wall in front of him, his hands touching strange indentations, like grooves swirling in some sort of design.

With his touch, the wall gave way and a soft, eerie light from within sent a shaft to meet them. Diego pressed forward into the room, where flame-colored liquid bubbled up in a central pool and the walls glowed with phosphorescence, where roots and rock formations twined and curled into strange designs in the elongated, rough shapes of animals and men, and where the humming was so loud, so perfect, so beautiful that after a while Diego thought he must be hearing the voices of the angels he had once read about—and they were telling him things. He listened so closely that he could not hear his father screaming.

4

Yana awoke the next morning at the cat's insistence. It stood by her head and, every time she tried to go back to sleep, poked its nose in her face. She seriously considered throwing it across the room, but then decided that both it and she needed something to eat. She could hardly inflict corporal punishment for a reasonable demand.

She had a collapsible pot in her survival kit and still had the water left in the thermos jug Bunny had loaned her. She set water on to heat and retrieved one of the fish from the hook outside her door, but from there on she had no idea what to do with it.

There were still some food pellets in her personal baggage, so she gulped down a green one and a pink one and set the fish on the stove to thaw. When it had well and truly stunk up the cabin, she gave it to the cat, who danced with delight.

"Don't tell Seamus," she said to the cat. "I think he meant for me to cook it, but between you and me, I never learned how to cook a meal, just get the basic pills I need down my gullet."

The cat looked up through slit eyes, purring and

growling over the fish at the same time, its expression clearly saying, "Your loss is my gain."

Yana was used to the close confinement of a living area within a hostile environment but found that despite her fatigue and illness she had trouble remaining inside her cabin for more than two hours at a time. It was cold outdoors, and the gear she had to wear to be outside was heavy and clumsy, but she could by God breathe the air, however gingerly.

During the few hours when the sun made the sky bright blue and the snow sparkle, she would have clawed her way through the door to get out if she'd had to. With all of its current landmasses clustered near the poles, Petaybee's light and darkness cycles closely resembled those of the polar outposts of Earth, where both extremes seemed to last for months at a time. Fortunately, she had arrived late in the dark cycle, so she got some differentiation between night and day, though not as much as she would have gotten in the artificially regulated watch cycles aboard company corps spacecraft.

She saw someone sliding past her cabin on long skis and rushed outside without her hat to ask them where they had gotten the skis.

The young boy flushed with more than activity. "They—uh—they're made around here," he said finally, but she could see the Intergal logo on his boots.

"Could I buy a pair at the company store, do you know?" she asked, thinking she had yet to find the damned store.

He didn't say anything but slithered hurriedly past, which told her they probably were neither made on

Petaybee nor sold at the store: more likely they had been "relocated" illegally from SpaceBase.

Down the street, someone carrying a package emerged from the doorway of one of the houses. The figure, of rather greater mass than most, walked-waddled-glided toward her on the ice, and Yana recognized Aisling, the blanket maker she had met at Clodagh's.

"Sláinte, Yana," Aisling said.

"Uh . . . sláinte, yourself, Aisling. Say, I'm trying to find my way around the village. Can you show me where the store is?"

"Sure. I just left there. Why, what do you need?"

"Nothing in particular. I just wanted to know what was available."

"Not much, but come on, I'll show you. Mostly, we try to make our own from what the planet provides. Some of us trade what we make at the store for the few things they have that we can't manufacture ourselves. Our stuff never stays in the store, though. I think they're sold for triple, maybe four times, what we're paid, on ships and space stations and to other colonies. So mostly we deal directly with each other. You know, one of my blankets for one of the good skinning knives Seamus makes, or Sinead will trade a moose hindquarter for a mountain sheep fleece for me or enough mare's butter for our lamps. Old Eithne Naknek often trades the sweaters she knits for food and wood, and we all trade hides to cut for boots and parkas. When I can get cloth, I can make real pretty things for latchkays. Used to do that a lot, but since the SpaceBase closed to civilians, you can't hardly get fabric anymore."

"I can see where I need to get to know who to go to for what," Yana said. She could also see that she was going to need some barterable commodity other than company scrip to get by. She had never tried hunting for food before. Most planets where she had touched down had still been too new for anyone to be sure what was palatable and what was poisonous; and anyway, there was always the awkward possibility of ending up inadvertently lunching on one's host species.

Aisling took her into the store. From the outside, it looked like just another house; inside it seemed even tinier, with the stove dominating the room and counters all around the edges. Flanking the stove were two tables, sparsely littered with bags of nutrient tablets and uniform neckties and buttons, as well as trousers in very small sizes. Aisling was scanning the shelves beyond the counters.

"Look, Yana. There's a good small pot. You better grab it. We've got one, but anything useful goes quick."

Yana purchased the pot. Looking further for something useful, she saw only small machine parts, burned-out chips, and multicolored wires.

"Sinead takes the wire and welds it into designs on tools and pots," Aisling told her as they left. "And uses the chips for jewelry. You should come over for supper sometime and we'll show you. Though everybody will be bringing things to trade or gift with at the latchkay."

Yana said she would like to do that, and Aisling continued on her way.

Two days later, as Yana was slowly waking up with a cup of hot watery beverage between her hands, she was jolted out of her semi-trance by the sound of dog feet and dog whines and howls outside. Bunny's face, framed by her parka ruff and mittens, appeared in the window. Yana waved at her to come in, and Bunny stuck her head in the door.

"If you still want to come with me up to Uncle Sean's place, come on. I'll wait out here with the dogs, but you better hurry. It's a good two-hour trip, and we may have to track him down once we get there."

Yana nodded and, after throwing two more logs in the stove for good measure, pulled on her boots and tugged her coverall and coat over her uniform. Grabbing mittens, hat, and muffler, she walked outside. The cat followed her.

"You sit there," Bunny told her, indicating the appropriate place in the sled. She wrapped furs and quilts around her. "It'll be cold sitting still. Later on, when you're feeling better, I'll show you how to drive dogs. Driving keeps you warm."

Then Bunny put in Yana's lap a pair of the big oval nets Yana had seen hanging over Clodagh's door. "You always want to have all your survival gear with you when you leave the village," Bunny said. "I don't think we'll need snowshoes, but you never know."

Something warm landed on Yana's thighs and burrowed under the furs. She bent over and saw a familiar orange face peeping out at her.

"Oho! Bunny, can you get rid of the cat?"

"It's okay. That's one of Clodagh's cats, and they go everywhere." With that she whistled up the dogs, pulled the brake up from the ice, and pushed with her foot, as if the sled were a scooter. With much wagging and anxious whining, the foxy-looking red dogs began pulling the sled down the icy expanse between the houses, around a corner, and out onto the river again.

For a while the ride was serene, the sled swooshing

over white still lit by the light of moons and stars, Bunny occasionally calling to the dogs or to Yana to look at one set of tracks or another and pointing out "snow goose," "fox," or "moose," accordingly. Then she whistled more sharply, shouted "Ha!" and the dogs made a rather sharp turn up over the bank of the river and through the slender, snow-draped trees.

The sled bounced along from there, the dogs frisking up hills and running down them, the sled sometimes suspended breathlessly in midair for a moment as it went over a bump. Bunny kept control with the brake and her voice, and once the lead dog, Maud, turned back to look at her and whined when Bunny called out "Gee!". Bunny promptly called out "Ha!" instead, and Maud, satisfied, turned back to the trail. Mostly the dogs trotted at a leisurely pace, and Yana got a good view of their excretory functions as they stopped to mark the trail every once in a while.

Finally, however, the trail turned downward for a long time, and then a vast treeless straightaway of ice and snow stretched clear to the horizon, broken only by huge, jagged, upright ice teeth that seemed to be shifting ever so slightly against the brightening sky. The howling of dogs close at hand occasioned answering howls from Bunny's dogs.

Bunny whistled the dogs to a stop then, and Yana saw that the coral-tinted squarish hill between them and the giant ice teeth was not actually a mound of snow kissed by the rising sun, but a building painted in that unlikely shade. As the dogs trotted to a halt, they rounded the corner of the building, and Yana saw a snocle similar to Bunny's sitting before half a dozen small houses, each with a howling red fox-hound on top of it, caroling a greeting to the newcomers.

"Here we are," Bunny said. "And it looks like he's at home, too."

Yana had formed no preconceptions about Bunny's relative, apart from expecting him to vaguely resemble someone of the blood kin she had already met. But Dr. Sean Shongili wasn't like anyone she had ever met, either here on Petaybee or anywhere else in her lifetime—despite the fact that she had the distinct feeling that she had encountered him before.

Bunny had rapped on the door, singing out a cheerful "Sláinte, Uncle Sean," a greeting lost in the canine chorus. She urgently beckoned Yana to hurry up, but Yana had to disentangle herself from the furs and the cat before she could stagger to her feet. That long, cold ride in a less-than-comfortable position had stiffened all her joints. She hated to appear less than agile and forced her body to move with something near a semblance of normality.

The door she approached pulled inward, and with snow glare impairing her vision, Yana could distinguish only a medium-sized form, for once not distorted by layers of clothing. The man was actually in a shirt with the sleeves rolled up to his elbows and the collar open.

"Uncle Sean, I gotcha home! I've brought Yanaba Maddock to see you. And I gotta favor to ask. In Clodagh's name." On those words, Bunny put a hand on Yana's back and propelled her into the house.

Blinking to adjust her eyes, Yana looked about a room that sprouted unusual shapes from every surface, wall and ceiling, a veritable djinni's cave of wonders and a heinz of unassorted utensils, tools, parts, and, as usual, felines. These were six times the size of the one left curled in the sled furs and not a one of them was orange-colored. Fine heads turned, and autocratic amber, yellow, and green eyes assessed her. In a basket near the fire, a black-and-white bitch with a harlequin face lifted her head, sniffing, moved her foreleg to hide the pups that nursed her, and remained alert the entire time the visitors remained in Sean's cabin. That was the sum of Yana's first impression. Then the man dominated the scene.

Sean Shongili smiled, and his eyes did, too: sparkly silver eyes that looked straight into hers, clever, "seeing" eyes that were bright with an unqualified welcome, a decided change from the superficial social manners that were usually all she was accorded and many degrees more kindly than Colonel Giancarlo. But Giancarlo had a mission for her, and he probably never regarded his mission personnel as remotely human.

Shongili wasn't much taller than she was; a subtle aura of great strength, intelligence, and charm emanated from him, though charm was a quality she had never trusted—until now. He was a lean man, which for starters she liked, with a narrow face, slightly broad at the eyes, which were wide-set and large; cheekbones that were more Magyar than Indian; a generous mouth with finely carved lips, white, even teeth just visible behind them; and a purposeful chin and jawline. Not a man easily persuaded from his purpose.

"Well, now, so you're Major Maddock," Sean said, and she hurried to pull off her right glove as he extended what looked like an abnormally long-fingered hand. But it was warm and grasped hers just firmly enough for her to sense, again, the unexpected resources in him. In fact, the touch of his skin on hers was slightly electric, stimulating.

Then the silver eyes blinked and something in the altered look made her frown slightly, confused, for all that there didn't seem to be any diminution of his welcome or smile.

"Has everyone on this frozen ball of ice heard of me now?" she asked, slightly petulant. She forced a smile on her lips to make her words seem more of a joke than they had sounded in her own ears.

"Good news travels faster than bad on Petaybee," Sean said. He moved with lithe grace to the ever-present stove of a Petaybee home, pouring three cups from the equally ubiquitous steaming pot. "Actually, I have the only radio link with the town around. Adak at the snocle depot gets downright chatty if anything interesting happens—such as Kilcoole getting a new citizen, and a war hero at that. Here's something to warm your guts after such a long sled ride, Major."

"Thanks," Yana said, ignoring the war hero comment and hoping to restore herself to his good opinion after that flash of aggro. "You're very kind."

His silver eyes glinted as he handed her the cup. "Bunny would skin me alive if I never asked you where your mouth was," he said, and winked with pure mischief before he presented Bunny with her mug.

"Too right, Unk," Bunny said, "and Sean makes a good bev."

Yana clasped it in both hands, to warm numb fingers, taking her time about sipping a liquid she knew would be too hot to drink immediately. The rising steam carried a spicily inviting odor to her nostrils.

"Charlie's gone, I hear," Sean went on, hitching his hips up onto the nearest flat surface.

"Yah! With barely time to say good-byes, and no song," Bunny said, then cocked her head at him, smiling winsomely. "Which is why we wondered if we could have the recorder. The major here knows all about equipment like yours, and she volunteered to help us send him a letter. To make up for his sudden departure, like."

Sean flicked a gaze at Yana, and she quirked her lips in a smile.

"Charlie-boy's not the one to irritate folk," Sean said. "Wonder why they posted him off-planet." But he put his cup down and, with a single fluid movement, spun on one heel to an overburdened wall cabinet from which he unerringly extracted a recording device. Not, Yana realized as she saw the face of it, an obsolete affair but nearly state-of-the-art from the last time she had been issued one. The cabinet was crammed with technological gadgets of all kinds, half of which she couldn't put a name or use to. She watched as Sean negligently pushed back into place equipment that would have been worth a small fortune on any planet, much less a technologically starved one like Petaybee.

"Half of it doesn't work," he said, without seeming to have noticed her attention. "Petaybee's hard on any kind of instrumentation and machinery."

"How do you manage your work then?" she blurted out.

He gave a diffident shrug. "I improvise. We do a lot of that on Petaybee." He handed her the recorder. "Do you understand this type?"

She examined the display keys more closely and nodded, deciding to limit her comments. "Had one almost like this on my last assignment." She slid the thin rectangle into a thigh pocket. Then she nodded at the big cats. "I haven't seen anything like them here."

"Them?" Shongili looked half-surprised, half-amused. "My track-cats. When they're of a mind, they'll even pull a sled."

"They're big enough." Yana moved slightly on her buttocks. She was near enough to the stove to begin to feel the heat. She shrugged her jacket open a little more. "Do they always look at a person like that?"

Sean laughed. "They're always interested in new things."

"Did you design them like that?"

Sean's mobile eyebrows developed a quizzical quirk. "Design them? They designed themselves," he said with a shrug.

"Yes, but I thought you and your . . ."

"Not them. What he did; what I do is check on adaptability, not evolution or even mutation, but something in between as each species makes subtle improvements to survive in conditions their ancestors never had to cope with. Petaybee is a prime example of survival of the fittest."

"He's off," Bunny said with an air of resignation, and let herself fall backward into the chair she had been perched on. There she struggled out of her outer layers, preparing to endure. She shot Yana a grin to quell any apprehension.

"Like cats whose ears are no longer susceptible to frostbite?" Yana asked, remembering Clodagh's offhanded comment.

"Exactly." Sean grinned. But the humor in his silvery

gaze held more than acceptance of her statement. He was probing, too, and a lot more deftly than Colonel Giancarlo could.

"Why haven't you done as much for the humans stuck here?" Yana asked, not quite certain she could tease this unusual man, but suspecting she could.

"Ah, them." Sean waved a hand. "We genetic manipulators aren't allowed to help humans. They have to do it the hard way."

"Have they?"

Sean cocked his head, his amusement not one whit diminished. "I'd say there have been ... adjustments made. Learning what furs, for instance, are most suitable for the purpose of keeping human bodies warm."

"That's intellectual, not biological," Yana said.

"Mankind's intelligence distinguishes us from the animals, my dear major. And allows adjustments much faster than animals can alter their genetic codes."

"Do they? Here on Petaybee?"

"Over the last two hundred years, they'd have to, to survive. Wouldn't they?" He drained his cup. "Of course, the original Admin was sensible about some of the species they sent, which helped."

"Which ones?" Yana asked.

Bunny snorted, obviously knowing the answer.

Sean grinned, a grin of pure unadulterated mischief. "Why, the curly-coats." When Yana cocked her head at him inquiringly, he beckoned to her. "I'll show you."

"They're his pride and joy, Yana. You're in for it," Bunny said, propping her feet up on a footstool and obviously not intending to join Sean and Yana.

"I asked."

"The curly-coats are equines," Sean said, and as he

cupped her elbow with his hand, she experienced the
same electric shock of contact. "Originally from the Si-
berian area of the Eastern Hemisphere. They exist comfortably in extreme temperatures, having a spare flap in
their nose that closes off frost. They survive on vegetation that wouldn't keep a goat alive. Small, sturdy, able
to maneuver on tracks even a sled has trouble running."

He led her down a corridor from the main room, past
closed doors, and into a link between the house and a
spread of other buildings that she took for research and
laboratory facilities. The link passed in front of other
closed doors, some with security keypads. She was
adept enough at sussing her immediate surroundings
without appearing to do so, yet she had the sense that
Sean was aware of her automatic scanning. They came
to the end of the link, which opened onto a paddock
with snow fences keeping the drifts from its surface. In
the paddock were a dozen small horses, curly-coated
to the point of being shaggy, with long fur icicled under
their throats, and long feathers curling down from their
sturdy barrels and down their short thick legs. At first
she wasn't sure which end was which, since the manes
were as long as the tails and just as thick. There were
several brown animals, but most were a creamy color;
they were all browsing on what looked much like the
icicled spines she had seen on the riverside three days
before.

"You'd never spot half of them in this terrain," was
Yana's first comment.

Sean chuckled, apparently pleased by her remark.
"They're survivors!"

"What do you use them for?"

"A variety of things. Their milk we can drink, fresh,

frozen, or fermented, or make into a butter which we use in our lamps."

"I have," she said, restraining herself from wrinkling her nose.

"It smells but it's better than nothing. Their coats we can comb and use for wool." Yana thought of the warm soft blanket she had seen in Clodagh's. "We can eat their flesh, drink their blood—" He glanced at her to see if that repulsed her, but she had eaten far worse than curly-coated equines in her time—worse and tougher than these little animals looked. "We can ride them, use them as pack animals, use them as extra blankets if we're caught out in bad weather. They don't object to sleeping with humans . . ."

She looked at him then, for the undertone to his comment was both risible and dogmatic. His silver eyes glinted with the mischief that seemed an essential part of his public self.

"They are amenable to anything we can think up for them to do. And they never complain or balk." That seemed to be of paramount importance. "They've saved many a team from hypothermic death and starvation. In fact, you can bleed them quite a bit before they are weakened."

"Useful."

"Indeed."

"Were they used by the teams that disappeared?"

Sean was surprised at that question and scratched the back of his neck. "Been given a few ghouly stories to keep you awake at night?"

"Not ghouly to me," she said with a shrug. "I've been first-team on a few company planets, a couple where I'd've been glad to have a few curly-coats along."

"Oh?"

She could see interest sparking the glint in his eyes. He leaned back against the plasglas, propping his arms on the wide sills, apparently not affected by contact with the cold surface, whereas she could feel the frost of it oozing into the semiwarm link.

She gave a laugh. "Don't get *me* started on that phase of my life. It's over." She made a cutting gesture with her hands.

"Then it's time to sing about it. You came through."

"Sing? Me?" She ducked her head in denial. "Not me—couldn't carry a tune in a bucket."

Sean smiled—almost challengingly, she thought. "Inuit chants can't be called tunes, not without a stretch of the definition, but they do grab the mind and make audiences listen. I think they'd like to hear your songs."

Yana was not affecting modesty: she just didn't think any of her experiences were worth hearing about, and certainly some of them she wouldn't talk, much less sing, about.

"I'm serious, Yana." He spoke her name with an odd lilt. She shot him a quick look and saw that he was, indeed, serious. Then his expression turned sly. "The spring latchkay's coming up soon. You'll be coming, and there are some folks hereabout would like to hear a song about Bremport."

"Bremport?" She went rigid.

He laid a light finger on her arm. "You were at Bremport. Charlie picked up on that when he got a copy of your orders and the briefing on your medical history."

"That should have been confidential," she said, feeling less guilty about Charlie than she had the day before.

"Charlie's older brother Donal was at Bremport, too, so it was of more than casual interest to him. So were three other sons of Petaybee and two daughters, and us here knowing nothing about their deaths but that they are dead."

Damn Charlie anyway. Giancarlo had been right to transfer him—the boy's loyalties had been too mixed for him to be an effective company representative here. Still, she couldn't blame him, but—damn. She remembered to exhale then, and swallowed hard on all the things she didn't wish to remember about Bremport.

The swallow was a mistake. Somehow it went down wrong and she started to cough. Hard as she tried to limit it to the one cough, another burst past her lips, and the next thing she knew she was racked by a paroxysm. She fumbled in her coat for her syrup and dragged the bottle out. But she moved too swiftly: it flew from her groping fingers and smashed on the stone floor of the link. As if the loss of the syrup were a signal, the coughing fit intensified. Sean's very strong fingers gripped her arms, supporting her convulsing body, and he began to hurry back the way they had come, though she had trouble keeping on her feet. She had to bring her knees almost to her chin to keep the spasms from tearing her abdominal muscles.

"What's the cause, Yana? The gas at Bremport?"

She managed to nod a yes. Then he was assisting her into a laboratory, flicking up lights, and settling her onto a nearby stool before he sprang across the room to the large array of cabinets there. Without fumbling, he poured out a dose of a clear yellow liquid and returned to her side.

"Something of Clodagh's that makes cowardly coughs evaporate on its fumes," he said. "We all take it now and then."

Yana was in no condition to object to anything anyone might consider remedial. Between one spasm and the onset of another, she knocked back the liquid—and rolled her eyes, inhaled, and then exhaled gustily, for the medicine had a kick in it that could only reduce any cough to tatters. And the next spasm didn't materialize.

Surprised, Yana took several short breaths, fully expecting each one to deteriorate into a cough. Sean regarded her with a growing smile curling his lips.

"See? Guaranteed effective."

"What was in it?" she gasped respectfully, still aware of the taste of it in the back of her mouth.

The mischief returned to Sean Shongili's eyes. "Well, now, that I don't know. Clodagh won't pass on the secret of her elixir. She just makes it."

Yana was aware of the plethora of laboratory equipment from slidetrays to electronic microscopes—and not obsolete ones, at that. She waved her hand at them.

"You look as if you could analyze the contents . . ."

"Ah . . ." Sean held up his hands. "It's unethical to plumb the secrets of another professional. I do animals; she does humans."

"But isn't there an overlap somewhere along the line?" Yana asked.

"How so?"

"Those cats of hers. And you've cats that are totally different."

Sean grinned so broadly that Yana knew she would

never get an honest answer on that score. "So I do." Then he turned from her and went back to the cabinet. He held up the bottle. "I can spare this since it seems to have been so effective for you."

Yana hesitated. She had had to use up far too much of her personal baggage allowance for enough bottles of the syrup to see her through her recuperation. But there was no question that Clodagh's was more effective. She sighed, cutting that loss and accepting the bottle. Maybe it would suffice to see the cough to an end before she had to go back to the prescription stuff.

"Clodagh makes it up in huge batches every fall to cope with coughs," Sean said, tucking the bottle securely in the inner vest pocket. "You can get more as you need it."

Yana felt another twinge of resentment against a system that did not supply her with enough money for even basic needs, much less medicinal niceties.

"Can you give me a few helpful hints about this place?"

He regarded her in surprise. "Bunny's good at that."

"Yes, but when I ask how I am to repay someone for leaving fuel by my door when I haven't asked for any, or giving me fish I don't know how to cook . . ."

He laughed with kindly amusement at her disgruntlement. "I see what you mean. It's so obvious to her that she doesn't realize how new and confusing it could be for you." He tucked her arm under his and guided her out of the laboratory, firmly clanging the metal door closed behind him. "Well, now, everyone knows you're new, and new to the ways of Petaybee, so they're helping you out. Old custom . . . especially for people they want to like . . ."

"Want to like . . ."

The silver eyes glinted. "They like heroes. No, they genuinely do," he amended when she snorted in disgust. "You're worth your weight as a role model . . ." Then he took a second look at her gauntness. "That'll improve," he said kindly. "So they'll sort of ease you into the environment the best way they can. What you do"— He held up one admonitory finger when she started to protest. —"is return the courtesies to the next stranger who arrives on our frozen shores. Or," he said, giving her that sly sideways glance that challenged her, "you compose a song to chant at the next latchkay."

"I don't think they really want to know about Bremport," she said very slowly.

His arm pressed hers encouragingly against his side. "They're tougher people than you realize. And they have a need to know, Yana. As much as you have a need to sing about it, even if you don't know it." His eyes were somber.

"Whatever," she said noncommittally, not willing to accept the truth, or the inevitability, of his suggestion.

They walked the rest of the way back to the main house in silence, a silence that was the most companionable one she had enjoyed in many a year. Sean Shongili was a most unusual man. Where under what sun could she possibly have encountered him before?

5

When they reached the house, they almost ran Bunny over: she was in the process of reaching for the door latch just as Sean flipped it up. Seeing her face, Yana knew that something had happened—something bad.

"Message from Adak, Sean. A hunting party found one of the lost teams."

"They did?" Sean took the hands that Bunny had held out in an unconscious appeal for comfort. "And?"

"There are five still alive . . ." Her voice trailed off.

"Which five?"

Yana read into that question that he was amazed that anyone had survived.

"Two of theirs this time, three of ours."

He dropped Bunny's hands and started to gather items about the room, cramming them into a pack at the same time he put on outerwear. He was ready in one circuit of the room.

"Where are they?" he asked.

"Clodagh's." As if that should have been a given.

"Drive us there, will you, Bunny?"

"Sure!" And the girl began to shrug into her wraps.

Yana wondered at how lightly Sean Shongili had dressed for a long drive in freezing temperatures. He

87

hadn't even rolled down his sleeves or done up his shirt collar, and the smooth pelted fur jacket he donned wasn't nearly as thick as Bunny's or hers. He grinned as he caught her expression.

"I'll be warm enough."

Then he hurried them out to the sled, where the dogs were already standing in their harness, yapping as if infected by the urgency that possessed the humans.

With deft movements, Sean settled Yana into the sled, bundled the furs about her, ignoring the cat's attempts to get into her lap, and gave her custody of his pack, telling her not to let it fall off.

Then he snugged his hood over his head, tying it under his chin, and shoved his hands in the thick fur mitts that were fastened by thongs to his sleeves.

"Come on, Bunny!" he yelled, and whistled at the team; the dogs strained against their harness even as Bunny wrenched the brake free of the ice and paddled with her foot to set the sled in motion.

The sled bumped forward, Yana clutching the pack for fear it would tumble off her fur-encased lap. If she had thought the outbound trip was fast and jarring, though she knew that Bunny had gone easily for her sake, the inbound journey was another matter. Sean ran beside Maud, the red leader dog, urging her to her best pace, chivying Bunny down steep inclines when she would have taken safer routes.

Yana hung on, determined not to close her eyes when the sled tilted at alarming angles and the landscape seemed to fly past her. She was particularly aware of the increased speed when the sled thudded from one hummock to another, crashing her bones together. Or when the cat, who had somehow crawled back under the rugs, sunk its claws through her pants leg to keep from being thrown about. Stands of hardwoods that had seemed miles apart during the outward journey streaked past her with barely an interval between them.

The abrupt arctic daylight had waned by the time they neared the settlement and saw its lit windows blinking welcomingly through the trees at them. The dogs slowed as they reached Clodagh's, making their way through a welter of other teams parked there. Sean grabbed the pack with a flash of a grateful grin at Yana and charged up the steps, Bunny right behind him as soon as she had hauled on the brake.

Grunting but telling herself that of course she understood their haste, Yana peeled back the furs and extricated herself from the sled. The cat jumped out and disappeared under the pilings. Oddly enough, as Yana straightened up she found that she wasn't nearly as stiff this time. She felt for the bottle of Clodagh's elixir and wondered what it contained. Then, hesitant about intruding, she climbed the steps to the porch. She could hear the subdued buzz of many voices even before she opened the door and slipped inside. The warmth was like a blanket surrounding her, but the press of people almost made her withdraw.

Peering over and around the bodies packed inside the room, she could see no part of the injured survivors, though there was a long clear space in one corner of the room where they might be lying obscured by the crowd. Clodagh's head and hips appeared from time to time, and once she saw what looked like the top of Sean Shongili's head. Bunny was standing by the stove, where she was precariously dribbling coffee into two cups, trying to keep from spilling any as she was repeatedly jostled.

Yana hoped one was for her, and it was: Bunny threaded her way through the throng and offered Yana a cup. She reached eagerly to accept it, for the warmth on her hands as well as her innards. She blew across the surface and at the first careful sip wondered if Sean used Clodagh's recipe or if it was the other way around.

"Could you see? Are they going to make it?" she asked, nodding toward the corner.

Bunny nodded, her eyes dark with worry.

"Ours'll recover a lot faster'n theirs, so there'll be more questions an' tribunals and inquests and stuff."

Which Bunny felt were irrelevant, Yana decided. "Isn't it just that your people are better acclimated?"

Bunny looked disgusted. "Of course they are and we try to explain that to them, but *they*"—the pronoun was used in contempt—"never admit the fact. Their people should somehow be better able to cope when most of 'em's never lived outside at all. And," she added with perplexity in her voice, "that's not the real problem anyway. The real problem is that they think they have to know everything about everything, and they don't. Even we who live here don't. But we know enough to pay attention to what the planet tells us, and they don't seem to pay attention to nothin'."

Yana sipped, letting the warmth thaw the ice in her blood. Maybe she would do better if she ran like the others did. She had done nothing but sit, and she was whacked—whereas Bunny's face was ruddy with stimulation, and Sean hadn't even looked puffed when he had grabbed the pack off her lap. Everyone in the room had settled down to what might be a long wait, one of many they endured with great patience. Yana felt her own running out, complicated by a growing sense of claustrophobia in a room packed with folk she didn't know well enough to wait equably with. She shifted her feet restlessly, wondering if she could withdraw without giving offense. Not that that was so much a problem, since she doubted anyone would notice one less body in the room except with gratitude. A more realistic concern was whether she *could* make it through this bunch to the door. And if and when she did, what would she do then, back at her cold and lonely cabin? That half hour in Sean's company had emphasized the disadvantages of solitude. She had felt oddly alive and on the alert in his company, the first time she had felt that way since Bry.

"Look, this might take hours," Bunny said, and Yana glanced sharply at her. "I've got to tend the dogs."

"Could I help, so I'll know something about their care?" Yana asked, hoping to delay the onset of bleaker hours alone.

"Sure." Bunny grinned, pleased at her offer. "It's not all that hard."

"If you say so," Yana said, and bundled back up in her winter gear to walk beside the team as Bunny drove it back over to the kennels at her Aunt Moira's.

It wasn't hard, exactly, but it required Yana to concentrate as she followed Bunny's example in removing the harness, checking it for wear, oiling it, and hanging it up properly, then checking the dogs' paw pads for any cuts and applying an ointment concoction of Clodagh's between the toes before chaining the animals up.

"You're lucky," Bunny told her. "I cleaned the dog

yard and put down fresh straw this morning already, so you don't have to do that part."

Having shown her what to do, Bunny retrieved some prechopped chunks of fish and other meat from a barrel outside her door and went into the house. When Yana had finished the dogs, she went inside and saw that Bunny was boiling the preboned meat, mixing with it what looked like hardened bread dough and fat. She finally crumbled up some suspiciously familiar pink-and-green tablets that looked like vitamin-mineral supplements of the kind issued to company troops. While the mixture heated, Bunny thawed snow on the back of the stove. Once it was melted, she and Yana used the same container to water each of the dogs in turn. By then the mixture was cooked to Bunny's liking, and they distributed it to the hungry animals.

Some of the dogs picked at their food like company diplomats at a high-level formal dinner; others wolfed it down with great gusto, growling over it, their jaws snapping as they ate.

"They—uh—seem to enjoy their food," Yana observed as the dog nearest her savagely gulped down his carefully prepared meal as if it were a bear, just-killed.

Bunny shrugged, grinning at the vagaries of her charges. "They do, right enough. And if one doesn't get it down fast, another'll try to snag it. That's one reason we chain them apart. Cuts down on meal fights."

"That cat of Clodagh's that followed me home seemed to want to eat the fish Seamus gave me frozen solid," Yana said.

"Nah! He might bat it around a little and gnaw at the edges, but he'll wait for it to thaw, or better yet, for you to cook it for him."

"The same way you cook for the dogs?"

"Of course not. The same way you cook for yourself."

"I don't," Yana admitted. "I'm ship-bred, you know. Food supplements and healthful nutrient bars for rations. Occasionally we get something else, but only the crew members assigned to cook for special functions learn to cook. So, how would *you* cook it to feed yourself and, uh, guests?"

Bunny grinned at the folly of the people who ran her world but didn't know how to feed themselves, then patted Yana on the hand and said, "Don't worry. It's not hard. I just stew it with a handful of my aunt's herbs and it makes right good eating."

Yana thought that over for a moment. Then, taking a breath, she asked, "Tell me which herbs make that sort of fish palatable."

"Sure, but you ain't had a chance to get any yet. So I'll scrounge enough. Meetcha at your place."

Yana had her stove fire going nicely when Bunny arrived with a small sack of the things she had filched from her aunt's kitchen.

"Aw, don't worry about a pinch of this and that," Bunny said when she saw Yana's worried expression. Then in short order, she demonstrated the art of concocting a fish stew from the herbs, a handful of rice, and chunks of what cooked into edible root vegetables. Bunny used all the fish from the string. "Because a stew gets better the longer it's alive. All you gotta do is freeze what's left overnight and thaw it on the back of the stove when you're getting hungry. I'll also show you how to make pan dough."

She did, and Yana ate a gracious sufficiency. Bunny

was still mopping up the stew juices with some of the pan dough when Sean's unmistakable voice called out, "Sláinte, Yana!"

Bunny was closer to the door and, at a nod from Yana, went to open it.

"Ah! Any left in the pot?" he asked, sniffing expectantly.

"Wouldn't Clodagh feed you?" Bunny asked, catching a plate and a spoon from the shelf on her way to the stove.

"She had enough, and I needed a little space," Sean said, undoing his coat and hanging it neatly beside the others on the door pegs.

"Who got out this time?" Bunny asked as he settled at the makeshift table so comfortably that Yana stifled the apologies she was about to make.

He paused long enough to ingest a spoonful before he answered.

"The Yallup group," he said, jamming a piece of pan bread down into the juices. "Lavelle, Brit, and Sigdhu made it; they'll be grand with some rest and decent eating, though Siggy lost another toe. The odd thing"— Sean wriggled his spoon about as if the movement would solve the oddity—"is that two of them made it."

"Yeah!" Bunny looked awed by that.

Shouldn't outworlders survive on this planet if their native guides were efficient? Yana wondered.

"Who?" Bunny went on.

"The team geologist the Yallups sent, father and son, Metaxos by name, Diego and Francisco. Damn fool brought his kid along for the experience." Sean spaced his phrases, eating in between gouts of information. Bunny snorted at the folly of folks' notions of experience; Sean grinned, light from the mare's-butter lamp on the table dancing in his silver eyes. "The son'll sing about it. The father ... now, that's where the trouble begins. He's aged. The boy said his dad was mid-forties. Looks closer to ninety."

"Ohhhhh!" Bunny drew out her exclamation, rounding her eyes, apparently finding great significance in this.

"Does hypothermia age you?" Yana asked.

"On Petaybee it can," Bunny said tersely. "So did they find anything?" She leaned conspiratorially close to Sean, her eyes glistening with eagerness in the lamplight. "The usual?"

Sean snorted, sopped up more stew on a piece of bread, and ate it before he answered. Yana thought he deliberated over his reply.

"More or less the usual. The kid gave some pretty concise descriptions. Caves, glistening lakes of free water, horned animals, sleek water beasts—you know, the usual." He broke off more bread, affecting keener interest in the business of eating than telling.

"Ahhhh!" Bunny let out another of her pregnant syllables.

"If you're deliberately speaking in parables, I'll go walk the cat," Yana said, rising.

Sean's arm reached out and pulled her back down to her chair, grinning an apology.

"People lost for weeks, gripped by hypothermia and close to the edge of starvation, tend to hallucinate."

"But you say he gave concise descriptions . . ."

"Vivid ones, though not necessarily accurate," Sean said, but Yana had the feeling he believed them. "Then the Spacebees arrived and took them all away. Rounded on Odark's people for not bringing them directly in to SpaceBase. But Terce was at the base and you were with me out at the lab, so what were they supposed to do? Clodagh's is certainly on the way, and closer." Sean took a deep breath, suppressing his disgust. "They needed aid as soon as could be. They got it. I'm not sure the geologist will pull through, though."

He chased the last of the juice in his bowl with the last of the pan bread. Yana debated the protocols in her mind and had her hand on the stewpot to offer more when Sean held up his hand.

"That does me fine, Yana, and you share a portion. More would be considered as impolite as too little." He pushed his chair back from the table, smiling at her.

"What did ours say?" Bunny asked eagerly, sitting forward again.

"Not much. Too busy warming up and far too glad to have been found to deal with more than that right now."

Yana nodded. She knew what Sean meant. "They'll be debriefed then?" she asked.

"Oh, and how!" He tilted the chair back, balancing himself with one foot on the table leg.

"Front, back, inside out, and outside in," Bunny agreed, shaking her head as if she felt sorry for the victims. "Did they find anything? I mean, anything real?"

"Like the deposits they thought sure they'd locate?" Sean's voice was level, but there was a silent laugh in his eyes, as if he knew something no one else did and treasured the knowledge. "No, they didn't find the sites, though Lavelle and Brit swear they should have, for they had updated and accurate readings and should have been right on site when the storm hit them. They dug in, of course." Bunny nodded, and Sean went on. "No time to make a decent icehouse, but Siggy's a damfine survival artist."

"They owe their lives to him, I'd say," Bunny remarked stoutly in support of Siggy's abilities.

"They do indeed, and the boy, Diego, said as much several times." Sean shook his head. "I hope they go easy on the kid with this debriefing nonsense. He was telling the truth or I've never heard it."

Bunny's mouth twitched irritably. "They wouldn't know the truth if it bit them."

"And it has." Sean and Bunny locked eyes, sharing some private knowledge. "I must get back," he said, rising and walking to the door to collect his things.

"Have you a light?"

He held up the long cylinder he extracted from a pocket. "I'll be fine. That rib-sticking stew'll see me home." He grinned at Yana, tipping the cylinder to his forehead in gratitude. "Yanaba, Buneka!"

The use of formal names surprised Yana, but she smiled and nodded in acknowledgment. He was gone in a swirl of cold air. Peering out her small window, Yana saw him, the cylinder held over his head as he jogged off at an easy pace, quickly lost in the night.

"Isn't he taking a dogsled back?" she asked Bunny.

"Sean? Not that little distance."

"That little distance took us nearly two hours."

"Oh, he's a good runner. Lotta times when we go out, he breaks trail for me. Sled'd only slow him up." Bunny lifted the thermos and shook it. "I'll bring you more water tomorrow. Thanks for the chow. G'night!"

A second swirl of cold air saw her away, leaving Yana alone, confused and with plenty to think over.

Over the next couple of days she didn't see much of

either Bunny or Sean, nor hear anything about the rescued men, although she did glimpse figures in Intergal regulation winter-survival uniforms lumbering through the streets more than once. The conversations she had with others in the settlement never touched on the subject she knew was in everyone's minds, as if the people thought they could will the incident into nonexistence by carefully avoiding it. Clodagh appeared on her doorstep the first morning, a lumpy bundle in one big hand and four cats at her heels. They promptly entered and did a quick recon before settling near the stove while Yana politely invited her in, though she was damned if she knew what to offer in the way of hospitality. She still hadn't had a chance to get in any supplies, and her fish stew was not going to last four days if that was all she had to eat, breakfast, lunch, and dinner. Her stomach was learning to demand food, not the bloat of nutrient pills.

"Did a quick round," Clodagh said, plopping the bundle down on the rickety table and untying it. A variety of small packets, some of them squares of cloth tied with a narrow thong, were revealed, and a half-dozen small jars. Three seemed to hold salves, pink, white, and green; the largest of the others held salt crystals, the second a dark powder, and the third a red-orange powder. "We've good salt supplies from the caves so don't worry about asking anyone for more when you go short but hot stuff"—and her big fingers closed about the dark powder—"is hard to come by, and you don't need much to flavor the pot. This"—she indicated the red-orange powder—"is good for the trots. Just enough on the tip of your finger put on your tongue and swallowed with a sip of water. Tastes awful but sure stops the bo-wells." Yana had never heard the word spoken quite that way. "When your crapper's full, just tell Meqo. She's manager of the dung heap this winter. The white stuff is good for frostbite. Use it even if you're not sure you're bit. Does no good too late. The pink is for chilblain—keeps 'em from cracking. Watch your toes for the itch . . ."

"I know about chilblains."

"Sure, and I 'spect most company soldiers do at that," Clodagh said amiably. "This greeny stuff is antiseptic. You might have some of your own—no? Well, this is better'n anything Intergal ever whomped up. These," she went on, gesturing at the small packets, "are spices, hots, sweeteners: reckon you can tell which is which by the smell of 'em." Then she hauled a much larger white sack from the folds of her parka. "Flour, single ration." A small tightly covered pot followed. "Risings, and soon's you take a schmerp, add some flour to keep it going. Keep it warm at all times." After a rummage in her clothing, a small quilted wool affair appeared, and the yeast pot was wrapped inside it. "Beans." A sack was pulled out of a pocket. "Three kinds. Puto says she has more she'll add when she gets back here. Navarana and Moira say you can join them in the woods when the time's right to collect your own wood pile." From another source, a hatchet emerged and was formally presented to Yana. "I'll need it back, a'course, when you can get one of your own. Aisling'll have some yarn for you." Keen eyes peered into Yana's. "Unless you don't know how to knit?"

Yana shook her head.

"Nah, a company person wouldn't need to, would she, drawing supplies direct from Intergal? Well, Aisling's patient, and there's nothing she likes better than to start someone off on the right foot, iffen they're willin'."

"I'm willing," Yana said firmly. "And thanks, Clodagh. I really appreciate all your help."

"Pshaw! You'll do the same in your own turn. Ippies stick together, cocking a snoot at the company for all they're so superior!"

With that she swung her ample bulk about with unexpected grace and was out the door before Yana could say more.

6

The wind roared down the pass from the mountains, through the foothills, and across the snowy plain that hid treacherous muskeg, rattling the snocle with bullying gusts. Bunny sat inside in full outdoor dress, watching the big shots prowl around and point as if they knew what they were doing.

They didn't. Even after they hauled Siggy's team back out here, way before the team had had a chance to recover from their ordeal, they knew no more than they had before. Of course, being stupid ips, Siggy and the others had no idea what the technical readings actually *said*, but this was where the storm swept down upon them, losing both ips and company men in a whiteout. Bunny had been in whiteout conditions herself several times along the river with the snocle and going back and forth between Sean's place and Kilcoole. White snowy ground underfoot, white sky overhead, and white haze and snowfall obscuring any other features of the surroundings, whiteout was disorienting and dangerous. It was a little like she'd heard space described, only white instead of black.

You could either keep driving, if you knew your trail, and hope you'd come out on the other side or find a landmark, or you just stopped and waited it out. The sensible thing to do, this far from any villages, would have been to bed the dogs down and wait it out, but the geologists had brought a lot of equipment and only allowed space for as much food as they felt they would need on the strict timetable they had set for themselves.

Lavelle told the company men, "We said, 'You better stop here until we can see something' but they said, 'Aw, no, we'll just be usin' our instruments.' Only problem was, their instruments broke 'cause of the cold."

The company men insisted that the instruments had been made for this climate and that it was impossible that they would break, and Lavelle had just shrugged. Thereafter she didn't know much except that the sleds had gotten separated, and the other three had been lost, drivers, dogs, geologists, equipment, food, and all. She had been driving the sled with the boy in it, so she had had room for a few more supplies. Brit had been driving the sled with the father, with Siggy running between them to keep them connected, as he had tried to do with the other sleds before they got lost back up to Moose Lake. Maybe they hit a thin patch of ice. Then, as they were coming down a pretty steep slope, the sleds overturned and both passengers were thrown out of the sleds, to roll down the hill and vanish.

"Didn't you think it was a little strange, them just vanishing like that?"

"No. What I thought was strange was that they couldn't find us. We were hollering like everything and the dogs were barking. Brit wanted to start searching, thinking maybe they were knocked unconscious, and we did look around where they should have logically been.

But when we didn't find any holes or anything, Siggy said the safest thing to do for everybody was stay put, light a fire, keep warm, and make noises all the time while the whiteout lasted."

"Trying to save your own skins, huh?" asked Colonel Giancarlo, the one who had sent Charlie away.

"No, no," said a younger captain with a handsome weather-beaten face and a much pleasanter manner. "Very understandable," he said soothingly to Lavelle, who had started to bristle. "What happened then?"

Lavelle looked straight at the colonel and said, "Then the weather cleared a little and Dinah kept whimpering, so I unhitched her. She run off and pretty soon we heard her howling; then she came trotting back with the boy. He said she dug through a drift to get him but his father was hurt and could we come and help him pull his father out. He got trapped in sort of a little avalanche, but fortunately, there was a cave in the side of the hill where he was trapped. They made it to the cave, but the snow blew back against the entrance again and it was real dark. The boy said he knew we wouldn't find them there but it was shelter and he'd been afraid to leave for help for fear he wouldn't find him again. He'd called out but we didn't hear each other for the wind."

"You didn't even try to find the others?" Giancarlo snorted contemptuously.

Lavelle had started yelling then, a rare event for the gentle and mild-mannered woman. "We didn't even know where the heck *we* were, mister! If Odark hadn't found *us*, I don't know if we'd have any of us made it back alive. Siggy couldn't even walk by then, and Brit and I would never have been able to dig the father out without the dogs helping us."

All the while the conversation was going on the boy, Diego, stood out there in the cold listening to them natter on, his face closed except for the occasions when something said or done seemed to make him angry; then his dark eyes would glow like fresh-stoked embers in the snow-burned red rawness of his face.

Bunny didn't know what to make of any of it, except that she was tired of acting just smart enough to drive her snocle, but dumb enough and friendly enough so that the big shots would keep talking in front of her, continuing their interrogation as she drove them to the ill-defined area where the party had been discovered. Terce was carrying on as if he had already become part of the inquisition, and the company men didn't make a move without consulting him.

It took two days on the snocles, driving them out to where the hunting party had run across the survivors, and then, with the recent snowfall in these parts and the wind blowing drifts everywhere, they could only approximate the location. Bunny shivered. She was out of the wind here in the snocle, and the sky was clear, but outside the wind picked up veils of snow and flung them across the landscape. Behind her, the trail was already drifted over in places. The company men had sent Terce back to make camp at the halfway point with Odark and Brit. Lavelle and the boy had remained behind to "assist with inquiries," and try to help them determine what had become of the other team members.

Bunny opened the door and climbed out of the snocle, trudging over to where the men stood arguing. Diego's adrenaline seemed to have run out while the company men wrangled around him. He had been radiating tension and at times anger at the interrogation, but now he slumped against Lavelle, who put her arm around him. He looked exhausted. He really shouldn't have been out here again so soon, but his father couldn't be moved. Siggy definitely had to rest and look after his frostbite, or gangrene might get the rest of his foot. Clodagh had given him some stuff, but the company men had taken him back to SpaceBase and "accommodated" him in a separate room from the crazy man, Diego's father, until he could be moved with the others to "another facility." Bunny didn't know what that meant, but she didn't like the sound of it.

"Excuse me, folks," she said to the party, "but we better make tracks while it's daylight."

"*I* say when we move," Giancarlo told her. "You do realize, young lady, that if I decide to, I can see to it that your license is revoked?"

"Oh, yes, sir. I know what an important man you are—how important all you people are. And that's why I'm telling you. If we don't get going now, I might lose my snocle instead of just my license, or another hunting party might have to find us. Our weather here, sir, as you may have noticed, is tricky. It has lots of—uh, different things "

"Variables?" the captain suggested helpfully.

"Yeah. Those. Lots of variables. And right now a bad storm's making. Also, sir, that lad looks to me as if he's all done in."

"She has a point, Colonel," the captain said. "Maybe we should make for camp now that we've seen the approximate site and come back better equipped when the weather clears."

The colonel glared but waved his mitten toward the snocle.

* * *

Diego Metaxos sat by himself in the corner of the shelter while the soldiers cross-questioned Lavelle. He wished they would let her alone. She had tried to help them—in fact, he thought, she had helped him a lot. And she could help him more, if only the interrogators would go away so he could talk to her.

Dad's delirious ravings seemed incredible to those men, and Diego knew they hadn't really believed him either when he had tried to tell them about the cavern, even though he was obviously unhurt. In a way he didn't blame them. Now the whole thing seemed like a dream to him—or it would have, except that his father had emerged from the same time and place looking as if he were still trapped in a nightmare.

Diego wasn't sure exactly *what* he and his father had gone through. All he knew was that their experience of that time in the cave had to have been wildly different for Dad than it had been for him, because while he felt fine, something awful had happened to Dad in there. Even after the icicles had melted from his hair, it remained white, and his face was drawn and sunken, like a skull's, the skin dried and far more wrinkled than it had been. The worst part was that except for the initial babblings, he wasn't responding to much of anything, just staring straight ahead, as if he couldn't see at all. The doctors said he was in some kind of severe shock, but how could that be? He and Diego had been together, and whatever it was Diego had experienced, it hadn't been anything to produce such an effect—at least not in him.

At first, he had told the rescuers and the company investigators everything, but when he saw their immediate skepticism, he had sense enough to clam up, beginning to doubt and second-guess his own perceptions. He needed to sort it all out, and he didn't intend to say any more until he was sure Dad would be tended to by someone who cared about him as more than an employee or a subject for study. Unfortunately, civilian dependent teenaged sons didn't have much clout with the company hierarchy. Dad needed Steve, and he needed him quick.

And maybe when Steve came Diego could talk with him and go over everything again in his own mind. But right now he shied away from thinking about it.

One thing was for sure, and that was that the company investigators weren't going to be able to answer any of Diego's questions. They were too busy third-degreeing everyone for answers to listen to questions.

The girl was looking at him funny. Most of the time she stared straight ahead, pretending to listen to the men as they talked amongst themselves or barked questions at Lavelle. But when they were looking the other way, or at each other, the girl's eyes slid sideways, trying to meet his, and her mouth opened, as if she were about to speak.

Finally she got up and went outside, and he thought she had to go check on her snocle or pee or something. When she came back, she casually sat down beside him. None of the company men seemed to notice.

"I'm Bunny," she said, sideways out of her mouth.

"I know. I heard them talking to you. I'm Diego." He realized he was talking out of the side of *his* mouth, too. But he felt relieved that someone was finally talking to him rather than around him, and he knew immediately that this girl understood that what had happened to him and his father was not just another academic problem or fact-finding mission.

Her eyes gleamed the same way the dogs' eyes had gleamed in the darkness, and her lowered voice reminded him of the whisper of the sled runners on the snow.

"I know," she said. "Are you scared?"

"No—well, scared about Dad, maybe. But otherwise, no."

"You ought to be," she said in a tone that implied she knew something he didn't know.

"Why? Is it going to storm again or something?"

"Probably. But I don't mean that, I mean them," she said, nodding to Colonel Giancarlo and the others.

Diego shrugged. "They're just doing their jobs, trying to find out what happened," he said. He watched Giancarlo's fierce expression as the colonel tried for the fiftieth time to catch Lavelle in a lie, and added, "Not that they seem to believe anybody."

"They're like that. Look, I'll be around. If you need anything, let me know, okay? I mean, with your da sick, is your mum going to come down here, too? Does she need a place to stay? My people would help."

He felt another flare of resentment and gave her a dirty look, then decided that wasn't fair. She was just trying to be nice—maybe nosy, too, but at least she wasn't browbeating anybody the way Giancarlo and the others were. "Nah, my mom's, uh, not available—but I think Dad would want Steve here."

"Who's that?"

"His assistant, and his partner," Diego said, daring her to make something of it.

But she just nodded and said, "Okay, I'll see if I can

find out what's being done officially, and if nothing is, we'll try to do something unofficially. I just wanted you to know you've got friends here. Night."

"*Buenas noches,*" he whispered back.

"You did good, Bunka," Clodagh said later, when Bunny had returned to Kilcoole. She had dropped Giancarlo off at the company station to await word from the head of the search party, and delivered the others back to SpaceBase before returning to the village. "The boy is alone. Do you think he saw anything, or was it just the father?"

"No," Bunny said. "I think he did, too. I can't say why—he's denying he remembers a thing now, but they wouldn't believe him if he told them the truth anyway. The father's in the high-security ward at the infirmary. The flot around SpaceBase is that he's crazy."

"Poor boy," Clodagh said, her eyes blinking rapidly through the steam from the teacup she held to her lips. "All alone. I can't feel much for his father, but the lad is so young to be left to the company wolves, especially when he has passed through what he has. If only we could initiate him, it would be better. Has he *no one*?"

"Just this Steve," Bunny said. "He is Dr. Steven L. Margolies, assigned to the same branch and regular duty station as Metaxos. I found that much out from Arnie's soldier boyfriend at the communications shed. He put up the name Metaxos on the computer and it was there, under the info on Metaxos. I don't know how we could find Steve though."

Clodagh shook her head regretfully. "It's not really our place to find him, but the boy will need help when he goes back out there—" Her head jerked up. "I wish Charlie was still here."

"Maybe Yana can help," Bunny suggested.

"Maybe," Clodagh said slowly. "But be careful. Charlie was one of us. He would know, the way you do, what the boy is going through, as well as how the PTBs are. We don't know Yana so good yet."

"Sean likes her," Bunny said.

"He does, does he? What did he say?" Clodagh smiled a very pretty smile that transformed her face, her eyes twinkling with gleefully prurient interest.

"Nothing, but I could tell," Bunny said. "Don't worry, you'll be the first to know—well, maybe not the first . . ."

"Yana could be a good ally, but she's real closed up. That's better than being too friendly, I guess, but I'd feel better about her being here if we knew more about her."

"Give her a break, Clodagh. It's not her fault she was born at the wrong time and place for you to have delivered her the way you've done half of us. I'm going to go down there now and see if she has any ideas. Don't worry. I won't give anything away."

Over the next ten days Yana gradually accustomed herself to the new environment. She slept a lot, in between the necessary chores of keeping warm and eating. She kept Clodagh's medicine near her so that every time she felt the tickle that was the prelude to a cough, she could take a swig and forestall a spasm. Whatever was in the stuff was far more efficacious than what the medics had given her on Andromeda. She practiced taking deeper breaths of the marvelous fresh air of

Petaybee, expanding her capacity, flushing out the last of the gas from the depths of the lobes. She would never be much use here on Petaybee if she couldn't even breathe without coughing.

She had just finished making another futile trip to the virtually useless company store when she saw the snocles pulling into corps headquarters way up the street. Some game or the other was definitely afoot, but until the trouble came looking for her, she would conserve her strength. She needed all she could muster to withstand her own cooking, she thought, as she attempted to make a meal for herself and the cat. Other than the fish she had been given by Seamus and the one pan she had been given, she had found damned-all of any use through company channels in Kilcoole.

The trouble did indeed come looking for her a short time later. She was in the middle of browning the fish when someone pounded at her door. She opened it to see Giancarlo standing there.

"Maddock, where the hell have you been and why haven't you reported in?" he snapped before she could invite him inside.

"Nice to see you, too, sir," she said with a growl, pumping his hand and pulling him inside. On the stove, the grease she was cooking the fish in crackled and spat. The cat scooted under the bed. For some reason, Giancarlo's appearance suddenly infuriated her. Maybe it was because she was frustrated trying to keep house with the charity of the villagers because the store was so ill-stocked there was little her meager funds could buy to keep her alive. Maybe it was because they were no longer on shipboard or space station and so it didn't *look* like the corps to her. Maybe it was because this guy was the kind of petty martinet she had always hated and had sworn she would get back at when she retired. Maybe it was because he was such a contrast to the polite and kindly locals. But she thought it was because after killing everyone around her and half killing her, the company still allowed brass-assed spooks like him to threaten to withhold medical treatment and to dump her unprepared in a place like this in order to use her. A couple of years earlier she would have taken it for granted that they had the right, that Giancarlo had the right. Now she felt anger rising up inside her high enough to choke her if she didn't vent a little of it.

"Do sit down and tell me how, *sir*, I'm supposed to contact you with no radio, no computer, no transportation, no contact person not even a bloody goddamn pen, *sir*, or a fraggin' piece of fraggin' bloody paper, *sir*. While you're at it, tell me how you expect me to maintain cover and gain the trust of the people here when you, *sir*, come barging in shouting my name like the ship's bloody paging program. Sir."

She sat down in the chair, leaving him to remain standing or sit on the bed, she didn't really care which, while she crossed her arms and glared up at him.

"I see discipline has relaxed after only a few days of pretending to be a civilian."

"I *am* a civilian, *sir*. Maybe an employee, if the company cares to issue me anything to do my bloody job with, maybe not."

"You, uh, seem to be feeling better," he said lamely.

"Yes, Colonel Giancarlo, I am. Even we invalids have our good days. A weapon. I forgot. If I'm doing espionage here, I ought to have a weapon. If for no other reason than to hunt my own fraggin' food. They do that here. They have to. Have you seen that company store? What's the company trying to do here, sir? Incite another Bremport?"

"That's enough of that, Major. What I want to know is why the hell you didn't inform us about this latest fiasco with the geologic team."

"Could be because I had barely arrived when it happened. Could be because I wasn't briefed on who was here and who wasn't to begin with. Could be because I have no means of communication, no liaison officer since you so impetuously dismissed the one who was already here—"

"We had reasons to believe his loyalties were divided," Giancarlo said. He was sweating now, bundled up in his outdoor clothing while the stove radiated heat throughout the room.

About then she realized that the stove wasn't just sending heat waves: the fish pan was billowing smoke. She began coughing, but she was so angry that, still bent double from the spasms, she grabbed her knife, stabbed the burning fish, and flipped it over in the blackening grease, still glaring at Giancarlo when her eyes weren't clenched shut from the spasms.

Giancarlo began coughing, too, and rose as she stumbled for the door and flung it open. They both stepped into the open air, breathing deeply, while the smoke rolled out the door.

"I want no repeat of this omission in the future," he said. "Meanwhile, I'll look into the problem of your special equipment. Good evening, Major."

She coughed and managed to blurt out "Colonel" only when he was well down the street. She covered her mouth and nose, reached around the corner of the door for the hook containing her parka, and grabbed Clodagh's cough syrup and her muffler. Downing a swallow of the syrup, she rubbed the muffler in the snow and, holding it across her mouth and nose, dashed back into the cabin. She forked the burned fish from the pan and flicked it onto the snow for the cat to salvage later. Then, with the door still open, she put on her parka and sat outside, waiting for the smoke to clear.

Fraggin' bureaucrat! He was one lousy grade above her and thought he was some kind of fraggin' deity. Idiots like him had assigned Bry that mission that had gotten him killed. Idiots like him had cut costs by shortchanging the colony on Bremer until the colonists had grown tired of watching each other and their children die of curable diseases and starvation, and had rebelled. What was that saying about "penny wise and pound foolish"? Damn!

"Are you okay, dama?" her across-the-road neighbor, whom she hadn't yet met, hollered out his door.

"Fine!" she called back.

"I saw smoke," the man ventured, diplomatically not referring to the rest of the row.

"Burned my dinner," she said.

"Want to come over while your house clears?"

"No, thanks," she called, trying not to sound as belligerent as she felt. "I'm out here for my health."

When she had literally and figuratively cooled off enough, she went back into the house. The odor of burnt fish was still very strong, but enough smoke had cleared so it didn't bring on another coughing fit. She kept swigging on Clodagh's bottle every so often to fend off hunger pains while she scoured the pan with her knife and fought off the cat, who kept climbing her leg, mewing piteously. It naturally wanted no more to do with the burnt fish than she did.

Bunny knocked on the door and let herself in before Yana could answer.

"Come in, sit down. No, better yet, I'll be glad to feed you fish if you cook the dinner," Yana told her.

Bunny shook her head and took the pan away from her, filling it with snow to melt on the stove and plopping the fish in—all of them. Yana had forgotten to take the rest of the string back outside, and they had all thawed.

"How did they expect you to live down here when they didn't teach you how to survive?" she asked.

"That's what I was just asking my good buddy, Colonel Asshole Giancarlo, when he came to give me his hail-and-farewell address."

"I heard," Bunny said.

"You did?"

"Yeah, all up and down the street. People thought you might be burning him at the stake or something until your neighbors saw him leave. They said you sure looked mad, dragging him inside. Then the smoke started billowing out of your house. You threw him out the door with burning fish and sat out in the cold."

"How could you know?" Yana asked, mortified at the picture she probably had presented. Some clandestine operative she was. Giancarlo would probably send some mercenary hit man after her after this incident, but it was worth it. Asshole. "It just happened."

Bunny shrugged. "It's a small town, Yana. By the way, your face is black all down the middle from your eyes to your chin."

"Shit." Yana pulled out the tail of her uniform blouse, dipped it in the fish water, and scrubbed. "Did I get it?"

"Not all. Your nose is still dirty."

That struck Yana as funny, and she began laughing so hard she started coughing again, realizing as she fell into hiccoughs that she was also slightly drunk from Clodagh's cough syrup. She collapsed on the bed.

"Oh, shit, Bunny, what a week," she said, her laughs subsiding into a flurry of silly intermittent giggles.

That started Bunny laughing, too. She put a plate on top of the pan for a lid and sat down at the table, laughing louder than Yana until her laughter started Yana off again.

"You're as bad as me," Yana said finally. "I'm a fine 'zample to the younger gen'ration."

"I sure would have liked to see you haul that Giancarlo in and kick him out," Bunny said. "I been driving him around for days and he's—he's—"

"Yeah, isn't he?"

"He's been browbeating Lavelle, even though she told him what happened. And he has poor Dr. Metaxos locked up in the crazy ward and won't believe what Diego tells him, and Diego's all by himself and can't find his other father . . ."

"Other father?"

Bunny nodded. "His father's partner, Steven Margolies. You know, they're like Aisling and Sinead, and they're Diego's folks, but nobody's even let the other father know about Dr. Metaxos. If Charlie were here, he could maybe have gotten a message to this Steve through people he knew at SpaceBase, but now there's no one in town who can help Diego, and you can bet Giancarlo won't do it."

"My my. You've sure taken up this Diego's cause in a short period of time. I thought he was in shock and half out of it."

"He's not. He's just worried about his da and nobody will believe him."

"What's he look like, Bunny?" Yana asked her.

"He has really dark eyes, very big, and his hair is—Yana, you're laughing at me!"

"Yep, I thought so," Yana said. "He's cute, is he? 'Sokay, Bunny. So you like this boy and nobody will help him and Giancarlo was his usual charming self to your buddy, so you're glad I told him off and you came to tell me so? Or did you really just come down to cook me dinner so I wouldn't starve to death?"

"Well, I was talking to Clodagh . . ." Bunny's face grew a little sly as she turned and pulled two steaming and fragrant fish out of the pan and arranged them on a plate. Carefully she picked the third one up by the tail. The cat was no laggard and had snagged it out of her hand before she could lay it on the floor for him.

"What I told Clodagh . . ." Bunny began, managing to stand between Yana and the fish.

"What?" Yana said, sobering now so that Bunny stopped playing and settled into the chair, handing Yana the knife so she could carve into her fish.

"Was maybe you could help Diego. You know, maybe you could ride in with me to SpaceBase next time I have a run and like wear your uniform and maybe Arnie's boyfriend would help you get a message to that man you said would help Charlie. Maybe *he* could let Dr. Margolies know what happened and—well, you did say he was in deployment. Maybe he could get him down here."

"Military deployment, Bunny."

Bunny shrugged. "It's all just PTBs anyway, isn't it? Can't they pull strings or something?"

"Hmm. Maybe they can. If anyone could, Ahmed could. Or if not, he'd find out *who* could." And in the back of her mind, it occurred to her that she could also use her full uniform and access to SpaceBase as an opportunity to "requisition" some of the equipment necessary to the duties Giancarlo seemed to think she was so derelict in performing. If at some later date he actually got around to issuing her duplicates, she could trade the items for other locally produced items. She wasn't really qualified for this kind of subterfuge, having never actually been a supply officer, but she figured necessity was going to have to be the mother of invention in this case.

Yana was very popular that evening. Bunny hadn't been gone more than a half an hour when there was another knock at her door. She opened it to find Sean Shongili leaning against the doorframe, astounding her again with how much less bulky he was than everyone else.

"Come in," she said. "You'll catch your death. A virus or something . . ."

The silvery eyes glinted with amusement and his mouth quirked at the corner. She had an unauthorized urge to brush back the lock of silver-brown hair that fell boyishly forward onto his forehead.

"I hear you've been taking on the Intergal high command," he said, stamping his feet outside and entering, shrugging off his light jacket before even closing the door.

"Oh, that." She waved her hand dismissively, pretending more nonchalance than she felt. She was probably going to have to do a little creative groveling over that sooner or later if she was going to be able to help the boy—or maybe not. She was no longer feeling so smug. The smart thing for Giancarlo to do was to cooperate with her if he wanted results; but, although he was far from stupid, for someone in his specialty, he did not seem to have learned the value of cooperation, though no doubt he found it in himself to cooperate with those of higher rank. She would worry about it later, she thought, realizing at the same time that the effects of the cough medicine's overdose hadn't quite worn off. She was using a lot of her mental energy to keep from throwing her arms around Shongili's neck and planting a kiss on the warm smile with which he was favoring her.

"Uh, sit down," she said, brushing her own hair back from her face and hoping her hands had gotten washed somehow in the midst of all of this and she wasn't resmearing herself with ashes. "Can I burn you some tea?"

"Please. I just got back from running with the search party."

"Any trace of the others?"

He shook his head and sat on the bed. She lifted a finger to tell him to wait, ducked outside, dipped up a pan of snow from a high drift, where animals hadn't been able to reach it, and returned to plop it back on the stove.

"No," he said. "Not a trace. And it started snowing hard again, so we had to give up for the time being. If your friend the colonel would just release Lavelle, I'll bet Dinah could help. She's the best leader of all of the dogs, and if our people are still findable, she'll locate them. We've been out for three days now."

"You must be exhausted."

"A little. I just came by to ask if you'd finished with the recorder yet."

"Oh, frag! No, I haven't, really. Clodagh came by once, too, but I completely forgot to ask her when she wanted to do the song for Charlie. If you need it, maybe I could—"

"No, no, that's okay." He peered over her shoulder. "Your water's boiling."

"Thanks."

He took a deep breath and said, "What I actually wondered was, well, while you've got it, have you given any more thought to making the song about Bremport?"

"Oh, Sean," she said, sitting back down hard. To her annoyance, she began to cough again, not because she had to but out of reflex. "Sean, I just can't do that. It's too soon. A lot of it's classified. And I just don't want to think about it. People here don't want to hear it, either, trust me."

He reclined on the bed, propping himself up on his elbow, and gave her a long hard look. "I could say the same thing, Yana. Trust me. You need to do this. We need to hear it."

"Sean, I can't. I'm no songwriter and I can barely stand to talk about it. Anyway, I only saw one small, awful part. The rest I've put together from what I was told before or since about Bremer."

"I'd like to hear about it," he said, quietly insistent.

"Did you have someone there? Did you know someone there?" she asked.

"You," he said, making and holding eye contact. "At least, I'm trying to know you."

That unsettled her for a moment. She put some of Clodagh's herbs in a bag and steeped them in the tea water while she thought. Maybe she *should* talk about it, not only because Shongili wanted to know, but because she was still furious about the whole thing. She couldn't keep popping off at superior officers on whose goodwill she was dependent and get away with it.

"Okay," she said. "Since you think it needs to be told to everybody else, let's turn on the recorder. I don't believe I could go through this twice." He said nothing, but raised his eyebrows inquiringly and she said, "My coat. In the pocket."

He moved with natural, lanky grace, rolling across the bed and onto his feet, striding the step or two to the doorway and extracting the recorder, rolling back across the bed with the machine in one hand. He set it on the table beside her chair and punched in the recording sequence.

She put the cup of tea beside him, then realized it was her only cup. Giving a shrug, she carefully raised the pan in both hands and sipped the tea from the lip before settling down again.

She could have gone next door and borrowed a cup, perhaps, but she didn't know the people and she felt that if she interrupted this moment, it wouldn't return. She might never again have the courage to discuss it. She certainly would never again have the kind of total attention she had from Sean Shongili.

"I'm not sure what's classified," she said to begin with. "Except that I'm not supposed to tell you how the terrorists infiltrated the station." She shrugged. "Hell, I don't know that for sure anyway, though I could speculate. The thing is, Sean, the deaths were unnecessary. None of those people had to die. None of them should have. The terrorists were after food, medicine, and supplies."

"How do you know?"

"Because I lay there on the floor playing dead, watching them loot the place, and that's all they bloody well took."

"We heard that they systematically ran through the place executing everyone they found alive," Sean said.

Yana shook her head. "There was no need of that. I think they did make sure of a few of the crew, but the station commander and supply officer just happened, by pure coincidence mind you, to be visiting another ship that day. *My* ship. It had just transferred supplies, and I was bringing fresh recruits over to familiarize them with a Class One station and demonstrate some of the equipment. I—um—I was just showing them how the snorkel worked."

"The what?" Sean asked, leaning forward.

Her voice had been clear and matter-of-fact so far, but suddenly she was having trouble forcing it above a whisper. Her throat began to spasm and she started coughing again. Sean held out the bottle of Clodagh's medicine, and she took a good swig before she continued.

"The snorkel. It's for short repair jobs in airless sections of the ship, so that you don't have to suit up.

There's an exchange unit in it that returns oxygen for CO_2, breath for breath, without the need to carry heavy tanks or wear a full space suit that might be too bulky to do some of the inside repairs in tighter places. Also, you can send snorkeled personnel into certain areas of the ship without having to flood the whole area with O_2. New invention. They discovered the exchange material on Bremer."

She stopped and watched him. She had lit the lamp earlier, and now its glow and that of the moons and stars through the window illuminated the room. The planes of his face were shadowed, and his eyes held hers, silently pulling more out of her. The tension was broken when the cat jumped up onto her knees and settled down, purring, as if knowing she needed reassurance that she was here, on firm ground, with living people and in no immediate danger, instead of back there.

He nodded slowly, an almost imperceptible movement.

"I stepped back into an air lock with the mask in place and let the inner door close. The students were looking through the view plate and watching me on the screens on either side of the door, as I explained the mask to them.

"I saw the vapor pouring in through the ventilation duct before any of them did, but I couldn't speak to them because of the snorkel. I signaled them to stand back and hit the O_2 button for the lock, waited a beat, and hit the exit panel for the door. But then I realized the vapor was pouring in behind me, too. I heard an explosion—felt it really—and the door jammed half-open between us. The recruits were coughing and crowding the outer door."

She stopped for a moment and took a swig of cough syrup, seeing the faces in front of her. "An eighteen-year-old girl blocked my way back into the hold. She was trying to get through to the outside, I guess, and was coughing so hard she couldn't straighten up. People were vomiting, crying. The girl's nametag said Samuelson and she had almost white hair, cut into a crew cut. You know, trying to look the part of a company cadet. Her scalp was bright red through her hair, and her eyes were bulging. I exhaled into the mask, tore it off, and tried to wrestle it over her face, but she fought me. I—uh—had to knock her down to get past her, into the room. I put the mask back on and breathed into it but the O_2 that came back wasn't pure. I must have let some of the gas leak in while I was trying to rebreathe her. The yellow vapor was still swirling, and through it I saw the viewscreens. Masked figures were running around, carrying weapons and containers, grabbing all the new supplies. My first thought was that they were station crew investigating the gas in the ventilation system. But that didn't jibe with the weapons and the way they were ignoring the people dying under their feet. I tried buddy-breathing with the nearest cadet who still had some life in him, and he seemed to realize what I was trying to do, but when he breathed into the mask, it fouled it, and he died too. They all died. Every damned one of them died and I just lay there, playing dead, on the floor breathing through the contaminated mask, exhaling the gas and CO_2, sucking in poisoned oxygen while the terrorists ran through the station.

The alarms were blaring and the station computer calling for help, but the last thing I saw was the masked face of one of the terrorists through the viewport leading to the main corridor. She looked surprised to see us lying in there. I had my face against the floor so the mask wouldn't show, and I was wedged among the cadets' bodies. I did—not—cover myself with glory."

She didn't realize until he pulled a rag out of his pocket and wiped her face that she had been weeping. She took the rag from him and scrubbed at her face vigorously, not wanting undeserved sympathy.

He withdrew gently, asking, "How did you get out?"

"The station computer alerted the ship's computer, and they sent medical teams and oxygen. It can't have taken very long, any of it, but I was unconscious by then. I woke up at Andromeda Station, unable to move. I was on an automatic respirator. Four or five of us survived, I understand, but we weren't allowed to meet. Once we were well enough to talk, we were questioned for weeks about how we managed to survive the others. At first I think they thought I was in league with the terrorists. But then some of the administrators on Bremer got scared and turned over the terrorists. We were exonerated, they were executed . . ." She shrugged, at a loss for any more to say. "Some song, huh?"

This time he rose from the bed and put his arms around her. She tried not to cry, not to play for sympathy. She had no need of it. But she developed a very sudden and crucial need for being held against Sean Shongili—since he had volunteered.

"I—um, I can't tell you anything specific about the kids from Petaybee," she said into his shoulder.

He hugged her more tightly and she relaxed into him, closing her eyes, relieved to have talked about it. Relieved that so far he hadn't told her what she should have done instead of what she had done to save the kids who were in her charge.

He surprised her then by saying, "Get dressed."

"What?"

"You're not tired, are you?"

"I wouldn't want to try to go to sleep now, no," she said, wiping her face with the heels of her hands so she could look him in the eye.

"I want to take you somewhere."

"Where?"

"A place we use for cleansing. Come on."

She pulled on her quilted pants and parka, her mittens, hat, and muffler, and stuck the cough medicine back in her pocket.

"Let's take this, too," Sean said, sticking the recorder into his own pocket.

"You don't still think I could *sing* . . ."

"We'll see what you think," he said, prodding her toward the door with a hand that lingered between the bottom of her cap and her folded-down hood, at the base of her hairline. A rush of longing for him made her feel weak-kneed and ashamed at the same time, as if she were exploiting the tragedy to hold his attention.

She sat with him in the cab of his snocle, the motor obscenely loud in the silent village. In a moment they were through it, past Bunny's sleeping dogs and Clodagh's house, past the company station and out onto the snowy plain.

The machine slid over the snow and parted drifts,

spraying white glitter in its wake, the engine's hum the only sound, as if they were riding the wind. After a few moments Sean leaned forward and pointed up, and she looked above her to see a long weaving band of rainbow-striped feathers undulating across the sky like the warbonnet of an old-time cinematic warrior.

They watched and rode in silence. A big cat sprang away from them; then the lights of their snocle snared a wolf and they had to tack around him to keep from injuring him. They didn't really need the lights, it seemed to Yana. The snow reflected back the light from the moons and stars and the aurora, casting deep shadows against which prominent objects were etched in a sharp relief. For the first time, she saw that the settlement was within sight of hills and mountains, off to the east and southeast. They passed between the first pair of hills and cut behind them, following a winding pass that didn't assail the mountains directly, but nudged gently into them. Within this shelter was more of the vegetation she had seen along the river, tall conifers and a great deal of brush.

It was darker here, in the shadows of the hills, and Sean stopped the snocle.

"We have to walk in," he said. "There's no way to get back there by snocle or sled, but it's an easy walk."

She nodded and followed, thinking she could use the crisp air to clear her head of cough-medicine fumes and the leaden emotional aftertaste of Bremport. She could taste the gas on her tongue again and smell it deep inside herself.

The air here was not as cold as that at the village. Stunted trees and brush grew along the man-made walkway fashioned of carefully pieced bits of flattened machine hulls and suspended over the snow and humped mounds of undergrowth.

Sean had been taking the lead, and now he reached back for her and pulled her forward.

"Look," he said, pointing to a large animal watching them from the shadows.

"It looks just like I do in this getup," she said of the burly furry form.

"That's because you look like a bear," he said, his voice husky, whether from whispering and cold or emotion she couldn't tell. "This is all muskeg underneath here, spongy, swampy. You'll soon see why. Berries stay on the bushes much later than elsewhere, which is what interests him." He nodded at the bear. "Come, we're almost there."

And around the next bend she saw the rising steam, curling above the snow-laden tops of larger trees, and two steps farther she saw the pools and the falls.

"Sean, it's beautiful," she said, taking in the upper pool, closest to them, where water bubbled up from the center in a fountain and formed a deep wide well reflecting the moons and stars in its ripples. Some hidden current sent the water cascading into a second pool and a third. A narrow path, almost free of snow, ran alongside the banks, leading in steps down to the lowest pool. Sean was already shucking his clothing. He turned and grinned at her.

"You'll dry out better if you only get your hide wet. If you can't swim, there's a lot of places where it's shallow enough to wade, but you'll prefer total immersion."

She had already begun to unfasten her outer clothing.

He jumped into the water with a flash of moonlight on his pale muscular backside. She caught a shadow-darkened glimpse of him sliding over the falls and heard him laugh.

Hoping this wasn't another of those instances where everybody else was freezing their butt off while Shongili was warm and under—or in this case un—dressed, she quickly finished stripping and much more quickly waded into the pool, then glided into the water. The pool by the fountain was indeed warm, almost uncomfortably so, and it unknotted her chilled muscles and soaked her through and through with its heat until she felt lazy and languorous. The water carried a hint of sulfur and mint. She kept as much of her under the surface as possible, diving repeatedly.

The diving caused a ringing in her ears that sounded almost like music. She swam underwater as long as possible, listening to it, hoping to remember which tunes it called to mind.

She surfaced long enough to catch her breath before approaching the waterfall. It wasn't a long one, a drop of just a few feet, and the lip of the fall was smooth beneath the tumbling water. If Shongili could do it, so could she, she thought, but she flipped over and went down feet first, her knees, belly, breasts, and face momentarily tweaked with the bite of the icy air.

The water in the lower pool was a little cooler, a little easier to swim in without falling asleep, but as she was surfacing, something flashed between her legs and up behind her.

She flipped around and grabbed, thinking to find Shongili, but her hand touched wet fur instead of wet skin and she found herself looking down into the laughing silvery eyes of a large gray seal.

She hadn't thought seals liked fresh water, especially not warm fresh water, and especially not inland streams, but perhaps this was another of Petaybee's permutations that Sean wanted her to see.

The seal flipped up and back under her and dived down into the lower pool. Where the hell was Sean? She felt a cold droplet on her face, and another, and looked up to see that light snow was floating down from a sky now only partially clear. She shivered and dove under, hearing the music again. This time, perhaps because of the closeness of the falls, she could almost hear the singing of lyrics as well.

The seal somehow or other had propelled itself back into this upper pool and now came up under her, as if inviting her to hold on to it while it swam around and around.

Yes! She did hear words, not lyrics after all, but spoken words, low and murmured. She thought perhaps Sean might have returned and was talking to her from the land. When she raised her head, however, he was nowhere near, though the murmurous words continued to the soft water music. She glimpsed the seal under the falls for a moment, and she decided she would get out of the pool. But first, she'd warm up beneath the water pouring from the hot pool above.

There was a narrow ledge under the pool, and as she climbed up on it, she saw the flash of gray fur again as the seal darted in and out. Ignoring the creature, she stood and let the deliciously warm water play over her face and hair, cascading down her shoulders, back, hips, and calves, caressing her face, throat, breasts, belly, and thighs. The water continued its tune, and listening for the rhythm, she realized suddenly that the air pressure had changed around her. It wasn't water alone that was caressing her, stroking her abdomen, counting her ribs with splayed fingers, cupping her breasts . . .

"By the powers that be, I welcome you home," Sean's voice said, as if reciting a line from a song or a poem. His lips slid beneath her ear and kissed her throat, and she turned in his arms, knowing full well that this was probably going to mean no end of trouble at some point but not caring at all.

His skin was slick with water but almost as well furred as the seal's. She turned in his arms and threw her own arms around his neck, kissing him hungrily. When the kiss was done, he held her for a moment, then looked down at her with silver eyes confusingly like those of the seal. She blinked and retreated a half step. The laughter in his eyes saddened briefly into wistfulness, then brusqueness as he held her away from him and said, "We'd better go now. You get out and get dressed. I'll be right behind you."

As if now was a time to be formal? She pulled away from him and dove back into the cooler pool, swimming briskly out and deliberately letting the cold touch her bare skin before dressing again.

Frag, what *was* it, anyway? Had her revelations been too much for him after all? Or had he really meant this little swim to be therapeutic and just gotten momentarily carried away when it became erotic instead? Maybe he had a serious interest elsewhere. Maybe he didn't like women. No, she had had definite evidence to the contrary. Angry and baffled, she pulled half-frozen clothing over her wet body and began walking very briskly indeed back down the pathway.

Halfway back to the snocle, he joined her, resting his hand lightly on her shoulder, the thumb of his glove brushing her cheek.

"I think you'll find you can write that song, now," he said.

She wanted to hit him but satisfied herself with pulling away and riding in silence all the way back to her cabin. But, after he left and her frustration died down, she realized he was right.

The frustration didn't stay with her. He had wanted her as much as she wanted him, she knew, and there had to be some reason why he had insisted they restrain themselves. When she thought back on it, she could see the cold snowflakes falling into the steaming water and hear the music beneath the falls again. She activated the recorder and spoke into it.

"Having only air for food,
They gave us poison to breathe
Even those who had never harmed them
Even those who would have helped them
Even those who were only children
Even those who were very like them.

"Holding a piece of their own world, I survived
Breathing through their own soil, I lived
I could not save anybody, not even all of myself.
They did not help anybody, not even themselves.
They died, as those around me died, and the
Food, and the medicine were taken back.
In the station, people choked and died

On the planet, people starved and died
When captured, the killers bled and died
I was sent here to die, too, here where the snows live,
The waters live, the animals and the trees live,
And you."

7

Bunny knocked on Yana's door early the next morning. "I'm heading out to SpaceBase. Can you come now?"

Yana had had very little sleep, between the ride out to the hot springs and back, and staying up late to record the poem. That had stimulated her far beyond her expectations; she had been unable to rest, kicking herself for not confronting Sean Shongili last night when it would have made sense. Now, except for a lingering twitchy nervousness, the encounter seemed hard to believe. She was both glad and sorry that he lived so far away: glad because she would not have to face him; sorry because there would be no chance meetings, no possibility of seeing him unless one of them deliberately sought the other one out.

What the hell! She had better things to do. She hauled herself out of her bunk and pulled on a uniform blouse that still bore insignia. She hadn't removed her rank from her fatigue jacket yet either, and she slipped it on under her parka.

"Are you feeling better this morning?" Bunny asked owlishly as they set out down the river.

"As opposed to what?" Yana snapped.

Bunny didn't seem offended; she just smiled and said, "Well, you were so upset over that Giancarlo making you burn the fish and then . . ."

"When you left me, I was doing fine, wasn't I? Was that supposed to change?"

Bunny glanced away from the river road and over at her, then back again. She looked disappointed.

Yana heaved a sigh and leaned back in the seat. She would have preferred to sleep until they reached SpaceBase. "I'd like to know who it is who's keeping a log of my activities and guests—then I could set the record straight when necessary. I'd hate for the whole village to be *wrong* about something. And that cough medicine of Clodagh's should be a controlled substance, by the way."

"He really likes you, Yana," Bunny said.

"Buneka, I'm not going to discuss this with you," Yana said firmly, settling herself and closing her eyes. After a few moments of not sleeping, she asked, "He hasn't always been by himself, has he?"

"Sean? Oh no, he used to have lots of girlfriends when he was traveling around the world. He almost married Charlie Demintieff's sister Ruby once, but she changed her mind at the last minute and married a guy from Baffin Point instead. How about you? Lots of old boyfriends?"

"Bunny!"

"Well, but have you had? We *know* all that stuff about each other."

"I've had a few boyfriends, I guess you could call them, yes."

"Anybody serious?"

"My husband," Yana said shortly, not wanting to dig

into her memories of Bry so soon after talking about Bremport. Couldn't these damn people leave anything alone? And why did she feel like she had to answer anyway? "He died," she said shortly.

"At Bremport?" Bunny asked almost reverently.

"No. Not at Bremport. Ten years ago. During a shuttle malfunction. Bunny, I *really* don't want to talk about it. Now then, what was the name of Diego's friend again?"

As Yana suspected, entering the base from the outside was different from being inprocessed through the cattle chutes. In places like this, with little of intrinsic value on the premises—by Intergal standards anyway— personnel were bored and security was lax.

"Whew, this is a hard, ugly-looking place," Yana said to Bunny as they pulled up to the gate.

Bunny's mitten described an arc around the perimeter. "There used to be lots of little businesses around here: bars, pleasure places, shops for the soldiers. Sometimes they'd bring in extra equipment that wasn't actually needed and trade it for something to send to families on other colonies or stations. But about a year ago, that all stopped and the company had the whole corridor bulldozed and you had to be a soldier or have a pass to come onto the base. We found out later about Bremport." She shrugged. "The elders were glad when the base closed. They said the soldiers were corrupting us, but heck, half of them were from here anyway, and related to us, so when their families were allowed out here, lots of us could go into the shops and buy cloth and other stuff that never makes it out to *our* store."

Yana's parka was uniform issue, and she opened it to

let her rank show as they passed the gate guard, who nodded at Bunny's ID and saluted Yana. The guard hut was a small "instant" building of composite material in a pale pastel. In the lights of the base—and the entire base was so strongly lit that Yana wondered that they couldn't see the lights clear from Kilcoole—she noticed that the buildings all had some sort of a pastel tint: anemic pink, bilious green, jaundiced yellow. All of the colors were watered down with the familiar omnipresent gray, so that the squat, rectangular buildings merely stood out in ugly relief from the snowy surroundings but achieved nothing so frivolous as beauty or gaiety. The buildings were set in precise rows, down which the arctic wind roared. Beyond the hunkering buildings, abandoned launch gantries towered awkwardly, swaying in the wind like the writhing legs of dying insects.

Bunny pulled up to a building much like the others except that it bore a letter and a number—C-1000. "There's my fare," she said between closed teeth, then jumped out, ran around to hold the door open for Yana, and said with a large obsequious smile, "I thank you for your patronage, dama. Please remember to ask that Rourke be sent for when you wish to return to our village again."

"Don't overdo it," Yana growled between *her* teeth and in a louder voice said, "Could you direct me, Rourke, to the infirmary and the communications depot?"

Bunny's fare, in the usual anonymous company parka and muffler up to the eyes, walked around the front of the snocle and squinted at Yana.

"Major Maddock? Yanaba Maddock?" he asked.

Startled to be recognized so soon after arriving on the

base, she counted to three and turned slowly to face the man, raising a rapidly icing eyebrow. "Yes?"

The man pressed his padding against her padding and gave her a stiff hug. "With all due respect, Major, I thought I'd never see you again. When I heard you were on Bremport . . ." He was struggling to unwrap his scarf and hood from his face.

"Rumors of my demise were greatly exaggerated, as the man said," she told him. By then, he had pulled the hood back to reveal the longer-than-regulation bronze hair and smiling brown eyes she recognized from her days with the survey teams. "Torkel!" she said.

"Small universe, eh?" It was a very tired but often true spacer's joke.

"What are you doing on Petaybee?" she asked.

"I was wondering that myself until I met you. Can I buy you a cup of something hot?"

"Sir . . ." Bunny began.

"I'll make it worth your while to—uh, cool your heels, Rourke. Shouldn't be too hard around here."

"Yes, Captain," Bunny said. Then she spoke more boldly, surprising Yana. "Sir, would it be possible for me to go see Diego? I mean, I just thought—"

"Good idea," Torkel said. "A pretty girl his own age ought to cheer him up some. Building ten-oh-six. If anybody questions you, tell them I authorized it."

Yana wasn't surprised that Torkel was confident in the amount of weight he swung as a mere captain. The fact was, as she and a few others had reason to know, his rank had little to do with his true degree of power. His family had developed the terraforming process used by the company to create colony worlds such as Petaybee, and his father currently sat on Intergal's board of directors. Torkel was a very competent officer, but he had been a captain longer than it took most to make general. Generals had a lot hidden from them, whereas captains tended to end up in the thick of things. No one had told Yana this, but she had figured it out, from shipboard conversation and a few remarks Torkel had made in jest.

It was a joy to sit across from him over steaming cups and energy bars in the dingy little canteen. They had removed hats, hoods, and mufflers but still wore their coats unfastened and peeled back, for the canteen was not well heated. Torkel studied her face as if he was memorizing her.

"It really is you. I can't tell you how I felt when I heard about Bremport, and then heard that you were there that day. I wanted to execute the terrorists personally."

"I know the feeling," she said dryly.

"You're looking wonderful. Better, really, than the last time I saw you."

"Really? It's amazing what a little toxic gas can do for a girl's complexion. I did lose quite a lot of weight and I haven't gained much back, trying to—" She started to say, "trying to figure out how not to burn my food," but he was already interrupting, leaning forward and looking deeply into her eyes.

"No, it's not that. You're more relaxed—less locked up inside yourself. I guess it must have been that we met each other so soon after your husband's death . . ."

"Or so soon after your divorce," she reminded him. He had been going through the female crew members at an astonishing rate by the time she had left for another unit. He had never come on to her before, though, but always treated her as a senior officer, with respect and what friendliness she had been able to allow. Still, if he thought she was less locked-up now, she had either become much better at hiding her feelings or she must have been more of a mess than she realized back then. "What brings you here, Torkel?" she asked, to get the conversation back on firmer ground.

"Oh, I'm sort of troubleshooting," he said. "Nobody's sure exactly what's going on. Minerals we can spot from space but can't locate on the surface, teams disappearing, unauthorized life-forms cropping up. The company asked me to evaluate the situation. I thought maybe you might be on the same mission, and we'd be working together again?"

"Well, I am in a way, but more covertly," she said. "I'm living in the village."

"Among the locals? That's pretty rough. How badly were you injured at Bremport?"

"I got a discharge, but I'm recovering," she said, and realized that it was the truth. The pains in her chest no longer plagued her and the cough was much less frequent, thanks to Clodagh's syrup. "Anyway, Torkel, I'm glad I ran into you. Giancarlo is a little unreasonable."

"I've noticed he was pretty heavy-handed dealing with that native woman."

"How's she doing, by the way?"

"She and the others are probably going to be sent offworld to be interrogated further. Nothing anybody says really adds up, Yana. Fifty teams have been sent down here in the past ten years, and this is only the second time that we've had any survivors at all."

"How *is* the boy?" Yana asked quickly.

"He's scared. Alone on a hostile world . . ."

"Torkel, I think Giancarlo's been filling you full of shit about the natives here. They're nice people, and they know a few things the company could learn to its benefit."

"Sure they do. That's what this is all about," he said with a wry lift of one side of his mouth. "And I'm not surprised to hear you have a high opinion of them. I'm sure you bring out the best in them. Even the ips know a good thing when they see it." He held her hand in both of his and kissed it, which both pleased and slightly alarmed her. If Intergal had a Prince Charming equivalent, it was Torkel Fiske, but she had never expected him to come after her, even in passing.

She patted his hands with her spare one, pressing her advantage. "No, they're very caring people. They're not only worried about Petaybeans who are being held, they're also very concerned about the boy. His father, too, of course. Has anyone gotten ahold of his father's partner?"

"Partner?"

"Yes, it's on the computer. A Steven Margolies, Metaxos's assistant."

"Yana, you're brilliant as ever. I didn't know anything about this. I'll have the man sent for at once. Metaxos is no good in the condition he's in now. The boy, now, he might help us if we keep him on-site and with Margolies, a man intimately familiar with Metaxos's work. That's a good rationale for relocating the whole family unit to Petaybee."

"Won't Metaxos need better care than the infirmary

here can provide?" she asked. "I heard his condition was pretty bad."

"Oh, care here's going to improve shortly. We're bringing in more troops and support teams to try to crack this case. Between the two of us, there's even some talk of evacuating the planet and doing some serious mining until it pays back."

"I thought it was a high-recruitment area."

"It is. Has been very good. But lately there have been fewer new recruits despite the austere conditions. Seems like the natives just don't want to leave." He smiled at her again, his eyes, even in this light, clear and a beautiful light brown, the color of Clodagh's tea. "If you're going to be here, I won't want to leave either."

"Good," Yana said, softening her briskness by smiling warmly at him. "I can't imagine anyone handier to run into right now. Giancarlo, as I mentioned, is being difficult. Now then, Torkel, repeat after me: 'Is there anything you need, Yana?' "

He leaned closer, and she could feel his breath as he said, stroking her palm with his thumb, "Is—there—any—thing—you—need—Yana?"

"I have a list," she said.

"What sorta hold you got on the captain?" Bunny asked as she helped Yana load the snocle. "He tol' me to come back and get you."

"It's called the 'old buddy network,' " Yana said, trying not to feel smug over the haul she had just made. "By the way, a burst went out to Steve Margolies. Diego'll have company here real soon."

Bunny paused in hefting the pack of "clothing, winter

wear, one of each" Yana had freed up. "That's great, Yana. Only how?" She gave Yana a searching look.

"I suggested that maybe the dad would come round faster if he had the support of his family unit." Yana hesitated then, not sure if she should confide in Bunny some of the plans for Petaybee that Torkel had mentioned. "You may be busier than ever soon," she heard herself adding.

"How so?"

"They're bringing in more troops and some support teams."

Bunny snorted. "What good'll those do 'em if they don't believe what they been told!"

"Intergal is trying damned hard to find those minerals they can see from up there."

"Yeah, they do keep trying, don't they?" That amused Bunny. "There. All your gear stowed safe and tight. Let's get home. I got dogs to feed." When they had reached the main road out of SpaceBase, she had other questions. "Who's this captain dude, anyway? The colonel really snapped to when he arrived, like he wasn't expected and not all that welcome, either."

Yana chuckled. "His name's Fiske, Torkel Fiske. Son of the family that developed the terraforming process used here."

"They did Petaybee?" Bunny turned very wide eyes on Yana. "How come you know him?"

"Served on the same ship a coupla times. That's all."

"That's *all*?"

"That's all, Bunny," Yana said in a tone to discourage further queries. And yet, it started her to thinking. Torkel had sure acted glad to see her. Now, when a guy like Torkel Fiske could bed practically any female he wanted, why had he been so attentive to her, Yanaba Maddock? Had he actually known, all along, that she was on a covert mission in the village? He had sounded genuinely surprised. Or was he just surprised to have run into her at SpaceBase? Had he meant what he said, about the possibility of evacuating everyone from Petaybee so they could blast the planet apart to find the minerals they had been after for so many years? "Ever wanted to get off Petaybee, Bunny? Get to see other worlds, where the living's a bit easier?"

Bunny shot her a quick glance. "Why would I want to leave Petaybee? I belong here, Yana. Not just because I was born here. I belong here! I belong to this planet." Then she clamped her lips shut and concentrated on her driving.

She had returned to her normal cheerful self when she slowed the snocle to a stop exactly parallel with the steps to Yana's little house.

"I'll unload, Yana," she said. "You go tend your fire. Some of this stuff won't do for freezing."

"Only if you agree to eat with me?"

Bunny grinned. "You mean, you want me to cook for you again?"

Yana waggled a package of dehydrated veggies at the girl in mock threat. "I got me things even I can't ruin."

There had been a most curious selection of foodstuffs available at SpaceBase, as well as basic things like flour, beetshug, and powdered yeast in a can big enough to supply the entire village for the next decade. She had several big tins of pepper and other hot seasonings. She would use those to trade. She had acquired a ream of paper, a box of inked styluses, and a ream of message tapes: the whole village could send one apiece to Charlie. Compared to the village store, the SpaceBase BX was a cornucopia of useful and occasional unlikely commodities.

In an inside pocket she had as neat a little pair of infrared night binoculars as could be found, just the thing for seeing distances on a snow landscape. She had a first-aid kit, though some of the contents had long since passed their expiry dates, but she had wanted the compact field instruments more than the medicines. She had a heavy-duty thermal sleeping bag, another quilt, clothing, skis, snowshoes, an ax, a hatchet, cross- and hacksaws, and enough nails and screws to set up a carpentry shop. And much to her delight, she had discovered, lying dusty on a bottom shelf beneath items of uniform apparel, several lengths of prettily figured fabric in bright colors, no doubt left over from the days when the soldiers' families were allowed to visit and trade on the base, too.

Also scattered among the more strictly utilitarian goods, she found other items apparently for sale or trade with civilians: beads, belts, glues for several different types of jobs, a carpenter's last in her foot size, three each of plates, bowls, and cups, a big skillet, two more pots, and a multiple knife with a six-foot run-out cord she had already attached to her belt.

She had a pail of multiple vitamins and minerals with an expiry date two years hence, and three boxes of the trail rations designed for Petaybee conditions. There had been cartons of those, newly shipped in, or so the quartermaster had told her. Plus a big can of freeze-dried coffee and another of real tea, and a few other comestibles that, as she had told Bunny, she knew she couldn't ruin in the serving.

She set about opening the cans she chose to serve, slopping the contents into appropriate pans and arranging them on the stove, which had not gone out. She had coaxed it to a more active state and was determined that this time she wouldn't be distracted from her task.

Clodagh's cat had watched her put things away with very interested eyes.

"Taking inventory, cat? How good do you count?"

The cat blinked insolently at her.

She had the meal prepared, rather proud of herself at producing more than a single pot of edible food. Bunny was certainly appreciative. Then, after dinner, Yana presented her with a length of the pretty fabric, the blue, which she felt would be a flattering color for Bunny. She was totally unprepared for the joy and prolific thanks, the hint of tears in Bunny's eyes.

"I never had anything this grand before, Yana," the girl said softly, holding the fabric to her face and rubbing it across her weather-chapped cheek. Then, with a wide smile, she beamed at Yana. "I'll be the belle of the latchkay in this." Her face dropped and she frowned. "That is, if Aisling can make it up in time for me. She's awful busy as it is."

"Aisling does your dressmaking, too?" Yana had been counting on the woman's services herself, and she ran through her barter goods to think what would be most appropriate.

"Yup, when there's something to do, and something to make with," Bunny said, still caressing the fabric in her lap. "What did ya get for yourself?"

Yana unfolded the deep-green-figured length.

"Ohhh, now that's ace, Yana, you'll look great in that!"

"Think so?" Yana held it up against herself. She hadn't had much in the way of feminine frippery in a long time, not since Bry, who had liked her in night-gowns. Which he promptly took off, a habit that had tickled her errant humor.

"Yes, I think so. And Sinead has some beads that would bring out the background green. Why, I can see it made up already. Wait a tic!" And Bunny was out the door, hauling on her parka as she went.

Yana folded her length up carefully, her fingers savoring the smooth finish, and set about clearing up the remains of their supper. She saved a dollop of the protein in the pan and put it down for the cat, who sniffed it then pawed around it as if trying to bury it.

Bunny returned with a flourish, Sinead and Aisling behind her. Without taking off her parka, she rushed over to the chair where she had put the blue and held it up for the two to see, letting the folds fall about her. "See? Isn't it the most gorgeous stuff you've ever seen?"

Yana thought she had never seen anyone get so much pleasure out of cloth.

The rest of the evening was taken up by discussions of styles and decorations for both latchkay blouses. Aisling had taken charge of the two lengths, holding them up against Yana and Bunny, draping them this way and that to see how the finished design would fall and, Yana noticed, smoothing the fabric as if her hands, too, had rarely felt such quality. Sinead was sent back to their cabin to bring up certain trimmings and beads, to be sure that the colors matched, and then that the patterns of beading and decoration were approved.

"Hear you got up to my brother's place," Sinead murmured when Bunny and Aisling were deep in the consideration of cut and style. Her eyes were intent on Yana's face. "Did he show you around much?"

"I think he did. Saw the curly-coats, and those great cats of his."

Sinead grinned, but her expression was as secretive as it was inquisitive, so Yana didn't know why Sinead had brought Sean up in the conversation. Could Sinead possibly know about their trip to the warm springs? That was *their* business.

"No seals?"

Yana managed to hide her reaction to that softly delivered query. She turned her head and met Sinead's keen eyes easily. "One. It seemed to like fresh water, though, which I thought was a little strange."

Sinead eyed her a long moment and then, with a cryptic grin, turned away. "We got a lot o' strange beasties on Petaybee."

"Oh? Why haven't I come across any yet?" Yana asked good-humoredly, despite the fact that her pulse had begun to race. This was exactly what Giancarlo wanted to know. Did Sinead realize that?

"I think you have to discover them for yourself. Like the seals. Tell you what, why don't you come check the traplines with me sometime? You might be surprised what you see when you know what to look for. Sometime soon maybe."

"Thanks. I'll take you up on that," Yana said, careful not to sound too excited.

Sinead turned back to arranging beads, wires, and trimming for Bunny to inspect.

Then, before Yana could quiz Bunny on the barter aspects of the new clothing, Aisling and Sinead had folded up the two lengths, cleared away the trimmings, and were out the door into the dark cold night.

"I didn't discuss price with 'em," Yana said to Bunny.

"Naw, that comes later, if you like what they do. And they're good, Yana. Aisling sews like a dream, and Sinead is a wizard with the beads and trims. You don't need to worry they'd muck up material like that! And gee, I've never had such pretty stuff for a latchkay blouse." The girl's eyes shone. "I can't thank you enough ..."

"Pshaw! That's *my* thanks for your help, Buneka. But the latchkay's coming up soon, isn't it? Will the blouses be finished in time?"

"Sure." Bunny grinned. "They left so they could start. You wait and see. We'll be the fanciest-dressed females there!"

Diego was surprised to see the snocle-driver girl again, but at the same time, in one part of his mind, he knew he had been waiting for her. Or if not for her exactly, he had been waiting for *something* to happen to relieve the heaviness that had fallen on him since he had returned to SpaceBase. He had come outside, the cold air being a change from the smelly stuff inside his quarters. It was also something to do, and the only sure way he knew to keep from trying to choke that dickhead of a colonel who kept on and on with questions Diego was sure his father didn't even hear. Why didn't they leave his dad alone?

"Diego? Hi. It's me, Bunny," the girl said, keeping her voice low and looking around her, as if she was worried about being seen.

"Hi. Did you bring me a cake with a file in it?"

"Huh?" she asked.

"Just an old joke I read in a book someplace. Sorry. Nice to see you again but—"

"Look, I just came to find out if anybody told you yet."

"Told me what?" Diego demanded. He hadn't meant to be surly, but that's how it came out. He was feeling pretty impatient with all of the guessing games and little hints being passed over his head all the time.

The girl merely looked at him, exasperated, then said slowly and patiently, as if talking to a very small child, which he supposed was how he was acting, "My friend, Major Maddock, got her friend the captain to send for Steve."

"She did?" Diego sat upright, staring at her. "How d'you know?"

"She told me. Didn't anyone tell you?"

"Nope. Wow, that's great," he said. He'd be okay, Dad would be okay, if Steve was coming. Steve would straighten everything out. Steve would believe him, even if the colonel and the others didn't, and Steve would know how to handle these assholes, get them to leave him and Dad alone. His relief was so intense it scared him. Maybe this was some sort of scheme, raising his hopes like this. "You sure?"

"Sure, I'm sure." She gave a disgusted flick of her

hand. "I don't go about spreading rumors. Wanna come to the latchkay?"

"Latchkay? What's that?"

"Party. Everyone's coming. Good singing, good music, good eating," she said, and Diego could see that she was excited.

"Dunno," he said. "I don't feel much like going to a party with Dad the way he is. Besides, I'm not sure Giancarlo will let me."

Bunny grinned smugly. "So don't ask him. Ask Captain Fiske. Just tell him that Major Maddock told me to ask you, and he'll let you come for sure. He likes her."

"Yeah? Well, as long as my dad's condition doesn't change or anything, you know, I guess I could. Nothin' else goin' on around here."

Her grin broadened. "You'll be glad you did," she told him. "Get to meet a lot of good people and hear some good songs."

"That'd be a change. Sure is no one here you could call 'good.' What kind of songs?"

"Ones my people know. Ones they write about us and our history. *Good* songs," she said.

If things had been normal, if he were back on the ship and his father had never come here and he had never come here and they had never found the cave, he might have made a smart remark, might have said something to make fun of her. But now that seemed like kid stuff. She was serious, and he felt as if he owed it to her to be serious, too. "What are they like?"

"Well, some are things you sing and some are things you chant. Some rhyme and some don't. But they all tell you stuff about things that happen to people, things that happen on the planet."

"Like poems?"

"I guess so. We just call them songs. What're poems like?"

He grinned and said, "Wait a minute," and went back to his bunk, pulling one of his precious hard-copy books from his pack. His nose was half-frozen, but he didn't care. He took the book back out and thumbed it open to a page. "Here's one I bet you'll like.

> " 'A bunch of the boys were whoopin' it up
> At the Malamute saloon . . .' "

He read her the whole poem, and she really seemed to like it, and then she recited something of hers, what she called a song. He had to admit it was pretty good, but he suddenly felt too shy to tell her then that he had tried a few himself. Besides, he was about to freeze to death standing outside the ugly blocky building talking poetry with a girl who dressed like a gorilla. "Guess I'd better go check on Dad," he said apologetically.

"Is he any better today?" Bunny asked.

"He'll be a lot better if Steve gets here. You sure you're not spoofing me about that?"

Bunny shook her head slowly. "I don't do that kind of trick, Diego. None of *us* would."

She left then. Diego watched her drive off in the snocle, wondering how a girl got the chance to drive one of the few decent vehicles on this iceberg. Maybe when Steve got here . . . He wouldn't let himself count on *that*. Not that he still thought Bunny would lie to him: Why should she? Why would she? But maybe it wouldn't be as easy as she thought. Maybe Giancarlo wouldn't let Fiske send for Steve. He liked Bunny, but she hadn't been around company crews like he had—she couldn't know how untrustworthy people could be, how unreasonable. She sure was a funny girl. And she really seemed to like this place.

8

A scratch on the door heralded Sinead's arrival at some O-dark-hundred hour. Yana was on her feet instantly and opened the door, dancing about on tiptoe as the cold of the floor ate through her bedsocks.

"I'll stir the stove," Sinead said, loosening her outer garments. "You'll need something warm in your belly today. Sometimes I think it's colder just before spring than it is midwinter. Good day to check the traplines though."

As she busied herself, pouring water from the thermos into a pot to heat, shaking down the ash from the embers, Yana inserted herself into the layers she felt she would need on this expedition.

"Wha ... arrrre ... we trapping?" she asked, her teeth chattering. She wondered that everyone in Kilcoole seemed to have whole teeth. She was certain one morning her front ones would crack off.

"Whatever's willing," Sinead said with a droll grin.

"Which leaves me no wiser."

"It's a good time to see what's available," Sinead repeated. "The time of year when some are more happy to die than live."

"How can you tell which is which?"

"You'll see. Here, drink this!"

Yana was quite willing to, cradling the cup in her hands and occasionally, carefully, holding it close to her cheeks to warm her cold face. As carefully as she wrapped her quilts about her prior to falling asleep, her face insisted on being out in the open, and was always cold in the morning.

Sinead had made a single serving of porridge, as well. "Aisling fed me," she said with a grin. "Can't get out of the house in the morning without being stuffed."

Yana grinned back, for a moment envious of Sinead, who had a caring partner who saw to her comfort. Then, warmed by the hearty meal, she was ready to go. Sinead had damped down the energetic blaze so that there would be coal to start up again when Yana returned. Clodagh's cat went out with them and whisked away on some business of its own.

"D'you have one like that?" Yana asked Sinead as she settled in the sled.

Sinead gave a snort. "No one has Clodagh's cats. They have you."

Yana agreed heartily and pulled the fur up to her face just as Sinead shouted to her lead dog, a big shaggy brindled female she had named Alice B.

There was no one else about as the dogs pulled the sled quickly down the main track of Kilcoole, though some houses showed lights. They were soon out into the forest, and Sinead urged her team to the left, down a long slope and then onto a wide expanse of white. Here and there Yana saw what looked to be the tops of square fence posts jutting up from their winter blanket and wondered if this was where the village grew its crops in the short summer season.

When she saw the leaders suddenly drop off into nothing, she just had time to take a firmer hold on the driving bow before the sled abruptly nose-dived down the steep slope.

They crashed past more of the spired vegetation she had seen on her first ride on Petaybee; then the surface became smooth again. Another one of Petaybee's many rivers? As they then traveled up a slope on the other side, she decided her notion was correct. Frozen bushes shortly gave way to trees, growing thicker as they progressed along the trail Sinead was following. The track led slightly uphill and then dipped downward again, across another clearing and into more forest, with Sinead pulling ever left, toward the slowly brightening eastern sky.

A time or two Yana's sharp eyes caught the glimmer of lights through the trees, and she smelled woodsmoke. On and on the dogs ran, barking now and then, evidently from sheer joy. Sinead would laugh and urge them on.

They had been traveling upward of an hour, in and out of forests, when Sinead called Alice B to a halt by a small shack. More of a lean-to actually, Yana thought, rising from the sled, rather pleased to find that she wasn't as stiff as usual. Nor had cold half crippled her. Was she actually becoming acclimated to this frigid planet? Probably she would become accustomed to the cold just as summer arrived, and by that time any temperature above freezing would roast her.

She helped Sinead unhook the dogs, check their feet, and set up their picket line. Then Sinead swung to her back the pack that had been Yana's cushion on the trip out. She passed a second, smaller pack to Yana. From the sled she took a long bundle, which she unwrapped to display three spears with sharp pointed metal ends and one with a wicked-looking barb and hook that Yana thought might be a harpoon, though she had never seen such an instrument before. Two bags and a large Y-shaped affair, which she could identify as a hefty slingshot, had also been packaged with the weapons.

"Ever use one of these?" Sinead asked, passing over the slingshot.

"I spent much of my childhood in domes where something like this would have been frowned on," Yana said, testing the feel of grip in her hand and the give in the slings.

Sinead gave a snort. "You handle it like you know anyhow."

Yana grinned. "One learns." She took the bag of small stones that Sinead handed over. "What's the other? Your slingshot?"

Sinead hefted the bag. "A variant—matched stones attached to long strings. You get them swinging in circles in opposite directions like this. When you've got enough momentum going, you twirl them overhead until the tension's right, then loose them to tangle the feet of whatever you want to bring down."

"I've seen that sort of thing a time or two. And where you'd least expect it."

Her pack settled, Sinead entered the lean-to and emerged with two sets of snowshoes, handing a pair to Yana. She knelt to attach hers and then they were both ready, Sinead leading the way into the dense forest, only slightly illuminated by the rising sun.

They had traveled about half an hour, Yana judged, when Sinead stopped to kneel by a heavy evergreen bush. Hauling the skirt of branches to one side, she pulled out the oddest-looking wicker contraption Yana had ever seen, with the smaller end turning back inside itself. It held two gray-furred long-eared animals of good size.

"Thank you, friends," Sinead murmured, and then with a deft twist of strong gloved hands she wrung their necks.

Yana was startled. "They weren't dead yet?" she asked, surprised more by that than by Sinead's quick dispatch of them.

Sinead shrugged. "They came to die." She hummed— though Yana was certain she caught the sounds of words, as well—while with quick movements she wound cord from an outside pocket about their hind legs and secured them to a hook protruding from her pack.

Then, continuing her odd humming, she put a handful of pellets in the oddly shaped trap and replaced it under the bush. By then Yana had figured out that the trap let the creatures in through the clever inverted neck, which, apparently, couldn't expand as an exit. Like a fish trap she had once seen, where fish could swim in, but not out.

"You don't trap them dead?" Yana asked when Sinead fell silent. She had the oddest notion that Sinead had been singing some sort of a ritual requiem.

Sinead shook her head. "No, we live-trap. It is our way. But it means I must run the trapline every three, four days, or they would also starve."

Yana shook her head, surprised. "You said it was a good time to die? Were those rabbits waiting here for you to kill them?"

"So it would appear." Then Sinead rose and started off to the left again.

They had emptied ten similar traps, and Yana now carried a share of the catch, when Sinead, holding up her hand for Yana to tread more warily, stole toward a thicket. Parting the branches so carefully that only a few grains of snow fell, she motioned for Yana to look into the small clearing. A large buff-colored reindeer stood there—on three legs, the fourth broken at the knee and hanging at an obscene angle. The deer had been cropping the bushes around it, and the snow had turned to muddy slush where it had trampled the clearing in its food circuit.

Sinead moved back, holding up one gloved hand to indicate Yana was to stay put. She slipped out of her pack, laying it quietly in the snow, and with spear in hand, she crept around the thicket. Yana watched as she disappeared into another portion of the undergrowth. Then she heard a grunt, a whirring noise, and a thunk as the spear found its target, and then an uninhibited crashing of bushes.

"Okay, Yana," Sinead called cheerily, and Yana pushed through the thicket and saw the spear sticking out of the deer's head, right between its eyes. "Grand pelt on this buck," Sinead said, running her hand down the side and back of the dead beast.

"This isn't one of your humane traps, is it?" Yana asked, looking about the clearing as she hunkered down beside the hunter.

"Not a trap, but I've seen does have their young in places like this."

"You're a mighty hunter, Nimrod," Yana went on,

observing how much of the spear's metal point had entered the beast's skull. "That was some throw."

"The idea is to cause as little pain as possible. Skull's thinnest right between the eyes. Minute the point hit its brain it was dead. Which it wanted to be with a break like that," Sinead said, pointing to the broken leg. "Hadn't done it but a day or two ago, either. Bone ends not frozen through. 'Nother thing about a head kill is the skin isn't marred. C'mon. We got real work to do now."

To Yana's surprise, Sinead had her help drag the carcass from the little clearing. "Doe might need it come spring, and it don't do to leave death scent around."

They gutted the animal, a procedure Yana found somewhat less distasteful than dissections of alien creatures she had witnessed during her search-and-discover days with company expeditionary parties. Sinead demonstrated the technique with almost ritualistic care and put the offal in a sack she had obviously brought for the need. She kept out the liver.

"Lunch," she said, "but I'll just put the rest of this— which we can use—where nothing can reach it." She hung the sack high on the branch beside the carcass, which was already stiffening with cold. "We'll come back for it. Gotta finish the line."

Then Sinead beckoned Yana to follow her as she took up her trapline again. They had acquired several more animals, two already dead in the live traps, when Sinead decided it was time to eat. She built a little fire and, with sharpened twigs, skewered slices of the liver.

The cooking smelled as good as the eating tasted. Yana licked her fingers, shoving them into her parka to dry them on her shirt when she had finished eating.

Sinead heated a pan of water and made some tea, which they took turns drinking.

"So," Yana said. "So far these all seem to be fairly standard critters, the kind that would have occurred in the northernmost parts of Earth back in the old days. I had kind of hoped for something a little more unusual."

Sinead looked across at her, a slight smile on her face. "Day's early."

"Do you ever catch those freshwater seals?" The shock of Sinead's reaction to that casual question made Yana try a hasty apology. "What'd I say wrong? You're the one asked me had I seen them."

"You see a seal, dama, and you be respectful." And there was no question of the menace in Sinead's manner.

Yana held her hands up in surrender and laughed shakily. "Sorry. Didn't mean to put both feet in my mouth. Are seals special?"

"Very," Sinead said in an unequivocal tone. Then she, too, lightened up, the tension draining out of her body. "Petaybean seals are one of the more unusual beasts: on the surface they may look like the ordinary Earth species, but they're very much a product of the planet and they must be protected. Not many people ever get to see a Petaybean seal." Unexpectedly Sinead grinned, her eyes intent on Yana's face. "You see one, you be respectful," she repeated pleasantly.

"You can count on that!" Yana said fervently.

Sinead rose and neatly covered their small fire with snow; and then they were on their way again.

Nine traps later, with some carcasses whose pelts had caused Sinead's eyes to glisten with pleasure, Yana realized that Sinead was swinging to her right. Maybe they were on the homeward leg. Yana hoped so. Her back and calf muscles were beginning to protest: individually the dead animals weighed little, but she had fifteen dangling from the pack now, and her legs were feeling the strain of unaccustomed snowshoeing.

There was no way she would complain, but she was tiring. Still and all, she had surprised herself with the day's work. Far cry from what she had been like first off Andromeda. A healthy life in the outdoors, with untainted air to breathe and decent food to eat, was certainly providing cures never found in an Intergal medical cabinet.

Yana heard the cracking sound almost as soon as Sinead, who dropped to her knees. Yana did likewise and watched with bated breath as Sinead crept forward. She motioned for Yana to come up, but also signaled her to proceed quietly. Yana had done her share of stalking—of beasts in her expeditionary days, of people in her days as an investigator—and moved appropriately. The cracking continued, a cracking and a thumping. Again Sinead moved forward, stepping with extra care, inserting herself into one of the ubiquitous thickets that grew everywhere. Yana let the branches close around her as she followed Sinead. Instead of peering up over the thicket, Sinead began to part the lower branches, crouching down to look through. She waved Yana to a point beside her, and Yana realized that she could almost see through to what looked like a riverbed. With exquisite caution, she slowly made an obscured peek hole in the branches and barely stifled her gasp of astonishment.

Animals that she first thought were some of Sean's curly-coated horses were standing about on the frozen river. One was butting at the ice, obviously determined to make a hole from which it and its companions could drink—and it was butting with a short, stumpy curled horn that grew out of the end of its nose bone. The critter was putting its all into the exercise, sometimes dropping to its knees with the force of its blows, then heaving back to all fours and springing from powerful hindquarters to beat again at the ice. The rear view exposed some obvious male appendages; checking the others of the group, Yana came to the conclusion that the horn seemed to be a perquisite of the male of the species. Suddenly it gave a triumphant bellow and began rearing up, coming down hard to stomp at the ice with its sharp hooves. The others in the small herd did likewise and then backpedaled as a black hole appeared in the white surface.

Sinead turned to grin broadly at Yana and then signaled her to withdraw. They jogged quite a ways down the track before Sinead stopped.

"Was that a unicorn I saw?" Yana asked, panting and wheezing just a bit from the exertion.

Sinead grinned with humorous malice. "There ain't no such animal and neither of us is virgin, though me more than you, I guess."

"I didn't see any in Sean's herd. And he showed me the stallion."

"This is a wild curly. They need the horn to get water in the winter."

"Does the horn fall off in the summer then?"

"Don't know. Never saw a horned curly trying to break ice in the summer." Sinead was off down the track before Yana could press her for more information.

Well, she had been promised unusual animals—and she'd got 'em.

To Yana's surprise they were back at the lean-to much sooner than she had anticipated. She helped Sinead hitch up the team to the sled and deposited the frozen small animals on the sled bench, and then they made a straight line back to where the deer was hung. Nothing had touched it.

By the time they reached Kilcoole, Yana taking turns with Sinead to ride the sled runners, it looked the same as it had when they left: no one about on the frozen track and lights coming up in the cabins as they passed.

"Need help skinning any of these?" Sinead asked as she deposited a fair half of the produce at Yana's feet.

"I wouldn't mind," Yana admitted. "Though I could probably figure it out, I've never really done it before. I have done a little trapping and hunting, but seldom for food; mostly it was for specimens that needed to remain intact for examination and analyses."

Sinead took charge, demonstrating the technique of placing the slits and peeling the coats back, stripping away connective tissue. "Ruining the hide wastes part of the critter's gift to you, so you want to do it right. Sharp knife helps." She helped Yana skin out her share, watching until she was satisfied that Yana had the knack. Yana found she learned skinning with a lot more ease than she did cooking.

Sinead pointed up to the crossbeams. "If you tie your catch up high out here on the porch, nothing'll get 'em. I'll bring back your share of the reindeer when we've butchered it. And its hide. You have more need of it than we do."

With Yana's profuse thanks trailing after them, Sinead and her dogs went on up the track to the cabin she and Aisling shared.

9

A week later, Yana noticed unusual activity at the Kilcoole meeting hall. When she went up to investigate, she was put to work by a laughing Clodagh, who was organizing every available body to assist in the good work. By midday the place had been swept clean, the floor washed, the trestle tables set up, and the chairs placed around the walls. The platform was erected where singers and players could be seen, and heat was pouring forth from the two fireplaces and the big fuel-drum stove. The breakup betting board had been hung from its accustomed hook, the dates and two-hour sections newly inscribed, waiting for folk to place their wagers as to the day and the approximate hour when spring would crack winter's ice and the rivers would once again begin to flow with wet water.

The latchkay stewpot, the biggest kettle in Kilcoole, occupied its burner, and every time the lid rattled with steam, a delicious odor wafted free. The big coffeepot was ready to go on—no need to do it yet or the coffee would walk out of the pot and demand dancing space. Mugs waited in platoons, and someone had donated a whole pail of sweetener. Soon the cakes and pies and other baked goods would arrive, and the other dishes the village's best cooks would provide.

With the hall set up, Yana hurried back to her cabin to complete the rest of her civic duty and prepare her hot dish. Bunny had suggested beans, probably because they were relatively foolproof, Yana suspected. However Yana, who felt she was doing quite well with the cooking lessons, not only seasoned them with the pepper Bunny had recommended, but actually got cocky enough to add garlic, just because she liked the flavor. She also threw in a heaping handful of dried tomato and capsicum flakes, because the dash of color made the plain beans look more festive.

She had just taken the beans off the stove when, rather to her surprise, Aisling and Sinead came by with the finished blouses. She was amazed that they had finished the garments so quickly, especially considering the intricacy of the ornamentation. Hers fit beautifully. Its V neck was tastefully decorated with beads cunningly sewn on to the material's design, a sort of appliqué. The full sleeves were gathered into a tight cuff, also beaded, and the bodice of the shirt fit close to Yana's lean frame, but not so close that it didn't soften the spare lines of her thin body. And there were pockets, also bead-trimmed, into which Yana could stuff her hands when she didn't know what else to do with them. The open collar was also cleverly decorated, with beads made from segments of some of the wires Yana had seen in the store. In exchange for the blouse, Aisling gratefully accepted Yana's proffered bags of those spices Bunny had said the two could most use.

By the time the other women left, it was time to bathe and dress for the main event. Usually, Yana just took a spit bath in kettle-heated water, but she wasn't about to put her new blouse on without a proper bath. The hot springs, while a few miles away, was not an impossible walk, and on several occasions since Sean had introduced her to it, Yana had trekked there for a dip. Usually there were other people enjoying the water, so she wasn't surprised not to encounter the "special" seal she must treat with respect. Had she been properly respectful that first time? she wondered. On this latchkay morning, the entire village was in and out of the pool, sprucing themselves up for the long-awaited celebration. There were such splashings and carryings-on that the communal bathing deteriorated into a sporting event. At which time Yana left, wrapping up well for the walk back to her cabin.

"Sláinte, Yana," Bunny called cheerfully as Yana reached her porch. "Want you to meet Diego," she said, pointing to the well-wrapped figure in her sled. "Here, give this to the major . . ." Bunny shoved a water thermos into his hands. "Major Yanaba Maddock, this is Diego Metaxos." She gestured with her hands for Diego to get a move on.

Yana felt for the boy, knowing how stiff a body could be after one of Bunny's sled rides, as he unfolded, a little awkwardly, balancing the water thermos.

"How's your father doing?" Yana asked, walking to the front of the porch to take the thermos from the boy. Seeing his haunted expression, she felt even sorrier for him.

"She"—and he jerked his mittened hand over his shoulder at Bunny—"said you'd made them get Steve."

"I didn't make anybody do anything, Diego," Yana said with a self-deprecating laugh, "but I did suggest—

to someone who has the power to authorize such things— that it might reassure your father and improve his condition. And yours."

"Yeah, thanks." He started to turn back, noted Bunny's frown, and turned back, a halfway smile tugging his cold and cracked lips. "I mean it, Major Maddock."

Now Yana could see why Bunny could be interested in the boy. Not only was he around her age, but he was tall and well built, with longish wavy black hair and intense dark eyes with curling lashes any girl would envy. And that little smile of his held a certain charm. It was certainly an improvement on his lost, haunted look. What had he seen in the caves that had produced *that* effect? Not that Petaybee wasn't daunting to anyone suddenly plonked down on its surface.

The two turned to go, but Yana suddenly remembered the blouse. "Wait! You'll want this for the latchkay," she said, ducking back inside. In a moment she handed the blouse to the girl.

Tears sprang up in Bunny's eyes. "Oh, Yana! For me? It's so beautiful!" She held it up in front of her parka and swung around to show Diego, who pretended indifference, but Yana thought she saw a flicker of admiration behind the boy's nonchalance.

Bunny hugged her. "Thank you! I'll go get dressed right now."

Yana watched Bunny, with Diego walking beside her, jump onto her sled and skim down the street, the plume tails of the dogs wagging as they knew themselves near home, and food.

With a satisfied smile, Yana went inside her nice warm house, to dry her hair and get ready for the latchkay.

* * *

To Yana's surprise, there was a knock on her door just as she was about to leave. She had been hearing people going past her door, on foot and with dogsleds, for the past half hour, though it was only midafternoon. She spent the time primping, trying to make her own appearance worthy of the blouse, admiring the way the garment added sparkle to her eyes and brought out highlights in her hair, even making her skin glow with unaccustomed color. The knock startled her. Bunny, probably.

Before she could reach the latch, the door swung slowly open and a well-snowed figure—for it had begun to snow again—stood in the doorway. She recognized the finely decorated gloves as Sean Shongili lifted his hands to push back the hood of his parka.

Yana's heart did an unexpected flip-flop. And got even more agitated as Sean grinned at her.

"If you thought you were going to weasel out of singing tonight, think again," he said, stepping inside and closing the door. "But I see you have dressed for the occasion. Nice shade on you," he added, nodding with approval. He stepped up to her, putting a finger on the beaded work of her collar and tracing the design. His smile deepened and his silver eyes gleamed. "A combined effort, if I do not mistake the fine Italianate touches of Aisling and my sister."

Yana swallowed, unaccustomed to being complimented on her appearance and inordinately pleased that Sean had. "They were very good to get it finished in time for the latchkay."

"Nothing Sinead likes better than a race against time," he said with a second cryptic smile. The intentness of his gaze reminded her of Sinead's regard across their trapping campfire.

"You—you should have seen Bunny's face when I gave her the blouse they made for her," Yana said, knowing she was babbling. She reached for her parka, which Sean took from her suddenly nerveless fingers and held for her. Feeling slightly foolish, she turned, shooting her arms out for the sleeves. Deftly he slipped the bulky parka up and onto her shoulders, settling it with a little flick of his hands across her shoulders. Then his fingers brushed the nape of her neck and she had to suppress a convulsive shudder. The memory of their hot-spring interlude flooded her, and she hoped she wasn't blushing. So she flipped her hood up, pressed shut the parka fastenings, all with her back to him, before she jammed her hands into her gloves and collected the bean pot. Turning resolutely, she smiled at him, just as if she hadn't gone through all kinds of mental acrobatics over the simple act of his helping her into her coat.

"Let's go. My debut awaits!"

"I hear the boy's alter-parent is on his way down. Good idea," he said as they stepped into the well-rutted roadway.

There were folks behind and in front of them, and every house had lights on to illuminate the way to the hall. Yana hadn't appreciated just how many people lived in and around the village.

"Is everyone on Petaybee here?" she asked, trying to estimate attendance from the steady traffic and the numbers of sleds already parked in front of the hall.

"Everyone who matters to Petaybee," he answered, grinning at her.

She mulled that over. "Why should I matter to Petay-bee?" she finally asked.

"Why shouldn't you?"

She wanted him to explain that remark and to stop being so cryptic, but before she could speak, someone hailed him from a passing sled. He cupped her arm in his, shielding her from the snow spray, as he called a cheery reply. Then they had to pick their way around sleds and sled dogs, careful not to tread on animals half-buried in the lazy snow that was adding new depth to the old.

They could hear the happy noise of many cheerful voices, the scrape of fiddles, the wheeze of an accordion, the tootle of a tin whistle, the bass thrum of a bodhran as they reached the front door. Light flared out onto the sawdust that coated the well-trodden snow as the door opened, letting out a puff of warmed air, redolent of leather, clean linen, and herbal scents.

As soon as Sean was identified, he was absorbed into a welcoming group that effectively divorced him from Yana. She shrugged, impressed by his popularity, as she hauled off her outerwear and tried to find a spare hook on the line down the left-hand wall. She gave up and tossed her parka onto the growing pile in the corner, then slid out of her boots and tied their drawstrings together before setting them down beside the pile.

An arm snaked around her waist and she was pulled into a tight embrace. She was about to struggle when she realized it was Sean. Then she was guided out and onto the dance floor and found herself, willy-nilly, pumped about in an energetic polka by her grinning partner.

Those on the sidelines seemed determined to encourage him to grander feats of speed and agility. She clung for dear life to his shoulder and his guiding hand as the room swirled in dizzying circles about her. Three or four weeks earlier she would have been coughing uncontrollably after the first turn about the room, but now she didn't even feel the need to reach for Clodagh's cough medicine. She was breathless, of course, but it was with the sheer momentum of the dance as she was swept away in Sean's arms while other dancers careered around them. She had better *not* have a coughing fit here. She could be accidentally stomped to death if she lost her footing! But it was all very exciting. She had never—not even when Bry was being extra sociable—danced quite this uninhibitedly. It was unbelievably exhilarating—dancing with a whirlwind. She didn't know how Sean kept his balance, much less how he kept dancing so lightly, and yet she who, a mere five weeks before, had barely been able to walk without doubling over with lung spasms could now—almost—keep up with him. Whether it was due to the romance of the moment or the beneficial effects of Clodagh's cough medicine she didn't know, but she loved it.

The dance stopped only when the musicians needed to catch their breaths and moisten their throats. Weak and breathless, Yana was obliged to hang on to Sean for fear of falling, and she shivered with reaction to the closeness of the hard, strong body that supported her, and the hands that clasped her body with a touch that sent peculiar ripples up and down her arms and legs. She knew she should pull free and didn't want to—not in this lifetime.

Sweat was trickling down her face by then, and she was afraid if she didn't attend to that she would disgust her partner. Except, just then, he laid an equally moist cheek against hers and laughed in her ear.

"You offworlders sure can rob a body of breath with your dancing!" he said.

"Me?" she exclaimed in amused outrage, and pushed back to be sure he was teasing her.

His silver eyes gleamed with mischief, and he pulled her back to him, leading her off the floor toward the immense bowl of punch, which no doubt consisted largely of Clodagh's blur-maker. Yana didn't care what was in the punch: she would welcome the moisture to unparch her throat. Fastidiously, she found her one cloth handkerchief and blotted the sweat on her face. Sean was likewise engaged, nodding and grinning at folks as he released her to get them two full cups.

"This is perfect," she said, after rolling the drink around in her mouth.

Sean's arm around her waist pulled her close against him. "Helps the nervous performer," he murmured in her ear.

"You had to remind me?" she demanded in a mock-accusatory tone. She had managed to forget that upcoming ordeal.

"Stick with me, babe," he answered in a mock-gruff voice, "and you won't need to worry!"

"You intend to get me suitably drunk?"

"No one gets drunk on Clodagh's punch," he replied with fake indignation, adding with another wicked leer, "but you'll be so blurred it won't matter."

"Here's to that," she said, and chugalugged the rest of the cup. He took it from her hand and passed it to the lady serving to be refilled.

"Hey, too much of this and I'll forget the words," Yana protested.

Sean shook his head, handing her the cup. "Some words you don't forget, Yanaba." He laid his fingers lightly on her shirt above her heart. "Some words come from there and, once spoken, can't be forgotten."

She gave him a long look, awash with a few un-blurred anxieties, like why he had insisted in the first place, why she had let him in the second—and in the third, should she go through with it?

"Have you placed your bet yet?" he asked, pointing to the breakup board and the knot of people about it. Someone had just chalked in a mark. Sean grinned. "Tolubi's out by two days and six hours."

"How d'you figure that?" Yana regarded him suspiciously.

He gave an indifferent shrug. "I'm not allowed to bet I've been right so often."

"Can I?"

Sean gazed steadily at her. "You could. But, knowing that I'm always right, would you?"

Yana returned his gaze. "If you're always right, I'd be taking an unfair advantage."

"You could still place a bet." His tone was bland and his eyes lazy.

"A sure thing's not a bet," she said. "And I'm *not* a betting woman anyhow." She gave him a droll smile. "I always lose, and I wouldn't want to spoil your record."

Sean laughed at that, his eyes twinkling, and she knew her response had pleased him.

"What would my prize have been?" she asked.

"Don't know what it is this year," he replied. "Usually credit at the company store, or pups, if there're some good ones due in the spring whelpings."

The music started up again, a two-step, and before she could protest, Sean had her out in the middle of the floor dancing with him, one strong arm clipping her waist so that she couldn't duck away, the other hand with fingers inextricably laced around hers.

She had time during that dance to see the crowd, standing and sitting around the big hall, and she wondered if the entire "native" population of Petaybee had somehow managed to assemble in this one spot. Kids raced about the edges of the dance floor, tripping over feet, howling with hurt and being comforted by whoever picked them up and dusted them off; babies were traded off as dancing partners were claimed. Little girls danced with their grandfathers and teenaged boys asked their aunties and grandmothers to dance or showed the steps to smaller cousins; a few of the older kids, looking self-conscious, waited to be asked to dance by a member of their peer group, but often little girls and grown women danced together, as did some of the men and boys—whoever didn't have a partner danced with any other available body.

Yana spotted Bunny, who was looking remarkably lovely and feminine, in close conversation with Diego near the food table: Diego had already started to munch on a meatroll, and Bunny was nibbling on a hunk of something in one hand.

Sean was an excellent dancer, possibly the best she had ever been partnered with, and for once her feet seemed to know which way to go. She dreaded stepping on his toes, especially as he had discarded his heavy boots and was wearing some beautifully beaded moccasins.

Between dances, Sean kept her mug full and piloted her about the hall as he met and exchanged some of his cryptic remarks with men and women.

"Who are these folks?" she asked in his ear as he maneuvered her to yet another couple.

"The parents of the Bremport victims," he said.

"What the frag! That's unfair, Sean." She tried to pull free, but his grip was implacable.

"Why? They know you're going to sing. They've wanted to meet you. They have. You're their last link with their dead."

"Oh, frag it! That's not fair. To me, Sean."

"Yes, it is, because now you'll know which faces to look for when you're singing."

"Is that why you're attached to me like a limpet?" she asked bitterly. "So I can't escape this ordeal?"

"It won't be an ordeal for you, Yanaba, but a release," he said softly and with such great tenderness that she felt weak-kneed. Damn Clodagh. She was blurring.

About then, she noticed that Bunny and Diego had not once parted company.

"Yes, Diego'll sing, too. You aren't the only one," Sean said, observing the direction of her interest. Then he chuckled. "Will the miserable like some company?" He began to propel her in their direction.

Some quality of the look with which Bunny was favoring Diego made Yana dig her heels in. "No, Sean, we won't interrupt them."

"No." Sean looked at the young pair, his mobile face

thoughtful. "No, I don't think we will. Bunny's handling him like a trooper."

"Handling him?" Yana bristled.

Sean shrugged, his expression bland. "Keeping him company, if you like. You know more people here than he does."

Just then Sinead and Aisling danced up to them, Sinead leading, as always. Both wore superb leather shirts, Aisling white, Sinead buff, with elaborate decorations which were so tasteful that jewels could not have been better displayed.

"Enjoying yourselves?" Sinead asked, her expression bland, but the slightly arch tone of her voice seemed to convey some hidden message evidently intended for Sean.

"Now that you mention it, I am," Sean said, equally archly, locking gazes with Sinead. "How about you, Yana?"

"Oh, I am, indeed I am," she replied. Sinead nodded and kept walking.

"What's up with your sister?" Yana asked Sean, as he whirled her in a pirouette to the other side of the room.

"Don't let her worry you for a single minute," he said.

She caught an odd twitch to his mouth, a twitch of minor irritation, she thought. Well, sisters had been irritants to brothers since the worlds began.

About the time she was beginning to wonder if the music makers had been trading off with others who looked identical to keep up such an amazing barrage of dance tunes and tempos, the current ones put down their instruments and left the little stage.

Somehow Sean had timed it so that he and Yana were

at the seemingly bottomless punch bowl as the last note died away. He pressed yet another cup into her hand.

"I'll be too blurred to sing," she said, trying to put it down.

"Drink it. You're on."

With what seemed to her like unceremonious haste, he then guided her across the floor to the platform.

"No, no, Sean," she protested, noticing herself to be the center of attention. In the sudden way these people had, everyone was settling into a quiet mode all around the room as Sean led her inexorably to the stage. Even the children were quiet, the babies remarkably all asleep.

"Yes, yes, Yana."

"Why me?" she protested, but her feet seemed willing to follow Sean.

"You're the hero."

She tried to wrench her arm free of his grasp, but his fingers merely tightened, and then she was stumbling onto the box that was the step up to the platform. She stood there, miserably aware of being the focus of so many eyes, so much unwarranted attention, of her coming ordeal. How could anything she said, or sang, help ease their losses?

Sean held up both arms and what little noise there was died completely.

"This is Major Yanaba Maddock," he announced, turning slowly to take in everyone patiently waiting. "You all know her. She will sing." Then, with an oddly formal bow, he gestured for Yana to sit on the single chair that was now centered on the stage.

She sank limply into the chair, feeling the hard seat

grind into her tailbone. Sing? She was supposed to sing now?

A soft beat registered, and she saw Sean, the bodhran in one hand, gently fingering sound from the skin. She blinked and suddenly began the chant that had come to her. She hadn't rehearsed it since that day, weeks before, when Sean had coaxed the words from her. But they were there, on her tongue, and in the proper order, in the precise rhythm of the drumbeat, and her voice was saying them. She was unaware of anything else because her mind was back there, in Bremport for those few surrealistically macabre and devastatingly helpless and horrible minutes, and she wondered that she could enunciate any words for the pain in her chest, the constriction in her throat, and the unwept tears that pressed against her eyelids. She wished she were even more blurred than she knew she had to be, to let go like this. To perform, as if by rote, any duties that had not been drill-inspired over centuries of practice.

She heard, from a distance, her own voice, and she had never realized she could sound like that: a husky rich contralto that dipped and rose. She wasn't really aware of what she was singing until she got to the final lines.

"I was sent here to die, too, here where the snows live
The waters live, the animals and the trees live,
And you."

As the last of that vowel drifted into nothingness, she bowed her head, tears streaming down her cheeks and falling into her hands. She couldn't move and didn't know what she was supposed to do next. Maybe Sean would liberate her.

Then a pair of work-roughened hands slid across hers, pressed gently, and withdrew only to be replaced by another set of hands. By the third pair she looked up, for their touch was like a benison, healing her grief, staunching her tears. She could even smile as yet another set of parents laid hands on hers to mutely offer their appreciation. Seeing the tears in their eyes—tears of an odd sort of sublimated sorrowing—hers began to ease, along with the constriction in her chest, the tight bands about her heart.

The little ceremony completed, Sean collected her and brought her wordlessly to Clodagh's bowl, where the woman herself ladled a cup for her and solemnly inclined her head in a regal bow of approval as the cup was handed from Clodagh to Sean and then to Yana.

Then Sean put his arm about her shoulders and drew her to sit in a space that magically appeared on a bench against the wall. His shoulder touched hers, his hip and thigh brushed hers. She felt drained but exultant, no longer sad but infinitely relieved. She sipped the punch, keeping her head down, unwilling to make eye contact with anyone as she savored what was, as Sean had said, a healing.

The little susurrus of soft voices, expectant, made her look up to see Bunny leading Diego to the stage.

"This is Diego Metaxos," Bunny said, arms above her head and turning around slowly to the audience just as Sean had done. "He must sing."

Yana hoped that she had shown as much composure as Diego did. He sat down with more grace than she had, his hands splay-fingered on his knees.

"I am new come, in storm, here.
A storm of heart and mind and soul.
I sought and found storm with Lavelle
She saved me when the sled crashed down.
With the heat of her body she saved me.
With the wit of her mind she saved my father, too.
Saved me to see the cavern that all say I didn't see."

His tone was rich in irony and his tenor young and surprisingly vibrant, though Yana suspected he had never sung before an audience either.

"But I saw the caverns and the water and the carving
of wind and water.
I saw the gleaming snow, like jeweled cloth.
I saw the branches waving, the water talking,
The ice answering, the snow laughing. I saw
The animals of water and earth and they were talking,
too.
They were kind to me and answered all my questions
But I do not know what questions I asked.
I do not know what answers I heard.
I know the cavern, the branches, the talking water,
The speaking ice and the laughing snow. I know
That you know it, too. So hear my song
And believe me. For I have seen what you have seen.
And I am changed. Hear my song. Believe me."

He threw his head back as his last passionate note died away, and threw out his arms, entreating their response.

It began as a very low murmur of approval, growing as more folk entered the answering chorus, as more people began to drum their feet on the floor, as a crescendo of sound beat on Yana's ears until she almost put her hands over them. But if she had, she would not have heard the answer.

"We believe! We believe! We believe!"

She had jumped up and was shouting along with everyone else. Because she could not doubt the boy. Everyone, at the same instant, swarmed across the floor toward him. Bunny was on the platform, hugging him, and suddenly he was crying, with the same sense of relief that Yana knew she had just felt.

Singing the Inuit way had much to recommend it.

Yana was still caught up in the emotion surrounding Diego's song when a voice spoke in her ear. "Now *that* was very moving."

The voice belonged to Torkel Fiske, who prevented her from turning with a light touch on her shoulders. Sean was no longer beside her. "Very touching. I'm so glad I convinced Giancarlo to let the boy come here today. Obviously he needed to vent his emotions and I do find it curious that when he insists here, in his poetic mode, that the nonsense his father has been babbling was real, the villagers agree with him."

"Maybe," Yana replied in a sardonic tone, "that's because the villagers are more observant than the company."

"Oh, but the villagers are the company, too. Perhaps a branch that's had insufficient attention in the past."

"Ooh, that sounds ominous," she said as lightly as she could.

"Maybe a little prophetic," he admitted, breathing into her hair. "I hope nobody will mind that I came. I just had to see for myself about this party you and

Diego were so excited about. Could I talk you into a dance, or are you able?"

"I seem to be managing," she said, looking around for Sean. "And there's no dance music playing," she pointed out, feeling ridiculous, standing there in her homemade blouse, uniform pants and stocking feet like something out of a gothic novel. "Look, Torkel," she said, shaking off his hands to turn in his arms. "You've been a godsend and I'm very glad to see you, and I'm flattered by your interest. Under ordinary circumstances I'd be very tempted, but, well . . ."

"Oho!" he said, his eyes smiling down at her while his mouth twisted with mock disappointment. "I'm not the only one to appreciate you, huh? I was hoping the locals would be too backward to notice. My estimation of this place increases by the minute."

Thank God his ego was strong enough that she didn't have to worry about losing his friendship—and his assistance—by declining to play. She kissed his cheek. "Asshole."

He prolonged the contact with a hug that ended with sagged shoulders. "Oh well, so much for the reasons I was looking *forward* to coming."

About that time Aisling approached them and held out her arms for a hug, too, giving Yana a graceful way to extricate herself from Torkel. "Yana, I just had to tell you how beautiful your song was, how much it meant to me and everybody else."

"Thanks, Aisling. And thanks again for making this gorgeous blouse."

Aisling flushed with pleasure. "That's okay. It looks beautiful." She glanced at Torkel inquisitively and with just a tad of something Yana took to be—well, not hostility, but suspicion.

"This is an old shipmate of mine, Aisling, Captain Torkel Fiske. He arranged for me to get the material and for Diego to be here today."

"Oh, that was real nice of you, Captain," Aisling said, sticking out a long-fingered hand for him to shake. Torkel, typically, raised it to his lips instead.

"Hey, Yana." Sinead appeared behind her partner and stuck her hand out to Torkel, too. "Tell this guy for me that Aisling and I share everything," she said.

Again, the tone was friendly but the undercurrents were guarded and, in this case, more markedly hostile— but not because Torkel was kissing Aisling's hand. Yana thought perhaps Sinead might be being possessive of her on Sean's behalf.

"Torkel, Sinead Shongili."

The two regarded each other like fencers assessing each other's strengths; then he kissed Sinead's hand, after which she surprised him by kissing his, then licking her lips.

"Um, hairy knuckles. My dad had hairy knuckles."

"I like her," Torkel said, turning to Yana and pointing to Sinead.

"Me, too," Aisling said, putting her arm around Sinead's shoulders.

"Listen," Torkel said confidingly, taking in not only Yana but Aisling and Sinead, "maybe you women can help me with something I've got to do which is going to be real hard. Maybe you'd even know if I ought to do it now or wait until this party is over."

"Sure, Torkel," Aisling said.

"What's the matter, man?" Sinead asked.

"I need to find out who is next of kin to a woman named Lavelle Maloney."

"Lavelle!" Sinead said. "Has something happened to her? Where is she?"

Torkel gritted his teeth and patted the open air with his hand in a calming gesture. "I really think I should tell the next of kin before I tell anybody else, don't you? But, well, I think they'll need your support when I've finished talking to them."

"Oh, no . . ." Aisling said.

Sinead touched her partner's forearm gently. "Why don't you go tell Clodagh and Sean they're needed and I'll take Torkel and Yana to get Liam." To Torkel she said, "Lavelle's husband has been sick a long time. He didn't come today. We'll get her boy Liam to come with us back to her house to tell his da. Her daughter lives at Tanana Bay, and her other son is in the Space Corps, stationed on Mukerjee Three."

Yana saw Sean then, one arm around Bunny and the other around Diego, herding the kids toward her, speaking earnestly to Diego. Close behind him came Clodagh, and Sinead stopped as she met them.

Clodagh held up her hand and twiddled her fingers impatiently, as if staving off Sinead's news. Then she, too, headed toward Yana and Torkel.

She knows, Yana thought as Clodagh sailed toward them like a liner through an asteroid belt. She already knows. But how?

Torkel was intercepting Sean and the kids. "Diego, son, you have great talent," he said.

Torkel looked so handsome and fatherly congratulating Diego, Yana thought. He had wisely chosen not to wear a uniform, despite the apparently official nature of his visit. He wore instead a heavy sweater patterned with moss green, rust, and cream that set off his hair and eyes to good advantage, and a pair of rust-colored woolen trousers. He was bigger than Sean, she saw, and more stockily built, and of course their coloring was very different; one russet, the other silver, like fire and ice. Except, she remembered with an inward blush, there had been *nothing* icy about Sean Shongili thus far in their acquaintance.

"Sean," Sinead was saying, "this man is here because something has happened to Lavelle."

Sean squeezed his eyes shut and his lips thinned with pain, but that was nothing compared to Diego's reaction.

"What? What's happened to her?" the boy demanded of Torkel, his eyes blazing and his fists clenched. "What did you dorks do to her?"

Torkel looked genuinely pained. "Nothing, son. We're not sure what happened, and won't know until we get the autopsy report."

Sean's head snapped up. "Autopsy?"

"I take it she *is* dead then?" Sinead drawled with a contemptuous roll of her eyes.

Torkel blew a deep and frustrated sigh. "Please. Let's tell the relatives first."

"Sinead," Clodagh said softly, and the woman plunged into the crowd.

Diego, who at first had seemed moderately pleased to see Torkel, suddenly blew a gasket. "Goddamn you guys, you *killed* her!" he cried. Sean had hold of him, which was a good thing, because Diego was lunging for the captain and spitting with anger. "You guys just kept after her and kept after her and wouldn't believe her or us or anybody. So you fraggin' tortured her to death or something! *Damn* you. Why couldn't you let her alone? Why can't you let us all alone? You don't know the truth when you hear it. *She* told you what happened. Dad and I told you what happened, and you beat her up because you didn't believe her and she died."

"No, son, I—"

"If you didn't have my dad there, I'd never go back to that place. Never! Let us go. You're too dumb to—"

Clodagh was interrupting him with soothing noises, but she didn't really know the boy.

Neither did Yana, but she knew the reaction. The boy had simply had one too many profound traumas in a short space of time. His singing had been a highly emotional probing for him, opening a deep wound for healing. Before the healing could take place, Torkel's revelation had assaulted him with a new pain on top of the other.

"Metaxos, listen to me," she said in a calm but very firm voice. "We can find out the truth. There'll be a report. They'll return her body. I'll go back with you to SpaceBase personally and find out what happened if I have to go retrieve Lavelle myself."

Diego jerked his head to turn his searing glare on her. "You're one of them. How can I trust you?"

"Oh, Diego, come *on*," Bunny said.

Just then Sinead arrived with a stony-faced young man in tow. "Captain Fiske, this is Liam Maloney, Lavelle's son."

"My mum's dead, isn't she?" Liam asked Torkel. In contrast to Diego, Liam seemed outwardly very calm. Almost as if he'd been expecting this, Yana thought.

"Well, yes. I wanted to tell you and your father together."

"No offense, Captain, but I don't think Dad wants to see any of you people right now. I'll tell him." He turned to Clodagh, who put her arm around him as if he were still a baby, and as they moved away, he buried his head against her massive breast.

"Okay, Captain, now that you've done your duty, I think the rest of us need to know what's going on," Sean said.

"Come on back to my place," Yana said quickly, including Sean, Bunny, Diego, Sinead, and Aisling in her invitation and finally, with a sympathetic glance at Torkel, adding, "I'll make us some *real* coffee."

10

"How did she die?" Sean asked.

"We can't be sure yet. The autopsy report wasn't in when I left SpaceBase," Torkel said. "Probably delayed effects of exposure. Acted like respiratory failure, apparently. The medic suspected she may have frostbitten her lungs while she was out there and nobody realized it until she had already been transferred via shuttle to headquarters. The old man isn't doing so hot either, although the girl, Brit, doesn't seem to be suffering any ill effects. They're to be transferred to Andromeda medical facility for further observation."

"Don't," Sean said. "Send them back here. Keep them at SpaceBase if you have to, but they will soon sicken and die if you send them off-planet. They're adapted to *this* planet and *these* conditions. They'll die elsewhere. Bring them back."

"I'm not sure I can do that," Torkel said, just a hint of belligerence creeping into his voice. He didn't say it, but Yana could feel the resentment building in him: here he was trying to be such a great guy and let the locals in on what was happening, and they tried to tell him how to do his job.

"Why not?" Diego demanded angrily. "Are you having too much fun questioning them?"

Torkel heaved an exasperated sigh. "Son, I'm trying to be patient with you because I understand how upset you must be about your father. Your dad's partner is on the way down to look after you and should be arriving on one of the first troop shuttles. But I've had about enough crap out of you. You've been raised by Intergal. Surely you know that we don't use rough stuff on our own people . . ."

He appealed to Yana, but she said nothing. The terrorists from Bremer had been interrogated. They had, at one time, been Intergal's own people.

Sinead said diplomatically, "It's just that we're a very close-knit community here, Captain Fiske. People will worry about Sigdhu and Brit even more now with what's happened to Lavelle. I'm not saying it was the company's fault, but you know, we're used to a different kind of atmosphere here than what you have on the stations and ships. Our air is fresh, even if it's cold, not endlessly reprocessed."

"Glad you enjoy it," Torkel said with an ironic lift of his eyebrow. "The company provided all of the amenities of this planet."

"We need our own back here on the surface, man," Sean said, and Yana realized that he was at a disadvantage not knowing who Torkel was. "*My* family has been accommodating the species of this planet to its peculiarities for four generations now and between you and me, the company hasn't provided a lot of what's here. There are major adaptation problems for our people . . ."

"And you are, sir?" Torkel asked politely, but with an edge in his voice to match the one in Sean's. They stood across the room from each other, each with his feet spread and his arms poised, like a pair of gunfighters squaring off.

The cat, which had been lounging on the middle of the table washing its underside, suddenly leapt up, sprang to the door, and meowed urgently to go out. Yana crossed between the men to open the door, and when she turned back, they had relaxed so that they were merely glaring at each other, but no longer posturing. She stepped quickly between them, gesturing to each to come closer.

"Captain Torkel Fiske, descendant of the terraforming Fiskes, this is Sean Shongili, descendant of the genetic-engineering Shongilis," she said quickly, as if officiating at a hailing party for newly recruited officers. "You guys want to go to opposite corners and come out flashing credentials?"

They didn't seem to hear her for a moment; then Torkel suddenly grinned fondly at her and reached out to squeeze her shoulder.

"Trust you to try to defuse a situation, Yana. God, I've missed you. Shongili, I am actually extremely pleased to meet you. Excuse me if I came on a little strong, but we were all shocked by that poor woman's death when she had been so instrumental in saving young Diego here and his father."

"I think I can help, Torkel," Yana intervened again. "Let me see that autopsy report when it comes in. And please, I think there's been enough evidence gathered so far to show that Petaybee is not exactly what the company ordered, and Sean may be right about the adaptive failures."

Torkel shook his head. "That doesn't make much

sense, Yana, when half the existing Intergal force was recruited from Petaybeans originally."

Yana shrugged and held out a cup of coffee, wishing she had acquired more cups from the BX. He took the cup in one hand, then took her hand in his other.

"The recruits are young, Captain," Sean said. "Their growing isn't over, nor full maturation reached when they leave Petaybee to join Intergal."

"That's as may be, Shongili. Yana, we'll talk about this later. I can see now that everybody's too upset to listen to reason."

"I can take you and Diego back, sir," Bunny volunteered. Yana noticed that her young friend had very wisely kept her mouth shut throughout the conversation, retaining an enviably neutral—at least as far as Torkel was concerned—stance.

"Thanks, young lady, but I brought my own," Torkel said. He turned to Diego as if to say something, but Diego's black scowl made him think better of it.

They were pulling on winter gear when there was a knock at the door. Yana opened it, and there was the cat, sitting squarely in the middle of the doorstep, and Clodagh, in only a light jacket, stocking cap, and knitted scarf, right behind.

"I'm glad I caught you, Captain, Diego," she said, with a slightly softer look at the boy. "Adak just got a message in and brought it to the latchkay looking for you. Dr. Margolies is at SpaceBase now."

Torkel nodded his thanks and started to turn to Diego, but Clodagh stopped him.

"Captain, I was thinking maybe, you know, if your doctors think Dr. Metaxos won't get any better, maybe he and Diego could come here to live with us? Dr.

Margolies, too, if the company wanted to station him here. Maybe he could do the work you need better if he lived with us?"

Yana wondered what Clodagh was thinking of. She knew the villagers had responded well to Diego at the latchkay, but in many close-knit communities, Dr. Metaxos would have been held indirectly responsible for Lavelle's death. Maybe these people were just unusually generous, but she couldn't imagine they would welcome a known company agent on the premises. On the other hand, theoretically Sean was a company man, too.

Torkel looked as flummoxed as she was by Clodagh's offer and said with his customary charm, "That's very kind of you people, and I'll certainly suggest it to Dr. Margolies and to Colonel Giancarlo. It might indeed be convenient to have Dr. Margolies based here in Kilcoole, at least for the time being, and good for young Diego to be around people his own age again. At least until the company comes up with some permanent solution for his problem."

Clodagh shrugged. "It's no problem to us, Captain. You might not realize it, but what happened to Dr. Metaxos has happened to quite a lot of people on Petaybee. This planet can be kinda hard on certain folks."

"Thank you for your concern, ma'am."

Yana had her coat on before he stepped a foot out the door. Hooking her arm in his, she said, "Tell you what, Torkel. How 'bout if Bunny takes Diego back to base and I keep you company on the way out and ride back with her?"

"I'd like nothing better," he said.

With somewhat forced heartiness Sean said, "Well, back to the latchkay for the rest of us. Bunka, make sure you girls are back in time for the night chants. Major Maddock will want to hear those."

For someone who had appeared so ardent earlier, Torkel Fiske was strangely silent during much of their two-hour snocle ride to SpaceBase. The river trail was wide and flat, streaks of clear ice showing black where the snow had drifted away, the moons gleaming white, mirroring the planet's surface. As the snocle cleared the trees and approached SpaceBase, white, blue, and red lights in the sky shot skyward or fell like multicolored snowflakes toward the landing pads.

"Looks like Kilcoole's not the only place there's a party going on," Yana said jokingly to Torkel.

"Hmm," he said, and in the closeness of the warmed air in the snocle, she could smell the musky cologne he wore. The man who has everything, she thought as she admired his classically handsome profile. She ought to be more moved, she told herself. She really ought.

"Yana? I thought you were medically retired here. Yet there doesn't really seem to be anything wrong with you that I can detect. Has it occurred to you that you needn't cut your career so short? I could arrange for light duty for a while, until you get back in the swing of things."

"What kind of light duty did you have in mind, Torkel? To tell you the truth, it's not bad here."

He snorted. "You could have fooled me. But actually, I thought maybe as long as you were here and you have the rank and the 'in' with the people, you could relieve Giancarlo. He's really blown it by letting that woman

die while she was offplanet. It's that kind of stupidity
that triggered the Bremport massacre."

"You've been reading my mail on that one," she said.
"That guy has zero finesse."

"Exactly. Now, I don't have to tell you that at times
you need a pretty heavy whip hand if you're going to
accomplish a mission that people may not understand
the rationale behind, or that may cause some temporary
inconvenience. People hate change. But I think someone who already gets along with them . . ."

"I see," she said. And she did. Someone who already
got along with them was in a better position to betray
their trust and kindness. Still, she might be able to help
ease any transitions, which would not be a concern of
Giancarlo's.

"And we could work together again. I need a strong
superior officer to keep me on the right track, you
know," he said, reaching over and squeezing her knee.

"Hoo boy, you were serious about that whip-hand
business, weren't you?"

He was negotiator enough to know when to drop the
subject and give her time to think about it, which she did
as they slid into SpaceBase, the lights from the landing
and departing shuttles spreading multicolored pools across
the snow for the miles surrounding the base.

While a holiday air had prevailed at Kilcoole, it
was definitely business even-more-than-usual at
SpaceBase, where parka-clad soldiers scurried from
the landing pads to a row of prefab warehouses that
had not been there on Yana's previous visit. In fact,
other troops were still assembling three more of the
structures, while heavy machinery moved crates into
the existing buildings.

"What's all this?" Yana asked. "Looks like an invasion."

"Watch your mouth," Torkel said, "if you want to be a positive influence for change. This is the expeditionary force I told you about. We're using SpaceBase as a supply depot for this continent. My father will be coming down later to supervise the more technical aspects of the operation but basically, from here, we'll launch probes and set up base camps close to the points we've identified from space as having the greatest potential for the resources we're seeking."

"Is this going on planetwide?"

"Not at the moment. Look, love, I can't say any more unless you choose to renew your active-duty status and your security clearance, okay? So think about it. And, by the way, come in for a physical so I can shove your status-change papers through in a hurry. You look pretty good for someone with banjaxed lungs and a medical discharge."

"It's all this clean air and country living," she said breezily.

"Great," he said, with a touch of grimness. "But don't be surprised if there are more traffic jams than usual around quaint and charming Kilcoole in the near future."

He plowed into an infirmary parking place willy-nilly and was out of the snocle and around to open the door for her before she could undo her seat belt. Bunny's snocle was already there, and she and Diego looked to be engrossed in urgent dialogue inside the vehicle.

"Can I meet Margolies without a security clearance?" Yana asked sweetly. "Just so I can reassure the populace as to Diego's family situation?"

"Of course," Torkel said. "I imagine he'll be in visiting Metaxos."

Bunny and Diego emerged, looking expectantly in their direction.

"We might as well form a welcoming committee," Torkel said with an overly hearty grin at the kids. "Come on."

Diego spotted Steve Margolies the moment they walked into the infirmary. He sprinted the length of the hall to embrace the older man, heedless of the presence of the medics, Torkel, Bunny, Yana, and even that of his father, lying on a hospital bed open-eyed and propped into an upright position with pillows. The room had only three other patients, and the ward on the opposite end of the corridor showed an unbroken line of empty beds.

Margolies, balding, bearded, and not quite portly, looked as glad to see Diego as the boy did him. "I came as quickly as I could, Diego," he said.

"I knew you would, Steve. I knew it."

Torkel stuck out his hand. "Torkel Fiske, Dr. Margolies. I had you sent for as soon as I learned of you from young Diego and this lady. This is Major Yanaba Maddock, currently retired and, uh—"

"Hi, I'm Bunny," Bunny said, also soliciting a handshake. "I hope you and Diego and his dad can come and live with us in the village."

"That's very kind of you," Margolies said, startled but amiable. "But right now I think Francisco needs the care he can get here."

"Have you found quarters yet?" Torkel asked.

"No. I came straight here after inprocessing."

"Well, then, look, Colonel Giancarlo and I are going to have to have a more extensive conversation with you later but I think right now the thing for me to do is to go make sure you are lodged at least in the same building with Diego. Yana, Bunny, I think we should leave this family alone, don't you?"

The infirmary corridors were teeming with new personnel and new equipment, and the building itself had been enlarged with newly attached modules at either end. Technicians were feeding data to computers, and medical personnel were stocking shelves and unpacking boxes. Yana wondered briefly why, with a half-empty infirmary, they were adding to it. She didn't like the look of that, actually. They must be expecting a great many more troops—and casualties.

They said their farewells, Torkel taking leave with just a hint of a lingering look in his eye for her as he strode off to do whatever it was he was going to do. Which Yana had a pretty good idea was not confined to simply seeing that the Margolies-Metaxos boys were comfy.

She and Bunny climbed in the snocle just as he turned around and waved, and Yana waved back until he was out of sight.

Then, as Bunny started the engine, Yana said, "Develop a mechanical problem, Bunny. I'm going to go back in there for a bit. If anyone challenges you, or stops to help you, drive off and come right back on base after a few minutes. I shouldn't be long."

Bunny gave her a hard, measuring look, then shrugged. "Okay, but whatever you're up to, be careful."

Yana flipped her an abbreviated salute and headed into the clinic.

For the first time since her release, Yana felt fortunate to have spent so long in a large medical facility. She walked back in as if she knew exactly where she was going. Purposefully, she pushed back thoughts of what would happen if she were discovered and her presence in the facility officially queried: Torkel might not even be able, much less wish to, bail her out, and she could easily lose her pension with Intergal and face time in a detention center. But right now was the best time for her to obtain a copy of Lavelle's autopsy—before anyone thought to doctor it up for official reasons.

She entered the Staff Only lounge, which was as empty as it was bound to be with so much activity going on outside, pulled off her new blouse, and hung it on a hook beneath a patient gown. Pulling on a scrub top and a paper cap, and paper shoes in place of her cold-weather boots, she hung a surgical mask around her chin and, taking a deep breath—without a hint of a cough, she noted distantly—to ease the tension in her guts, padded briskly back down the hall.

At Andromeda, as at most company infirmaries, convalescing patients did routine, nondemanding chores to save the professional staff work. Even officers did it, and were glad of it, for it helped stave off the boredom of being separated from their own work and their own lives. During her own convalescence, Yana had spent considerable time helping in medical records, requesting and transmitting data from central files. She could at least see if the autopsy had been performed on Lavelle yet—and if it had become a classified file or not.

She walked straight into the vacant ward opposite the one containing Diego's father, careful to keep her back to the boy and his guardian, and sat out of sight, around the corner, at the nursing-station computer. She typed in the access code she remembered from her days in the hospital—no longer than six weeks ago, which seemed incredible, considering how well she felt and how far she had come. She breathed a sigh of relief as the code worked. In a closed system, where for the most part only company troops and employees had access to the facility, the need for security was not as tight as it would have been on a world containing a variety of corporate or military entities. On shipboard, space station, or wholly owned planetary subsidiary, Intergal was the only game in town.

ACCESSING FILE: MALONEY, LAVELLE, DECEASED

NO MEDICAL RECORD.

Then the machine purred along for a moment and she punched in AUTOPSY REPORT, and suddenly the screen filled with data. She hit PRINT, scanning while the document printed.

The lungs had been congested, so Lavelle had indeed had pneumonia, but that was not listed as cause of death. Her immune system had suddenly and fatally collapsed, unable to cope with half a dozen systemic viral infections. The autopsy noted that this alone was surprising, since tissue samples—muscle, blood, skin, and bone marrow—all indicated that she had been in the physical shape of a woman half her chronological age. Also, a small inexplicable node had attached to the medulla oblongata. That was strange enough, but the autopsy report also cited the presence of an unusually large and highly developed lump of "brown fat" weighing an astonishing 502 grams: its blood vessels had ruptured. A footnote by the examining physician explained that while two hundred grams of brown fat were normally present in human babies at birth—to ensure NSHP, nonshivering heat production—the substance atrophied when babies grew big enough to adjust their own temperatures to cold. It was odd enough to find the brown fat active, and far odder to find it so enlarged. There was also a thin subcutaneous layer of a dense fatty tissue. A minor mutation to protect inhabitants against the cold? Then she remembered seeing a similar fatty layer, thin but present, in the animals she had skinned after the trapping expedition.

Reading on, she was vastly relieved to see that there was no sign of any external injuries or evidence of drugs in the system that might have indicated that Lavelle had been tortured or abused in any way during interrogation. Stuffing the printout in her pants pocket, she shut off the computer, rose, wiped her eyes like any machine-weary tech, and made herself shuffle back down the corridor to the lounge to change again into her latchkay blouse before rejoining Bunny in the snocle.

11

"How do we know that this is for real?" Bunny asked when Yana showed the autopsy report to Sean, Sinead, and Clodagh.

"It is," Sean said unequivocably.

"Then you know about this brown fat stuff, the node, and the anomalous fatty layer?" Yana asked.

Sean nodded and Clodagh's eyes glistened.

"It's why only the young can go off Petaybee," Clodagh said.

"Their brown fat hasn't developed the same mass that adults' have?" Yana asked.

There was a long pause while Sean, Clodagh, and Sinead exchanged secretive, and almost embarrassed, glances. Bunny just looked from one to the other, perplexed and hoping to find an answer in their faces.

Finally, Sean nodded. "Something like that, Yana. It's pretty complicated, and frankly nobody, including me, understands all of the functions of the adaptations. You may have noticed my research facilities for anything much beyond simple animal husbandry are a bit limited. A lot of it the planet simply seems to do on its own. I haven't found anything about deliberately introducing such changes as the brown fat and the node in any of the notes my predecessors left behind, but I do know they exist from examining the corpses of other Petaybeans."

"I can understand how you might not know how the changes got here or what they consist of if you're not responsible for them, but there are still a few things I think you *can* explain," Yana told him.

Had she not grown up on space stations and ships, where humans were the dominant life-form but by no means the *only* life or even the only sentient life, she might have been a little more shocked by what they were implying, that humans were being altered by a planet to suit itself. As it was, she was vaguely annoyed with herself that she was reminded of old vids of aliens who took over the bodies of innocent earthlings.

She took a deep breath and began confronting the issues that disturbed her concerning Lavelle's physiology. "Let me get this straight. You folks here on Petaybee are all Earth stock, right?"

"That's right," Clodagh said. "My ancestors were sent here from County Clare, County Limerick, County Wicklow, and Point Barrow, Alaska. Sean's and Sinead's are from Kerry and Dublin and northern Canada."

"You know all that?"

"If you'll remember right, Yana, I told you most of us can't read or write. It's part of my job here to remember these things." Clodagh grinned. "An old Irish profession."

"Well, tell me this: if you're Earth stock, like me and like most of the company corps, how come only you people can't be moved from where you were sent? I mean, even if the young can go and the older ones can't, it hasn't always been that way, has it? Why is that brown fat stuff affecting you now and it didn't to begin with? Surely at first the company occasionally recruited people who were a little more . . . mature."

It was Sean's turn to look perplexed—and somewhat worried. "Yes, they did. But mostly they've preferred to recruit the youngsters, and it's never seemed to do them more harm than military service does anyone, that we know of. And you have to understand, Yana, that our people have been adjusting to the planet and the planet to us for a couple of hundred years now. The physical changes found in Lavelle's body were *adaptive* changes to this world. Some people adapt more readily and more completely than others—and the more exposure they have, the longer the period they have to become accustomed to something, the greater the chance of a profound adaptation. Lavelle was very much a woman of this planet. She lived most of her life outdoors, she ate only what she caught or grew, like many of us, and she was well into her fifties. Here, she was very tough. But her body was used to *cold* weather, Petaybean midwinter cold, far colder even than you've experienced so far, to clean air and pure water and real food. I'm afraid she had lost whatever resistance she had to other conditions in the process of becoming suited to the extremes of Petaybee. Our peculiar weather conditions would never have killed her, but in exchange for that protection, her body relinquished certain other immunities. Besides which, she had a very strong emotional attachment to her home place."

"I hardly think emotional attachment alone could have caused her death," Yana said.

"It's possible, Yana," Clodagh said. "It's possible. It's

hard to explain to you when you've been here such a short time but maybe when you witness the night chants, you'll understand a little better. With Lavelle being the kind of woman she was, I knew, Sean knew, really all of us knew, that she was as unlikely to survive away from Petaybee as that colonel would out in the mountains without a parka. If we'd known that they'd planned to take her off-planet, we'd have protested, tried to stop them somehow."

"*Lavelle* would have protested," Sinead said in a bitter voice, her small rough hands knotted at her sides. "She must have told them. She didn't need to know what her insides looked like to know she would die offplanet."

Yana gave a gusty sigh. "And much as I hate to say so, she could've told them till the sun turned cold and they wouldn't have believed her."

"Now they do?" Clodagh asked, her face impassive.

Yana shook her head, in anger, frustration, and a whole lot of other conflicting and negative emotions. She was tired. She was confused and disappointed and even somewhat disillusioned, something she had never thought would be possible again. This had seemed to be such a simple, happy place, and now *it* had a secret. All she wanted was to get some rest.

"It's time to go now," Sean reminded the others as he tucked his hand under Yana's elbow. "You haven't missed the chanting, Yana. It will revive you."

Feeling the familiar surge of attraction for him mingle with all of the doubts, fears, and unanswered questions rolling through her mind, she wondered if he could be lying, if in spite of his protestations he was somehow tampering with these people's genes so that they would never be able to leave. She had the oddest feeling that he was definitely hiding something, and that worried her more than any of the other secrets Petaybee held. Was Sean responsible for the problems Giancarlo had mentioned when she had first arrived? And if these people knew they were being changed, as some of them seemed to believe, why did they put up with it?

Yana regarded Sean for a long moment as his silver eyes appealed to her. Gazing up at him, she tried to see him as some sort of psychopath mad-scientist monster, and all she could think of was how wonderful it had been to dance with him tonight, and before that, their encounter at the hot springs. His expression grew less sad and serious as he watched her face, and she knew he could see her resolve to stay detached melting.

Then, with her voice wavering with unaccustomed indecision as much as weariness, she said, "Oh, frag, Sean. I'm really bushed. Nothing short of eight hours' sack time is going to revive me."

A sly smile kindled in his eyes and curved his lips. "Wanna bet?"

Clodagh unexpectedly touched her shoulder, her eyes gentle with sympathy. "You come, Yana. You'll see."

The cat came out with an authoritative "meh!," provoking Yana to an exasperated laugh. She rubbed her forehead with an impatient gesture.

"You guys are bent on brainwashing me into a proper Petaybean, too, aren't you?"

"Something like that," Sean said in very good humor. He knew he had won. If he hadn't exactly convinced her, she would at least let her wishful thinking override her better judgment for the time being. With a deft movement he closed the opening of her jacket, flipped her parka hood onto her head, and started pushing her hands into her gloves.

"Lemme do that," she said, feeling a surge of almost childish rebellion. She didn't want to feel *completely* manipulated just because she was willing to be reasonable. But she didn't resist as he guided her along, following Bunny, Clodagh, Sinead, and Aisling back to the hall, which was still resounding with the sounds of merriment within.

Outside the door, a girl stood chatting with a man who was stirring the contents of a huge metal drum, set up over a small, fierce fire. As they passed, the man nodded, smiled, and smacked his lips appreciatively at the odors wafting up from the delicious-smelling concoction, soup or stew, in the big barrel. Clodagh took an exaggeratedly deep sniff, fanning the aroma toward her with both mittens.

When they entered the meetinghouse, Yana had to pause to adjust to the temperature—and the odor—of the hall, which had been packed solid with energetic folk for the past eight or nine hours.

If these dancing, singing, talking, gesticulating, laughing, crying people were really the cruel victims of a malign curse that doomed them forever to bondage to a hostile planet, they were either blissfully unaware of it or they plainly didn't give a rat's ass.

And suddenly, neither did she. She liked this lot better than the whole Intergal company corps and the board of directors put together, and if there was something wrong with them, well, she had been told to investigate and that was what she was doing. Sort of.

The room was hot, but she didn't mind; it was redolent with food, sweat, and other odors, but there was also a sensation that defied a name, although she thought it had something to do with the great good humor, the fun, the joy these people were projecting. How they had kept it up the whole time she had been gone, she didn't know. But patently they had! She grinned up at Sean and saw that he was sweating; she felt the first moisture beading her brow, too.

As if their entrance were a signal, the music ground to a wheezing stop and the dancing couples stood looking toward them expectantly. Clodagh, Sean, and the others stripped off their parkas, and Yana removed hers. In a corner of the room a bodhran rumbled like marching thunder and a banjo began playing in a minor key. Someone began singing in a husky tenor, as if his throat had endured too many cold winds and the smoke from too many fires. He sang a lonely, homesick sort of song about the green fields of planet Earth, then followed with a rollicking, humorous parody contrasting Earthbound living to life on Petaybee. The next song was a similarly silly one about the last man on the planet who could read, which Yana knew was an exaggeration since at least the company-sponsored people read memos and orders and such.

That song changed the mood of the evening, and every instrument but the drum stilled. The drum slowed from the bouncing beat of bodhran to the steady muted thump of a heartbeat.

Without exchanging another word with anyone, Clodagh began singing the song she had sung for Yana over dinner the first night.

Thump. Thump. Thump. Thump.

The drum pounded in even, measured time as

Clodagh was joined by everyone else as soon as she had
sung the first line.

Thump. Thump. Thump. Thump. The air swirled with
smoke from the fire, on it riding the evaporated breath
and sweat of the two or three hundred people cramming
the hall. Yana felt them so strongly around her that it
was as if they all wore the same skin; the drum was the
beat of their collective heart.

As the last droning word of Clodagh's song died
away, someone else took up a new song, one that Yana
had not heard before.

> *"Lost the song, lost the words, lost the tongue*
> *Lost the skill to read our own tracks.*
> *Lost the skill to mark our trail.*
> *Lost the symbols to read the spoor of others.*
> *Lost the pictures that once replaced them.*
> *Lost the voices that told us we did not need them.*
> *Lost the earth for want of the songs. Ajija."*

The voices swelled around Yana as several more
drums took up the beat, so that the walls of the lodge itself seemed to pulse with the tempo. Sean's voice sang
in her right ear, Bunny's in her left, Clodagh's in front
of her, and Aisling's behind her. She found it difficult to
think of the report, difficult to think of anything, in fact,
except exactly what was happening all around her, inside her. She breathed in the air that the others had
breathed before her, she swayed to the beat of the drum,
and although she didn't know these songs, she realized
that her own mouth was opening with all those other
mouths. This was a sort of spiritual communion, with
those around her, that had nothing whatever to do with

a religion, or a ritual of any sort. Happening, that's what it was. A Happening. It was happening just as much to everyone else in the hall as it was to her. Words were irrelevant: feeling was important. She just had to be singing *something* as the song continued, a new voice leading it.

> *"The new song stained the soles of our shoes*
> *The new song bathed us. We drank the new song.*
> *We breathed it, taking it into ourselves for life*
> *And for life to the song giving forth breath."*

And another voice, older, cracked, sang:

> *"The new song spoke to us in the new tongues.*
> *The howl of a dog, the curly-coat's whinny,*
> *The fox's bark.*
> *The new song walked on the feet of the cat.*
> *It spoke of its secrets in the death-squeal of*
>   *the rabbit.*
> *It sings its secrets from its own mouth*
> *To the ears of those who can listen.*
> *Let's not leave it to sing alone any longer*
> *But go to the center and add our voices*
> *To keep it company for a while*
> *And learn from it new harmonies. Aja ji."*

Yana had no idea how long or how often the song had been repeated, but suddenly everyone was putting their parkas on and, to the continued beat of the drum, filing through the door, out into the night. A brilliant band of light snaked overhead, punctuated occasionally by small dots of colored lights descending. More traffic at SpaceBase, she realized. It seemed incongruous and unreal after the chanting to think about ships landing.

Sean was nudging her forward, sandwiched between himself and Clodagh. "Is it over now?" she asked.

"Not yet."

"Where are we going?"

"To the hot springs. We chant as we walk. You'll see. It's very beautiful."

He squeezed her shoulders encouragingly, and she was not at all surprised, for some reason, to find that she was no longer tired.

With the beat sustaining her, and everyone else, they marched on; totally unlike any Christian soldiers, she thought irreverently. She was surprised when they reached the hot springs in what seemed like a very short time. She had thought the springs were much farther away from Kilcoole. The rising steam occluded any details that daylight might have illuminated. The procession—no, procession was *not* the right word any more than "ritual" or "religion." Okay, she thought, this informal early-morning-after-the-night-before gathering made its way around the spring and seemed to disappear. Startled, she blinked, felt Sean's fingers tighten in reassurance, and then realized that the line led *under* the waterfall. She hadn't suspected before that there was any access there. But then with the steam and the sheeting of down-spilling water, she hadn't looked.

There was just sufficient space for a body, knowing where to go, to sidle past the actual cascade of water without getting more than a dusting of spray. Then she had to adjust her vision to a curious lambent light that was both soft and clear. She could see the walls of a passage curving gradually downward, and the bobbing of heads as people descended. The air was remarkably fresh and invigorating.

The downward movement continued, with people silently merry. Yana tried to figure out why those words seemed so appropriate: "silently merry." But they all were *glad* to be here, together, and moving toward whatever destination lay down there. She became aware that Sean was giving her occasional quick glances, as if reassuring himself that she was accepting this "happening." She didn't know what else she could have done but go along with everyone else, if only to discover what she could of the hidden places of Petaybee, and its secretive inhabitants. Yet . . . the palpable merriness of everyone around her denied the prospect of threat or harm. And she felt so good about coming!

How long the downward slope wound its way, she couldn't tell, for the soft rhythmic beat of the bodhrans urged them onward, yet the drum sound did not echo, but was oddly absorbed by the walls. Then, suddenly, they were there! In a vast luminous cavern, all blues, greens, soft pastel variations of those hues in serrated layers, streamers, bands, patterns. She wished she could ask Diego if all of this looked familiar to him. She was certain she was in the cavern he had described—if not the same one, then a similar one. For there was the water he had mentioned, the odd formations that did look like natural vegetation in their apple green, and ice-sculptured animals in weird and bizarre shapes. People were seating themselves in random groups, murmuring pleasantly, merrily, to each other, with an air of expectation about them.

Clodagh moved to the right of those in front of her

and Sean guided Yana in that direction. Sinead, Aisling, and Bunny veered, too. Clodagh went beyond any other group, to a sort of promontory of pale sea-green ice, and plumped herself down, cross-legged, a position that Yana found both remarkable and enviable in a woman of such proportions. Clodagh settled herself solidly and smiled as Sean, propelling Yana in front of him, moved beyond and above her. He motioned for Yana to be seated. She was somewhat surprised to find that the surface wasn't the least bit cold. Sean folded himself down beside her, close enough so that their shoulders were touching. She wondered about his constant tactile contact with her: she had never noticed him being touchy-touchy with anyone else. She didn't know if she was offended—no, she wasn't. Not at all. When he wasn't being just plain reassuring, even possessive, she found she *liked* Sean touching her for any reason. She had always maintained a physical aloofness with most people, male or female, saving touch for caress, rather than for identity or possession. When Bry turned touchy-touchy, she knew what would soon follow. She folded her arms about her legs and hooked her knees up to her chin. Sean assumed a similar posture, as close to her as possible. He grinned and gave her a totally impious wink.

The surface under her buttocks seemed to get warmer. She wiggled, realized the heat was all over, and undid her parka, only then noticing that everyone else had already done the same. A steam or mist seemed to be rising all around them, hiding the people on the other end of this crescent. She didn't think the body heat of even so many people could have such an effect on this huge cavern.

Sean was watching her, a half smile curving his lips as if he expected, and was pleased by, her actions.

"So? What now?" she asked, leaning into his strong shoulder so that only he heard her.

"Relax, Yanaba. Just take it easy, and take it all in. We're including Petaybee in the latchkay and introducing you. In a moment the planet will respond—just accept it, okay?" His lips barely moved, but she heard each word distinctly. His fingers flicked out in a subtle gesture.

That was when she became aware of the change in the lighting. Whether it was a trick of the mist or not, the lambency had taken a deeper, golden hue, and through her tailbone she felt a vibration. Conversations died off, and a respectful silence spread. Clodagh seemed to elongate from coccyx to poll. Bunny, too, straightened her spine. Much as she wanted to, Yana could not turn her head to see if Sean was responding, for she herself was caught up in whatever it was. And what was it? she asked herself, as she felt each vertebra in her back stiffening. Vibration and warmth pulsed up her spine to her brain stem. Then she was taking deep breaths, inhaling from the gut, filling her lungs—lungs that could now expand to full capacity with neither pain nor wheeze.

She had the weirdest sensation that her brain was expanding, too, the scalp lifting from her head bones—not at all an uncomfortable feeling; more as if she was lightening up all over. Of their own accord her eyes closed—so that she could concentrate on these internal expansions. She was aware, too, of her blood flowing in her veins, juices moving throughout her organs, as if some agency was cleansing her inside out—the way one inflated a mattress, a survival bubble tent, or the tire of a ground-effects machine. There was no pain or discomfort involved—only this sense of being filled in every physical crevice and bodily cavity, this lightening.

She was then inexplicably *aware* of a different sensation: one of completeness, one of belonging, one of perception and acceptance beyond her physical self. She fought that briefly, lost, and was rewarded with a euphoria she had never experienced even in her closest moments with Bry. It was like, yet unlike, orgasm; inexpressibly satisfying and rewarding. She exhaled slowly—for the lightening feeling had apparently occurred during the course of her one deep inhalation. Immediately she pulled air into her lungs again, wishing to achieve that almost vertiginous state of full extension, that delicious lightening, that . . . quasi-mystic belongingness.

Something very gentle, like a feather flicking dust from a delicate surface, flowed across her mind, chiding her for being greedy. All she really needed would be given.

Yana blinked her eyes open, for the thought was alien to her: it had been implanted in her mind. She blinked again. The mist had dissipated. And so had the people who had accompanied her to the cavern. Clodagh was gone, Bunny and Diego, Sinead and Aisling! Before she could panic, there was pressure against her right shoulder.

"I'm here," Sean said, a ripple of laughter in his low voice. When she turned her head, his silver eyes caught hers and then he nodded. Exhaling a totally worldly sigh, she let herself sag, no longer upheld by whatever had had her in its thrall. She felt a shaft of regret for what was no longer in touch with her.

"How long?" she asked Sean, gesturing about her.

"How long did it feel?" he asked, taking her hand in his warm one.

"Like one deep breath."

He nodded again, his eyes slightly hooded, but his smile was full of satisfaction. Then he held her hand up, examining it closely before he turned it palm up and kissed it. She could not control the shudder that crackled up her spine. He laid her palm against his warm cheek and made eye contact.

"It was more than one breath, wasn't it?" she asked.

He nodded, and she could tell from his caution that the time that had passed had been much longer than he felt it safe to admit, before gauging her reaction.

Slowly, carefully, sorting through her memory of the experience and her reactions, reaching the logical conclusion of something that defied logic, she asked, "You people weren't just being poetic when you said Petaybee is alive, were you? It is, isn't it? And it—it hypnotizes you or puts you in a trance or something. Like Diego?"

Sean nodded. "Most of the time it's like it was for you and for Diego, but for those too rigid to accept the possibilities, it can be extremely traumatic—induce shock, madness, even death. Not just with outworlders. You may have noticed young Terce, the other snocle chauffeur?"

Yana nodded. She hadn't seen much of Terce since she had arrived, but she remembered Bunny saying the boy wasn't too bright.

"He didn't react well to this experience. Most children easily accept it, but Terce . . . Maybe he just had too linear a turn of mind or something, but it terrified him and he's never tried again. He sometimes lurks on the edge of the latchkays but he won't join in. But there was no malice involved—just a . . . lack of communication." He shrugged. "There's much more to this planet than instrumentation can detect, Yanaba. You've experienced a central part of it tonight."

"A rite of passage?" She wanted to sound skeptical or cynical or even facetious, but that wasn't the way her words sounded even in her own ears. She dropped her voice to a whisper. "I passed?"

Sean laughed with such real mirth that she had to grin. Then he pulled her against him, arms tightly cradling her body to his chest, rocking both of them back and forth.

"What do you think?" he asked teasingly.

"I don't know what to think. I'm not exactly the religious type . . ."

"Religion has nothing to do with it, Yana. We weren't worshiping. The planet is alive. It's only courteous to communicate. There's—a relationship involved," he said, quite lightly and happily. She realized that he was more relieved than he cared to admit that she had come through her—introduction—without trouble. He continued his rather nonchalant explanation while draped around her, nibbling her ear. "The company wants us to think that everything on the planet came from them, but that's not the case. This planet has a mind, and has developed resources, of its own. Living here, most of us know that and accept the gifts, the protection, and in return, we offer it companionship and—I don't know, expression, I suppose."

"But why? Why does it not only accept you but give you so much? If it really is a living, thinking being, it could as well resent you for occupying its surface. What does the planet get out of you—us—being here?"

He smiled lazily again and ran his finger the length of her spine. "Scientifically speaking? I haven't a clue. But I do have a theory: I think that the reason probably is—maybe—that Petaybee *likes* us."

"That's it? It provides for you, lets you live here and allows you this . . ." She searched for a word. "This *blissful* form of communication just because it *likes* you?"

"That's about the size of it." He nodded. "And it protects us from its own extremities as well, don't forget, with the adaptations." He gave her a delicate nibble on the back of her neck to punctuate his remark.

"That didn't ultimately provide enough protection for Lavelle," she reminded him, trying to sound rational when all she wanted to concentrate on was how to twist in order to nibble him back.

"It can only protect its people here, Yana. Miracles are seldom things."

"Will I grow the adaptations? The—what was that ugly term?—brown fat and the protective layer under the skin?"

"If you need them."

She pressed a thumb roughly across his bare forearm and gave him a quizzical look.

"Oh, yes I have it," Sean said comfortably. "And a few other accommodations you'll just have to find out for yourself. Some of us are more fully adapted than others. I, for instance, am even more a creature of Petaybee than Lavelle."

"I don't believe it! You don't look different. And you don't carry an extra ounce of flesh anywhere," she said, almost accusingly. She was remembering his body all too vividly.

"Are you sure?" he said in a teasing voice, and his hands began to wander across the skin of her back and arms.

That was the first moment she realized that she was as naked as he was. When had that happened? Yet their nudity did not surprise her, seeming as natural as if they had just shared a sauna—and she *had* wanted to see his finely muscled body again. Did this damned planet grant three wishes? Had she taken hers without knowing what she really wanted?

Of their own accord, her hands began to caress his warm silky flesh, the muscles excitingly firm beneath her fingers. Then Sean added the persuasions of his lips to those of his hands, and Yana responded with an ardor she thought she had lost too long ago to ever regain it. He was so silky, so strong, so agile, suddenly so demanding, and she found she had a few demands of her own. His chuckle seemed to beat against her diaphragm and against her breasts, forcing an echo from her as he rolled himself into her with a speed and skill she had to admire. He filled her as she had never been filled before, and the ascent into ecstasy was almost more than she could bear ... than they could bear, for Sean, in mind and body, was subtly, and impossibly, linked to her in a way that she had never experienced before. She was herself, matching the urgency of his rhythm; she was him, sheathing and unsheathing with a power that he, too, had never encountered in a long life of couplings.

They both called out at the same time, in the same voice of joy that was colored with an agony of regret for so ephemeral a moment. As they clung to each other, breathless, unbelieving, that moment seemed uncannily elongated—and all too brief.

"Yana!" Sean murmured in her ear, his tone reverent.

"Oh, Sean!" With strengthless arms, she pressed him against her, burying her face in his neck. The million things she wanted to tell him remained unsaid, for words would shatter the sense of bonding and she felt she had to preserve it, extend it.

For the first time in her adult life, sleep overcame her after sex. Sometime later, Sean shook her gently by the shoulder, kissing the corner of her mouth.

"Hmmmm." She didn't wish to move. She wanted more of him and put her hand out to pull him back to her. But he was dressed. That effectively brought her fully awake.

"We *must* leave now, Yanaba," he said, his eyes tender and his hand gentle as he began to dress her.

That, too, was a novel experience, being *dressed* by a lover. She helped him even though she didn't want to.

When she was jamming her boots on, he took her hand, pressing it against his leg, and with his free hand, tilted her chin up so she met his eyes. She had to catch her breath against the lovingness in their silvery depths. He stroked her cheek with a touch that reminded her of another one.

"Sean, if you were taken off-planet—if they hauled you in for questioning like Lavelle? Would you die, too? Torkel was—"

He put a finger to his lips. "I know. And I can't stay here—" And she knew he meant Kilcoole, not just this cavern. "But I *will* return to you"—and the slight emphasis made her heart bump—"whenever I can, Yanaba Maddock." He dropped his hand to her breast, over her heart, and pressed in hard. "Am I in yours as you are in mine?"

"Yes." Why she could admit it so easily she didn't know. Except that it was true. And it didn't matter if he never did return to her. She would love Sean Shongili for the rest of her life.

His lips brushed hers as gently as he had stroked her cheek.

"Come, we have to hurry." He turned abruptly and led the way out.

As they moved up the slope, it seemed to her that the light behind them gradually dimmed. It was dawn when they ducked out from under the cascade. Dawn of which day, Yana wondered.

12

Yana was still pleasantly disoriented from the experience in the cave and bemused by lovemaking as they walked back to the village. She was not exactly sure how far they had come from the hot springs when Sean pressed her hand in farewell and disappeared into the trees. Considering their conversation and his sudden insistence that they leave the cave, she was hardly surprised.

The sky resembled a healing bruise, staining the morning with yellow-brown haze and, even out here in the woods, smelling like a spaceport, which was unusual. Mostly the smells about Kilcoole were delicate and crisp, refined by the cold to mere essences, but now the stench of hot ship-shielding filled the air and cast a pall over the woods. How many troops had landed since she left SpaceBase?

As she walked out of the woods and into the long clearing preceding the village, one of Clodagh's cats— the one who lived in her own cabin? she could never be sure—trotted up to her, and a short time later Clodagh appeared.

Her beautiful smile livened her face as she embraced

Yana and kissed her cheek. "Welcome, neighbor. I knew
there would be no problem for you."

"Sean's gone, Clodagh."

"Very wise. You should find somewhere to go, too,
Yana. The soldiers are all over the village now. They
came the morning we returned from the chant."

"When *was* that, Clodagh?"

"Yesterday. Don't worry. It didn't take you long for
an offworlder. Giancarlo has gone up to Sean's place
with the others, but he was asking for you, too."

"I need to find Torkel Fiske before Giancarlo finds
me. Is he here, too?"

"I don't think so. Bunny will know."

"Where is she?"

"Somewhere between here and SpaceBase. They
been keepin' her and Terce and Adak all awfully busy.
Adak will know where she is though."

As it turned out, they didn't need to go to the snocle
shed. They met Bunny, accompanied by another of the
cats, coming down the street toward them through a village that had changed during the time Yana had been in
the cave. Snocles ferried uniformed and parka-clad figures up and down the streets, and similar figures wandered between the houses, trying to look as if they were
patrolling something. Snocles were parked willy-nilly
along the streets. Many of the vehicles were loaded
with equipment, and Yana saw two trains of the machines heading away from the village. Several houses
farther on, winter-uniformed corps members were slapping together another of the prefab buildings.

"As you can see, we've been invaded," Clodagh said.
"Sláinte, Bunny."

"Sláinte, Clodagh. Yana! Oh, Yana, you did great.

Isn't it wonderful?" Yana was momentarily confused all over again as Bunny gave her a welcoming hug, then realized that the girl's words referred strictly to the earlier portion of Yana's encounter with the cave, not to the more private events occurring afterward. Still, the relief behind Bunny's joy reinforced Yana's recognition that not everyone found the communion wonderful, or even pleasant. The cave—no, the planet—could and did damage those it rejected, or those who rejected it; she wasn't sure quite what the criterion was. She was just immensely glad to have been found satisfactory.

She grinned back at the girl. "That it was. Even more wonderful than you can possibly imagine. But right now, Bunny, I need to find Torkel Fiske fast."

"That's dead easy," Bunny said. "He just left the station for SpaceBase. I'll take you out there. I'm trying to be there when Colonel Giancarlo is here, and here when he's there, so he doesn't remember his threat to take away my license."

The usually silent riverbed was now a high-speed thoroughfare, vehicles skiing back and forth, passing each other. The ride to SpaceBase was nerve-racking, because it was obvious, even before Bunny began to veer out of the way of poorly driven snocles, that not every driver was as capable as she was on such a treacherous surface.

Bunny dropped Yana at the headquarters building and drove off even more cautiously through a great deal of snocle traffic, toward the infirmary, where, she told Yana, she hoped to find Diego.

As opposed to the bustle outside, headquarters was quiet—stripped of personnel, Yana thought. The door to an inner office stood open, and through it she could see

Torkel's bronze hair shining in the light from his console.

"Hello, Yana," he said when she strode in, closed the door behind her, and sat down. He barely looked up at her, which under most circumstances would have been a rather refreshing change from his pronounced attentiveness of the past few days. "I'm on comm line with my father. I'll be right with you."

She waited while he returned to his conversation.

"Great, Dad, see you soon. Over and out," he said aloud, tapping the final key. He was still smiling as he turned expectantly to Yana and asked, "What can I do for you?"

"You offered me Giancarlo's job. I want it."

He grinned. "Is it my turn to say, 'But this is so sudden'?"

"Torkel, he's making a balls of the whole thing. Listen, we have got to talk seriously about what's going on here on Petaybee and the company's interface with the natives."

"Yana, let me remind you of a point that others seem to be forgetting: the natives are transplants of barely two hundred and fifty years ago from Earth. Johnny-come-latelies as our projects go. And from my conversation with your buddy Shongili, it seems to me they're awfully damned possessive for sharecroppers on company property."

"That's because you only know part of what's been happening. Look, Torkel, Giancarlo told me to find out what's been going on with Petaybee and the unauthorized life-forms, and I think I have. Both the natives and my own experience confirm my conclusions. I think you'll agree, after we've talked, that the mining operations can't be started precipitously, and any mass transfer of the inhabitants of this planet is out of the question."

"Excuse me, Yana. Dear. The company makes the decisions; not you, not me, and certainly not the illiterate dregs the company was kind enough to resettle here." He gave her his best company-negotiator's poker face. The set-to with Sean had either done some serious damage to his goodwill, or that goodwill had been an act.

"Torkel. Dear. At least hear me out, okay? You *did* ask."

He relaxed again. "Okay. Shoot."

"Before you slap my wrist, let me remind you that I was retained by the company to investigate, and I took that as my authorization to do so, not only in what's happening here on Petaybee, but also in company records pertaining thereto."

"You accessed Lavelle Maloney's autopsy file?" he asked with a one-wolf-to-another-wolf grin.

"That's a roger."

He shrugged. "I would have preferred you to go through channels, but I see your point. And if you can explain to her friends that birth defects caused her death, rather than our interrogations, so much the better."

"They weren't birth defects, Torkel."

"No?"

"No. According to Shongili and the others, they were anatomical adaptations engendered by contact with Petaybee."

"Really? Is there any proof of this?"

"Tests on any mature Petaybean will yield similar anomalies, Sean says."

"I see. We can run the tests on Sighdu and the other woman then, I suppose."

"You can, but you need to bring them back to Petaybee ASAP and run the tests here. From what I understand, the adaptive mechanisms making the inhabitants suitable for a cold planet of this type would make them exceedingly uncomfortable in temperatures you find normal. And recycled air would contain viruses and bacteria which their immune systems couldn't handle. That's what actually killed Lavelle Maloney, and what may soon kill the other two if they aren't returned here." Before he could say anything, she continued. "Torkel, until the company can figure out a way of adjusting these peoples' highly sensitive immune systems to all of the free-spinning viruses and bacteria on satellites or other planets, the kind of move you say the company's proposing would amount to genocide."

"That's a fairly dramatic statement to extrapolate from the autopsy of one off-planet Petaybean, Yana. Besides, it's the Petaybeans themselves who are making this necessary, with their guerilla sabotage against our geographical and mining exploration expeditions."

Yana cocked a cynical eyebrow at him. "There're no guerillas on Petaybee, Torkel, no sabotage! If anything, it's the other way around."

"How so? The company owns the planet. The company terraformed the planet. It has the right to extract mineral deposits."

"The company might own the right to inhabit the surface of the planet, Torkel, and under normal circumstances, it might have the right to harvest certain resources the terraforming process sowed. But owning the planet itself?" She slowly shook her head. "This planet was here way before Intergal was formed or terraforming was invented. You *don't* own this planet."

Torkel gave a scornful snort. "If the company doesn't, who does? Not the inhabitants that the company put here."

She awarded him a pitying glance. "No, they just occupy it. The planet owns itself. It's sentient, Torkel. A living entity."

"Now you sound like Metaxos and his boy." Torkel threw up his hands in exasperation.

"That's because I've seen what they saw. Or, rather, 'seen' isn't exactly the right word. Felt it, experienced it, heard it, been touched by it. Whatever. The locals say it's a way of communicating with the planet, and you have to be willing to be touched by it or you can become disoriented enough to be in the same shape as Metaxos. Or, like some of the other missing teams, if you're too far from help, die as a result."

He regarded her a long moment. "And Metaxos aged in this process?"

"That's a possibility. The phenomenon can take a lot out of someone who resists it." Something occurred to her suddenly. "Do I . . . look any older to you than I did the last time you saw me, Torkel?"

"No. Younger if anything. There's a glow about you that, if you had ever given me any encouragement, would make me jealous." He briefly dropped his lids over his eyes.

She smiled like one of Clodagh's cats after a snootful of fish. "Other than that?"

"No. So you contend that you've been through the same thing as Metaxos? And didn't fight it, so came out revived? So where did this happen? In one of these illusive mineral deposits?"

"I didn't find any deposits." Yana was unsettled by that shot. "I—found—myself in a quite ordinary cave formation, same kind I've seen other places occurring naturally under hills. According to the spatial map I received with my briefing, the cave isn't in one of the spots where your instruments have detected mineral wealth." She tried another tack. "Look, the locals accept me to a greater degree than you, Giancarlo, or anyone else. That makes me the best qualified to organize this operation in a way that won't be harmful to the natives or the planet."

Torkel gave her one of his suave smiles, which she had begun to find infuriatingly smug and condescending. "Yana, get real! We own the planet, and the natives are technically nothing more than employees. Also, it seems to me that you're treading—you should pardon the expression—on thin ice here. Are you really offering to do this job, or have you, in fact, gone over to the side of the people you were supposed to be investigating?"

"Why does it have to be sides?" she asked, leaning forward and willing him to keep making eye contact with her. "If this is a company planet and the inhabitants are company employees, isn't the company interested in the potential above and beyond the usual? This may be something entirely new here, Torkel. Something that would be useful without the expense of reterraforming a planet." She could see that "expense" was a key word, and he was definitely mulling over the "entirely new" notion. "At any rate, we'll need to delay any evacuation or even the transfer of a single Petaybean until we've developed some means to compensate for their dependency on the planet."

"Fresh air, freezing temperatures, and no microbes to attack their disabled immune systems." Torkel shrugged. "That should be easy enough."

"If that's all there is to it," she said darkly. "That's what I know now, and I'm only scratching the surface. Please go carefully here."

"Oh, we're being careful okay. Since you're so concerned, you'll be glad to know that my father has been following all of the events here, too, and he's seen the Maloney woman's autopsy report, as well. Since he understands the brief evolution of this planet better than anyone, he's decided to personally conduct an investigation to rule out any malfunction in this planet's development resulting from the terraforming process as a cause for the aberrant occurrences you mention. That's Dad— nothing if not conscientious. And he likes nothing better than a new scientific mystery. Me, I'm a simple, practical kind of guy. I think the explanations for all of this are probably traceable to fairly uncomplicated sources."

There was a knock on the door. Torkel stood and walked over to it, stepped into the hall, had a few low words, then opened the door wider.

Giancarlo stood there, along with Terce, the snocle driver. Torkel shrugged.

"I'm sorry, Yana. And very disappointed to have to say this to you. However, Terce here corroborates Giancarlo's suspicions that you've entered into a secret pact with the guerillas and betrayed the company. I'm afraid we're going to have to hold you for questioning, pending complete physical and psychological examinations and testing, as well as the standard interrogation."

"Torkel—" she began. "Captain Fiske. That young man is one of the fai—"

"In light of our conversation," Torkel said, cutting her off midword, "I'll see to it that the investigation is conducted here on Petaybee for as long as possible, but it may be necessary to move you to more sophisticated facilities."

She stood and did an about-face, forbearing to tell him that being moved would probably not harm *her* in the same way it would the Petaybeans.

Giancarlo glared as she started past him. She kept her eyes straight ahead, focusing slightly over his left shoulder, as if he weren't there. With a hand jarring against her shoulder, he stopped her in her tracks, his expression guarded but hostile.

"We're also looking for Dr. Shongili, Major Maddock. You could save yourself an extra charge of obstructing investigations if you'll give us some idea where he might be found."

She said nothing.

Bunny Rourke's snocle was her dearest prerogative, if not possession, but she didn't bat an eyelash when she saw it was gone from the place where she had parked it.

She had been all set to take Diego and Steve Margolies back to the village, to let Steve meet Clodagh and the others and talk with them about what had happened to the Metaxoses. Steve had the same specialty as Dr. Metaxos and, if only he could be convinced to keep an open mind, that would give them one more ally to avert what Bunny knew in her gut was going to be a catastrophic change in Petaybean lives.

She had felt it in the cave during the night chant—just the least tremor, nothing someone unacquainted with the planet, like Yana, would notice, but the planet was worried, fearful. Sean had felt it, too, she knew, but she was also sure he had been clearing his mind of any negativity to help Yana. They were waiting for Steve to finish talking with Dr. Metaxos's doctor, so she and Diego had gone to start the snocle while they waited.

"I've got to go now," she said, turning to Diego. "They've taken my snocle, but I think you and Steve should get the first ride to Kilcoole you can."

"Maybe the major can get one for us from her buddy, that Fiske guy," Diego said, not understanding.

Bunny shook her head even as she pulled away from him. "No. If the major was okay, my snocle would still be here."

"I'll come with you." Diego still didn't get it.

"I have to go on foot. You'd freeze."

"Nah, it's warm today. I—"

"No. Meet me later. Bring Steve and we'll introduce him to Clodagh. I got to go before they catch me, Diego. Bye."

She didn't hear whether or not he returned her good-bye as she ducked between the buildings, behind piles of unassembled equipment, her white-and-gray rabbit-fur parka blending with the snow as she circled around to the river and headed back toward Kilcoole. There, she would pick up Charlie's dogs and go somewhere: Sinead's old trapper's cabin, maybe, the one Sinead had lived in before she had hooked up with Aisling. The PTBs wouldn't know the location of that one.

She hoped Diego would tell Yana what she had done, and then she realized that what she had told Diego was true: Yana wasn't okay. That redheaded captain, the nice one, either hadn't been able to help her or hadn't been as nice as he seemed. All the more reason she needed to get back to the village and try to get help. Behind her she heard more shuttles landing and smelled the fumes from the hot housings on the spacecraft as they touched down. There were so many of these company people with their machinery and equipment and all of Intergal's resources. The company men acted as if her people had to do anything they said, and for the first time, she was scared that they might be right.

She didn't run: running attracted attention. She tried to move with the rhythm of the wind and the snow, except that today the snow wasn't blowing, it was melting. Diego was right. It was a very hot day. She shed her parka as soon as she thought she was safely out of sight of SpaceBase and the river road.

She could hear the roar of the snocles on the river; an altered sound now, sort of muted, wet, splashy, accompanying the sound of the engines and the swish of snocle skis on ice. The day was really *very* warm. Warmer than it ever got even during the middle of the short Petaybean summer, when most of the snow was gone and it was no longer necessary to have a fire in the house. But how could that be? Actual breakup usually didn't come for weeks, and then usually gradually, a crack in the ice one day, a soft spot the next, and then the ice began to move. *Never* was it this hot so early in the season.

In the distance, the sound of an explosion was muffled but audible. She wasn't surprised. She had seen the explosives loaded in corps snocles setting out from Kilcoole in a northerly direction earlier in the day. They claimed to be "exploring," which meant they were blowing sores on the face of the planet.

Though the explosion sounded distant, the shock waves made the ground beneath her feet shudder.

Her boots were made of hide, suitable for dry snow. She had another, waterproof pair she wore for early and late winter, but she hadn't thought about changing into them yet. She could have used them now. The soft moosehide soles of her boots were soaking up icy wetness from the melting snow. If she didn't reach Kilcoole by nightfall, when, despite the unseasonable warmth of the day, the temperatures were likely to drop below freezing again, her feet would freeze. Maybe she should have stuck closer to the river. But she thought that it would be quicker, and safer, to cross country to where Uncle Seamus was ice-fishing. She planned to ride the rest of the way home with him.

A breeze blew against her, but it was a warm breeze, soft and friendly. She took off her hat and mittens and stuffed them in her parka pocket, unbuttoning her outer sweater as she walked.

There was another distant explosion, and the ground bucked under her feet as if the whole planet had writhed in agony. Why did they have to do that? It occurred to Bunny that somehow the planet was generating the unusual heat, the early breakup, in response to the assault on it. Such a thing had never happened in Petaybee's inhabited history, but then, that history was relatively short.

The ground continued to tremble as she walked, more cautiously now, through the woods. Here she could keep close enough to the riverbanks to avoid getting lost. Where the snow hadn't drifted too deeply against the riverbanks, she even caught glimpses of the snocles through the trees.

How long had it been since she had taken Yana out to SpaceBase? Only a few hours, surely, and already the river had changed. The ice looked patchy now, long blue streaks showing where the runners had carved their tracks. And it didn't look like the rest of the ground anymore. It was shiny, with a glaze of melted snow over the top. She didn't remember the river ice ever melting so fast, but then, she didn't remember ever seeing as much traffic on the river, either. All that friction and weight surely added to the melting process. And this was the warmest day for this time of year she could recall in her whole life.

She was across the river from where Seamus usually set up his ice-fishing tent when she heard the sharp *Crack!* as if someone had fired a pistol right beside her head.

Some of the people in the speeding snocles were trying to brake on the ice, others slowing, veering in confusion. Yet others who had experience with such treacherous conditions were trying to pilot.

She ran closer to the bank, plunging into the snow up to her knees. Seamus was running from his tent, at first moving wildly about, then stopping, staring at the ice, and finally darting out in front of the snocles waving his arms, urging them toward the banks. Two yards beyond where he stood, between him and the oncoming snocles, the ice parted in a foot-wide gap, the side nearest town already buckling under the weight of the snocles that had just passed over it.

"Get off! Get off!" Seamus was yelling to the snocle drivers. "Drive onto the banks!"

A giant icy chunk broke off and plunged into the blue water bubbling up between the slabs. The ice, which had been substantial enough on the drive to SpaceBase with Yana, looked glass-thin! Along the edges of the river, it was creaking and she saw cracks forming there, too. The level of the river seemed to be rising.

One driver, either not understanding or not believing Seamus, zoomed straight for him, and plunged nose-first into the crack, the snocle runners and windshield submerged in the swirling water and wedging the crack even wider.

Seeing the tail sticking up out of the river alerted the next few drivers, but unfortunately not before three more, two coming from SpaceBase and one from Kilcoole, skidded out of control. The one from Kilcoole ran into a snowbank on the edge of the river. Bunny plowed through the snow to reach it, hopping over a two-inch-wide crack in the ice, feeling the surface, which only hours before had been solid, bouncing under the sopping soles of her boots.

The other two snocles had both torn into the back of the partially submerged vehicle, sending it deeper into the river. Fortunately, snocles had reinforced cabins and the drivers of the two that still had their runners on the ice scrambled unhurt from their seats. But Seamus was leaning across the crack, trying to pry open the sinking vehicle's door to extricate the driver.

Bunny pushed the snocle on her side of the crack back toward the center of the river. The vehicle slid easily on the ice, even laden as it was with equipment. Bunny knew the trick of it, having had to haul hers from deep snow or off black ice.

The driver clumsily wrenched open the door and

spilled onto the ice, scrambling ineffectively to gain his feet.

"Get back in!" Bunny yelled to him. "Go get help from town!"

"No *way* am I gettin' back in that thing, babe!" the soldier yelled at her and ran for the bank.

More snocles were jamming to a stop just short of the crack, which was widening by the minute as pieces crumbled into the river. The drivers crowded toward the crack, trying to help Seamus save their comrade.

"Lie down! Form a chain!" one driver yelled—the first smart thing one of them had done, Bunny thought.

Torn between climbing in the snocle to drive to the village for help and going to the aid of her uncle and the driver, Bunny chose the latter. She dove into a belly flop, skidding across the ice faster than any of the other would-be rescuers could walk, and grabbed one of Seamus's ankles just as he managed to snag open the door of the imperiled snocle. The driver half jumped, half fell out of the vehicle and into the river just before the ice cracked wider. A piece of ice broke off, and the turbulent waters enveloped the rest of the snocle, the outstretched arms, head, and upper torso of the driver on the other side of the crack, and all of Seamus except the ankle to which Bunny was clinging.

His momentum dragged her forward but she held on, flailing in the water with her other hand, trying to grasp some other portion of him. She knew her actions might be holding his head underwater, but at least she could keep him from being pulled under the ice.

Something grabbed at *her* hand then and she caught her uncle's arm, letting go of the ankle to grab his forearm with both hands. It was then that she suddenly realized that the water was warm! Not ice cold, as it ought to be, but almost hot. She had no time to think about what had caused *that*, because Seamus's head broke the surface just as Bunny felt the ice under her chest loosen.

"Here! Over here!" cried the soldier on the other side of the crack. By then they had already hauled the driver of the sunken snocle out, and some of the other soldiers were hurrying him up the bank. "Come over here, old man, that little gal can't handle you."

Seamus, nodding in agreement, lunged away from Bunny and over to the soldier, who was immediately joined by a second man. Together they pulled Seamus from the river.

Bunny slithered backward until she felt more solid ice under her. She slid until she came up against the abandoned, still-running snocle. Levering herself onto the driver's seat, she gunned the snocle down the softening ice so hard it flew across the gap at the side of the river and up onto the bank. She kept to the woods on the way back to Kilcoole to warn the village of the unseasonably early breakup, all the time wondering how *that* had happened.

After Bunny's precipitous departure, Diego Metaxos and Steve Margolies headed back to their quarters.

"So, what is it with you and this girl?" Steve asked in a kidding tone. "Are her intentions honorable?"

Diego felt himself flushing uncomfortably. He had thought once Steve got here everything would be okay, but even with Steve, he felt edgy and uncertain. The only time he had felt good was that day in the village, when he had chanted his poem and all of the people had understood it. After he had met Steve, and Steve had spent some time at Dad's bedside, Steve, Captain Fiske, and Colonel Giancarlo had spent hours closeted together, and that bothered Diego. The last couple of days, except for short visits with Frank at the hospital, Steve was occupied in organizing what he called his expedition.

Diego hadn't had a chance to talk to him about that and seized the moment.

"What are you planning to do when you go back out there?" he asked Steve when they were safely back in their quarters.

"The same thing your dad was trying to do, only with more support. Locate the deposits, mark the spot, take samples."

"Must make you feel good, taking over from Dad," Diego said. His voice contained a bitterness he hadn't known he felt—at least not toward Steve.

"Hey, son." Steve stopped stuffing articles in a bag and turned to face him. His brown eyes looked wounded. "It's not like that. I'd like nothing better than for Frank to be well and leading the expedition, but he'd want me to carry on his work, now, wouldn't he?"

Diego shrugged. "Maybe. Maybe not."

"What do you mean?"

"Did you ever think that maybe he's like he is because he didn't want to keep on?"

"What? You mean, he willed himself into the state he's in now"—Steve was clearly incredulous—"because he didn't do a good job the first time? Diego, my boy, that is not clear thinking."

Diego shrugged again, a disgusted lifting and dropping of his shoulders. It hurt to think about Dad. It hurt to think about Lavelle. He didn't even want to think about losing Steve the same way and he realized he was pulling a number on him, trying to guilt-trip or scare him into not going.

"I don't know, Steve. Maybe the mission isn't such a good idea, huh? What are they going to do if you find the stuff?"

"You've been too much in the company of Bunny and the villagers, Diego. Be sensible. The company has a lot of bucks invested in this planet."

"You haven't given it a chance," Diego shot back. "I thought you would take care of Dad when you got here but all you've been doing is taking over his job. You're just like all the other company geeks. You don't give a damn about us, this planet, or anything else except the fraggin' company!"

"Diego . . . son."

"I'm *not* your son," Diego said hotly, storming toward the door. "Good-bye. I'm going to see my dad. And hey, if you come back in the same shape he's in, I'll get you an adjoining bed!"

When green-coated men and women decide to give you a going over, you let them get on with it, cooperating when you have to. Especially when hovering over the proceedings is a block-shaped marine with piggy, close-set eyes: the kind you just know likes to twist arms and has some mighty painful nerve blocks he's dying to practice on a live and wriggling body. So Yana went along with the procedure, privately resenting every intrusion, draining, pricking, probe, and order. When she could, she sneaked glances at the scans, trying to remember from all-too-recent experience if she could

detect any alterations, improvements, or changes in the
results. She did better with X rays, and could even find
the thickening around her innumerable repaired broken
bones. Then one of the medics, the skinny woman with
the jaw like a vise, altered the screens so she couldn't
see the ones of her lungs—the ones she most wanted to
check out.

"It's my body," she said in a growl of complaint. "I
got the right to look!"

They ignored her, as they had done since she had
been ordered into their presence. She did catch terms
like "unusual remission," "minimal scarring," "regener-
ative," and "improvement": the last two words she liked
hearing very much, but she would have liked to know
where the improvement and regeneration had happened.
Actually, she didn't need them to tell her that her lungs
were sound again—lungs that she had been told would
never completely heal from the gas she had inhaled on
Bremport. Petaybee had done that for her. Would they
believe it had been the planet? Probably not!

The medics were deep in consultation for a long
while after the last of the examinations had been completed. One or another kept glancing at her as if she had
grown tentacles or oozed slime or perhaps turned into a
new sort of humanoid specimen they could dissect for
the good of Mankind.

Ignoring the tension in her guts, Yana forced herself
to relax—as much as anyone could on the hard examination table. She succeeded well enough so that she was
jerked out of a doze by a rough hand.

The one she had come to think of as "Ornery-eyes"
indicated, with a grunt and a jerk of his thick thumb,
that she was to accompany him. The medics didn't

pause in their discussion to observe her departure. Then she noticed that Ornery-eyes was sweating, great circles under his armpits and down his shirt back. Out in the corridor she could appreciate why: they must have turned the heat up as high as it would go. He jerked his thumb in the direction they were to take.

Automatically she memorized the turnings as he prodded her left or right, or straight ahead, and down the stairs. She wished she'd had a chance to see a layout of the SpaceBase complex. It was ingrained in her that she should never waste the opportunity to dekko a place, even if she might never need the info. Then she felt a series of concussive shocks through her paper-slippered feet, and she winced. That wasn't from any hard landings—unless someone was being awfully careless with shuttle vehicles.

Her escort grabbed her arm, pulling her back a pace and jamming her right up against a door. The thumb indicated she was to enter. She pondered briefly about knocking, but when the thumb jerked threateningly again, she shrugged and opened the door.

A man of medium age, medium build, and medium coloring, with the unmedium insignia of a bird colonel on his collar, sat at a small desk, studying the small screen. To her surprise, he looked up the moment she entered, waved the marine out of the room, and beckoned for her to be seated on the only other piece of furniture in the nondescript office. He also turned off the screen.

"Major Maddock, I'm Colonel Foyumi Khan, that's K-H-A-N," he said with a trace of a smile.

"Psych?"

He nodded. "Routine reassignment testing," he said

in a manner designed to reassure—but somehow she wasn't. "You appear to be in excellent physical shape considering your condition just six weeks ago. This planet seems to suit you."

"It would be more accurate to state that I suit it."

His eyes widened just slightly. "Oh?" he asked encouragingly. "How do you construe that?"

"My improved health, of course," Yana said, trying for innocence. This shrink was altogether too smooth. She was almost flattered that Intergal had assigned her an interrogator of his quality. "Great place for R and R."

Through her feet she felt another of those distinct tremors. Khan noticed it, too, and he frowned slightly, glancing down, then back up at her. She returned his regard quizzically, though she had already decided that the quakes were not being caused by someone crashing a shuttle onto the landing field. Somewhere blasting was going on, and Petaybee was wincing away from Intergal's latest assault on its mineral wealth. Damn Torkel! He hadn't heard a word she had said.

"And you feel that this ... ah ... planet is totally responsible for your improved physical condition?"

"Well, breathing fresh air that hasn't been recycled for who knows how long with what additives from however many stations it's been serviced in is a good start when you've burned lungs. Then there's regular hours, clean living, a natural diet free from technological additives, winter sports, and stress-free companionship. Those're surefire prescriptions for renewed vitality."

"I see. And this stress-free companionship? It means a lot to you?"

Yana shrugged. "I'm a company employee. I go

where I'm told, do what I'm told, and when it's pleasant duty with nice folk, I'm grateful."

"Grateful enough to sell out the company to retain the nice folk?"

She chuckled then, noting the evenness of his return gaze, the blandness of his face. Behind those sat a very smart man.

"Why should I sell out a company which has provided me with what I need? Especially when I'm trying to convince the company that they're about to throw the baby out and recycle the dirty bathwater."

"The bathwater?"

"Colonel, I was sent out to see what I could learn. I learned something that Captain Fiske finds unacceptable. He's evidently quite ready to take the word of the man he originally intended I would replace and a short-witted snocle driver with a beef against me. All because he's run smack dab into something he can't understand."

"And you understand it?"

"No, not at all. But I do concede that it's happened, along with my" — She chuckled —"inexplicable return to health."

"So you're grateful to the planet for this?"

She could see him grappling with that notion and nodded. "The planet is more than Fiske is willing to accept."

"But you do?"

"I do. And, if he'll only credit an old shipmate with the sense to tighten bolts when she sees 'em loose, he'd do himself, the company, and me a stupendous favor."

"Which is?"

"He—and Intergal—can gain a lot more from Petaybee than consumable minerals!"

"And what can they gain?"

"Working knowledge of a new sentient life-form."

"Which is?"

"This planet."

He brought his chin forward in a nod that ended abruptly. He looked at her and smiled: not a really reassuring smile, but the kind one might give someone who might not be playing with a full deck. Yana raised an eyebrow and deliberately laid one arm on the desk, hand relaxed on the surface, as she hooked the other arm along the back of the chair, assuming as indolent and relaxed a position as she could. She had given enough of the psych tests she knew were upcoming to know how to act: open, relaxed, easy, as if she hadn't a care in the world. She even hauled her right ankle up to her left knee, as if to leave herself completely open. This room was hot, also, and she didn't want to show any perspiration—even if the bird colonel was.

He shot the expected questions at her and she gave him back the answers, pausing briefly now and then to consider—as was wise of her to do—but not pausing long enough for him to consider it an evasion or hesitation. It was working, with him and with her, because the more complicated the shrink-questions, the more she relaxed, since she knew exactly the sorts of answers required. They hadn't really looked at her records, had they?

Suddenly, in the middle of posing a question designed to reveal any sexual aberrations she might have, he stopped and stared at her—as if seeing her for the first time.

"You know all the parameters of the answers, don't you?"

"Wondered when you'd figure that one out, Colonel."

He leaned back as far as the uncomfortable chair would let him, crossing his arms on his chest. "So what's behind all this? Give me a straight answer."

"I already did, Colonel. I've known Captain Fiske a long time. He asked me to do some nosing about for him since I was billeted in a Petaybean village. I did. I gave him my report. He doesn't care to believe it." She shrugged at such vagary. "It's not the first time commanders have refused to believe reconnaissance reports and taken more comfortable rear-echelon theories." She shrugged again, reaching up to scratch her head as if puzzled by such irrationality. She was sweating, and that wasn't the way to put across her point of view. Except that the colonel was sweating more profusely than she. "Hey, did they turn up the heat around here just so I wouldn't get a chill in my paper wrapping?"

Now the colonel was free to take out a cloth and mop his face and neck. "Heat's been rising steadily. I thought this was the cold season down here."

"The locals are already taking bets on the exact day and time the ice on the river will crack and be carried away downstream."

He gave her a side look, then grinned. "How'd you bet?"

"Me?" She chuckled. "I don't have enough money to waste on foolish bets, Colonel. But the earliest of those dates chalked up is weeks away." They felt another rumble underfoot, one considerably more authoritative than any of the others.

The colonel clutched at the edge of the desk as the

monitor rattled on its stand. In the same second, Yana grabbed the side of the desk.

"Someone's planting too much semtex," the colonel said with a frown.

Yana grinned, having thought of another answer to the whammy they had just felt.

"Spill what you know, Major," the colonel advised, "while there's still a chance for you to get straightened out on this. Unless, of course, you think the planet's fighting back?"

"If, that is, I was a bettor, Colonel, I think my money'd be on the planet."

Just then the door burst open—resisting a little, for it was slightly off kilter from the last quake—and Fiske came in, his eyes narrowed in anger. Behind him were Giancarlo and Terce.

"All right, Yanaba, where is he? How's he doing this?"

Yana took great satisfaction in maintaining her calm while three sweaty, angry perturbed men threatened to overwhelm her. "I assume that the 'he' you refer to is Dr. Shongili?"

"You know it is." Fiske, jaw out, took the necessary step to loom over her in the chair.

"I don't know where Dr. Shongili is, Captain Fiske. How could I since I've been . . . involved . . . here for the past four or five hours."

"He's somewhere on this planet . . ."

"I hope so," Yana murmured.

". . . and I'm going to find him and find out how he's doing this." Fiske flicked his fingers at the ground.

Yana did not have to pretend surprise. "You think he's blowing his planet up to thwart you?" She actually had trouble suppressing her laughter. "He's got no explosives. The company has 'em all. And why would he want to blow his planet up?"

"I don't know how he's doing it, but he's responsible."

"Using what?" Yana fired back at him. "Or, maybe," she said, turning devious, "he's told the planet to resist, to hamper, to impede your efforts to strip it of its natural resources."

Fiske jutted his jaw out again, clenching his teeth over whatever it was he wanted to blurt out in frustration. Instead, he transferred his feelings to the grip of his fingers on her arm as he roughly hauled her up from the chair.

"You're coming with me!" And he began to frog-march her out of the room.

"Like this?" she asked. Part of her paper skirt, soaked with her perspiration, had been left on the seat of the chair. She had also lost one of her paper shoes in his haste to get her moving.

"Captain!" the colonel barked in a tone that could not be ignored, even by Torkel Fiske. "You will permit the major to dress before she leaves this installation."

13

No doubt in an effort to humiliate, harass, or annoy her, Giancarlo signaled Ornery-eyes to stay in the room where Yana was to dress herself. It would take a lot more than Ornery-eyes to perturb Yana. She was slightly flattered that Giancarlo thought it would! Ignoring her audience, she took advantage of the dressing-room shower to enjoy a quick wash before she dressed. She smiled as she noticed that she had been given ordinary-issue clothes, not winter gear. Torture could take many subtle forms: freezing wasn't a common one.

When Ornery bustled her down the corridor to the assembly point, Yana was reasonably sure she'd had the best of that deal. For when they got outside, it was nearly as warm as the facility had been—and she was far more comfortable, in the lighter garments, than any of the others were.

She was shoved, just ducking her head in time to keep from cracking it on the doorframe, into a ground vehicle, which was already inhabited by several squads, sweating in their winter gear. They were conveyed out to the field where a troop copter waited. She caught a glimpse of other air-assault vehicles and some big land cruisers. She also saw two dark circles, one of considerable size, where the field, plascrete and all, had subsided. She wondered if the planet knew what to target or if it just pulled the plug where the terrain made it easiest.

They had barely gotten settled when the bulky vehicle tilted to one side.

"Lift! Lift! Lift!" Torkel yelled as the pilot made as if to investigate the damage.

Yana privately enjoyed the planet's antics very much, though she was crammed in the backseat between Giancarlo and Ornery-eyes's massive torso. The latter had folded his arms over his chest and was staring straight ahead, ignoring the almost-180-degree view afforded by the bubble-shaped Plexiglas windshield. Yana, however, took the scene in eagerly.

Craters pocked the surface of the great field. As the vehicle came around and headed north-northeast toward Kilcoole, she saw the village below; then, as the copter angled off toward the mountains, she gasped as she caught glimpses of the river, seamed with dark, steaming cracks. Its surface was littered with snocles, either capsized into the cracks or stranded on larger blocks of ice. A few, back toward SpaceBase, were being offloaded by men stripped down to their shirts, while farther ahead men and women scrambled to save each other from drowning and pulled each other ashore. A couple of snocles were attempting to find snow firm enough for the runners to ski on while one soldier broke trail, planting markers to show where the snow had not yet turned to slush.

Yana hoped that Bunny's snocle wasn't out there among the stranded, or that the girl hadn't been arrested when Yana was. She also wondered just where Sean was, but one thing was sure: he wouldn't be where this copter was taking them.

It landed in the pasture that had once held the curly-coats. She thought she caught sight of one of the dark ones, hiding in the copse, but it could have just been a big brown-branched bush the height of a curly-coat. The house, when the troopers entered it, weapons drawn, had the feeling of a deserted place. At least that was what Yana sensed from the still, cool air inside. Not so much as a whisker of one of Sean's unusual big cats, either. Torkel led the way down the link to the laboratories, Giancarlo with him, Ornery hauling her along in their wake.

"I want every disk, file, paperwork, notebook, everything," Torkel called over his shoulder to the lieutenant in charge of the squads. "Everything taken back to the base. I want this place under strict surveillance and rigged to catch anyone who steps inside."

"The animals are all gone," Giancarlo said savagely. "He obviously got back here to let them all loose. We could have learned something from them."

Yana could see from the condition of the pens that they hadn't been occupied for a while. That must have been the first thing Sean had done when he had separated from her.

"You certainly didn't expect to find them here, did you, Colonel, tamely waiting for us?" Torkel asked, resuming his pose of amused condescension.

"Dammit, Fiske, I told you we should have moved in on him earlier, right after that all-night binge the natives had."

"But I thought that was too good a chance for my undercover operative to miss," Torkel said, leaning against the wall. Just where Sean had leaned, Yana thought, the first day they had met. "Is that where everyone got their orders, Yana? Is that where you switched sides?"

"I haven't switched sides, Captain Fiske. I'm still a company woman, trying to help the company all I can."

Giancarlo raised both fists, and she stared back, daring him to carry through his threat.

"You both wanted me to see what I could find out. I did just that," Yana went on. "Not my fault I can't tell you what you want to hear. No one's told me what that is."

"Terce said you'd sold out," Giancarlo shouted. "He saw you go with the others, to plot treason."

"Where'd he see us go?" she asked, hoping her hunch was correct. "We were in the hall until daybreak and then most of us went to the hot spring to clean up."

"That fat woman, the one with all the cats, is the ringleader."

"Clodagh?" Yana allowed her incredulity and astonishment full rein and laughed. "If that's what Terce told you, Colonel, you must be the only one on Petaybee who doesn't know that he isn't playing with a full deck."

Just then the comm unit bleeped, and Torkel toggled it on. He listened, and in the next moment, disbelief, consternation, and finally horror swept across his face.

"Back! Back to the copter!" His arm swept them before him with great urgency. "Shuttle's crashed!"

Yana wondered from Torkel's reaction if his father, old Whittaker Fiske, had been due to arrive in that particular shuttle. Briefly she considered departing in the confusion. Ornery was up ahead of her in the corridor: she could slip away very easily right now. But she was certain she had weakened Giancarlo's accusation. She could do more if she hung about. Maybe, with a little luck, she might get Torkel to listen to what she was saying. And, if his father wasn't dead, maybe she could beat some sense in that old man's head. She would certainly prejudice the case she had been making by doing a flit right now. Petaybee ought to have one advocate in the company's court. Sauntering, she caught up with Ornery just as he realized she wasn't nearby.

"Miss me, big boy?" she asked, and walked past him, out to the waiting copter, where she slid in next to Giancarlo, leaving Ornery to compress his mass into the space between her and the copter's bulkhead. Ignoring the commotion and Torkel's demand for more information on the accident from the copter pilot, she was perhaps the only one looking out past Ornery toward the river, newly freed from ice thrall. She sat up straight, unable to believe her eyes, as a dark object that she first thought was a boulder turned into a seal and suddenly moved with astonishing speed and grace to slip into the water.

Now, how long had that been there? Had it actually been watching the house? Or was her imagination working overtime?

"The regeneration is all the more remarkable as it's so totally improbable," the medic was saying to his companion as they preceded Diego down the hospital corridor. "Never saw anything like this. And in such a short time. Woman was hacking her lungs out and not likely to live the year out."

The man beside him asked a question that Diego

could not hear, but he figured they had to be talking about Yana.

"No, no, can't be a transplant. I'd believe *that* more than a natural remission but there're no scars: not even a 'scope hole."

They turned to the right at the next corridor and he went on, thinking hard. Bunny had mentioned that Yana's health had improved since her arrival on Petaybee. He snorted. His father's sure hadn't. What if . . . And he halted in his tracks for a long moment. Then he was jolted out of his reverie by tremors underfoot—which reminded Diego of other half-understood remarks by Bunny. Why wasn't she around when she was needed? Why had she skitted out of the base as if something was after her?

More than anything now, he wanted to get Dad to Kilcoole and Clodagh. Petaybee had messed his dad up and now Petaybee could damn well cure him, like it had Yana!

It was, as Diego had hoped, slack time in the ward. Dad was sitting up in his chair, and dressed, which might have been a battle. Diego had stuffed another parka under his own, a real drag with the heat so high. Even his dad was sweating a bit. Diego got the wheelchair and, for the benefit of the other men in the ward, started his chatter.

"Dad, you wouldn't believe the weather out today, so I'm goin' to take you for a little stroll. See if we can't chase the cobwebs out of your head. Here now, easy, you just sit tight, huh?"

His father, as usual, didn't acknowledge his words with so much as a lifting of the eyes.

Diego wheeled him out of the ward, down the hall, and onto the ramp outside the infirmary.

For the first time he became acutely aware of how noisy it was at SpaceBase, of the change in the temperature and the air. Snocles that had once zipped down the snowy paths between buildings were racing their engines to escape being mired in slushy, melting snow. New vehicles, forklifts and track-cats, toiled to move the tons of equipment freshly delivered to the loading docks. One of the smaller track-cats was trying to shift a snocle entrenched in a snowbank.

Suddenly the ground bucked, the boardwalk collapsed at one end, and the wheelchair jerked from Diego's grasp and rolled down onto the ground.

Diego jumped down and caught it before it turned over and dumped his dad in the slush. People ran past him, ducking for cover, as another jarring crash from somewhere nearby shook the ground. When he looked up, he saw that both the track-cat and the mired snocle, engines still running, had been abandoned by their drivers. The track-cat was just a few yards away, but the wheelchair was stuck in the slush.

"Come on, Dad, you're going to have to help me," Diego said, his fingers fumbling to unstrap the wheelchair's safety belt. He placed his father's arm around his own shoulders and tried to haul him to his feet, but Francisco was dead weight. Diego looked from the aged, uncomprehending face to the alluring track-cat.

He changed tactics. He slid his father back into the chair and darted for the track-cat. It couldn't be much different from driving anything else, and he already knew how to drive hovercrafts and had watched Bunny drive her snocle. He released the tow chain and flung himself into the driver's seat, fumbling for the throttle.

After a little experimentation, he managed to get it into reverse and backed it over to where his father sagged in the chair. Leaving the snocle idling, he hopped down beside his dad, pulling the limp and unresponding arm back across his shoulders and attempting to hoist the older man up once more. This was hopeless! Dad just hung limply and could do nothing. In another minute the driver would return, or someone would pass by and see them, and then this perfect chance would be lost.

"What the hell are you trying to do?" someone said suddenly behind him.

Diego nearly jumped out of his skin, then recognized Steve's voice just as his father's partner stepped in front of him.

"I've been searching all over for you. I heard the explosions . . ."

"We're fine," Diego said hotly. "And we'd have been even finer if you hadn't caught us. I've got to get Dad out of here and I will somehow." He raised his chin defiantly and stared Steve straight in the eye.

Steve stared back, looking at Diego as if he were crazy; then all of a sudden he shrugged. "Okay, Diego, it's your call. But I go, too." And he picked Diego's dad up in his arms as if the stricken man were a baby and climbed up on the companion seat in the track-cat.

Diego scrambled into the driver's seat and, after a try or two, shifted the cat into forward gear and headed toward the village.

* * *

Bunny roared into the snocle shed. Adak was red in the face and waving his hands, arguing with a uniformed soldier, but she had no time to be polite about interrupting them.

"Adak, quick, we've got to rouse the village! The river's breaking up way early, and a lot of snocles are trapped on the river. Seamus fell into a crack bigger than a tree saving one of the drivers, and the others pulled him out."

"You run and tell Clodagh, Bunka. She'll let the village know, and I'll get on the radio for help."

"I told you, sir, I'm relieving you of duty," the soldier said.

"Good. Then you get on the radio," Adak said. "And I'll use this vehicle to try to rescue the stranded drivers."

"You can't do that, sir. That's a company-issue snocle, and not a private vehicle," the soldier said. "Besides, I don't know how to work this thing," he added, staring at the microphone.

"Fine, then I will, and you go help the drivers, but keep your snocle off the river and for pity's sake stop standing about arguing, man," Adak snapped.

Bunny grinned as, without further argument, the soldier climbed into the snocle and gunned it back down the tracks it had just made. Bunny sprinted out of the shed as Adak was pulling on his headphones and picking up his microphone.

Whatever he was saying over the radio was lost, however, because all over town the sled dogs had begun to howl with the plaintive screams of tortured souls. As Bunny passed by Lavelle's place on her way to Clodagh's, she was even more surprised at the antics of

Lavelle's dogs. Still tethered to their kennels, some were standing on the roofs and howling; others were lying on the ground, whining and baying in turn. Dinah, the lead dog, had become a frantic canine acrobat. She raced to the end of her chain, then back and forth and in frenzied circles until her lead was tangled in her legs and around her collar, and her neck would soon be rubbed raw from the friction. Bunny stopped to untangle her.

Poor Dinah. She really missed Lavelle, Bunny thought, but then, when she stopped to touch her, she got an urgent flash of hot, panting thought: *The boy, the boy, gotta go, gotta go, gotta get the boy, oh let me get him, gotta go, needs me, friend, friend, needs me, needs me needs me, gotta go, go go nowoooo . . .*

"Shh, Dinah, shhh," Bunny said. It didn't feel strange to be talking to a dog: she did it all the time. But it did seem odd that the dog seemed to be talking, too. "Diego's okay, Dinah. I just left him. Look, tell you what, you come with me and we'll find Clodagh, okay? Don't run off now when I unsnap you. Maloncys have had enough pain without losing you, too."

The more of Dinah she untangled, the more the dog calmed, tail wagging cooperatively; but when the dog was at last free, she snatched herself out of Bunny's grasp and bounded off toward the river.

"Holy cow, sir, where did that volcano come from?" the pilot asked Torkel as the copter sped toward the westerly crash-site coordinates provided by SpaceBase. They were still a good distance away when he pointed to the port side.

Since his comments had crackled through the headsets everyone was wearing, Yana looked, too. The fiery glow, the pall of the ash hanging in the air, was plainly visible. The air was still full of turbulence from the initial eruptions, and the lightweight copter shook and tossed about like a Ping-Pong ball.

Beneath them the ground rolled and fissured while ash and smoke pumped from the newly blown cone, born on one of the low mountains to the west. Visibility was poor with airborne smuts that were beginning to build up on the ground. Yana realized that some of the quaking she had felt back at the clinic must have come from this eruption.

Sandwiched as she was between Giancarlo and Ornery, Yana had a clear view between the pilot and Torkel, riding in copilot position. She wasn't at all reassured by the panorama. It looked like someone's terraforming gone wrong, and she thought they would be smarter to make tracks *from* rather than *to*.

As the copter drew nearer to the new volcano, a thin line of people emerged from the grayness beneath them and started waving frantically.

Torkel picked up the copilot's microphone. "This is Flying Fish. We have you in sight. Please identify yourselves. Is Dr. Whittaker Fiske with you? Over."

Rather to Yana's surprise, a response came back immediately. "Flying Fish, this is Team Boom Boom. We see you. We have two severely injured people in our party. That's a big Mayday. Please transport to SpaceBase pronto. Over."

The pilot clicked the transmission button on his own microphone. "This is Flying Fish, Boom Boom. Gotcha. We're setting down one-zero-zero meters due east of you. Over."

But Torkel clicked on the copilot's mike again before the stranded team could respond. "Boom Boom, this is Captain Torkel Fiske on the Flying Fish. Is Dr. Whittaker Fiske or any member of his team with you? Over."

"Negative, Cap'n Fiske. Petaybee blew its top about the time the shuttlecraft was landing. The turbulence from the volcano blew the craft off course and we had to initiate evacuation procedures before we could search for survivors. Sorry, sir. Over."

"Boom Boom, Flying Fish here. I'm sorry, too, but you'll have to hang on while we radio SpaceBase for another craft to retrieve you. We need to look for the survivors soonest."

"I can't fly into that, sir," the pilot said, glancing anxiously at Torkel. "It'd clog the jets. Let me pick up the wounded and get ground support."

"Finding my father is number-one priority," Torkel told the pilot in a command tone. Yana couldn't see his face. She wondered briefly if Torkel wanted to save his father because of his importance to the mission, or simply because Dr. Fiske *was* his father.

"Flying Fish, you can't leave us here. Our wounded are in bad shape and the rest of us are having trouble breathing from the ash. It's smothering in there, sir. Please, at least pick up the wounded. Boom Boom over."

The pilot, heedless of Torkel's commands to fly into the face of the billowing ash clouds, began circling to land. Yana saw Torkel reach for his sidearm, but the pilot had anticipated a problem.

"Sorry, sir," the pilot said, pointing a pistol at Torkel, "but you and the others will have to get out while we load the wounded. I'll call for another aircraft and some ground support for you as soon as we're in the air."

Ornery started to draw his weapon, but his attention was on the pilot, not on Yana. With a well-placed chop to his wrist she numbed his hand and relieved him of his weapon before either he or Giancarlo could react. She stuck the muzzle of the gun under Giancarlo's ear with one hand and extracted his sidearm from his holster with the other in a series of rapid movements that would have made her hand-to-hand combat trainer beam with pride. Ornery leaned menacingly toward her, but his numbed hand wasn't following orders. She shook her head and jabbed Giancarlo meaningfully with the gun.

"This section of the aircraft is secured, pilot," Yana said into her mouthpiece.

The pilot gave her a thumbs-up and said to Torkel, "I'll take your sidearm, too, sir. And just in case you gentlemen want to claim this is mutiny or anything, I'm sure superior-officer types like yourselves are aware that, by chain of command, I am the pilot of this craft. I am therefore the temporary CO. Thanks to you, ma'am."

He set the copter down and the stranded people surged toward it. He lifted a foot and kicked Torkel's door open. "Out you go, Cap'n. You there, Corporal, open your own damn door and disembark. You too, Colonel. Under the circumstances, we'll belay the ladies first shit."

When the others had jumped out of the copter and the pilot turned to watch her go, Yana saw that he was a warrant officer, a green-eyed, lean-jawed man with curly black hair, broad prominent cheekbones, and the slight tilt to his eyes she had begun to identify with people from Petaybee. His nametag said O'SHAY.

14

The track-cat lumbered down the riverbank and into the trees, surely and slowly—much too slowly to suit Diego. What if someone caught them and tried to take them back? What would happen to them then? Would they send Dad off-planet? Would they split them up? Would he be charged with the theft of the track-cat?

Hours seemed to pass as the vehicle rolled, slowly but staunchly, up small hillocks and forded freshets of water and melting snow running toward the river.

The track-cat was open to the air, too, so it was a good thing the day was exceptionally warm or they all might have frozen. Diego's dad lay inert against Steve, who clung tightly to his clothes to keep him from bouncing out of the vehicle.

The slushy, icy terrain was tough going even for the track-cat. Diego nursed it up a hill and down over the other side, only to lodge with one edge of the track in a ditch.

"Try rocking it," Steve hollered. "Forward, reverse, forward, reverse! Let it dig its own way out."

But the tracks could not bite or budge. Diego put it in neutral and climbed down to see exactly what the problem was. That was when he heard the noise from the other side of the trees and realized they weren't the only ones in trouble.

He pointed to show Steve where he was going and, leaving the vehicle running, trudged through the slush until he was clear of the trees.

The snowy road that the snocles had been so blithely using had become separated from the bank by a foot of open, steaming water. A soldier waved his parka to keep oncoming traffic from adding to the twenty or thirty vehicles already slewed crazily over what remained of the iced river. Beneath snocles and the feet of the drivers, huge steaming cracks yawned and pieces of ice broke off and floated in the blue-black water.

As Diego watched, the ice broke and a snocle shifted, unbalancing its ice raft so that it and one of the men both slid slowly into the river.

Groaning at this new emergency, Diego raced back to the track-cat just as Steve slid out from under Francisco and fastened the safety harness around the flaccid body.

"What the devil's going on over there?" Steve demanded as he sprinted toward Diego.

"The ice is breaking, and there's people stranded on it," Diego told him, panting and pointing urgently toward the river. "They need a lot of help and fast. We've got to let the village know right now."

But Steve had to see for himself and swept past Diego to crash through the brush and look at the river. Diego followed uncertainly, torn between the crisis on the river and his father's helpless body left alone in the snocle.

On the fracturing ice, maybe a half-dozen people now lay on their bellies, hands and feet linked, forming a human chain to fish for the man who had fallen into the river. He still had a perilous hold on the ice floe, which bobbed about, having tipped free of the snocle.

Steve stood poised on the bank for just a moment before he took a grip on Diego's shoulder. "Get your father to the village on the double, Diego, and send back help. I'll lend a hand here."

"But, the track-cat's stuck," Diego reminded him.

"Deal with it," Steve commanded in the same kind of gruff tone Diego had heard him use to talk to shipboard staff. Diego glared at him, resentfully. Steve, seeing his face, added, "That's our expedition team down there. See? The big fellow with the red bandanna? That's Sandoz Rowdybush. And I think the guy on the ice is Chas Collar. Your dad and I have worked with them for ten years. I'm not about to desert them."

"No, but you'll desert Dad."

Steve took a deep breath. "He's got you, too. Go back to the cat. If you can't get it moving, stick with your father till I can come for you. If you make it to the village, tell them this river is having a serious meltdown problem and we'll need all the help they can muster."

Not quite mollified but having no other option, Diego sloshed back to the track-cat. Sure the guys on the ice needed help, but what if help from SpaceBase came and found Diego's stuck track-cat? Then Dad would never get the help Diego was now convinced was his only hope. There were plenty of *other* guys out on the ice already—why did Steve think they needed him more than Dad did? Angrily, Diego kicked at the brush surrounding the track-cat—which gave him an idea on how to free the vehicle. He tore into the vehicle's locker, strewing a number of items on the floor until he found a hatchet, which he used to lob off enough branches to cushion the treads and give them some traction. Then he cleaned the mud out of the tracks as well as he could, all the while muttering to himself, as much to keep his own spirits up as to vent his frustration and anger.

Just about the time he had the cat ready to go, he had reached the conclusion that Steve had really had no other option but to go rescue his friends. On the other hand, there was no way Diego was going to wait tamely here. Not when he risked being found by the company corps, who might resent his appropriation of their vehicle. More importantly, they would take Dad back to the clinic, where *nothing* was being done for him, and Diego knew with a certainty he couldn't have explained even to himself that he *had* to get his dad to the village, and away from the company. The people in Kilcoole understood what had happened to his dad, and they could cure him. He *knew* they could. They had to.

He didn't realize how tense he had been until he broke the track-cat free of the mud. Hoping his spontaneous shout of relief had been inaudible among the shouts and cries coming from the river, he immediately changed directions, driving across the gully and back into the woods. Now he steered away from the riverbank, keeping to the trees, avoiding anyone who might be struggling ashore and also avoiding surveillance by airborne rescue parties.

Half an hour later, with the light beginning to wane, he was far enough from the river that, when the ice finally completely gave way, all he heard was a dull roar, like a far-off crowd cheering some sporting event. And he heard that only because the engine of the track-cat, which had been left running day and night since the vehicle had been commissioned, had run out of fuel.

He stopped and listened to the distant roar, tasted smoke and ash on the air mingling with the released ozone smell of open water, felt the ground trembling beneath the track-cat as if it, too, would break open at any time. Birds screeched through the trees as if crying warnings.

His father's inert body looked uncomfortable in the harness that was keeping it upright on the seat beside him. Diego tenderly rearranged the passive limbs into less grotesque positions. He didn't think his father could have been hurt by the rough journey, but he really hated to see his dad, once so athletic and fit, collapsed like a disconnected android.

With no more fuel, the vehicle was useless. Diego let out a deep sigh. Despite his detours, he couldn't be that far from the village at this point. He glanced around, sniffing and finally noticing the odd smells in the air: acrid, oily, definitely nonregulation. Usually by now the air started to chill off, but it was still as warm as it had been all day. Strapped as he was in the seat, Dad wouldn't be in any real danger from chilling for at least another half hour, Diego estimated. He reached for the coat he had removed during his exertions to get the track-cat moving again and tucked it around his father, patting it in place, remembering his father doing the same service for him when he was smaller. Maybe he shouldn't leave his father here. There *were* wild animals on Petaybee, wild animals strong enough to break into the track-cat, maybe. Would they be more afraid of the machine smell than they would be hungry? Suddenly

Diego wasn't sure he could take the risk. Not with his father so helpless.

But he couldn't just sit here, halfway to nowhere. Fretting more than ever, he turned to rummage through the track-cat's locker, hoping there might be something useful in it. There was nothing: nothing to use to build a fire, no emergency rations, not even a canteen of water, but then the cat had been used around the Space-Base, where such supplies had always been at hand. It wasn't as if the motor pool had anticipated the cat being stolen for a cross-country escape. Totally demoralized, Diego flopped down on the driver's seat, wondering *how* he was going to cope now. If Steve did keep his promise to come after him, he wouldn't *be* there anymore. Would Steve be able to come looking for them? What could he do? He'd only wanted to *help* his father!

As if to seal his depression, the first keening howl sounded through the evening.

Bunny didn't have to alert the village: the dogs' wailing did it for her. People poured out of their houses to see what was wrong. She didn't have to tell them the river had broken up. Anyone born on Petaybee and raised with Kilcoole's long winters could smell breakup in the air, could feel the change in the pressure, and if that wasn't enough, the ice melting from the roofs and the slush seeping through the soft soles of their boots made it all too evident.

Bunny ran up to Lavelle's door first. Liam opened it. "Liam, the river's breaking early and people in snocles are trapped."

"The planet take them, then." Liam shrugged angrily and started to shut the door in her face.

"Seamus is out there helping, and Dinah's got loose and ran off toward the river. Please, Liam, if you won't help, at least spread the word!" When he reached for his parka on the hook by the door, she caught his hand, grinning. "You don't need it. Come *on*."

She didn't wait to see if he followed but ran straight to her Aunt Moira's. Moira and her three oldest sons, Nanuk, Tutiak, and Tim, were already hitching up Charlie's dogs while Maureen and 'Naluk, the oldest girls, carried blankets and other provisions to the sleds. "Auntie Moira, the river's breaking up—"

"I know, Bunka. Don't just stand there! Help us! Seamus is out there on that river."

"He's okay for now, Auntie. The soldiers pulled him out. But they all need help."

Tutiak growled at her. "What do you think we're trying to do?"

"No need to be rude to your cousin, Tutiak," Moira said, slapping at him. "He's sorry, Bunka. We're taking Charlie's dogs to go help now. Okay with you?"

"Fine," Bunny said. "I have to go tell Clodagh."

"Hmph," Tim grunted. "As if anyone ever needed to tell Clodagh anything."

Bunny paused at Aisling and Sinead's, first noticing that the dogs were missing from the yard, then that the long daylight was finally waning. The door opened on her first rap to reveal Aisling wearing her waterproof breakup boots, with her arms full of blankets.

"Breakup's come early, Aisling, and—"

"I know."

"How?"

"Alice B heard from the other dogs. Sinead and the dogs are on the way."

"It's getting too slushy for dogs even. We're going to need the curlies."

"Have you asked Adak to call Sean?"

Bunny felt something inside her wrench suddenly. "No! I— Aisling, the soldiers kept Yana. I think Sean's in trouble."

"Warn Clodagh," Aisling said. "I'll tell anybody else who hasn't figured it out yet and meet you there."

With a wave, Bunny ran on through the dusk to Clodagh's house. Clodagh was holding a lamp when she opened the door. None of the cats were in sight; then one appeared, taking immediate advantage of the open door to brush past Bunny and jump up on the table, where it began mewing piteously.

"Marduk says Yana hasn't been home to feed him," Clodagh translated.

Breathless, Bunny collapsed in a sprawl on Clodagh's bed. "She was goin' to try to reason with Captain Fiske for us, but it mustn't have worked. Clodagh, the river's breaking—"

Clodagh nodded with some satisfaction. "Of course it is. The river ice has been SpaceBase's quickest connecting route to us. The planet's protecting us—and itself."

"Seamus almost drowned trying to help one of the soldiers," Bunny said, without asking how Clodagh knew what the planet knew, or was trying to do. She just did, that was all. She always did.

"That Seamus," Clodagh said, shaking her head. "Of course he would try to help. Is he okay?"

"He's out on the ice with the others. They're all still stranded. And not only that, Clodagh, but when I stopped by Lavelle's to untangle Dinah from her harness, Dinah—well, it was like she *talked* to me. She was all upset about some boy. And that has to be Diego, but *he* should be safe at the SpaceBase. What are we going to do, Clodagh? Everything's coming to pieces." This last came out of Bunny almost like the howl of one of the dogs. That made her realize that she was very tired and keyed up to the highest possible pitch. She would give anything to be able to sleep for a week—if only someplace felt safe enough to sleep in! Even Clodagh seemed different somehow, her eyes glittering and her customary expressions underlain with agitation and a hard anger that had nothing to do with Bunny. Clodagh, Bunny felt, was actually glad about the river and wouldn't have minded if everyone—well, not Seamus, but everyone else—had drowned. Bunny suddenly realized that she, too, wouldn't mind if they all drowned, if all of SpaceBase suddenly sank into the planet and disappeared and the company moon vanished from the sky. They were bound and determined to ruin Petaybee. Everything Bunny cared about and counted on was changing, coming apart the way the ice, usually as much to be depended upon as the ground this time of year, had broken away beneath her.

Even Clodagh's house no longer felt like the haven of comfort and reassurance it had been for Bunny ever since her parents had died and she realized she could no longer live among her cousins.

"Bunka," Clodagh said, touching her shoulder.

"Why couldn't they leave us alone, Clodagh? Why couldn't they leave Petaybee alone? Did they have to ruin everything?"

"They've ruined nothing yet, Bunka. Oh, they set a

few charges about here and there, and sent soldiers out to the mountains. But until they stop and pay attention, they're not likely to learn anything about Petaybee worth the knowin'. And meantime, the planet has means to protect itself."

"Clodagh, have you ever *been* to SpaceBase?" Bunny asked. It hadn't occurred to her before that she had never seen Clodagh outside the village except for a time or two on journeys to Sean's house. Clodagh couldn't possibly understand the power the company *had*.

"Of course not, *alanna*, now why would I want to go there?"

"They have thousands of soldiers there right now. Yana says they mean to evacuate us. By force! Just without a by-your-leave make us all go into space someplace. Then they'll keep blowing up things on Petaybee until they get all the minerals and stuff they want. Clodagh, I've seen the shuttles and the ships. I know lots of the soldiers. They *can do it* if they want to. They own Petaybee."

"Nonsense, Bunka. Nobody owns Petaybee but Petaybee."

Bunny was about to argue the point when something landed with a heavy thud on the roof.

Marduk, the cat who had been living with Yana, stood on his hind feet and pedaled his front paws at the ceiling, chittering and mewing as if looking for a rafter to jump onto.

From outside the house came a sound like a well caving in, a roar with a deep echo to it. Bunny recognized it at once as the voice of one of Sean's big cats.

She, Clodagh, and Marduk were at the door all at once, but before they could go outside, a huge shape landed softly in front in the doorway. The black and white bewhiskered face of the big cat regarded them quizzically.

Marduk, far from being frightened by the larger feline, stepped forward to rub noses with it. Each brushed scent glands on the side of his face into the other cat's fur.

Clodagh stood away from the door, and the big cat padded inside, leapt to the bed, and circled about on her handmade quilt to make a nest for himself. Marduk hopped on top of the larger creature's back and chirruped autocratically. Clodagh produced a pair of thawed fish and a pan of water for the cats to lap. While they ate, Clodagh sat beside them on the edge of the bed and stroked their backs.

She crooned especially to the big cat, and it looked up from its meal with narrowed eyes and purred thunderously back at her. Marduk, annoyed at being left out, butted her hand with his head before he continued to eat.

"Do you suppose it knows where Sean and Yana are?" Bunny asked. "When I petted Dinah, I felt as if she was talking to me."

"Come here, Bunka," Clodagh said, and put Bunny's hand on the cat's head. "Have you an answer for Bunka, Nanook?"

Why else would I bother coming? the cat asked her in a velvety, rumbling voice.

The words weren't spoken; but Bunny heard them nevertheless, inside her head, the way she had heard Dinah's. Nanook's diction was much better than the dog's.

Clodagh regarded Bunny speculatively.

"It talked to me," Bunny told her, blinking rapidly.

"This cat is a he, not an it," Clodagh told her. "He talked to you because you can understand him. Marduk, also, is a he. In fact, on our whole planet, there are no its. Some things have no gender, but they are not without names. It's only polite to learn those names."

Bunny shrugged. "Well, I guess I knew that." She had played with the big cat since he had been a kitten, actually, every time she had gone to visit Sean. She petted him again. "Sorry, Nanook, I didn't mean to hurt your feelings."

Having cleaned his chops of fish residue, Nanook began to tidy up the white fur of his chest. The house suddenly shook, and from under the counter came the sound of crashing glass. Marduk jumped down, and Nanook stretched beneath Bunny's hand.

Sean's gone swimming, he said. *Yana came with soldiers, but their chop-chop bird squawked and the soldiers took her away again. They do not have good feelings for her. They have even less good feeling about Sean. They did not like those of us who live with Sean and tried to find us, to take us away with them. We were not found. Then the ground shakes and I smell smoke-that-is-not-cooking. And shedding time is early. What are people* doing *to our place?*

The last thought was accompanied by a plaintive roar that sent a blast of fishy breath into Bunny's face.

Diego found a sturdy branch, though he knew it wouldn't be much good as protection against wild animals. Hefting it in his hand made him feel somewhat less vulnerable, however. He could hear the river roaring, along with a crunching and grinding of the ice that set his teeth on edge. He prayed Steve would be done with his rescuing of other people and remember he had a duty to rescue his own family. Darkness was closing in.

The distant howling picked up again and became separate sounds: keening, howling, and plain crying, like the ghost of an all-too-familiar memory. Diego glanced over at his father. For a moment he thought he had seen a flicker in his dad's eyes, but the older man sagged against the harness as limply as ever.

Another howl, much closer now, was answered by several others, still distant. Diego swung his stick like a baseball bat, placing himself between the track-cat and the hostile woods. As an afterthought, he reached inside and switched on the lights, grateful that the battery wasn't drained yet. Then the lights picked up a ring of shining eyes in the woods, closing in on him.

The howling took on a triumphant note, and suddenly something dashed from the woods and straight at him.

Cocking the stick to make his first blow count as much as it could, Diego released it at the top of his swing as the lights picked up the red fur of the dog. Dinah crushed him against the grill of the track-cat with the weight of her body. She licked his face and the hands he tried to protect his face with and whined her relief.

He couldn't have said how he knew the dog was Dinah instead of any other, except that Dinah had done this sort of thing before. And behind her came answering whines and howls and a man's voice crying "Whoa! Down, dogs."

Diego freed himself from Dinah's embrace in time to

see a sled pulled by four dogs break through the trees into the lights of the track-cat.

The man driving the sled wore no coat and frowned when he saw Diego, but Dinah ran frantically between the cat and the sled until the man relaxed.

"You're the boy who was with my mother, aren't you?" the man asked.

"Your mom was Lavelle?" The guess wasn't hard, with Dinah bouncing between them.

"That's right."

"Then please help us. I have to get my dad to Clodagh's. He's been dying at SpaceBase like Lavelle died when they took her off-planet."

The wind blew and the planet shook, whether in fear or anger or both Bunny couldn't tell, but inside Clodagh's house a phenomenon was taking place that Bunny would have only partially understood the day before.

A taciturn Liam Maloney, whined and howled into submission by Dinah and the other sled dogs, had delivered Diego Metaxos and his father to Clodagh's just after dark. Now Diego nursed a cup of tea, while his father sat tied into Clodagh's rocker.

Liam had returned home to feed the dogs, although Dinah had whined and made her peculiar "oooo ooo" sound when pulled away from Diego. Bunny wondered what she would hear if she stroked her. She wondered if Diego could hear Dinah yet, but thought he probably couldn't. After all, she had lived fourteen years on Petaybee, and she had always known communication existed between certain aspects of the planet and its people. Come to that, she had communicated with the planet like everyone else during the hot-springs interfaces at the end of every latchkay.

Everyone knew that *some* people, like Clodagh and Sean, could talk to most of the animals. Others, like Lavelle, could certainly understand their own lead dogs. Bunny had always talked to the animals, all of them, having been brought up to think it was only polite to do so. But today was the first time the animals had ever struck up what could be called a conversation with her. Maybe it was because she had bonded with her snocle instead of to dogs or cats or curlies, or maybe Dinah was just an unusually telepathic dog. Anyway, although Dinah was evidently tuned in to Diego, the dog had talked to Bunny first, and underlying all the worry and trouble, Bunny felt a marvelous elation about that.

The big cat, Nanook, had bounded past her as she held the door open for Liam and Diego to carry Francisco Metaxos into Clodagh's house. Bunny had caught a flutter of thought, *Wonder what's happening out there now . . . ,* as the cat passed by.

Darkness blanked the windows and the wind blew fiercely, carrying the scent of ash and fresh water, thawing earth and smoke. It howled around the house like a team of hungry dogs and rattled the roof. Inside, the stove kept the house almost stiflingly warm as it kept Clodagh's caribou stew simmering in her biggest pot.

Diego was wolfing down his second bowlful and Bunny making short work of hers while Clodagh stirred fresh ingredients into the pot.

"Want to have enough for when people come in off the river," she said. "Some of them are bound to stop by."

The cozy domesticity of the scene was reinforced by

Clodagh's cats, who had returned from whatever business they had been about when Bunny had first arrived.

Diego had one on his lap, while another, Bearcat, napped on Bunny's knees. And, of course, one of the more enterprising members of the pride twined around Clodagh's ankles as she cooked. Marduk and the remaining five seemed fascinated by Francisco Metaxos.

Marduk sat on the scientist's lap, kneading and purring and gazing raptly through narrowed eyes up into his face. Another cat sat on the scientist's shoulders, its rust-striped cheek and white whiskers snuggled against the man's right ear, front paws pedaling his shoulders while the ringed tail curled possessively around Metaxos's neck from the other side. Two more cats flanked Metaxos on either arm of the chair, licking his fingers and hands and grooming him, while another pair alternately wove about his feet and settled across them like house slippers.

You'd have thought the man was made of catnip the way the silly animals were carrying on, Bunny reflected. Whether it was coincidence or communication, at the moment the thought formed she drew an indignant dig from the cat in her lap.

"Can I have a bowl of stew for Dad, please, Clodagh?" Diego asked. "But maybe it'd be better—" He broke off and looked at Clodagh's back imploringly.

She turned and gave him an impassive half smile. "Yes?"

"If you'd feed him? Bunny says you're good at taking care of people and things and, to tell the truth, he never eats very well for me."

Bunny, who had watched Diego feed his father a couple of times, suspected that half the problem was that

Diego found spoon-feeding his once-brilliant and vigorous father a disgusting process. She knew it made him sad and angry: that would be the way she would feel, she knew. Unnerving, too, to have to shove food into the mouth of a grown man as if he were an infant.

Clodagh regarded Diego with understanding and sympathy. She looked at the bowl she had filled and then handed it to him with a kind smile.

"No, it's better if you do it, son. Someplace inside your da he still knows you and loves you. If he'll eat for anybody, it'll be you."

"I guess so," Diego said dispiritedly, and pulled a chair opposite his father. Bunny noticed he was careful not to disturb any cats, though Marduk raised a paw as if to snag the spoon carrying food to Metaxos's mouth.

Grimacing, she looked away as the spoon neared the man's lips: that was the disgusting part, when stuff fell off the spoon and down the chin and had to be wiped off before it messed up the shirt. At least Diego didn't have to actually pry open his father's lips to get the food in. But, as she was turning her head, Diego suddenly said, "Hey, Dad. All right! That was great. Try another bite."

When Bunny looked back at them, Diego had a grin of satisfaction on his face: his father, eyes still dull, face otherwise slack, was chewing the soft diced bits in the stew. Encouraged, Diego replenished the spoon with more bits; the cat on his father's shoulders sniffed as the spoon passed his nose, but didn't try to snag it. Dr. Metaxos's eyes even looked a little more focused when he chewed, Bunny thought. Food was the best thing he could concentrate on right now; maybe he was even tasting it. She hoped so: it was a shame to waste a good

Clodagh stew on someone who couldn't appreciate the fine taste of it.

Just then the door burst open and Aisling swirled in like a one-woman typhoon, followed closely by Steve Margolies. Through the door behind Steve, Bunny saw Sinead talking into the ear of one of the curly-coat horses that stood around about the house.

"Clodagh," Aisling called cheerfully, "Sinead and the curlies did some right fine towing work at the river, getting snocles out of trouble. Everyone's out now and on their way back here. We left all the snocles at Adak's, but he's so busy, I thought I'd see if you had something cooked up for him to eat. He's going to be there all night. And it's not just the river breaking up early, either. You know all that smoke we've been seein' and the ground shaking? Well, that's from a volcano eruption over by where Odark found Lavelle and Siggy with your lad here and his da." She grinned at the expressions of disbelief and amazement. "And the miners and engineers and company men that went out that way to start work, they got caught right under that volcano." She grinned so broadly at the effect of that news that she had to lick her lips.

Of them all, Clodagh didn't seem surprised.

"*And*, there's a shuttle down, almost right on top of the volcano, to hear Adak tell it, and the survivors yelling like stuck pigs for help. Well, that smooth red-headed captain who was sniffin' after Yana took her and Giancarlo and some other soldier to go see if anyone got out of the shuttle. They made it to the miners and then"—Aisling's expression changed to indignation—"that captain wanted to leave behind the injured miners and all, right where they were being bombarded with ash and hot mud, so's he could search for the shuttle. Can you believe the man's sand that he'd abandon wounded, his own people, mind you? And crazy enough to want to make a copter fly into all that heat and ash and smoke? But as luck would have it, and such good luck I can scarcely believe myself, the pilot was Rick, you remember Orla O'Shay's oldest boy that went into the service fifteen years ago? He and Yana Maddock made the captain and the colonel and the other bloke with them get out and load the wounded. He radioed back for a pickup for them and the other survivors, and Adak was just talking to him as we came in. Sinead says she has it from her sources that Sean's gone missin', too, and she's *that* worried about himself and Yana. The O'Shay boy says Yana disarmed the colonel and his lad neat as you please and not a moment too soon. Dr. Steve here wants to rustle up some transport. He feels he's got to get out there to eyeball that volcano while it's growing."

She paused to take a deep breath and then, with a grin, added, "Seems like Petaybee's not supposed to have volcanoes in that spot."

"Bunka, take a bowl of stew over to Adak and see if there's any more news, will you?" Clodagh said in a tone that was not a request.

"Sure, Clodagh," Bunny said.

"You're the one I'm to ask about transport?" Steve Margolies asked, looking perplexedly at the big woman.

"Eat first," Clodagh said hospitably, and handed him a bowl before filling a bigger one for Bunny to take to Adak. "You need good food after that stuff at the river, and for anything else you want to do."

Steve dragged a tired hand across his face as if he

had only just remembered an essential like eating. He accepted the bowl and found a spot to sit, then took a good look around the room.

"Frag!" Steve Margolies exclaimed, his eyes wide with astonishment. "Look at Frank. He's *petting* that cat."

"Sure, it's fine exercise for his fingers," Clodagh was saying matter-of-factly. "Everyone knows animals are good for distressed folk."

Bunny was grinning, too, as she carried the stew bowl out the door on her way to Adak.

Despite the lid to keep the heat in, she had to walk carefully to keep from spilling the stew. It would keep hot long enough, however, for her to make a few short stops on her way to Adak's. She slipped in at her own place, where she traded her soaked and stiffened hide boots for her breakup muckers and put on a kettle of food for her dogs. She looked in at Moira's window. The cousins and the dogs must have come and gone again, for Seamus was sitting large as life by the stove, shoveling Moira's soup and bread into his face. Moira was busy cooking. Now that Bunny knew that Seamus had made it back okay, she could continue with an easy heart.

Passing Maloney's again, she was greeted by Dinah's unhappy howl. She would pet and reassure the dog on the way back. Right now, not only was Adak's stew cooling but also a clever dog like Dinah might try to have first grabs at it. So she simply clucked reassuringly at the dog and kept going.

Six or seven snocles sat parked outside Adak's shed, but they had not been cleaned, serviced, or fueled, and were still covered with melting slush, water, and mud.

Inside, Adak, headphones over his ears and microphone at his lips, was hunched over the radio. Bunny slid into a chair beside him and shoved the stew in his direction. He looked a little startled to see it appear in front of him, but accepted it without question. Lines were etched deeply into his face and his eyes looked hollow, but his whole body was taut with nervous energy. Early breakup and a new volcano a-borning might be considered catastrophes, but the end result was that today had produced the most excitement Kilcoole had seen since the first expeditionary team had been lost in a tsunami down on the southern edge of the ice pack.

"Well, I'm sorry about that, SpaceBase," Adak was saying with a certain amount of agitation, "but until the next hard freeze, the snocles aren't reliable as transportation for a trip clear out there. Over." He managed to spoon some stew into his mouth. "Oh, sure and they'll run on the snow, that's not the problem. The problem is the rivers, you see, and if you don't believe me, you can ask yer lads as got fished out of them today. Over.

"Is that so? Well, I'm sorry to hear that, too. It's a shame about Dr. Fiske's shuttle crashin' and to be sure we *do* understand the urgency and all. Over." He hurriedly ate some more.

"No, of course flyin' over it is impossible if the ash and smoke are as thick as you say. My suggestion would be to get yourself some of them crane-copters and have them hoist the snocles to the edge of the affected area and then see if the snocles'll drive at all in the ash. You're still going to be havin' the same problem with slushy going as we have here though. Over.

"The rivers of course, man! Petaybee has more rivers and lakes than you can shake a stick at, and who knows which ones are thawin' this early? Normally the high country would stay frozen longer, but a volcano, now, that's a chancy thing. I'm not a scientific man like yerself, but it seems to me such a thing would warm the country considerable. Over.

"Like I said, air-hoist a snocle to where O'Shay picked up the wounded. I'll wager Yana Maddock can drive it even if your two officer lads don't know how. Over.

"They *what*? When? How'd you find out? Uh—very well, over.

"Yes, then, I do see the urgency. Look here, I'll try to get some of the local folk on it in the meantime. The point is, machinery just doesn't do awfully well in some of the conditions we have hereabouts right now. That's why we use animals. I'll get back to you. Right. Over."

"What," Bunny asked impatiently, "was that about Yana?"

"Well, seems O'Shay radioed for help as soon as he was airborne and the other copter passed him at the halfway point. He was almost to SpaceBase when they radioed back that they were bringing in the rest of the survivors, but that Fiske, Giancarlo, and Corporal Levindoski overpowered Major Maddock and forced her to go with them into the flow area to look for Dr. Fiske. The higher-ups are that frantic to be after them, but the ash would clog any machines they got and it's not that good for the beasts either."

"I'll bet the curlies can do it, if anything can," Bunny said staunchly. "They were bred for sand and snow back on Earth, and they can close off their nostrils if they need to, and their eyes have a protective lid."

"Maybe so," Adak said, taking a slurp of stew. "Hard to figure why anybody'd want to risk a good curly to go after some company bigwig, though."

15

Gun in hand, Yana held off Giancarlo, Torkel, and Ornery until the wounded were loaded. Torkel had relented enough to help, while Ornery and Giancarlo stood by, glaring malevolently at Yana. The last thing O'Shay did before he slammed the door shut was to fling out a red-and-white-striped rectangle. Picking it up, Yana identified it as an emergency rations pack and blessed the pilot's thoughtfulness. The four remaining survivors of the expedition were suffering from shock, and the high-energy rations would do much to revive them.

"If he thinks that's going to save him from a court martial, he's got another thing coming." Giancarlo snorted as the copter lifted off. To Ornery-eyes he barked, "Don't just stand there, Levindoski. Commandeer that pack. We'll need those supplies on our search and rescue of Dr. Fiske and his party."

"Uh-uh," Yana said. "Not so fast, Colonel. You're not commandeering shit just yet. These folks need to chow down first." She pointed to the nearest survivor, a gaunt-faced man whose pocket nametag was half burned off. "Connelly?" she said, reading what was left. "Why don't you distribute? You'll want the yellow ones—they'll replace electrolytes and boost your energy levels."

Keeping one eye on her and the gun she held, Connelly retrieved the sack. With a pang of pity Yana saw that he was sufficiently fatigued so that it took him three yanks to break the tabs, and half the bars and drink packets spewed over the ground. She stepped back and motioned for the others to help.

"Wait!" Torkel cried with a tinge of desperation. Yana turned to him. His eyes, watching the survivors scoop up the supplies, reflected a struggle with his emotions for the sort of control and charm that had always been a hallmark of his command personality. "Yana, please be reasonable. You know we're going to *need* those . . ."

"Torkel, if I was you I'd shut the frag up," Yana said, waving the gun at him. "You didn't exactly cover yourself with glory trying to take the copter away from the wounded and you're not improving things by trying to prevent the distribution of emergency rations to these survivors. As for me, I ate a while back."

Connelly, who had been handing the packets out to the others, contemptuously threw four at Torkel's feet. "Sorry, buddy. Didn't know you'd missed your bloody lunch."

"It's not that," Torkel said, wisely leaving the packets alone for the moment. "She's distorting this incident to make us look bad in your eyes, hoping you'll aid her."

"Which you are now doing by eating those rations," Giancarlo said sternly. "If you value your careers, you'll listen to Captain Fiske here and cooperate with our mission."

"Careers!" said another man, whose ashy parka bore

the name "O'Neill." "Sure now, Colonel darlin'," he went on, his face angry, his words soft, and the Irish in his accent dangerously broad, the way the Petaybean accent became when mocking the stupidity of higher-ups. "We're that worried about our careers havin' just outrun yer volcano there. Seems to me that if it's our lives we're after valuin', the dama's the one to be listenin' to." He deliberately and defiantly chewed and swallowed a large hunk of his ration bar.

"Colonel Giancarlo, please," Torkel said. "I know you mean well but you're playing into her hands."

Watching his face, in which the desperation she had seen before was now suppressed, she saw him begin to calculate the effect of each word and attitude on the survivors. He was smart enough to know that he had alienated them initially, and smart enough to know that if he wanted to regain control of the situation he was going to have to have them on his side. "Folks, you'll have to forgive Colonel Giancarlo. He doesn't mean to sound callous but he's absolutely right. Our mission is one of the utmost priority and this woman has sided with the Petaybean insurgents creating this catastrophe!"

His arm swept across the devastation behind the survivors, the pulsing mud in the valley at their heels, the glow of the volcano visible even through the ashy miasma cloaking the area.

"Right," Connelly said, "one skinny little woman, with or without help, caused a volcano? I'm a mining engineer, Captain. Pull the other one."

The third man coughed both to clear his lungs and to get attention. "They might have set strategic charges that *triggered* the volcano."

"Th-that's right," the last survivor, a woman, stammered. Until she had eaten her ration bar, she had been trembling so violently that she had looked on the verge of convulsions; now her fearful glance centered on the presence of the authorities as represented by Torkel, Giancarlo, and Ornery. "Teams have disappeared here before. It can't all be natural."

"Damned right it's not," Torkel said, following up his advantage. "We were interrogating Maddock here, trying to get information from her to head off this disaster, when it blew up in our faces. Meanwhile, my own father, Dr. Whittaker Fiske, was coming to join a team in your vicinity to suss out the situation."

"In case you don't know who Dr. Fiske is," Giancarlo put in, "he's assistant chairman of the board, direct descendant of the man who developed the terraforming process that transformed this rock into a viable planet, and is the company's top expert on the environmental development and stability of all of Intergal's terraformed holdings."

"He's the one man who can save this project and everybody involved with it, which is why you *must* help me find him," Torkel said, adding with a catch in his voice that could have even been genuine, "and he's my father. That's why we tried to supersede your need to move your wounded and effect your own rescue. Another copter would have been here for you immediately, of course, but this woman"—he jerked his thumb at Yana—"took advantage of the pilot's humanitarian instincts to turn the situation against us. But if one of you will guide me to where the shuttle came down, she won't be able to stop me from going in after my dad and saving this rock."

"Okay, who's it going to be?" Giancarlo demanded. "We need to move here and move fast. You heard Captain Fiske. We need volunteers to take us to the crash site."

"Say what?" O'Neill asked, not believing what he heard. "We come out of that"—he waved to the steaming valley—"by the skin of our teeth and you're after us to risk our necks again? You're bloody nuts!"

The third man just shook his head tiredly. His shoulders were stooped under the weight of a variety of cameras and other instrument packages, as well as under the weight of the terror and pain he had just lived through. The straps kept Yana from seeing all of his name but "Sven" was part of it.

Torkel shook his head firmly, staring O'Neill down. "No. I'm not nuts. I'd never ask you to risk yourselves except that this is absolutely vital. It is imperative to the well-being of this planet and the personnel on it that we find my father with all possible dispatch."

"Find him? In that?" Sven demanded in a voice rasped harsh by smoke.

"There's no alternative, man!" Torkel was getting agitated as he looked from Sven to Connelly and then to the other two, the stocky O'Neill and the stammering woman. "You did see the shuttle go down, right?"

Sven and Connelly both nodded.

"Well, where did it go down? Point me out the direction from here. I've coordinates, but they're only good in a copter."

Sven gave Connelly a long look and then, angling himself, he faced in a west-northwest position. "Near as I can remember it. We were scrambling ourselves by then."

"Why bother?" O'Neill asked, a trace of exasperation in his voice. "Captain, the shuttle was trying to land just as the volcano blew. The shock wave hit it like a ton of fraggin' bricks. I saw the craft knocked out of the sky with my own eyes. There's nobody could survive that." He obviously felt his own survival was miracle enough for one day.

"That's not true!" Torkel said, his voice suddenly wild with denial as he grabbed O'Neill's coat front and began shaking him. "My father has to have survived, you bloody idiot!" Then he realized what he was doing and loosed O'Neill with one more plea. "Don't discourage me, man. Help me, for pity's sake."

Yana had been watching this, also making certain that neither Giancarlo nor Ornery made any sudden moves toward her. She thought maybe Torkel's emotional display was genuine, but the man was devious—it could as well be a diversionary tactic. She couldn't take any chances. "Chill out, Torkel," she said. "These people are exhausted and in shock. They're not going to be fool enough to risk their lives going back in there."

But if Torkel was acting, he was doing it with enough conviction that he ignored her waving the gun. "You didn't actually see the volcanic blast destroy the shuttle, did you?" he demanded of O'Neill.

"No," O'Neill said tiredly. "It was intact when the force of the blast blew it off course."

"Ah, but it blew it away from the path of the debris, right?"

"Well, yes. It was debris, too, as far as the volcano was concerned," O'Neill told him.

"But there could have been survivors of the crash?" Connelly, who Yana sensed was slowly being convinced by Torkel's insistence, told him in a weary but not unsympathetic voice, "That was three *hours* ago, Captain, and that volcano's been raining down and spitting mud out . . ."

Torkel heard the sympathy in the man's voice and pounced on it. "Will you guide me?"

But he had pushed too hard. Connelly withdrew and favored him with a disbelieving look, shaking his head. "The only one I'm guiding is me, out of here, when the copter gets back."

"Listen up, Connelly, and the rest of you, too," Giancarlo said. "Captain Fiske is not just any military captain. As son of Boardmember Fiske, he also holds the position of ranking executive on this planet at this time. Failure to cooperate with him and with this mission will have serious repercussions on your career."

"So," Connelly said, "will death. I'm not sticking around here waiting for that mountain to blow again for the *chairman* of the board. Besides, in these flying conditions"—he waved his hand off to the north—"no copter, any copter, would stay airborne for more than ten, maybe fifteen minutes." He snorted. "You'd do better using your feet."

When Giancarlo started toward him angrily, Yana spoke up again.

"I wouldn't, were I you, Colonel," she said. "They've done enough just making it here. And you both should know," she added, flicking a glance at Torkel, "how useless it would be to fly a copter in there!"

"Then, by all that's holy"— Abandoning his frantic make-'em-see-reason attitude, Torkel drew himself up into a noble-against-adversity stance. —"I'll make it on foot. Your packs there," he said, pointing to the pile slowly accumulating a cover of ash, "can be replaced at company expense when you get back to base. They won't be of much future use to *you* considering their present condition, but I would very much appreciate being able to scrounge what I need from them."

Connelly and Sven exchanged looks and shrugged. The woman, with an anxious look at Yana's gun hand, darted over and extracted a small sack from the pile, skittering back to the protection of her colleagues.

"Might as well. There's not that much there," Connelly said, "and if the company'll make good . . ."

"Of course the company will make good," Giancarlo snapped. "Your equipment was company issue to begin with. Who else do you think would replace it?"

"I promise you it won't be debited from your pay," Torkel said quickly. "And any personal effects you've lost will be replaced, as well. The company takes care of its own."

O'Neill flicked him a resentful glance. "The way you were going to take care of the wounded?"

"Frag it all, O'Neill, I'm not some kind of a monster," Torkel said, even as he gestured for Giancarlo and Ornery to help him collect the packs. "I told O'Shay to radio for another bird for your wounded and for yourselves. A few minutes would have made no difference to them. You'll all get out safely. My father, and the crew of that shuttle, are still out there in that inferno."

Yana couldn't believe Torkel's gall, trying to guilt-trip the survivors. He sure was a company man: give with one hand, shuffle the shells, and take with the other! But she had no objections to him going after his father, as long as he didn't force anyone else to do it, too.

"Knowing how important it is, won't even one of you guide us?" he implored one more time as the air began throbbing with the sound of an approaching copter.

"Captain," Connelly said, "we really couldn't help you. All landmarks will have been destroyed by now, and none of us saw where your father's craft actually crashed. You've got the compass and the coordinates of where it was originally supposed to land." He scanned the sky anxiously with reddened eyes. "I hope you find him."

The unmistakable sound of the approaching copter grew louder: it was a Sparrowhawk, if Yana read the sound of it right. Those usually had room to seat the crew members and three more, but there was ample room for others to sit on the floor. Maybe, with a little luck, she could just manage to squeeze herself on board, too.

She relaxed her guard just enough to glance up at the sky, and that was when she was jumped. She had been so busy watching Torkel, Giancarlo, and Ornery that she hadn't paid any attention to the survivors, and Sven used the distraction of the chopper to grab her gun hand and twist. Before she knew it, she was on the other side of the weapon, nursing a numb wrist.

"Good man!" Torkel cried, leaping forward to relieve Sven of the gun, only to be waved to a standstill.

"He is that," O'Neill said. "Too good to let you get the drop on us again and try to get *this* helicopter away from us as well, for all the good it would do you."

Sven was evidently in agreement, for he backed over to the rest of his colleagues in a show of solidarity.

"I wouldn't have let them do that," Yana told Sven. "I made them surrender the other copter, didn't I?"

Sven grunted and shook his head, waving her back to the others.

"We're sorry, dama," O'Neill said. "You did help before and we're that grateful, but maybe you were only doin' it to get clear of them? Maybe you'd be after commandeerin' this bird for yourself to make your getaway. We can't chance it, and we don't need any more trouble today."

"At least take me with you," Yana urged.

But at that moment Giancarlo hooked her left arm and whipped it around and up under her shoulder blade, leaving her far more occupied with pain than argument.

"You're not going anywhere, Maddock," he murmured in her ear. "We haven't finished with you yet."

O'Neill and Connelly looked as if they were about to jump in and defend her, but Torkel spoke up again.

"You people go on. Take the copter, but leave her with us. She knows more than she's telling, and maybe when she sees what her rebel friends have unleashed, she'll have the good sense to help us save this planet."

"If she knows where other charges are planted, we'll get it out of her," Giancarlo said grimly.

"It *is* true that there wasn't supposed to be any natural seismic activity where we were setting up the mine," Connelly replied cautiously, with a glance first at Sven and then at the approaching copter.

"Right!" Torkel said, yelling over the copter's noise. "Everything that's happened is unnatural. You tell them at SpaceBase that there's a massive conspiracy afoot on Petaybee, and that Maddock's changed sides. She's in league now with the perpetrators. If you hadn't disarmed her, she would have gotten away, and who knows what trouble she would have caused."

The copter was slowly settling to the ground a discreet distance from the knot of humans. The survivors began backing toward it, Sven keeping the weapon trained on the company tableau of Torkel, Giancarlo holding Yana prisoner, and Ornery.

"They're nuts," Yana yelled, appealing to O'Neill. "You said yourself, nobody can jumpstart a volcano!"

O'Neill shot her a guilty glance, and he and Connelly exchanged looks, but the woman laid her hand fearfully on Sven's arm and he shook his head.

"No," he hollered. "We've risked our butts enough for one day. I'm not risking my job any further for someone in trouble with the management. You got into this mess, dama, you get yourself out without our help. You people sort it out among yourselves."

When the survivors were aboard the copter, Torkel leaned in the open door to yell at the pilot.

"You tell them at SpaceBase that I said this volcanic eruption is part of a plot to undermine our investigation and to kill a member of the board. And you get them to send out ground transport as soon as possible. Get it to the volcano site! We'll meet them there! Tell them that my father, Dr. Whittaker Fiske, is out there and it's vital we rescue him. Absolutely vital!" The pilot began lifting off and Torkel jumped down and backed off slightly, but repeated himself, yelling through cupped hands. "Tell them we've gone ahead to rescue my father. They're to follow us!"

The pilot gave him a thumbs-up signal and waved him away from the rising aircraft.

They all watched as the copter whisked away, disappearing into a maelstrom of wind, ash, and smoke. Giancarlo released Yana abruptly when it was out of sight, and she fell to her knees. As she rose, she gingerly worked her shoulder to be sure Giancarlo's enthusiasm hadn't wrenched muscles. As near as she could tell, she was still in good functioning order—at least for now.

Without so much as an eye blink, Torkel tossed her one of the packs he had been filling.

"Grab the rest of those ration bars, Maddock," he ordered.

She didn't mind. It gave her the chance to get something in her own belly. She couldn't fault the survivors, but she sure hoped they didn't believe the crap Fiske had been shoveling in their ears: that she was "in league with the perpetrators," "had caused all these unnatural phenomena." Trouble was, she thought with a snort, those poor devils were shocked enough to believe every word. Rather ungrateful of them, though, especially when O'Shay had made it plain that she was the only reason the copter had been able to land to pick up their wounded. Whatever! Torkel had turned them against her sufficiently to banjax her one chance of getting free. Free—and she had a private grin—to foment riot and rebellion back at the SpaceBase, or even with all those dangerous allies she had joined forces with.

She hoped they were all right at Kilcoole. Then Giancarlo brought her back to the present with a shove in the direction of the valley filled with blistering mud and smoking ash. Torkel was leading, then Ornery with Giancarlo behind her: not exactly where she preferred him, but she was in no position to make requests, was she?

Although there were still safe places to walk where the mud hadn't yet spread, Yana wondered how far in toward the volcanic site they could get, where the damage was fresh and the flow still boiling hot. If the planet decided to set off its new volcano again, they would be right under it. Actually, she thought, smiling to herself, the planet was doing such a complete job of dividing and routing the "enemy," that she wouldn't mind going under to such an admirable opponent.

"We'll be okay," Torkel said to no one in particular as he trudged forward. "But Dad won't if we don't reach him soon."

His voice was still taut with anxiety, though it projected less heart-wrenching filial devotion than it had when he had spoken to the survivors. Yana wondered why he was really risking their necks—but the answer was fairly obvious. Torkel was a pretty good company spy and a fair administrator, but he was not a creative scientist like his father, and without the elder Fiske, he was not apt to carry the same weight in the corporate structure. Of course he wanted to find old Whittaker. He was once again protecting his interests.

She was thinking about that as she kept a close eye on where she was putting her feet. She tried not to cough in the ash-laden, sulfury-smelling smoke. She hadn't had her lungs healed just to mess them up again inhaling this sort of crud. She tore off a piece of her shirttail and tied it across her mouth. The others did likewise, but cloth was a flimsy filter against the thickly laden wind, unlike the protective masks the company would have issued if such conditions had been anticipated.

Their progress was slow. They could not see the sun at all, and when Yana checked her watch, she had to rub the face clear of clinging ash to read it, but even then the face remained dark and empty; the ash no doubt had worked its way into the mechanism and clogged it. Fortunately, the compass was better shielded and more reliable. For hours, they picked their way forward through the maze of paths that terminated abruptly in mudflow, forcing them to double back and find a new path, then following that one forward until it, too, gave out. Occasionally the volcano would spew forth a gout of fiery red and orange matter, giving them a terrible beacon to their progress. The air was also getting closer, hotter, and that slowed them down, too. All were perspiring heavily, and the three men had torn shirttails into sweat bands around neck or forehead.

Just about the time Yana was beginning to wonder if the crash site was a myth to lure them into the certain death of the volcano field, Giancarlo yelled and pointed. There, ash-dusted and protruding from what looked like an ocean of the gray muddy guck, was unmistakably a delta wingtip that had to be part of the downed shuttle. They rushed forward, stopping just on the edge of the bubbling mud.

Yana looked up at Torkel and saw his eyes harden and his mouth twist in pain. That sort of anguish was not generated by a career anxiety alone, she realized. Whatever personally pragmatic motives he might have for this search, he truly did care for his father.

They had to spend a long time circling the crash site, looking for any sign that someone might have escaped. Torkel circled and paced like a crazy man, trying to find a way across the mudflow to that protruding wingtip, though what good that would do, Yana didn't know. They had no rope or cable to secure the tip to keep it from sliding farther into the mud, and the four of them certainly couldn't have pulled it, and the rest of the shuttle, free. Then Torkel obviously realized that this activity was futile and began methodically inspecting every inch of what solid ground there was for traces that survivors had exited the shuttle before the mud had drowned it.

The world was silent, except for the men's harsh breathing, and even that was muffled. Yana tried not to hold her breath, but she hated every ounce of contaminated air she had to drag into her lungs. When would Torkel give up this useless search? If there had been survivors, they ought to have had sense enough to get out of this vicinity with all possible speed. The likeliest explanation for the lack of traces leading away from the crash site was that there had been no one to make them. Surely Torkel had to admit that possibility. And it was equally unlikely that their tracks would be discernible with mud and ash constantly falling to cover such traces. Meanwhile, conditions were deteriorating from minute to minute as the mud and ash built up. If they weren't awfully careful, someone was going to take the wrong step and end up mud-baked.

She felt the ground flutter beneath her feet and took a step backward.

And quite unexpectedly she found herself touched by an amazing sensation. It was similar to what she had felt in the cave: staunch, reassuring, welcoming. She swiveled around, not knowing what she might find in such an unlikely place. There was only the giant boulder she had just stepped around. It was shaped like an enormous top, the point plunged deep into the ground. Its mass had separated the flow of the mud, leaving a wide, clear, somewhat sheltered space.

The mud around her gave a mighty heave and she shot an apprehensive glance at the boulder for fear it might topple over onto her. But it didn't move an inch. Was that what the planet had been reassuring her about? That the boulder was safe? Then Ornery shouted, and whipping around, she was just in time to see the wingtip slowly sinking out of sight into the mud. Torkel, standing a few paces beyond her, yelled in anguish and reached out as if to grab the wing. He was off balance when the surface heaved once more, and he was thrown sideways. Instinctively, she leapt forward, catching the fluttering edge of his torn shirt with one hand. With a second desperate lurch, she caught hold of his pack strap with the other and hauled him into the shelter of the top-shaped boulder.

The tremors were the prelude to another eruption of the volcano. Particles of ash rained down faster, ever faster, rapidly developing into a deluge of red-hot flying stones. Then, with a roar much louder than a ship blasting from a launchpad, scalding mud, scouring ash, and rock-strewn dust flew past them. Yana cried out, whipping her left arm under cover as the downpour ignited the fabric of her sleeve. She beat out the sparks and crouched down as tightly as she could against what protection the boulder gave. Beside her, Torkel let out a yowl as his vulnerable right side was also lashed by burning embers. The hot ash was pervasive, and there seemed to be no way to avoid it. In desperation, she unslung her pack and covered her head with it. Squeezing tight against the boulder, she felt the ground tremble again. Fleetingly she wondered about the advisability of clinging to a boulder, no matter what the planet suggested. At any moment the huge stone could roll over and crush them. But alternatives were not available. She let the pack slip farther down to protect her back from the hot and painful dusting.

Every muscle taut and every nerve stretched, she endured, as Torkel did beside her. She really should have made her escape at Sean's, she decided. That was her first mistake! She could have used one of the curlies or the comm unit or *something* to get her back to the village. Her second, she thought grimly, was not watching the miners and letting one of them take her weapon. Again, if she had played her cards better she could have been safely back at Kilcoole, where she knew she had friends and where she would have had a chance of finding Sean. If half of what people said about him was true, if what she *felt* about him was true, he would know what this was all about.

Then, miraculously, the roaring abated, a gust of side wind blew some of the smoke and ash away, and a light rain began to fall.

Maybe, Yana thought with small hope, it would rain harder, clear the air a bit, and cool the mud off enough so they could walk out of there.

When at last she dared to peel herself off the boulder, she did a damage report on herself. Burns stung, rock scrapes ached, she was covered with ash, blood speckled here and there. Then she looked at Torkel, who looked much the same way she felt. Only . . . her hand went to her head and she was relieved to find that she had more hair left than he did. Torkel had lost quite a swath, including his eyebrows, down his right side. And most of his shirt. The back of his fatigue pants, made of a supposedly indestructible material, looked more like mesh drawers. His right arm was a mass of tiny blisters, and her left one was in no better shape. Both packs were smoking, riddled with burn holes. She was putting the remains of the pack out where the rain could douse the final sparks when she saw Giancarlo lying unconscious, half-buried in the runnel of mud. He must have been trying to make it to the shelter of the boulder, too. There was no sign of Ornery-eyes.

The copters and other aircraft were grounded by falling ash, the snocles could not run over rivers and muddy slush, the tracked vehicles were too slow, and the runners of the sleds would not slide over broken ground. Rivers had changed their courses so that travel by water was unreliable to the point of insanity.

Therefore, the little string of sturdy curly-coats, each bearing either passenger or pack, traveled alone across the vast emptiness of the uninhabited northwestern sector of Petaybee, toward the mountains stretching up from the plains on one side; on the other, down onto the ice pack to the north and on to the open sea.

The lead curly, Boru, carried Sinead, while the next, the largest and the sturdiest of the beasts, carried Clodagh, wrapped in a poncho that covered both her and her mount so that she looked like a mountain on hooves. Behind her traveled Bunny, then Diego Metaxos, who was still fretting about leaving his father in Aisling's care. He had been badly torn between the honor of being asked to join the rescue party and his responsibility to supervise his father's steady improvement. He had left his father absently stroking one of the several cats, who had continued to adhere to the man like leeches. Both Clodagh and Aisling had assured him that this was a very good sign and told him to let matters proceed at their own pace. Diego couldn't hurry the healing process but he had extracted a promise from Aisling that she would take his father down to the hot springs as soon as possible. Steve Margolies had insisted on coming along as the "technical" observer to the phenomenon. He carried the only concession to modern technology, a comm unit, for contacting Adak in Kilcoole and SpaceBase.

Bunny thought it was the most ill-assorted rescue party imaginable, but, what with all the injured being tended at Kilcoole, these five had been the only ones available. Sinead would have gone by herself, if no one else had accompanied her to rescue Yana, hoping to find her brother, too. No sooner had Bunny told Clodagh what Adak had said about Yana being in trouble and the shuttle crashing than Sinead had barged into the cabin, muttering that Yana was in trouble and she had to go help.

"Sean send for you?" Clodagh had asked, her gaze unusually piercing.

"Not just Sean," Sinead had answered, biting her words off. She glanced about, measuring the occupants for suitability to her need. "This is it, Clodagh!"

Clodagh had nodded once and brought her meat cleaver down so hard that it quivered, stuck, in the board. "I go with you!"

"You?" Bunny couldn't believe her ears, but Clodagh was already taking off her apron, striding to the litter of parkas and boots by the door, and searching through them for her own gear.

Her statement had galvanized the others. Nothing

would have kept Bunny from following Clodagh, though her insistence astounded Steve. But he repeated his assertion that he had to make observations of the phenomenon. When Diego vacillated, obviously distressed, wanting to go, yet unwilling to leave his father, Aisling had volunteered to look after Francisco.

As they went outside to select curly-coats from the herd Sinead had rounded up, another volunteer made it plain that he was coming along: Nanook. A quick smile lit Sinead's anxious face, and she laid her hand in a brief gesture of gratitude on the animal's black-and-white head.

Dinah joined them, too, using drastic measures to get her way. Seeing them ride out of the village, she had howled so piteously and continued to yelp at such an earsplitting volume that Herbie must have given in and ordered Liam to let her loose. She came charging up to Diego just as they dipped down in the valley northwest of the town, and she maintained a position beside his mount throughout the trek.

Nanook had taken it as his right to lead the expedition and ranged way beyond Sinead, now and then padding back to them as if hoping he could speed up their progress. But the slush and mud made the going slow, and even the clever curly-coats got trapped now and then in melting drifts.

On the first day, when the ground shook again, Clodagh lifted her hand to signal a halt. Laboriously she dismounted and slowly lay down, arranging herself flat on her belly, her right cheek pressed onto the snow-packed ground. After a long time, she rose, wiping her face clean before she pointed west. "That way."

Clodagh also had other means of communication and Bunny watched, fascinated, as she employed them. She sang. Using tonelike sonar, she sang to the birds and the rocks and the plants:

"Friends, have you seen our friend, Yanaba?
She met the enemy and was taken into battle with him.
See that she comes to no harm."

If the addressee was a raven, it promptly flew away; if it was an animal, it ran purposefully off; a stream, it kept about its business, but Bunny swore that the ripples changed pitch; and if it was the ground beneath the hooves of the horses, it simply absorbed the songs, listening. Clodagh listened, too, and then she would alter their direction a compass point or two. They would continue for a while on the new course until she found something else to sing to.

In this way, despite Margolies's demanding explanations of this quixotic form of directions, they traveled for two days and two nights and half a day again. They got what sleep they could in their makeshift saddles, stopping only to feed the horses, and for ten minutes in every two hours to rest their mounts' backs. The horses kept moving tirelessly, mostly at a walk but occasionally, where the terrain had been swept free of snow, breaking into their smooth little canter.

Very early on the rescuers had to cover their mouths with pieces of cotton cloth that rapidly became clogged with dust and ash and had to be shaken often. Even the food they ate during their brief halts tasted like more of the same. Soon everyone's eyes went from stinging to being red and swollen. When they could dig down to clean snow during the rest halts, they bathed their faces, trying to relieve the irritation.

Everything was mud gray—the sky, the ground, the air—and the people and animals moved like big ashy lumps in front and behind. Bunny was so tired and so full of ash and smoke that only her sore tailbone let her know that she was not traveling in a dream. Then Nanook began racing forward and back to them until they quickened their progress in anticipation of what he might have found. He led them to a place where the snow and ash still bore faint indentations of human feet, the long flat marks of copter skids, and a pile of discarded effects, all but the metal reduced to scraps of melted or fused material. Fingers of cooling, hardening mud crept up the side of a canyon wall.

Nanook leapt the few feet from the edge of the canyon to the mud, and Bunny caught her breath, fearful that Nanook might be risking injury. But the cat was far from stupid, and he landed and solemnly stretched out on a surface that was apparently comfortably warm. He began licking his filthy paws as if he were back in Sean's laboratory.

"Trust him to find the perfect spot to relax," Clodagh said, amused.

Dinah also settled down to lick her paws clean. She had trotted dutifully by Diego's mount, her red coat barely visible under its ashen cover.

They slipped the saddle blankets and hackamores from the horses and fed them. They munched trail rations as they unstrapped the snowshoes that they hoped would give them better footing over the ash-covered mud and snow. While they made a final check of their packs, Steve Margolies called their position in to Adak. Bunny only hoped the transmission was better than the reception. All they could hear was a hiss and crackle a little louder than the wind, which was blowing steadily east.

"I hope they got all that," Steve told the others. "I didn't hear exactly what they said but, having done a personal on-the-spot review of conditions, I think they said this is a no-go area. There was also some gibberish about there being no one in command to give orders."

Clodagh gave a contemptuous sniff and, with a groan, once more began to spread herself flat on the ground. The others stood about for what seemed a very long time—at least the curly-coats had moved a good distance away in search of any grass the mud and ash hadn't buried—before she moved again.

She hauled herself up, mopped the ash from her face and neck, brushed it off the front of her clothes, and then pointed. "That way."

"The volcano's that way," Steve protested, pointing elsewhere.

Clodagh moved her arm slightly toward the north. "The volcano is that way." Then she dropped her snow-shoes to the ground and stepped into them. Scooping up her pack and twitching her shoulders so that it settled on her back, she started off in the direction she had indicated.

Bunny looked at Diego and shrugged. Sinead jerked her head at the perplexed Steve, and very shortly, all were following her down into the valley, Dinah sticking right at Diego's heels. In several leaps, Nanook caught up and passed the humans. Clodagh took particular notice of where he put his paws. For all her bulk she moved with unexpected agility as she followed the cat's tracks.

16

Yana and Torkel dragged Giancarlo back to the uncertain safety of the boulder, the three of them hostage
to the hot mud surrounding them. Yana bound up
Giancarlo's pulped arm and leg, but the heat of the mud
and flying rock had pretty well cauterized the wounds
inflicted by the blast—or so she would have to hope,
she thought ruefully. The colonel would be lucky to live
long enough to get infections.

Torkel had taken a worse beating than she, for although her back was pretty well skinned, her hair hadn't
been as badly singed and her scalp hadn't been pep-
pered with ash because she'd had sense enough to protect her head. Torkel's face was scored and swollen
where rock had hit it before she had pulled him down,
and he was ravaged with grief besides.

She had had to prod him painfully to get him to
move enough to help her with Giancarlo.

"Look, Torkel," she said in her best bracing tone. "If
your dad survived the crash and the first blast, it's likely
he survived the second one, as well. At any rate, we
can't do anything about it one way or the other unless
we survive. Here, eat this so we do!" She thrust a battered ration pack at him, somewhat amazed that the

wrapping was still intact. It seemed years ago that she had stuffed them in the front of her shirt.

She wasn't sure when she slept, but she knew that sometime within that interminable period, the searing heat from the mud dissipated and the sunless air grew cold again. She and Torkel Fiske put the unconscious Giancarlo between them and hunched over him, sharing their warmth with him. In her sleep she dreamed that she was holding Sean rather than Torkel, and he was bathing her wounds with water from the hot springs, telling her, "I'm here, Yana. Trust me. Nothing of this world means you harm. Listen to its voice. Remember now ..."

The dream and others like it repeated as she slept or half dozed, shivering, clinging to the warmth and life in the two other bodies for more time than she could count or was conscious of.

Then, without knowing how or when it happened, she woke from the dream of Sean, feeling warm again. She smelled a freshening in the air and realized that her hand was touching something cool, hard, and smooth; and, rousing, she found that she was touching the once scalding mud.

Torkel was still sleeping, and Giancarlo moaned in a fever. Yana sat up and placed both palms against the mud. The sensation wasn't unpleasant. It still retained some warmth, but was otherwise hard and seemed stable. Standing, she tested other areas, pressing her fingers into the layer of ash overlying the previously steaming rivulet. It gave with a slight hiss and a hint of smokiness, but once the crust was broken, solid hard mud was only an inch or two down. She carefully hauled herself up on top of the flow and found that it held her weight.

The air *was* clearer. She could definitely smell and see the difference at this height. A strong wind whipped at her, blowing the ash back away from them and over to the north and east. Torkel sat up and blinked lashless eyes at the sudden change. Yana rubbed cautiously at her arms, avoiding the burn blisters but needing to increase blood circulation and reduce hypothermia. She was glad of the visibility, glad of the ability to travel again, if only they knew where they were going. Then she opened the remaining ration pack, twisted it into two more or less equal halves, and let him choose.

"We'll have to drag Giancarlo," she told Torkel when they had finished their scanty meal.

"He'll slow us down," Torkel said.

"You want to leave him?" she asked. She didn't like being directly responsible for anyone's death. On the other hand, if she *was* to be responsible for someone dying here, she wouldn't much mind if it was Giancarlo.

Torkel looked down at the colonel, then shrugged and bent to hoist him by the arms up the wall of mud, where Yana helped support the unconscious man.

"We'd better get him back to where a copter can land, then," Yana said.

But he shook his head stubbornly, unreasonably. "Dad may still be out here."

"You can come back afterward," she insisted.

But just then a fresh gust of wind from the west carried a raven toward them. The bird swooped, diving so low that its wing brushed Yana's hair.

Its cry was no doubt only the usual raucous caw, but

to her, wounded, shocked, and probably a little delirious, it seemed to be saying " 'ana, 'ana," or maybe it was "Sean, Sean." Then it made an abrupt turn and flew back the way it came. Abruptly she recalled Sean's dream message.

"Okay, you win," she told Torkel. "But we spell each other dragging the son of a bitch and you get first shift."

She was pleased when the crow's west eventually turned out to be the right direction. Even so, both she and Torkel were at the end of their strength from dragging Giancarlo's heavy and unresponsive body when she caught the first gleam of open water. She hadn't realized how parched she was until that moment. Then her throat took over, reminding her that she was so dehydrated it didn't know if it would ever come unstuck. Up closer, Yana saw that the water was a little stream, running from one edge of the mud and on into the side of a hill. Yana fully expected the water to be milky with ash and mud and clogged with debris, but in fact it was so clear she could see the stones at the bottom. Somehow this stretch had escaped all of the ravages of the volcano. Where the stream emerged from the hill, she could make out a deep, cavelike opening, into which her crow guide disappeared as she watched.

Judging by the way the ash had drifted, Bunny thought that the wind had been westerly for some time, possibly the entire two and a half days it had taken them to make it this far. Nanook even began to touch down on the mud from time to time, and when the humans walked on it, they felt only a tolerable warmth through the soles of their boots. It certainly wasn't hot enough to damage the snowshoes, which were proving their worth through the heavier ash deposits.

They were moving steadily to one side of the smoldering cone. Smoke or steam was windborne away from them to the east, so that the air was not so clogged with ash and sulfur stench.

Seen from this safe distance, the volcano didn't, to Bunny's way of thinking, look all that dangerous. It was actually not very big.

"It doesn't have to be big to be dangerous," Steve said when she voiced her observation. "I'm no expert on vulcanism—Petaybee is not supposed to be labile," he added in a sourly amused tone, "but, on a world which does have considerable activity, a volcano can rise up one day and disappear the next. After raining ash, lava, rock, or whatever all across a landscape. We're just lucky this is only an ash-and-mud type. Some rise for the one blowoff and then remain dormant."

"Is this one dormant now?" Bunny asked, eyeing it nervously.

"We hope," Steve said with a grin.

"Clodagh?" Bunny persisted.

Clodagh shrugged and plowed on tirelessly. Nanook skirted a vast lake of hardening mud that steamed more than did most of the rivulets and puddles of the stuff.

The volcano was almost out of sight behind them, obscured by the foothills, when Nanook suddenly picked up the pace, from an amble to a working lope. Then, abruptly, he halted at a fast-running stream to lap up the clear water. The others were glad to follow his example.

Clodagh did more than drink: she immersed her face in the stream. She was so long about it that Bunny got worried, but when she finally lifted her dripping head, she wore a broad smile.

"That way," she said, pointing uphill in a more northerly direction as she wiped her face, leaving dark gray smudges on her forehead and down her cheeks.

Ash clung to all their clothing and rendered their complexions ghostly gray.

"Let me see if I can get a message through, Clodagh," Steve said, starting to unsling his radio equipment.

"Not now," she said, shaking her head, and began to follow the stream. Steve shrugged and resettled the radio equipment.

The stream disappeared into a narrow opening at the bottom of the first terrace of the cliff. When Clodagh indicated that they would have to climb, they discarded the snowshoes. Bunny marveled that Clodagh calmly prepared herself to climb, hitching her skirts high enough so that her sturdy legs, clad in woolen pants knitted in a variety of quite lively colors, were visible. She was slow, true enough, but she made certain progress upward. Nanook reached the top of the terrace in three graceful leaps, Dinah scrabbling close behind him. Fortunately they didn't have all that far to go. On the second terrace, Nanook turned to his right and led them around an escarpment, ducked into a hole in the stone, and disappeared from sight. Only then did Clodagh groan, for she would have to go down on hands and knees to follow the big cat. She did.

Once inside, they could all stand up again. Clodagh paused, leaning against the wall to catch her breath. Bunny thought the pace was telling on the large woman. It was certainly beginning to wear Bunny down a bit, and she was much more used to running about than Clodagh.

"Hey, this is like the other place," Diego said, looking about him. A curious luminescence gave enough light for them to see.

"Quite a few subterranean networks did appear on the last scan that was made of this planet," Steve was saying as he examined the rock walls, wiping off a light film, which he rubbed between his fingers. "They weren't on previous ones, but they do account for the subsidences. Or do they? Most unusual. I wish Frank had been well enough to travel with us. He's more familiar with such geological anomalies than I am." He walked on a few more strides before he stopped completely, forcing Diego, walking behind him, to hurriedly step aside. "Or perhaps there was a flaw in the original terraforming that has produced unforeseen long-range crustal defects. A shame that Dr. Fiske was killed on the shuttle crash."

"We don't know that for certain," Bunny said. "Only that Captain Fiske was going to try to *find* his father, so he could still be alive."

"Is Fiske's father the company big shot who's supposed to know more about Petaybee than anyone else?" Clodagh asked, pausing to lean against the stone.

"Yes," Steve said. "He's Dr. Whittaker Fiske, grandson of the Dr. Sven Whittaker-Fiske who developed the Whittaker Effect, the process that perfected the accelerated terraforming technique used to make Petaybee habitable." When Clodagh gave Steve a long and thoughtful look, he corrected himself. "Or at least he *thought* he had perfected it."

"Why didn't he name it the Fiske Effect then?" Bunny asked.

"He named it for his mother, Dr. Elsie Whittaker. I guess he thought it was appropriate, considering the generative nature of the project."

Clodagh gave a satisfied grunt and, pushing herself off the wall, was about to move forward again when she stopped, holding her hand up for silence. "Listen!"

The sounds were muted but obviously human. Bunny and Sinead dashed forward, Diego, with Dinah at his heels, just behind them. The voices had suddenly risen in excitement, and as Bunny turned the next bend, she stopped in surprise. Nanook had found Yana and was attempting to lick any part of her he could!

"Yana! You're alive!" Bunny cried, but she had taken no more than one step before she realized that Yana was not the only inhabitant of the large, low cave. And judging by the way the camp had been set up, Yana and her companions had been here a few days. "Who're all of you?" she demanded.

A sturdy man in a torn uniform and a bandage covering almost all his black hair stood up by the fire, where he had been stirring a pot. "Captain John Greene of the shuttle *Sockeye*," he said with a wry smile. "Who're you?"

"Buneka Rourke of Kilcoole," Bunny said in stunned courtesy.

"From Kilcoole? Of all the bloody luck," groaned a disgruntled voice, and a battered, blistered, half-naked, filthy man barely recognizable as the dapper Torkel Fiske rose painfully from his seat on the ground. He placed himself protectively between the rescue party and an older man, who had one arm bound across his chest.

Before either Bunny or Sinead could respond to Torkel's hostile reaction, Steve Margolies, and Diego, and an excitedly barking Dinah rushed into the cavern, followed more slowly by Clodagh.

To the man behind him, Torkel said, "Just keep calm, Dad. I'll handle this. These are the rebels I was telling you about. The ones who brainwashed Maddock into helping them."

"Nonsense, son," the older man said, stepping gently but firmly past his tottering son. "That's Steve Margolies there, and Frank Metaxos's boy, Diego. They're no more rebels than I am."

"Dr. Fiske," Steve exclaimed, rushing toward the older man and pumping his good hand excitedly. "I can't believe you survived."

"Neither can I," the older Fiske replied in a droll voice.

"Dr. Fiske, in the past few days, Diego and these people have showed me the *most* amazing developments. You simply won't believe what I have to tell you . . ."

"I'll be the judge of that," Dr. Fiske said. "Stop posturing for a moment, son, and sit down before you fall down." He gently pushed Torkel back to the floor. "And for the love of Mike let these people clean you up and dress your wounds. You're no damned good to me dead. You, young Diego, lend me a hand here to clean up my son's wounds before they fester. I've only got the one that's useful now, myself. I'll debrief Dr. Margolies."

"Yes, sir," Diego said, taking over the bowl of water and the cloth. Having learned a few things from caring for his father, Diego went about the duty both gently and conscientiously, cleansing the portions of Torkel's body that Torkel couldn't have reached. The captain wearily protested every dab, as if Diego were deliberately trying to inflict more pain than was absolutely necessary. Diego's private opinion was visible on his face: the captain was acting like a big baby.

Dr. Fiske settled down to one side of Torkel, and Steve hunkered down and began talking in a rapid-fire explanation full of words Bunny didn't understand even when she could make them out.

Yana caught Clodagh's eye and urgently beckoned the healer over, indicating Giancarlo's bundled figure on the ground by her feet.

Clodagh examined the colonel's terrible burn wounds briefly, pursing her lips at the irremediable damage.

"I can do something to make him comfortable, no more," she said, shaking her head. "Intergal may know something." She started to work, pulling various unguents and potions, bandages and splints from her knapsack.

Yana would never have expected to be sorry for a man like Giancarlo, but she was. Hurting as badly as he was, he had not uttered a sound.

For herself, Yana was so glad to see Clodagh and the others from Kilcoole that she could have cried. She and Torkel had made it to the cave several hours before, and she had been unutterably relieved to see the shuttle crash survivors. However, once Torkel had reassured himself that his father was safe, he began ranting about Yana's treachery and warning the shuttle crew to ignore anything she might say and to watch her. Considering the fact that Yana had obviously taken on most of the physical burden of dragging Giancarlo, as well as supporting Torkel, as they staggered into the cave, the shuttle crew didn't pay much attention to his ravings. Still, the atmosphere had been extremely tense. Even the cave itself seemed to be holding its breath, waiting for something. The calm before the storm? Yana wondered. A lull before the mountain blew again? It didn't feel exactly like that, and she was too tired to analyze the feeling, but it definitely added to the tension.

Once Clodagh finished ministering to the unconscious Giancarlo, she rounded on Yana, clucking over the scabby sores crusting Yana's left arm and over her appearance in general.

"When did you eat last, girl?" Clodagh demanded.

"I had a piece of ration bar just before we got here," Yana said.

"You look like you could eat a whole moose by yourself and sleep for a month. You were skinny as a skeleton when you got to Kilcoole, but we fattened you up good. Now you look like a lame doe after a hard winter again."

Yana jerked her arm away from Clodagh. "Don't fuss over me. I'm all right. There are others who could really use your help, Clodagh." She nodded beyond her to others wearing makeshift bandages. "The shuttle survivors have been here for three days, and they've had zip to look after themselves with. All they could do for Dr. Fiske was immobilize his arm and wash off his wounds."

"Is that him over there Steve's talkin' to?" Clodagh asked. When Yana nodded Clodagh said wryly, "He looks better off than Torkel to me."

Sinead joined the two women then, her face anxious. "Have you seen him?" she asked Yana. "I thought he'd be with you."

"No, if you mean Sean," Yana said with an odd smile. "But I'll tell you both something. We didn't *find* them"—and she gestured to the crash victims—"we were led to them."

Hope bounced back into Sinead's eyes. "Led to this place?"

Yana nodded. "What's more, they swear they were led here, too. I can only think of one person not here at the moment who might have engineered this rescue, and I've been wondering, Sinead, how the hell he did it." Her eyes were keen on the other woman's face. "Dr. Fiske told Torkel he believes that there's an underground network of rivers. That's why there were so many subsidences when the mining charges weakened subterranean supports. If there's a network, one river flowing into another, then someone who knew his way around could go from one end of the system to the other without ever being seen—couldn't he?"

Sinead gave Yana a long look. "If there was such a network, that's possible, I suppose. I don't go underground much. I like horizons." Then she reached to heave her pack off her back and began rummaging in it. "I've got spare clothes you can use. And some stuff Clodagh will want."

"No one looked beyond this cavern?" Clodagh asked with quiet urgency.

Yana shook her head. "We'd enough to do without going exploring!"

"That's as well," Clodagh said with a satisfied snort, and asked Yana who was the worst of the injured. She cleansed, stitched, anointed, and listened as gradually the two separate incidents were reported in detail.

The shuttle had been on the point of landing when the volcano blast had caught it, throwing the vehicle heavily to its side. Nine passengers had not survived the impact, but the others, hastily mobilized by the resourceful young pilot, Captain Greene, had got the living out of the shuttle before the air locks were submerged. They had managed to leave the area, the hot mud only centimeters from their heels as they plunged out of the western end of the valley. They had paused only to distribute supplies and attend to burns, scalds, and broken bones, before force-marching themselves as far from the erupting volcano as their strength would take them. The wind was easterly: they had picked the only safe direction to flee. And that had been only by chance, since the pilot had thought he was directing them toward the mining site that had been their destination, but a knock on the head, from the crash landing, had skewed his sense of direction.

"Remarkable that we were all led to this particular spot," Steve Margolies said. "This appears to be the opening of a vast system of caves. The two parties could have ended up in widely separated spots. Are there other entrances to this particular cavern?" he asked, glancing toward the back of the cavern.

Greene shrugged. "Could be. We didn't need to explore with that fresh stream right outside."

"We'll return later, properly equipped, and do a thorough investigation," Dr. Fiske said in a firm command tone. "Right now, we'd better report these coordinates and get our wounded back to SpaceBase. I believe this may be one of the places for which our teams have been searching all these years. Dr. Margolies, I trust you brought some means of communication with the base, didn't you?"

"Of course, of course," Steve said. He jumped to his feet. "We'll have to go outside and get some height for the best possible signal—" Then he stopped, as Torkel latched on to the comm set at his belt and hauled himself wearily to his feet, using Steve to balance himself.

"I initiate any communications," Torkel said curtly. Then he caught his father's frown and managed a ghost of his old diplomatic smile for Margolies. "That is, I'll report in while you and my father continue the debriefing."

Captain Greene nodded to the least injured of his crewmen, a short black man, who helped Steve and the fumbling Torkel untangle the comm set from Steve's belt.

"And while you're exercising your jaw, Dr. Fiske, I'll just see to your arm," Clodagh told the scientist. She crouched down in front of him and began untying the sling.

"Dama, I've waited this long," Fiske said with great dignity, resisting her ministrations. "I can certainly— Ouch! How did you do that?" He stared at his newly set arm and then at Clodagh, eyes wide with respect.

"It's a knack I've developed," she said. Then she dipped a length of bandage in a pot of her boneset potion and quickly and deftly wrapped the area about the break. By the time she had done that and rinsed her hands off, the bandage had hardened. "This will be more comfortable for you until you get back."

"But this hardened . . . I don't believe this," Fiske said, tapping the shell experimentally.

Gently but firmly taking his arm again, she replaced it in the sling and tied it across his chest. Then she began to undo the blood-soaked bandage on his thigh.

"This wants stitching," she said, examining the gaping wound.

"It's been cleaned and dressed," Fiske said testily, inhaling quickly at the sight of his parted flesh.

"That was well done," Clodagh agreed, and let a handful of a moist salve slip onto the wound.

Fiske started to hiss and then stopped in surprise. "That didn't hurt."

"Medicine need not hurt, or taste bad, to be effective. Never did know who started that stupid old superstition," she said with all the scorn of an experienced practitioner. From another packet she took a needle already threaded and began to make neat sutures.

Despite an initial distaste, Fiske gradually became fascinated by her swift movements. "Where did you get your training?" he asked respectfully.

"Living on Petaybee teaches you many useful things," she said serenely, and tied off the last stitch. "Not perhaps what your medical folk might use, but it works. That's all we ask of any medicine, isn't it?" she added. "Anywhere else?"

He had a less serious laceration farther down the leg, and she put in two neat sutures to close that. Then she applied a wet aromatic compress to the swollen, bruised flesh of his ankle.

While Torkel and the crewman called for a copter and Clodagh fussed over Dr. Fiske, Yana helped Bunny warm up some of the provisions the rescue party had brought with them. By the time a rich meaty stew had been reconstituted with water and was simmering in a flight helmet stripped of its lining, Clodagh had finished administering to Whittaker Fiske. Yana offered the old man some of the stew, and he thanked her without a hint of his son's surliness.

Yana had food for Clodagh, as well, and put it into the healer's hands with a firmness and a look in her eye that told Clodagh that she had better eat or else!

"Is it just that I am very hungry and tired of energy bars, or is this really as good as it tastes?" Whittaker Fiske asked amiably.

"Hunger is a good sauce," Clodagh said. "Here's a spot of seasoning that'll add an extra zap to it." From her capacious medicine bag, she took an herb bottle and sprinkled some powder into his bowl and hers, then offered it to Yana.

Settling down beside her, Yana grinned around her spoon. "Clodagh's far too modest, Dr. Fiske. Food generally tastes better on Petaybee because most of it's fresh! Even the frozen stuff."

"I thought the growing season was a little short for that," Whittaker Fiske said, chewing thoughtfully.

"Yes," Clodagh said. "But we get more daylight than usual during our growing season, so things get big fast. And the fishes and animals we eat grow all year-round."

"And maybe *you* have a lot of access to hydroponic gardens on the space stations, Dr. Fiske," Yana said, "but to me anything that hasn't been freeze-dried and stored in a food locker for several ship-years tastes downright ambrosial."

They had just finished eating when Torkel and the crewman returned to the cavern, Torkel's step somewhat more confident than it had been.

"All right, everyone, gather what you want to take with you," he began.

"Not much of that," one of the crash survivors muttered.

"There's a jumbo copter on the way with medical staff," he continued, frowning as he tried to identify the wit. Then he saw that Yana was sitting next to his father. "Maddock, you're to consider yourself under arrest."

Yana looked up at him quizzically.

"Oh, come now, Torkel," his father said with some asperity. "Surely you can't hold any of these people, least of all Major Maddock, responsible for Petaybee's geological vagaries! I tell you quite frankly your allegations have no scientific foundation."

"Sir, you manage the planet and I'll manage the investigation. Maddock's turned against the company and is actively aiding the—"

"Who, you say, make their headquarters in Kilcoole?" Fiske asked in a mild tone, looking up at his son who towered over him. "The same town that organized this very efficient, if unorthodox"—and he smiled at Clodagh—"rescue party? I find that hard to believe."

Clodagh chuckled, and Torkel gave a deep, disgusted sigh and sank down beside his father.

"You wanted me to get to the bottom of the team disappearances . . . sir," Torkel said with exaggerated patience in a hoarse weary voice, "and the biological anomalies on this planet. You saw that big cat that came with these people, the one that's even now sunning itself on the ledge outside this cave? And keeping watch, I wouldn't doubt. That cat's one of those same anomalies. It's one of Shongili's little pets, and there'll be no mention of such a breed in your files. Major Yanaba Maddock's been thick with Shongili since shortly after she arrived here, and I believe she's fallen under his influence and become his accomplice. I don't have Shongili, but I do have Maddock, and with her in custody I'll get my hands on Shongili, too."

Fiske raised his hand to silence Torkel, but he looked directly into Yana's eyes.

"Are you guilty as charged, Yanaba Maddock?"

"Me, sir? No, sir," Yana replied with a wry smile. "Trouble is your son didn't like hearing what I had to report."

"Sir, this is neither the time nor the place to discuss the situation," Torkel continued in a low, strained tone, his eyes boring into Yana as if his stare could force her to silence. "It's *not* what it seems!"

"I'll go along with that," Yana said fervently.

"Sometimes when you create life, it does not fit the form you chose for it," Clodagh said with an enigmatic smile at Whittaker Fiske.

"What's that supposed to mean?" Dr. Fiske asked, frowning.

"You'll be given to understand that soon." She rose, putting an end to that subject. "Come, Yana, we must speak to Sinead. She, and perhaps Bunny, better drive those curly-coats back. They won't find much to eat around here now that the volcano's finished."

"The volcano's finished erupting? How can you know that?" Fiske tried to get up, but he was stiff from sitting so long and couldn't stop her.

"She's bad as the rest of them, Dad," Torkel said, looking rather pleased that Clodagh had damned herself out of her own mouth.

"Bad?" Whittaker Fiske exclaimed. "Bad doesn't come into this, son! Margolies, a word with you!" He limped over to Steve, who, with Diego, was helping get some of the injured ready for transfer.

Yana remained near Clodagh. Captain Greene snagged Torkel to organize an orderly transfer of the survivors from their cave refuge to the nearest possible copter landing site, and that kept the captain occupied. There was a flurry of activity when the copters arrived, stretcher bearers whipping back and forth, people getting loaded. Yana noticed Clodagh in deep conversation with Sinead, Greene, and Bunny, but she thought nothing of it. She just made damned sure she stayed out of Torkel's way, a task made easier when Greene strong-armed the exhausted man aboard the copter while insisting on giving him a preliminary report.

"I left my medicine bag in the cave," Clodagh said just as the last folk were waiting to load up.

"Sure thing," Yana said, turning back to the cavern entrance. But inside, she found Sinead, apparently gathering up the last of the debris. Sinead smiled at her, an odd sort of smile, and then Yana heard voices in the passageway.

"It is something that you must see right now, Dr. Fiske," Clodagh was saying as she entered the cavern, the scientist limping impatiently beside her, "to begin to understand what Petaybee is beneath the surface you folk gave it."

"Beneath the—what are you talking about, woman?" Fiske, anxious to return to SpaceBase, was getting grumpy. "Are we going to miss the copter?"

"It will wait," Clodagh said easily, and Yana realized

that the big woman had come on a mission that had an urgent purpose extending beyond the initial search and rescue.

17

Trailing behind Clodagh and Fiske, Yana heard the copter lift off. She paused, listening until the sound was barely audible, then turned back to follow Clodagh. As she started walking, she became aware that the atmosphere inside the cave had subtly altered and lightened: the whole cavern was flooding with a sense of release— the exhalation of the breath she had felt it holding since she had first arrived.

At the same time something splashed and she swiveled, but she could see nothing, and decided that the sound must have come from outside the cave. Backtracking, she peered out along the little stream that flowed into the cavern, through the low, dark opening.

Something was rising from the stream out there. Sparkling droplets of water splashed around a long, silver-brown body energetically shaking itself dry as it rose from the water. Yana watched in fascination as the droplets flew, clearing a finely sculpted head with ears flat against the skull and bright eyes that seemed to search the entrance of the cave. Then the moisture was gone and the head seemed to, well, fluff out, she supposed, and the body lengthened into that of a man—a man who seemed to be wearing a fine silky pelt of hair.

Or, perhaps, a gray wet suit. But as he walked closer to her, she saw with joyful surprise that the man was Sean, clad in nothing at all save volcanic ash, which he must have been trying to wash off in the spring before coming inside.

"You always travel that way?" she called out, not quite trusting what she *thought* she had seen and hoping that either he would explain sometime soon or she could somehow find a subtle way to ask.

He grinned down at her. "Not always, but it's very convenient if you know how." He looked down at himself. "Can get a little drafty once I'm out of my element, though."

The cave was littered with bits of uniform that had been discarded by survivors as not worth transporting. Sean rifled through them until he found a flight suit riddled with holes. He pulled it on, and it served as a social covering.

"Ashes as disguise and swimming as transport? Clever of you," she said, making a wild guess.

"More or less," he said, coming to stand very close to her and putting his hands on her shoulders.

She wasn't quite ready yet to be distracted by his touch, still bewildered and intrigued by the way he had appeared and by what she felt surely had to be her perfectly ridiculous perceptions of it. "You know—I was wondering about that raven that guided us here—I sort of had a sense of *you* then. You don't by any chance own a black wet suit and hang glider, do you?" she asked, lifting her brows in a query that practically demanded that he confide in her.

He remained amused and enigmatic. "And make myself small, as well? Gracious no, I couldn't do *that*. I don't go in for wings. I've a definite water affinity. But I do have friends in high places."

Yana decided to pursue that mystery later and concentrate on more urgent matters for the time being. She laid a hand on his arm and said, "Sean, I'd better brief you as to what's happening here. Torkel Fiske is ready to court-martial me for trying to defend Petaybee and Clodagh's taken Torkel's father into the cavern—"

"I know, Yana, I know. And I'll explain as soon as there's time. Right now we'll do better to help Dr. Fiske and Clodagh."

His hand made a reassuring warm spot on the middle of her back as he guided her toward the passageway.

Yana became suddenly aware that the sound of the helicopter, which had grown faint by the time she had found Sean, was suddenly louder again. Instinctively she lengthened her stride. Sean heard it, too, and increased his pace to match hers until both were well within the passage.

The luminescence was brightening, and ahead of them she could hear Clodagh saying soothingly, ". . . someone who wants to meet you, Dr. Fiske."

The copter thud grew louder and louder, then suddenly began fading again, but from behind, Yana heard quick footsteps entering the cave.

"Come out with your hands up, Shongili, Maddock! I saw you rendezvous!" Torkel yelled. "And my father had better be unharmed or—"

"Are you with me?" Sean asked Yana quickly. She nodded, and they stood, one on either side of the passage, flush against the wall, while Torkel, forgetting all training in his agitation, barreled into their ambush. Yana disarmed him easily and caught him in a wristlock, while Sean, on the other side, did something that made Torkel sag against them. Other footsteps could be heard in the outer cave then, but Sean ignored them as he dragged Torkel onward. Yana stepped forward to help, and together they steered him through the passage and into the inner cave, where Clodagh, Bunny, Sinead, Nanook, and Dinah surrounded Dr. Fiske.

A warm mist was already rising from the rivulets running down the cavern walls and along the sides of the floor. It was scented with earth, ozone, plant life, both green and decaying, and the faintest hint of the perfume of exotic flowers. The mist trickled along the floor and twined up the knees of the people in the cavern, gently tugging them down.

The luminescence on the cavern walls danced with shadow play as if lit by firelight; the walls themselves seemed to pulse. The mist thickened and rolled up around them, veiling their faces: heavy, warm, scented mist; the distilled essence of the caves, the ground, the water, the air, moving in and out of their bodies with each breath they took.

Feet shuffled briefly behind Yana, and the disturbance in the air pressure told her that yet others had entered the room. They said nothing, and when she could bring herself to glance over her shoulder, she saw that the late arrivals were cloaked by the mist as well, their nostrils and mouths and lungs and hearts adding to the rhythm with which the cave pulsed.

Every sound was magnified, the trickle of the water rattling like rain on a roof or rustling leaves, a whispered accent to the measured throb in the cave.

Suddenly Torkel writhed in Yana's hands, and she

felt him wake, heard his ragged breathing tear against the fabric of the thing that was happening here.

"No!" he cried. "No, stop! This is how they brainwash you. Dad, don't listen!"

Dr. Fiske's voice sounded muffled and distracted as he answered, " 'M fine. Don't be such a horse's ass."

And Clodagh murmured encouragingly, "You're both just fine, just fine."

From behind Yana, other hands joined hers on Torkel and other arms wrapped around him—in reassurance, not restraint.

"Don't fight, Captain," Diego's voice whispered. "Please don't fight. Listen. It doesn't mean to hurt you, it just wants you to listen."

"I'm here, Captain Fiske," Steve Margolies whispered in a less solicitous tone. "I'm a scientist, and so is your father. If this is all bull, we'll know. You're safe with us. Greene and the other pilot just joined us. You're safe."

"You're safe and well and here because Petaybee has much to tell the sons of those who first woke the planet to life," Clodagh said.

Torkel started to struggle again, and the whole cave suddenly vibrated with a thumping tremor that repeated over and over to the beat it had established from their breathing. The walls swirled with images, and Yana once more felt the jolt of contact running up her spine, exploding in her nervous system with blossoms of pure joy as she experienced a greater unity than she had ever known. A part of her heard Torkel gasp as he was infused with it, too, and then others became included. Contact was made with them now, each touching another; warm skin or warm cave, warm mist or warm breath, all were mingled in the heavy beat of the planet's great heart.

In the cold cave floor she felt the ice-and-rock shell that had once imprisoned that heart. Then a shock rocked through her, over and over again, the world's greatest orgasm, *this* world's great orgasm. She was so full of life and joy that her body could not contain it all and lovely things began growing from her skin, her hair, her eyes and mouth and ears and nose, her womb and anus and fingers and toes and hair, giving birth to thousands of new beauties every second, flowering things and furred things, winged things and hoofed things, soft dense creeping mosses and towering trees with undulating sweet-scented fronds. And through each thing, with no more than a whim of a try, she could speak and sing, act and dance, love and laugh and live. Even dying was a kind of life, and she felt that, too, with regret but no grief.

Lovely things sent shivers over her skin, caressed her surfaces, brought warm pleasure to her orifices, dove and swam through her blood, nourished her. And all was well and all was one and she was glad of life.

Then a little pain started—just a small one, near her heart. At first it only troubled her once in a while. It grew worse when some of the things that grew from her were removed, though she could bear even that at first. But it grew worse and worse as time passed and other, sharper, deeper pains shot through her, as if someone had suddenly plunged a knife into her. She seized up and screamed and tried to cry out through the things growing on her, and some heard and cried for her and some were scorched by the force of her cries. Panting, she waited for the pain to pass and it did, until the next time.

Then the first pain, the main pain, the central pain, a pain much like the start of the ecstatic release that had freed her from her ice and rock, intensified, deepened, drove through her until she could stand it no more. At last she lanced her own boil by applying more and more pressure, sending blood and the strength of her muscle and bone, igniting nerves until the area blew, and she lay bleeding, but relieved. The things that nourished her surface rushed over her and centered on the spot to console her, and she felt the consolation, the oneness, the comfort of releasing her pain through those who had first released her.

Gradually the images of a volcano erupting on her left breast dissolved into the image of the pain flowing through the pores of her skin and out. That image dissolved into one of herself accepting Petaybee's pain from within it and releasing it through herself, until she lay spent on the floor, Torkel Fiske sobbing on one side of her with Diego between them, Sean and Steve Margolies on the other side.

The mist had vanished now, and Dr. Fiske sat looking up at the luminous walls, tears coursing down his cheeks, his bad arm draped awkwardly across Clodagh's back and the other one around Bunny.

Slowly they rose and left the cavern. O'Shay and Greene, as last in, were first out to reboard the waiting helicopter. Yana hauled herself aboard and crowded in next to Giancarlo's stretcher, where Nanook lay stretched lengthwise next to the colonel, purring and doing the job usually reserved for his marmalade brethren. Then Sean squeezed in on her other side, and they made the journey in silence.

"What was terraformed, Dr. Fiske, was a sentient entity which just happened to be a planet," Sean said when they were comfortably reassembled in Clodagh's house.

"Scientifically, I find that very hard to believe," Dr. Fiske said, sitting as erect as possible on Clodagh's bed.

Clodagh, meanwhile, was stirring up another batch of medicine for the abrasions and burns suffered by Torkel and Yana. Giancarlo had been delivered to the hospital at SpaceBase. O'Shay had taken off again, neglecting to mention to the receiving officer that he had several other passengers, passengers who were attempting to digest a great quantity of new information. He landed the copter at Kilcoole, and those who had been present for Petaybee's revelations disembarked.

Torkel was slowest to revive from the experience, remaining extremely quiet and contemplative when he did. But he also quietly and contemplatively used Steve Margolies's comm unit to order from the contingent of soldiers stationed in Kilcoole an armed guard around Clodagh's house.

He was confused, Yana thought, and she didn't much blame him. She was a little confused herself, and at the same time much more enlightened as to the nature of the bond between this planet and its people. She had, after all, directly experienced in microcosm everything the planet had experienced.

"Scientifically, there probably is no explanation," Sean said, calmly agreeing with Whittaker Fiske. "And I've spent most of my boyhood and all my adult years examining the pertinent sciences with little success and no . . . scientifically acceptable . . . answers. I just know that Petaybee works for us, and for itself, in a unique symbiosis."

"Yes, it could be a form of symbiosis, at that," Whittaker Fiske said, nodding as he absently stroked a marmalade cat. "A most remarkable one. Definitely unique. However, I would still very much like to have more details: Was your grandfather aware of the planet's sentience and reactions? Did he establish whether or not its sentience occurred during, or after, the terraforming process? How did you become aware of its sentience, and most of all, what protocol is now involved? I don't believe that Intergal has ever encountered such a phenomenon in any system it has explored to date. I do, at least I think I do, understand now why our totally unprepared and scientifically oriented teams could not psychologically cope with their—shall I call it . . . psychic initiation to Petaybee's sentience? Poor Francisco Metaxos is a good scientist, but he has always been extremely didactic."

"He's better, by the way, Whit," Clodagh told the man. "Better all the time and now, I think, he's more accepting."

A curious, affectionate sympathy had grown up between Clodagh and Whittaker since the event in the cave. Dr. Fiske had held Clodagh's hand all the way back to the copter. The pair had sat together, staring out the copter window, now and then exchanging long, searching looks. Yana would have liked to exchange similar searching looks with Sean—but not with a crowd of people around.

"Aisling will bring Frank over," Clodagh went on,

"soon's they've finished feeding and grooming the curly-coats. Any chance of bringing Colonel Giancarlo to Kilcoole, too, when he's stable? Being contrary the way he is, he'd never have survived the cave in his weak condition, but strengthen him up a bit and introduce him to Petaybee gradual like, he might even come to understand a bit."

Whittaker nodded, though Yana thought Clodagh was being uncharacteristically and unrealistically charitable toward Giancarlo and far too hopeful about his adaptability. The man was as rigid as the company rule book.

"I'll tell you what I can, Dr. Fiske," Sean said, leaning forward to plant his elbows on his knees. "And what I've learned about Petaybee. First, we've never tried to keep anyone deliberately in the dark about this, but as you can imagine, it's a little hard to explain and make anyone believe us. All we know is this: when your great-grandfather's terraforming process had been completed and the planet ready for occupation, a proper ecological mix was determined by the Intergal specialists."

Sean had washed off the last of the ash and was wearing pants and a gray cable-knit sweater borrowed from Sinead. With his silver eyes and silvery hair, he reminded Yana of the way she had seen him on the shores of the little stream when she had mistaken him for a seal. She ran her hand softly down his arm from elbow to wrist, and he captured the hand in his own and squeezed, as he continued speaking. "My grandfather, as the Intergal biogeneticist, was asked to make what biological changes were necessary to adapt animals who could function in this planet's harsh climate and be useful to inhabitants where machinery and technology would prove inadequate. He did so, supplying us with an ecological chain that includes plants, trees, grain, food beasts, and those that could be used in a variety of tasks, such as the sled dogs, curly-coats, moose, deer, the other small food and fur animals, birds, insects: all viable on this cold, snowbound planet. All of us here, the vegetation and we more movable creatures, were influenced by his work."

"But he went much further than he should have," Torkel said, less belligerently; more in dismay.

"Not deliberately. He was, like yourselves, a scientist, and he didn't reckon on the planet being a part of his equation. Once awakened, it had its own agenda and entered into the spirit of the changes—taking the ones Grandda made and improving on them now and then, when it felt these alterations were necessary. Those of us who have lived out our lives on Petaybee, like Lavelle, are more affected by those changes than the young people who volunteer for service off-planet. I have never left Petaybee. I know I never can." He smiled with great charm. "I don't wish to leave Petaybee. It has made me part of it, the way it is part of me."

Torkel shook his head, half denying, half agreeing. "That's not enough for me, Shongili. What *happened* to us in there? It wasn't brainwashing—not as I know it," he added, puzzled.

"The planet was telling you how it felt about what you've been doing to it," Sean said.

Torkel twitched, grimacing, seemingly unable yet to accept that explanation. "Well, I still don't understand how you got the planet to do what it's been doing over the past few days. Starting volcanoes, earthquakes, breaking up the rivers six weeks too soon ..."

Sean shrugged. "I didn't get it to do anything, Fiske. It planned its own defense. I've done nothing but see that its messages are delivered."

"Which only you can interpret?"

Sean shook his head. "You and I had the same experience there in the cavern, Fiske. You can interpret it as well as I can, if you just stop trying to deny what you felt. You can't deny what you personally experienced, can you? If you had rejected it as completely as you're trying to, you'd be in the same shape as Frank Metaxos. All I did—all any of us did—was to try to protect you from your own stubborn idiocy and put the right people in the right place at the right time for Petaybee to deliver its own message. It did that in the cave."

"And what, exactly, was the message that we both received, as you understand it?" Whittaker Fiske asked, his face full of lively curiosity rather than challenge.

"The message is that Petaybee is a living and sentient entity, Dr. Fiske," Sean answered imperturbably. "It does not wish to have its skin blown open, its flesh dug and taken away, its substance reduced, its children hunted, harried, or removed against their will. It is pleased to have been awakened, and it is more than willing to share itself: including, I might add, some valuable processes, which can benefit you and your superiors, that you're not even aware exist on this planet."

"Like Clodagh's medicines," Yana chimed in. "I'd think the company would have a lot of use for a cough medicine that can actually heal lungs as badly damaged as mine were."

Torkel regarded her with surprise, then turned thoughtful while his father nodded sagely.

"Not to mention that boneset stuff," Dr. Fiske added,

running his fingers across the hardened cast. "Simple things that have multiple applications and no side effects. Go on, Shongili."

"Petaybee has been particularly distressed," Sean said, "by the increase of traffic at the SpaceBase. The planet was able to buffer the area under SpaceBase to allow a certain amount of necessary comings and goings, but that amount has now exceeded the safety margin and must cease. Petaybee does not wish to have to feed and supply the numbers now massing in the SpaceBase, as these numbers would be a burden on its resources, especially this time of year, before the growing season."

"It was glad to see that some of us who left here as kids have come home, at least to visit, though," John Greene said. He and O'Shay had been wolfing down a casserole Aisling brought over earlier. "I was given a real welcome in the cave. Didn't know it remembered me."

"You and O'Shay have a lot to answer for, Captain," Torkel said. "Like why you didn't place everyone under arrest when you saw that we were being detained in the cavern."

O'Shay shrugged. "Like the man says, Cap'n, we're native-born. We got more sense than to interfere when a latchkay's starting."

"You're natives?" Torkel stared at them. "No wonder I didn't get the support I required." He rounded on Sean then with a resurgence of his old belligerence. "Did you arrange that, too, Shongili?"

Sean shrugged. "You give me more credit than I deserve. The presence of Captains Greene and O'Shay is pure serendipity, Fiske. No harm's come to you, so I don't see that the personnel involved matters."

"I don't put anything past you, Shongili," Torkel said, and striding to the door, he opened it and beckoned a guard inside. "I want one of those portable comm links from headquarters. Bring it here on the double. We'll just check out a thing or two about the disposition of Petaybeans on this project."

The guard snapped a salute, and Yana thought she saw a little smile playing at the edges of his mouth. Yana wondered about that, and began to suspect what Torkel would find about the disposition and composition of Intergal troops currently on duty in Petaybee. She noticed that Steve Margolies was looking exceedingly thoughtful: he kept glancing from Torkel to Sean to Dr. Fiske, but whatever was worrying him he kept to himself.

"You keep speaking of these adaptations, son," Dr. Fiske said to Sean, with an air of getting back to important matters. "Just what do they consist of?"

"The most important," Sean said, his voice filled with the sort of excitement that the other two scientists, more than anyone else in the room, were best equipped to understand and share, "is how Petaybee—not I or my grandfather—improved, beyond their previous capabilities, the perceptions of some of the more intelligent species."

"Like the pussycats here with Frank?" Steve Margolies asked.

"Yes, and like this," Sean said, and lifted his hand and closed his eyes. In a moment there was a scratching at the window and a whining at the door. One of the guards opened the door to admit Dinah, who was leading a weakly smiling Francisco Metaxos, followed by Aisling. Clodagh opened the window to admit Nanook, who jumped down across the sill in one fluid motion, walked calmly over to Whittaker Fiske, put one saucer-sized paw on the man's uninjured arm, and said "Meh," quite clearly.

"My word!" Dr. Fiske leaned away, staring at the cat. "You asked it to come and do this?"

Sean nodded while Nanook gave a burst of purr, marched to Torkel, and repeated the performance.

Torkel started to shove Nanook away but stopped, giving Sean a puzzled look. "It's telling me that Giancarlo is resting well, thanks to it."

"Him," Sean said. "Nanook is male. And he likes his ears scratched. Most of the felines here have the ability to soothe troubled, or sick, minds. They'll carry messages, lead people across dangerous terrain, and hunt when that's necessary."

Dinah, tongue lolling from her open mouth, waited until Metaxos was safely deposited in a chair between Diego and Steve, then pranced up to Fiske. She gave a bit of a whine before she pushed her nose at his arm and held it there a moment.

"Talking cats and dogs?" Dr. Fiske asked, eyes round with amazement.

"Telepathic, actually," Sean said. "When they choose to be. Dinah, as a lead dog, had no trouble communicating about trail conditions and finding her way across frozen wastes. She had bonded most effectively with Lavelle, the woman who died when Captain Fiske and Colonel Giancarlo had her removed from Petaybee. Nanook has a close bond with me, but is actually a pretty social creature."

"And Clodagh's cats—" Yana began, but Clodagh shot her a look and she subsided. No need to tell the offworlders everything. Not more than they needed to convince them. Not just yet. So Yana made no mention about unicorned curly stallions, intelligent seals, and trained ravens. Sean's hand dropped to the back of her neck and kneaded it gently as he watched the reaction of the Fiskes and Margolies.

"Telepathic sled dogs and felines . . ." Dr. Fiske said, shaking his head.

"Your granddad was one busy guy." Torkel snorted. Nanook dug his claws into Torkel's leg, ever so slightly. "Ouch!"

"Grandfather developed several types of large felines and canines suitable to this icy climate, but, as I said, Petaybee improved on his work many times over the years. Give Petaybee a chance, and it will improve on anything you ask it to. Isn't that much better than blasting the planet apart for mere minerals and ores which the company can surely find on lifeless asteroids and planets?"

Dr. Fiske sighed. "Ah, now I suppose we come to the crux of all this. If I understood it correctly, Petaybee is extremely grateful for its life, but not grateful enough to endure our resource development plans? That's why the teams have disappeared or been killed?"

Frank Metaxos cleared his throat and said in a rusty voice, "It wasn't intentional, Whit. I—freaked out, as Diego would say, what with the blizzard followed by that intense psychical input. I understand now that what I sensed in the cave was only this same explanation. And—incredible as it seems—something of an apology.

Perhaps Petaybee could adjust its climate a bit for those of us who aren't used to such extreme conditions."

"Actually, Petaybee's extremely hospitable, if you're willing to take the hospitality on its own terms," Clodagh told him. To Dr. Fiske she added, "Petaybee offers you more than you could ever take from it by force. This doesn't have to be a fight."

"That's right," Yana said, leaning forward and talking with all the persuasion at her command. "The company's just been trying to develop the wrong things so far. This planet offers absolutely unique opportunities to study its inner life—providing you can find some extremely dedicated people able for the challenge. And that's the resource the company most needs to develop—the people."

"I suppose we could send scientists down to instruct them in the proper procedure," Dr. Fiske said slowly.

"You send them," Clodagh said, nodding. "*We'll* teach proper procedure. But you'll see, it will work."

"We'll send equipment—comm units, computer linkups."

"Some maybe," Clodagh said. "But not too many. Too noisy. Petaybee wouldn't like it. Just send a couple of teachers who don't mind the cold and can teach us reading and writing. That's quieter."

Just then the guard returned with the comm link Torkel had sent for. Torkel accepted the equipment and set it on his knees.

"Now then, we'll see what's going on here," he said. "Computer, I want files on O'Shay . . ."

"Richard Arnaluk, sir," O'Shay helpfully provided.

"And Greene . . ."

"John Kevin Intiak Greene the Third, sir," Greene

told him. "My crew members were Corporal Winona Sorenson, deceased, Specialist Fourth Class Ingunuk J. Keelaghan, deceased, Lieutenant Michael Huyukchuk, wounded in action—"

"Wait a minute," Torkel said. "These names sound Petaybean."

O'Shay shrugged. "They are—native-born or Petaybean stock. Same's true, I think, for most of the replacement troops shipped down with me. And the survivors we picked up near the volcano."

"Computer, access personnel list for troops transferred to planet Petaybee, code name Operation Mop-Up. Cross-reference by planet of origin or descent and provide statistical data of composition of total numbers."

After a moment of frantically scanning the screen, Torkel looked up suspiciously at Sean. "This can't be right. Unless your planet can manipulate troop movements by remote control."

"Why? What does it say?"

"Eighty-eight percent of the troops deployed here for Mop-Up are of Petaybean origin."

Sean gave a low whistle. "Imagine that. I didn't know we'd sent so many people away. Did you, Clodagh?"

"I sure didn't."

"Computer, audio, please. Explain how such a large percentage of personnel assigned to Operation Mop-Up are of local origin."

"This system cross-indexed physical and psychological requirements necessary for ground duty on an arctic-type planet. The personnel selected were the best qualified to function at appropriate levels on such a planet."

"Torkel," Yana said, leaning forward and slightly to

the side to watch the screen. "While we're on the subject of the *quantity* of Petaybean troops involved, why don't you check statistical data concerning the service records of those with Petaybee as planet of origin as compared to those of the corps as a whole?"

"Computer?" Torkel asked, and gave it the data request.

"Petaybean personnel on the average receive seventy-five percent more commendations, sixty percent more bonuses, and eighty-nine percent more decorations than troops of other places of origin. However, they are promoted through the ranks ten point five times slower than other personnel, and only twenty-one point eight-nine-five percent of Petaybeans become senior officers."

Yana lifted her eyebrows at Torkel and permitted herself a small, smug smile. "See? These people are definitely worthwhile to the company, and definitely worth developing."

Torkel raised an eyebrow back at her. "As long as they're never removed from the planet to do what they're worth developing *for?*"

Sean broke in. "Many of our people are perfectly happy to serve the company and see the universe. You just have to recruit them early."

"And I think if the company worked *with* Petaybeans on the research, compensatory devices could be used to offset the incompatibility between Petaybean adaptive characteristics and space travel," Yana said. "*That* is what I was trying to tell you before."

Torkel shut down the comm link with a snap, and Sean grinned broadly.

"It's okay, son," Dr. Fiske told Torkel.

But Torkel shook his head uneasily. "It's not okay, Dad. We're in an intolerable situation, disadvantaged. There're not only more of them, they're the company's best troops but, being here, their loyalty is compromised. We're at their mercy."

"Fortunately for you, Captain," Clodagh said, handing him a cup of hot drink and a hunk of bread, "we're extremely merciful around here. Sprinkle a little of this on your bread. You'll see how tasty it is." She passed over an herb jar and, unusually compliant, Torkel shook it over his bread.

Dr. Fiske smiled at his son as one of the marmalade cats jumped into Torkel's lap and began purring. For a moment, Torkel stiffened, wavering briefly between rejection and acceptance. He took a sip of the drink and a bite of the bread. After several more sips and bites, he gave a deep resigned sigh and finally relaxed, leaning back in his chair, the cat firmly in charge.

"Look here," O'Shay began tentatively, appealing to Clodagh, "if there're that many Petaybeans come home to roost, d'you think we could have a latchkay to celebrate?"

"The very thing," Aisling agreed happily.

"Now that," Sean said, "is one of the best ideas I've heard in days. It would undoubtedly settle a lot of qualms and answer some of the questions you haven't thought of yet, Dr. Fiske, Steve."

"Well," Yana said, rising, "since confusion has died down to mere chaos, I'd really appreciate a decent bath and change of clothes." She looked askance at the riddled remainder of her shirt.

"I'm not exactly as clean as I'd like to be either," Sean said. Also rising, he took Yana by the arm and began leading her to the door. Then he stopped. "You wouldn't mind dismissing that guard now, would you, Captain Fiske?"

"I will," said Whittaker Fiske, rising and doing exactly that.

Yana could not believe the relief that washed over her as she and Sean stepped out into the fresh air. The whilom guard had dispersed like snowmelt on a hot day. She inhaled, half expecting the previous days' exertions to result in a paroxysm of coughing.

"You won't have that trouble ever again," Sean said as he guided her toward the path to the hot springs.

"Wait, I'll need clothes," she said, half towing him in the direction of her house.

"There's always something left about at the springs," he said, and pulled her back to his side, grinning with a boyishness that surprised her.

Laughing, she let herself be held. "Is it wrong of me to want to wash some of Petaybee off?" She asked, buoyant with relief and with his presence.

"You can never wash Petaybee off completely, Yanaba Maddock. Not now! You're stuck with us, love." And then he threw back his head and gave an odd call.

Two curly-coats broke out of a nearby copse and trotted up to them.

"Local transport," Sean said. When the curlies stopped beside them, he lifted Yana onto the back of one before he vaulted astride the other.

"You just called and they came?" Yana asked, bubbling with laughter, as she laced her fingers tightly into the mane. She knew little about riding, but she felt no fear.

"Sure thing," Sean said, grinning like a fool. "Let's go!"

To her surprise and delight, Yana found the curly-coat's rocking gait to be extremely comfortable, its fur soft on bare skin. She tried not to see how fast the terrain sped by as they went hell-for-leather down the forest track to the hot springs.

They reached their destination in moments, sliding off the mounts, who then wandered away as amiably as they had come. Sean was discarding his clothing and stood before her, sleek, faintly silvery-tan, waiting for her to shuck off the tatters she wore. Then she held out her arms toward him.

Smiling with a luminosity to his silver eyes that made her breathless, he enfolded her in his arms, pressing her head into his chest so that she could hear the beating of his heart.

"You've heard what Petaybee had to say. Now hear what I have to say to you, Yanaba Maddock." He tipped her head back to look at him. "You are courage, you are beauty, you are honor, you are strong and kind. You are also loved. By more than I." He bent to kiss first one eye and then the other, then her forehead. "Petaybee healed you because it had need of you. I have my own need of you, and of the child you carry for both of us." He touched her breast then, gently but as if in benediction.

"Child?" She tried to struggle free, appalled and aching with hurt and disappointment. If he wanted a mother for his children, he would have to find someone else and she couldn't bear that thought. "Sean, I'm past all that. It may have escaped your notice, but a person doesn't become a senior company officer until middle age. My body is just not—"

"Well, love, as long as we're talking about what bodies are and are not, I think you should be aware of a thing or two about mine. So much has happened, I didn't want to spring it on you all at once, but back in the cavern, when we were all joined with Petaybee, I knew . . ."

"Knew what? Sean? Sean!"

But he dove into the water, and as it sluiced over his skin, instead of the gray-brown ashy color subsiding, it deepened, blurring his skin so that she felt she was looking at him through mist. Scan rolled himself into a ball, dove under the water, and when he surfaced again, his silver-brown hair covered not just his scalp but his face—and his form had changed!

Before she could say anything, the seal who was Sean climbed back out, playfully flipped her with the water on his sleek hide, and unfolded once more into her lover.

She took one involuntary step backward, then stepped toward him. "What—exactly—happened there?"

"My grandfather did, as Torkel suggested, go a little far. Actually, a lot far. There are some special notes in his personal diaries, which I have hidden in a safe place. He was fascinated by old Native American and Celtic tales of men who could change their shapes to protect themselves and suit their environment—of course, these were magical tales, but he always maintained they were just an extreme form of adaptation. Of course, he wasn't supposed to experiment on people at all—he didn't realize at the time that the planet was already producing substantial adaptive alterations in us—

but he *did* do a bit of manipulation on himself that has carried down in my chromosomes, so that I, at least, adapt—er, quite a lot more drastically—than others on the planet. I 'adapt' or actually, in most ways, transform, at times into the marine animal most suited for this climate. I'm what they call in the old Celtic folklore a selkie; a man on land, a seal in the sea, or in my case, in the water."

"And your sister?" Yana asked. "Does she transform, too? I wondered why she bit my head off when I mentioned seal hunting."

He shook his head. "Not that I know of, and I think she would have told me. She's the only one who's actually seen me change, except for you, though Clodagh knows. As you saw, the seal shape can be very useful when it's necessary to navigate the underground riverine network." He gave her a half-uncertain, half-rakish smile. "Clodagh and Sinead even seem to feel it makes me one of the more versatile individuals on the planet. But the woman whose opinion on the subject matters the most to me is you and—I wasn't sure how you'd feel about it, which is why I hesitated to make love to you the first time we came here, although I wanted to very badly. I meant to tell you all of this before we made love after the latchkay but . . ."

She laid her hand on his cheek, and he caught it and held it as if she were throwing him a lifeline. He took another deep, ragged breath. Obviously confiding this secret to her scared him as none of the dangers they had braved together had done.

"I—hope—that after what you've seen, you can see that it's this dual nature of mine that gives me my particular special bond with Petaybee. And that because of it, when we were all joined with the planet, I sensed that within our common union there was an extra person present, the child you carry. Our child."

"But I can't *have* a child," she said, still trying to absorb his astonishing revelation. A little dizzy with all the changes taking place, she leaned against his water-slick body, her cheek damp against his shoulder. "I *can't*."

"You can and *are* having our child," Sean said in such a fiercely tender voice that she melted against him. "Petaybee healed that part of you, too, because our children will be even closer to it than most. The planet wants your children—and mine." He turned her in his arms, and again she saw the anxiety—no, fear—cloud his silver eyes. "Or do you not want mine?"

Yana gulped. "I think . . ." she began unsteadily; then she cleared her throat so what she could manage to say was audible. "I think that first I need a bath. After that, anything you want, I want, too!"

"Then you don't mind?"

"Being pregnant? No, I thought I'd never get the chance."

Relief mingled with the anxiety in his face now. "Then you do *want* the baby? You don't mind that I sometimes . . . change into a seal?"

She searched his face, so strong and full of integrity, intelligence, and humor. She thought of their lovemaking and his strength and kindness through everything they had endured together. She shook her head slowly, rather amazed to find that in the face of all of that—in the face of her love—she had damn few fears, and even fewer doubts. She put her arms on his shoulders, looked into his face with a quizzical little smile, and gave a small shrug of nonchalance.

"A seal? A man? Whatever," she said. "Nobody's perfect."

Coming to bookstores everywhere in July 1994 . . .

POWER LINES

by Anne McCaffrey and Elizabeth Ann Scarborough
Published in hardcover by Del Rey Books.
Read on for the opening chapter of
POWER LINES. . . .

1

SpaceBase occasionally still rumbled underfoot, as if to remind everyone that Petaybee planet was by no means pacified. The riders from Kilcoole village had kept well to the wooded trails farthest from the steaming, freshly thawed river, now merely rimmed with ice like a frosting of salt along the top of a glass. Several times on their journey, the planet shook and shifted, as if reminding them of the urgency of their mission, but by now the Petaybeans calmly accepted the planet's new mood.

Major Yanaba Maddock, Intergal Company Corps, Retired—well, mostly retired, anyway—looked around at the faces of her lover and her new friends and neighbors. Their own mood was both happy and expectant as they dismounted in front of the SpaceBase headquarters building. Clodagh Senungatuk, Kilcoole's healer and one-woman information center, dusted her divided skirts while her curly-coated horse gazed impassively as flurries of its freshly shed hairs floated on the unseasonably warm air.

Sinead Shongili, Yana's own beloved Sean's sister, assisted Aisling, Clodagh's sister, from the saddle while Buneka Rourke held the reins of her Uncle Seamus's and Aunt Moira's horses as they dismounted. The churned mud that formed the roads at SpaceBase was dotted with stones and boards and pieces of metal to be used as steps. Hopping from one of these to the next, the party of Petaybeans made their way into the building.

They all had such high hopes for this meeting, Yana thought, almost with irritation. Personally, she hated meetings. Always had. Most of them provided no more input than could be contained in a two-second burst on a comm link. Waste of time, ordinarily. She took a deep breath and neatly tucked in the shirttails of the uniform blouse that Dr. Whittaker Fiske had suggested might be the politically tactful costume for the occasion. Partisan as she was, she was the most neutral person attending the meeting. While the company she kept announced her leanings, the uniform would remind the bosses of her long-standing company affiliation.

Sean Shongili, sensing her tension, reached up briefly to knead the back of her neck, and she gave him a nervous smile. As the chief geneticist for this area of the planet, Sean was a key member of the Petaybean delegation. He and the others seemed to think that it was predestined that the company men would see reason and accede to the requirements of their planet and its people. Sean, who despite his profession was no more experienced at being a prospective parent than she was, had already suggested that her premeeting trepidation was in part at least a hormonally stimulated response. He was wrong, but as he had been born and bred on the planet, she could hardly expect him to understand.

Petaybeans gathered only to entertain themselves and each other or to discuss a problem and arrive at a consensus for solution. Company meetings were far more often power plays where the issue was secondary to whose view prevailed. But then, she had never before been to any meeting where the issue was the survival of a sentient planet and its people.

Two deep breaths, and she followed Sean into the building and on into the conference room. As the Petaybeans and Yana entered, Dr. Whittaker Fiske stood, forcing the other dignitaries to do likewise. Here most of the cracks from the earthquakes had been sealed. The screens along the walls were still slightly askew on their brackets but functional. There wasn't enough seating for all the Petaybeans who had been invited, but the major players ringed the beautiful table, handcrafted from native Petaybean woods.

As nominal chairperson, Whittaker Fiske sat in the center with his son, Captain Torkel Fiske. Yana, Sean Shongili, Clodagh, and the Petaybean survivors of the last ill-fated exploratory mission sat to the left of the Fiskes; Francisco and Diego Metaxos and Steve Margolies were placed to the right, along with various other company dignitaries. The latter looked considerably more confused than the Petaybean group, who were, to a person, optimistically resolute.

A bare half hour later, when the comm link with Intergal Earth had been established, the optimism on many faces had been replaced with disgust and dismay at the unreasonableness of certain officials.

"And you actually have the unmitigated gall . . ." declared the occupant of the main screen, Farringer Ball, the secretary-general of Intergal's Board of Directors, "to tell me that the planet is making these demands on us?" His round, fleshy face had taken on a reddish orange hue.

Yana thought some of that color had to be generated by the faulty connection or the disrupted innards of the comm screen. No human flesh could turn such a shade.

"Yes, Farrie, that's what I'm saying," Whittaker Fiske replied, smiling gently as a fond parent might to an erring child. "And I've proof enough that I haven't lost my marbles or melted my circuits or any damned thing else you can think up to account for such a—" Whittaker Fiske paused and grinned before he added, "Delusion. Delusion it isn't!" He said that with no smile whatever and a very solemn expression. "We may not have encountered such a phenomenon before, Farrie, but we have now, and I don't need my nose rubbed in it any more than it has been. So let's get on with—"

"We'll get on with nothing, Fiske," Farringer Ball said explosively, and a thick finger rose from the bottom of the screen, followed by a hand that was shaking with anger. "I'm sending a relief company down immediately, with a squad of medics to check out every single—"

"Just be sure none of the company or the medics happen to have Petaybee as their planet of origin," Torkel interrupted.

"Huh? What's that, Captain?" The secretary-general shifted his scowl slightly to Torkel.

"It'll be hard to do, Secretary Ball, since most of your best men and women come from this planet."

"I don't believe what I'm hearing." Farringer turned away from the camera to address others on his end of the communications channel. "We've got a planet issuing orders, respected scientists gone barmy, and now

362

captains telling secretary-generals how to choose rein-
forcements! This situation is now Class Four!"

"You never were reasonable, Farrie," Whittaker Fiske
remarked in an amiably placatory tone, "when you
come up against something remotely unusual."

"Remotely? Unusual?"

"Like I said . . ." Whittaker glanced around the
screens at the other people who were attending the conference from a distance. "You can't handle what isn't in
the book. This isn't. I came here myself to sort out what
looked like a minor glitch. And it's the majorest one
I've ever encountered. However, keeping both mind and
options open, I'd still like to get on with the substance
of this conference. Take a trank, Farrie, and listen, will
ya? I'll explain if you stop interrupting me."

"We do owe Whittaker the courtesy of hearing him
out, Farringer," said one of the other board members, a
woman of elegant bearing and composure. She had a
beautiful countenance, sculpted on classic lines that
owed nothing to surgical skills. Her black hair waved
back to frame her heart-shaped face; even the harsh colors of the comm unit could not hide the porcelain fair-
ness of her complexion, or the clear, bright blue of her
eyes. Her makeup was discreet, and the only hint of
her high rank was the exotically set firestones that she
wore as earrings. Marmion de Revers Algemeine had
made several fortunes on "hearing people out." "I rather
fancy the idea of a planet knowing what it wants, and
doesn't want! Sentience on a vast scale." She leaned
forward, elbows on the surface in front of her, and
rested her chin on her fists. "Besides, Whittaker never
gives boring reports."

She flicked her glance sideways, but as the speakers

were in different offices, at widely separated locations, it was impossible to tell if she was looking at someone in her vicinity or one of the other attendees.

"This won't be the least bit boring, Marmie," Whittaker said, grinning. "Torkel sent me an urgent call that there was a breakdown in the terraforming on this planet—we used Terraform B, which has never before broken down—so I figured that a simple adjustment would suffice, but I certainly wanted to be on hand . . ."

"Yes, yes, we know your grandmother developed that program," Ball said testily, flicking his fingers impatiently.

"The point, then, my impatient friend, is that no breakdown has occurred. Unless one counts evolutionary development of a quite extraordinary nature as breakdown." Whittaker said the last triumphantly, and Yana saw some of the Petaybean contingent nodding in agreement and looking relieved.

"Am I missing something here?" Ball demanded. "Have you found a way to extract the minerals we require after all? Or located the missing members of the teams?"

"No, but one surviving team member, who has made quite a spectacular recovery, is sitting here in this room. Dr. Metaxos?"

"Secretary-General Ball." Francisco Metaxos nodded to the screen. Metaxos's hair was now spectacularly white, but otherwise he looked much younger than he had when he was first found, closer to his true age of forty-some-odd years. When Yana had first seen him, she'd thought him a man of seventy or so. The only change that hadn't reversed was the hair. It had been, when he landed, as black as his son's, or so Diego had said.

Marmion Algemeine suddenly smiled. "Frank! We heard you were . . ."

"I was," Metaxos said, returning her smile. "But as happens with many maladies, once the cause of mine was made clear, the appropriate treatment was administered and I'm fine now."

"Why is everybody talking in riddles?" Ball asked, almost plaintively.

"If you'll allow me, sir," Torkel cut in, "I think I have the explanation. It seems that all of us, myself included, have been under some sort of massively induced hypnotic illusion. It is quite strong, quite real-seeming. Under this illusion, one becomes *certain* that this terraformed rock on which we stand is actually a sentient being. That is, of course, impossible, a bit of superstitious nonsense, but I assure you the quality of the illusion is exceptional. I feel that it is induced primarily through two of the inhabitants of this area, the woman called Clodagh and this man, Dr. Sean Shongili. Even our own Intergal agent, Major Maddock here, has fallen under their influence and—"

"None so blind as the man who will not see, son," Whittaker Fiske said sadly.

"Even my father has been taken in, sir."

"Excuse me," Yana said. "I thought we were here to present evidence, to talk over solutions. There is the evidence of Lavelle Maloney. The autopsy report is objective enough. There were physiological changes in Lavelle's body that the doctors couldn't explain. Dr. Shongili here can. Whether or not the company accepts the explanation is another matter, but you should at least hear Dr. Shongili out."

Ball waved a dismissive hand. "We've seen the reports and the treatise he sent in with its highly imaginative explanation of Petaybean adaptation. Still smacks of obstructionism. Besides, Shongili is one of the ringleaders down there, if certain parties are to be believed."

The Petaybeans cast resentful eyes on Torkel Fiske, who smiled, a wronged man vindicated.

The elegant Marmion spoke again in her slow, considered way. "Tell me, Doctor Shongili, Ms. Senungatuk, are your perceptions that the planet is sentient shared by other Petaybeans, planetwide?"

Clodagh nodded, but Sean looked dubious. "We aren't in direct contact with the southern landmass," he said.

"Not directly," Clodagh said, shrugging. "But they know."

"You seem so sure."

"How could they not know a thing like that?" Clodagh asked. Yana had the distinct impression that Clodagh was hedging, unwilling, for some good reason to divulge more just then. Knowing Clodagh, that would not be out of character. The woman was like the planet: round, subtly active, and full of mysteries. In Yana's experience, they were mostly comfortable, benign mysteries, but mysteries nonetheless.

Marmion let that drop for the moment, but another member of the committee, whose balding, ponytailed head had been turned to the comm screen, turned to face them. His eyes were a beautiful celestial blue, but his mouth was a thin hard line, the upper lip beaking over the lower like a snapping turtle's.

"We must ask them, certainly," he said. "We must conduct a survey all over TBeta and inquire of its inhabitants what their beliefs are concerning the planet and what experiences they have had there. It is a study long overdue." His speech contained a slight lisp and an odd intonation, an accent perhaps, mostly erased.

Yana thought Marmion and Whittaker Fiske might find support in the man's suggestion, but instead, Whittaker visibly scooted his chair farther from the table and the comm screen, and Marmion let the tip of her tongue show against her upper lip before answering carefully. "An excellent suggestion, Vice-Chair Luzon. I shall go personally."

"And I, as well, will go, Madame Marmion," Luzon said. "I am most interested in the belief patterns and customs of colonial peoples, especially those who have been without the benefit of extensive company contact over the years."

"I'm sure you'll find Petaybee a fountain of information, Matthew," Whittaker Fiske said with a somewhat strained attempt at his customary amiability.

Matthew Luzon. Yana had heard the name often before, she realized suddenly—and not in a positive light.

"Your investigations and attempts to correct the thinking of colonists are well known, if not widely appreciated," Whittaker said. "But I think an actual fact-finding expedition, led by Marmion here, is in order now. Her delegation could take advantage of the warm weather to use audiovisual recording equipment generally too sensitive for the climate on this planet. I think the more subjective material could wait until later."

Luzon allowed the corners of his mouth to curl in his version of a smile. "Oh, no. I think my presence will be of great assistance. Come, come, Dr. Fiske. I do not take up so much room. I will accompany Madame Marmion."

The floor trembled beneath their feet and the screen wobbled on its brackets for a few moments. Yana glanced at Clodagh and saw that the big woman was watching the image of Matthew Luzon with a certain studied wariness that Yana had never seen on her face before. It wasn't fear exactly; dread, perhaps. That was when it hit Yana who Luzon was. And she was instantly appalled to learn that he had risen to such prominence in the company.

Luzon was trained in cultural anthropology, a discipline that should have made him more broad-minded and accepting of others. Instead he had the reputation of using his eminence to condemn the "less civilized" or "unenlightened" peoples, using their cultural differences as cause to withdraw or withhold company support or cooperation. Saved the company a lot of money, she supposed. His name had been bandied about when the inhabitants of the central continent of a world called Mandella had been herded into tenements so the jungles and bogs they had formerly inhabited could be tapped for fossil fuels. The tenements had not been well built, and the reeducation program had not included instruction in the use of the modern implements in the new homes, including the sanitation devices. Those Mandellans not killed in the great fire that raged through the tenements died of the communicable diseases that swept through later. Luzon's reports had been what allowed the company to sidestep its responsibility when dealing with the Universal Court. In fact, Yana thought she recalled hearing something once about Luzon being under consideration as a judge for the court.

And now the man was proposing to come looking down his nose at Petaybee!

"Well, I'm not coming down there," Farringer Ball was saying. "Lot of damned nonsense. I have a company to run here. Can't go traipsing around to every backwater bush planet whose colonists get a little peculiar. Hell, if they weren't peculiar, they'd be in the corps or out in space."

Marmion raised an eyebrow and he desisted. "Anyway, I can't and won't interrupt my work to go. But Matthew's done some crack investigating before, and Marmie will bring back the goods. I'll be guided by their evidence."

"That's a relief," Whit snapped. "You sure as hell haven't shown any inclination to be guided by mine, or that of Metaxos and Margolies."

"Of course I have. I read the reports and I haven't evacuated the place and stripped it back to rock yet, have I?"

"Sir," Torkel Fiske said. "What about the additional troops? And I insist that Major Maddock face an official inquiry and possible court-martial for her actions."

"We're already talking about an official inquiry, Captian, or hadn't you been paying attention? If the inquiry determines that there's been subversion or sabotage, I doubt Maddock will have gone far, and she may be able to assist the investigators. Now then. There'll be an escort with Madame Marmion and Dr. Luzon, of course, and additional technical personnel. If we decide to evacuate, we'll call in more then. Meanwhile, you've got enough manpower on hand already, I should think. It's not like an army's going to be any help stopping earthquakes and volcanoes. This meeting is concluded."

Goat-dung knew that she was evil, willful, spiteful, malicious, and would someday, if she didn't mend her wicked ways, be prey for the creature from the bowels of the planet. She had been told so often enough, as the welts from the Instrument of Goodness impressed the lessons on her backside.

For her crimes, she usually got the hardest, dirtiest work to do of any girls her age; but when the warming came, melting the ice falls on the sides of the cliffs and turning the floor of the Vale into a great lake, the rest of the community joined her in scrabbling up the sides of the Vale to higher ground, carrying with them the teachings of the Shepherd Howling and all of his sacred implements, plus what food, clothing, and housing materials they could salvage for the community. All of the greenhouse gardens were lost and many of the animals had drowned.

For days the waters rose up the icy walls of the Vale, creating slush and even mud underfoot and also a steaming mist that made it impossible to see. Goat-dung and the other children, packs strapped to their backs, climbed the walls of the canyon and carried dripping parcels to the adults, then splashed back down in the bright cold water to try to retrieve other articles.

Bad as she was, even Goat-dung was so used to obeying the will of the community, the will of the Shepherd Howling, that she failed to see the possibilities for escape in the situation.

She'd just climbed back up again after falling three times back into the water. Shivering with cold, muddy and scraped and bruised, half-naked, she huddled by the fire and ate the bowl of thin soup she had at last been permitted to ladle out for herself. The soup was mostly cold, and the fire, a pitiful stinking thing of still-damp animal dung, was nothing but a slightly sultry draft that failed to chase the ache and chill. It didn't banish the goose bumps, never mind the frigidity in her bones.

For once, no one else was better off than she, however. The one hundred or so followers of the Shepherd huddled along the rim of the steaming Vale of Tears, their lives and homes inundated by the Great Flood the Shepherd claimed had been sent to try them.

"The monster seeks to subjugate us to its will in this fashion," the Shepherd said over and over again. "We shall not succumb. When the waters subside, we'll return to our Vale and continue to defy that which would corrupt us."

The Shepherd, instead of staying within his offices and superior quarters, was now among the flock organizing, counseling, exhorting—and observing. Feeling the disapproving eyes of the rest of the flock on her was bad enough, but twice Goat-dung looked up from her misery to see the Shepherd himself watching her, and his regard made her colder than the waters in the Vale.

She rested from her last climb, as the still-short day drew to a close and the mists from the Vale crept up over the edge of the encampment. She heard soft footsteps approach and Concepcion, her belly still as flat as it had been before the Shepherd married her and her name was still Swill, squatted beside her.

"Good news, little sister," she said.

Goat-dung said nothing. Until she knew what Concepcion wanted, silence was safest.

The other girl, a bare four years older than Goat-dung, held forth a piece of metal. "You've been chosen," she said simply, and rose to go.

Goat-dung stared at the piece in her hand. It was cut into the shape of a heart. The Shepherd had chosen her to be his wife.

"What? When?" she called after Concepcion.

"Tonight," the older girl called back and was lost in the mist.

And that was when she did the worst thing she had ever done in all of her wicked days. She ran.

The mist covered her trail and the slush muffled the sound of her steps. She ran as hard and as long as her exhausted, undernourished body could. She had no idea where she was going. She had known no other people but her own, though sometimes the Shepherd made allusions to others, outsiders, those who had fallen into error. They were horrible people, the Shepherd said, who would sacrifice girls like her to the Great Monster.

Better that than be a dutiful wife to the Shepherd, like Swill-Concepcion and Nightsoil, now known as Assumpta. Wives of the Shepherd, though they were no older than children, were given adult names, usually related to the Teaching.

Assumpta, once a rosy-cheeked, titian-haired angel of a girl, full of childish agility and grace, was now old at thirteen. She had lost four children to a bleeding disease and had been beaten after losing each one. She no longer walked very well.

Concepcion, on the other hand, was still barren at fifteen, and she was beaten for that, as well. Their own mother, Ascencion, was another of the wives, and supervised the beatings herself.

Goat-dung's mother had also been the Shepherd's wife, although Goat-dung was not one of his own lambs. One reason she was so wicked, the others told her, was that her parents had been outsiders. She had been too small when her mother died to realize it, but it was said that her mother had been an extremely unrepentant outsider who had not wanted to be the Shepherd's wife and had been prevailed upon to accept the blessings of union with him only through the firm kindliness of the flock. No one among them had met Goat-dung's father, who had died in ignorance and error and slavery to the Great Monster.

Goat-dung ran and ran, splashing through slush, hot with her effort as long as light remained in the sky, then running to keep from freezing as the night swallowed the planet. The moons came up and she stumbled on by their light. She ran on and on, down and down, as if she were running into another Vale. Looking back, by the moonlight, she saw the peaks of the mountains behind and above her: the monster's back, its snout, its teeth.

She dragged herself farther. Down here the slush gave way to mud in places, and a stream ribboning down the mountain steamed just as the water in the valley floor did. As she drew near it, it gave forth warmth, and when she touched it, it was as hot as if it had been heated in a pan and only cooled slightly.

She eased her way into it. It was deeper than it looked and had quite a current. It buffeted her along, lapping her with warmth, until it ran into a kind of tunnel, carrying her with it.

373

She was too tired, too full of lassitude from the water, to avoid being swept into the side of the mountian, and remembered, just before she hit her head on a rock and all became blackness, that the Shepherd taught that this was the very sort of place never to be caught.

ABOUT THE COLLABORATION

The inspiration for the arctic background of *Powers That Be* came several years ago when Hugo and Nebula award–winning bestselling author Anne McCaffrey visited Fairbanks, Alaska, at that time the home of (future) Nebula-winner Elizabeth Ann Scarborough. When the two weren't working on a writers-in-the-school project for the Fairbanks Arts Association, Scarborough saw to it that McCaffrey tasted the adventures Fairbanks in the winter had to offer: a dogsled ride, the northern lights, a movie about dogsled racing, and (thanks to her friend Hilda's hospitality) moose spaghetti.

In the beginning of 1992, McCaffrey invited Scarborough to Ireland to conduct some folk music research. Inevitably, the two writers talked about writing, and folk music and the Irish, and the idea for *Powers That Be* "just growed" despite McCaffrey's busy schedule and Scarborough's exploration of Irish music. The manuscript bounced back and forth down the hall at McCaffrey's new home in County Wicklow, with story conferences occurring over the breakfast table before the milkman arrived. The two took turns writing and rewriting the manuscript to make the transitions smooth, each section being written in turn by whoever was most excited about that particular passage. The book was completed before the end of Scarborough's '92 visit, and McCaffrey's editor, Shelly Shapiro, who was visiting at the time, promptly put dibs on the joint project for Del Rey. The story will continue in two more volumes, which are to be written in the next two years on subsequent visits.